THE PALUCCI VENDETTA

THE PALUCCI VENDETTA

GENEVIEVE LYONS

Macdonald

A Macdonald Book

First published in Great Britain in 1991 by
Macdonald & Co (Publishers) Ltd
London & Sydney

Photoset in North Wales by
Derek Doyle & Associates, Mold, Clwyd.
Printed and bound in Great Britain by
BPCC Hazell Books
Aylesbury, Bucks, England
Member of BPCC Ltd.

British Library Cataloguing in Publication Data

Lyons, Genevieve
The Palucci vendetta.
I. Title
823[F]

ISBN 0 356 19509 0

Macdonald & Co (Publishers) Ltd
165 Great Dover Street
London SE1 4YA
A member of Maxwell Macmillan Publishing Corporation

This book is for Tom and Brigid McCabe,
with love and gratitude.
And for Michele.

Prologue

The man stood in the shadows watching the house. Snow was falling thickly, powdering the shoulders of his mackintosh and melting on his black hair, plastering it to his skull. The house he watched so intently was a large mansion set a little back from the street. It glowed with lights, jewel-bright in the darkening twilight. There was obviously a party in progress. Fat black limousines drove into the street from Fifth Avenue, dropped guests dressed in evening clothes, then moved sedately out from the other side of the drive and into Madison and away until needed again to pick up their well-heeled passengers and take them home.

The man stood motionless on the snow-covered pavement, watching the bejewelled women and top-hatted men, chattering and laughing excitedly in expectation of the party to come. They waved to friends and greetings were exchanged as they mounted the short, wide flight of stone steps that led to the front door. The man's shadow fell before him, elongated in the light from the streetlamp, his face in shadow under the brim of his hat. He was thin, the bones of his face barely concealed beneath his skin, gaunt, haggard. His eyes burned deep in their sockets. His breath left clouds of vapour on the crisp icy air.

When the door was opened to the guests by the butler, the watcher across the street could just glimpse the Christmas tree in the hall.

Down the street he could hear a group of carol singers trilling out 'Good King Wenceslas,' ever so slightly off-key.

> Where the snow lay roundabout.
> Deep and crisp and even.

It *was* deep and crisp and even, thought the man under the lamp-post. And it was cold. His hands were buried in his pockets, his coat-collar turned up. Occasionally he took his left hand from his coat pocket, took the cigarette from between his lips and blew a stream of smoke into the crisp freezing air. His right hand stayed gripped in his pocket.

He was holding a gun.

The snow had eased up a bit. It fell lightly now, the flakes fine as sifted flour where before they had been large as silver dollars. He glanced at the house again. The women wore furs and they turned their faces towards their escorts, laughing. Most of them had covered their coiffures with wisps of lace. They hurried into the house out of the cold, white night. As each couple entered they invariably cried out a greeting. Again and again he heard the name: 'Palucci.' For half an hour the watcher heard the name constantly reiterated and the greeting 'Merry Christmas'. Behind him he could hear the carollers now singing 'Silent Night' as they came nearer and nearer to where he stood.

He had been waiting there for the last three days, always in the shadows. But the man he sought, the man who lived in that mansion across the road, had not emerged. He was either ill or away. The watcher decided on the latter because no one with a doctor's black bag had entered the mansion.

The watcher did not mind waiting. He waited in anticipation, a heightened excitement possessing and sustaining him. This was the best time – waiting. Once it was over, blackness would descend and then there would

8

be nothing. A void. An empty space. He knew that but he did not care about it now. The cold did not trouble him; his hunger he assuaged at the hot-dog stand and with lousy coffee from the deli around the corner. He could still see the mansion and all who came and went through the deli's plate-glass window. The entrance had never been out of his sight for a second and when he had to go to the toilet he had paid the paperboy to watch for him, holding out a dollar and saying, 'If a man, medium height, dark, distinguished-looking, comes out of that house you are to run like hell and fetch me, hear? At once, see?' And snapping his hand closed over the bill the boy replied, 'Yes, sir.' The boy was eager-eyed, hooked on the American dream, determined to be a millionaire one day. The watcher knew his type. Terrier-sharp, set on success, he could be trusted now if not in ten years' time.

When the watcher emerged from the wash-room the boy was still there, waiting, pointed nose quivering, eyes fixed on the house. He handed the boy another bill.

'Tomorrow? Same time? Same place?' he asked. The boy nodded eagerly. Every cent counted. And the next morning as the watcher drank his scalding coffee, trying to get rid of the chill in his bones, the boy's face had suddenly appeared at the window of the deli, blocking his view. He motioned the boy inside.

'Gimme ten minutes to finish my breakfast, then come back here and take my place.'

'Buy me a coffee?' the red-nosed urchin asked cheekily.

'OK.' The man sounded grudging.

'An' the dollar?'

'OK.'

If things went on like this he might have to pay the boy again tomorrow morning, but he did not think so. There was a tingling in his blood and he felt a thrill of excitement course through his body.

He had been away, the watcher was sure. He had been

9

away and he would come home soon. He had to. There was a big party in the house. It was on the cards that, any minute now, the man he waited for would arrive. He could feel it in his bones.

'Home he comes, the hero, from his wars. Battered, proud, with a princess of Troy in his arms.' The lines floated into his head. Agamemnon. He had had an unpleasant homecoming too, the great warrior. Clytemnestra, a bath and then murder. Well, the man he waited for was in for an equally terminal arrival!

His heart beat fast in his body, its throbbing ricocheting from wrists to throat, from temples to chest. His hand was clammy around the revolver. He smiled. He had all the time in the world and nothing else at all on his mind.

~~~~~~

He knew the car was arriving before it appeared. He knew it would turn the corner from Fifth any minute now. His nerves had reached a crescendo of tension, everything ready, all senses alert.

Out there in the darkness it travelled slowly past Central Park, nearer and nearer to East Eighty fifth, nearer and nearer to him.

Suddenly he became aware of the other shadow, waiting. He had been aware of something, someone moving at the edge of his vision, something lurking at the corner, not the usual sights and sounds of the area, but a new element.

He had been accustomed to the comings and goings of the neighbourhood. He knew the servants, and which house they were employed by. He knew the vendors, the delivery boys from the smart shops of Fifth Avenue, Park and Madison. None of them had noticed him. He was adept at preserving his anonymity, a chameleon that took on the protective colouring of his background. Now he was aware of a strange presence in the immediate area. In

10

the darkness, darkness moved. Shades and shadows trembled, reassembled at the stirring of something. He could see nothing except movement.

The shadow had come from Madison Avenue and it displaced the air near the privet hedge that boxed in the gravelled forecourt of the house at the other end of the street. The shadow moved and shifted again, moved nearer.

He could not see if it was a man or a woman or even what kind of human being it was. It could have been a child. He was annoyed. His concentration was fragmented by this unforseen interruption. Who was it that hugged the shadows in a similar fashion to himself? He peered to his left, and there it was again! The movement quick and ephemeral as a ghost, a sudden displacement, then a blending with the night.

He looked to his right. Yes, he had been correct. A shiny black limousine was turning slowly into the street from Fifth. He looked left again. The shadow had crossed the street and was standing under the lamp-post.

He uttered a cry. The face was clearly spotlit in the lamplight. He let out a cry softly on strangled breath. He knew her. He had seen her photograph. Her pale forehead, the line of her brows, the high cheekbones and tragic mouth gave her face the stamp of nobility. She too had lace over her hair. She stood as still as the watcher, and she too was intent on the limousine's slow progress down the street. The car was large and it moved at a sedate pace. A prosperous pace, the watcher thought, dignified, king of the road.

He glanced rapidly back to the girl beneath the lamp, then to the car again. Fool, fool, what in hell was she doing there? What did she hope to accomplish? What was her purpose? Was it the same as his? It did not seem possible.

She was terribly in the way. She could ruin it all for him. All those days of discomfort and strain would be wasted.

He crossed the street as the limousine drew to a halt in front of the mansion. He drew the gun from his coat pocket. The girl moved forward. He could feel her. The watcher cursed her.

'Get back. Get back.'

She turned quickly, bewildered at the sound of the voice calling out in the dark street. She looked at him, puzzled.

'Jesus Christ!' he cried. 'Get back!'

There was a dawning horror in her eyes. 'No!' she called. 'No. Oh, no!'

The driver had got out of the car, opened the rear door nearest the house. The head and shoulders of the man stooping to avoid the car roof could be seen emerging. The girl ran towards the hearse-like vehicle. The man stood on the steps to the mansion, facing the street.

The watcher had thought he would have his back turned. But on the steps in the cold, clear night he had heard the girl's hurried approach and the watcher's warning to her. Such noises were unusual in this neighbourhood. So the man stood on the steps of his mansion, looking to right and to left, peering into the darkness, trying to decipher what had caused the rumpus. He seemed totally unperturbed. A beautiful woman stepped out of the limousine.

The watcher raised his gun, saying, 'Jesus help me. God help me.' He held it steady and calmly pulled the trigger. The bullet hit the man on the steps and he let out a surprised cry, his puzzled eyes still searching the shadows. The watcher fired again in case the first shot had not been fatal. His own sight was blurred.

The snow had begun to thicken, falling into his eyes, blanketing his vision momentarily. He blinked and threw the gun into the hedge behind him.

He did not delay any longer. He could hear someone crying, sobbing heartbrokenly in the still silent street, and after a second realized it was himself. Then he heard the carol singers.

> God rest you merry, gentlemen,
> Let nothing you dismay . . .

He could hear the sound of revelry from the mansion and saw figures in the lighted windows as if they were in a movie.

But now the door had opened and people were coming out on to the steps. Someone screamed. Someone cried, 'Ring the police!'

The watcher could wait no longer. He turned back into the shadows and disappeared into the night.

PART I

 *Chapter One*

Giuseppe Palucci fell in love with Maria Assumpta Castiglioni the moment he laid eyes on her. She was a tall, voluptuous woman who carried herself like a queen, her back ram rod-straight, her head set proudly on the long white column of her neck. Her hair, a rich mahogany shade, was parted in the middle and drawn flat and tight against her skull, where it lay in a neat little coil pinned firmly with combs. Her face was that of the Madonna in the great cathedral in Palermo: fine-boned, slim-nosed, and chiselled mouth, firm, generous and strong. Her eyes were the same colour as her hair, lively, dancing passionate eyes. They drew him to her.

Giuseppe was a small man. His monkey-like face was permanently creased in wrinkles, his eyes twinkled with the joy of life and he had abundant energy. It was a palpable asset and would take him where he wanted to go, and further. He only came up to Maria's shoulder but it did not matter to him at all. He loved her, and to his everlasting surprise she returned his love.

Maria was staying with friends in the small village where Giuseppe lived. He loved it and planned a wonderful life for himself within its confines.

His haste to marry her shocked Maria's friends for the little man appeared to be penniless although they could see he was very ambitious. There was no impropriety in his wooing, simply a concentrated urgency. He was in a terrible hurry to get her to agree to be his wife. It seemed

17

he could not rest until she gave her consent. The truth of the matter was that Giuseppe Palucci always knew precisely what he wanted and when his mind was made up he was incapable of taking no for an answer.

Giuseppe's father had lived in the village all his life, a labourer on the lands of the Duke d'Abrizzio. A simple man, humble and unambitious, he rented a small cottage half-way down the hillside where the woods ended on the south side of the d'Abrizzio estate. Giuseppe proposed to Maria at the edge of that wood behind the little hut that all his life he had called home. When she said yes he let out a great whoop which, his father said later, they could hear half a mile away in the village. Then he kissed her reverently on her rich full lips, and said, 'You'll never regret this Maria Assumpta, never.' And, to her amusement, he went down on one knee. 'Not *before* he proposed, like a sane man would,' she told her friends at home, 'but *after* he proposed he knelt to me, and gave me a pledge . . .'

She rolled her warm dark eyes, emotion catching at her throat. 'Such a pledge! You would not believe.'

When they urged her to tell them what this wonderful pledge was, she shook her head and refused to discuss it.

'You would not believe it,' she said, 'but I do. I do. So you would think me a fool, and I am not. But my little man . . .' She sighed and smiled to herself. 'He is wonderful!'

What Giuseppe had said to Maria that fine afternoon outside the hut at the edge of the woods was: 'One day, Maria, one day I will own the land as far as you can see. Do you see those olive trees below? Left to die, neglected, unkempt? Well, I'll bring them back to fruition, and I'll plant vines there to grow along with the olives. And to the right, I'll have lemons.'

'But the land is not yours, Giuseppe *mio*.'

'I will buy it,' he said confidently. 'And I'll extend the house. We'll build as we need to but you will be comfortable. You will have a fine kitchen to cook in and a

18

bedroom fit for a queen. I am sending you home to your parents, my beloved, until I can bring you to the kind of home you deserve.'

Maria's heart had faltered. It seemed impossible that Giuseppe could fulfil his promise to her for a long time. Would she have to wait years to become a bride?

'Cannot I work alongside you?' she asked, and he nodded.

'Yes,' he replied, 'but when we are married and you have your home and I will not be ashamed before you. *Then* you can work with me. And we'll be married soon, I promise. It will not take me long to build a kitchen for you, and a bedroom over it, and some furniture to go into it. Then you will come, then we will be married, then you can help me in the work.'

She trusted him implicitly. He inspired faith. So she did as he asked and went home.

Giuseppe's mother had died giving birth to him and afterwords his father had cared for the child with all the tenderness of a mother. He fed him, bathed him, told him stories, and carried him around on his back while he laboured. At first the other men laughed at him, but he paid no attention to them and after a while they took it for granted: the worker with his little son strapped to his back. The men made the time to tickle the little boy, making him laugh. They pretended they were too tough to bother about children but Giuseppe became their mascot and they took turns to play with him. He developed confidence, becoming trusting and unafraid.

Giuseppe's father sent him to school. Everyone was surprised for it was not the custom, but the father was illiterate and he did not want his son to be as ignorant as he.

'I get you an education so you can have these mad ideas?' he asked his son on hearing his plans, but mildly for he was secretly pleased by Giuseppe's audacity. He

19

loved his son so much that anything he wanted to do found favour in his father's eyes. But he felt it his duty to protest and perhaps be able to cushion Giuseppe's disappointment when his hopes and plans were smashed, failing as his father knew they would be.

'The trees are not yours, Giuseppe. The Duke will be angry if you use them to build a house and furniture.'

Giuseppe shook his head. 'No. I told his son and Antonio agreed with me. The forest is too thick. Like everything else on the Duke's land it is unhealthy through neglect. I will only take a little wood. It will do the forest good, and some day I'll repay the Duke.'

His father laughed and sucked his pipe and shook his head. 'You'll never manage it,' he said complacently. But Giuseppe did. He built the little three-bedroom house. He made a bed from the wood of a cedar and a table and some chairs from pine. He carved the bed-head and the backs of the chairs with simple indentations and curlicues, and he worked with love.

When it was ready in all its simplicity, the kitchen pegged firmly to the living room, the bedroom built above it, he sent for Maria.

Her parents came from Messina for the wedding. She brought a good dowry with her. Her father and mother were shocked when they realized how poor Giuseppe really was, but Maria was adamant about marrying him and he managed to persuade them that he had great potential. Besides, the wine was flowing and everyone in the village honoured them. Also Maria had shown no interest in any of the men at home and they certainly did not want her to remain a spinster.

Fra Bartholomeo married them in the village church. There were tears in Giuseppe's eyes when he promised Maria all his worldly goods, and the villagers sniggered behind their hands for the total sum of Giuseppe Palucci's goods was nil. Except perhaps the bed he had made and the other items of furniture, but even those poor objects were made from the Duke's wood, so technically did not belong to him. He possessed nothing.

They were soon to realize that their scorn was misplaced. Giuseppe, with his wife's dowry, at once purchased from the Duke their little homestead and the tiny plot of land in front of it. It was the law. If a family lived on a smallholding for a certain number of years, they had an automatic option to buy.

The deed of sale was signed in front of the Duke with Signore Gitano the attorney present, representing Giuseppe's rights. The following Sunday, he took his wife to church.

All his life he had gone to the village church every Sunday. All his life he and his father had sat at the back. It was customary for the Duke's labourers to sit there. This first Sunday after his purchase of the cottage, and with Maria on his arm, he found to his surprise that he was being ushered up a few rows. He was placed among the homesteaders and farmers. He was very gratified. He beamed at his wife who smiled down at him tenderly and felt himself to be the luckiest man alive.

~~~~~

For the next two years Giuseppe laboured with unremitting zeal. He worked all the daylight hours God gave, hiring himself out to the highest bidder, labouring wherever he could find work, Maria beside him. Every penny they earned was put away in a safe hiding place. Maria was frugal and soon they had a lump sum of money, augmented considerably by the sale of Giuseppe's carved furniture.

He made his furniture at night before he took his four hours' sleep. He fashioned from wood stolen from the

Duke's land, excusing himself on the grounds that the nobleman was letting his land go to rack and ruin.

The d'Abrizzio family were great aristocrats who lived on top of the hill in a pillared mansion that sizzled beneath the heat of the sun. There were no trees nearby to give shade. The d'Abrizzio's forest circled the estate well below the ancient crumbling walls and was no use at all to the inhabitants of the *palazzo*. The architect was an idiot, Giuseppe decided, and obviously not used to the weather in Sicily. They had to keep the shutters closed up there against the fierce light and the heat of the sun for the greater part of the year. Even the balustraded terrace was high up on the first floor over the library. Upon its wide, shadeless expanse Giuseppe could often see the old Duke sitting at a wrought-iron table, sipping his coffee and reading his paper. He imagined the architect had thought having this loggia so high would mean it would be cooler and catch the breeze, but it was hotter there if anything, and the wind was dusty and sand-laden, so the place where the family gathered was extremely uncomfortable.

It was a grandiose folly, this palace on top of the hill, naked and proud under the sun's ardour, offering no protection at all, whereas Giuseppe's farmhouse was a cool and peaceful place shaded by eucalyptus and cypress. He never ceased to praise the Lord and the Madonna for giving him the sense to be content with his cottage and not eaten up with covetousness for the grandeur of the palace shimmering in the heat above them.

Giuseppe had only to watch that highborn family to realize that the unveiled sun that beat down on their heads had addled their brains.

If Giuseppe thought the whole d'Abrizzio family mad, he never said so openly. He was a discreet man. One had only to possess a modicum of intelligence to realize that the family had no common sense. They spent their cash in hand and whittled away their inheritance recklessly,

22

without a thought for the morrow. The d'Abrizzios were profligate and bit by bit had been forced to sell off the land they owned in order to support their idle, extravagant lifestyle. They neither worked nor laboured but spent their time riding, dancing, reading, playing music, and in other such pastimes which were, in Giuseppe's opinion, a useless waste of time, accomplishing nothing. Everyone had a duty, he felt, to add something to the world they lived in. To take all the time, and never to replace, was wanton extravagance and it appalled him. Nevertheless, it had the distinct advantage of allowing him to purchase from the impoverished family some of the most fruitful land in Sicily.

But first Giuseppe had gone to the old man asking him for more work, now that he was married. The old Duke had sent him away with a clip on his ear, for all the world as if he were a nipper, telling Giuseppe that he had no money to spare to pay for having his land looked after.

'You could not conceive of the expenses!' he screamed at Giuseppe, two spots of red on his cheeks. 'We'll go bankrupt, shouldn't wonder.' Giuseppe didn't know what he was talking about and hurried away, seeing no hope for him there.

The Duke's son Antonio, who was some eight years older than Giuseppe, told him that his father drank a lot. He imparted this fact through pursed lips, in disapproving tones.

'Makes him irritable,' he said, reloading the rifle he was carrying. They often went shooting or fishing together. They were friends of a sort and had known each other since childhood, yet there was no intimacy between them. There was certain mutual respect but they were not close. Antonio was a cold person, not at all affectionate, and Giuseppe the exact opposite. They were always slightly uneasy in each other's company.

It was Antonio d'Abrizzio who told Giuseppe that he could cut down some of the trees in the wood.

'Father will never know,' he said contemptuously, 'and it is necessary. You will be doing us a favour. The wood needs to be cleared, thinned down to produce healthier trees.' Then he cocked his head to one side and looked at Giuseppe with eagle eyes.

'But don't get caught. If you are, I shall deny I ever spoke to you about it.'

Antonio was full of how he was going to change things when his father died, but in the event everything seemed to continue as usual. The old Duke passed away, life went on, nothing changed except that Giuseppe did not steal any more trees.

By that time he had the sum of money he had aimed at saving, and Maria was pregnant.

He went to see the new young Duke who had also married and whose wife was similarly pregnant. Rumour had it that he had been cheated and his wife, whom he had believed to be rich, was in fact as poor as a churchmouse, something that did not come to light until after the wedding. Anita Demarro who worked in the *palazzo* said that the Duchess was one of those infinitely well-bred persons who are constantly ill, and that she and the Duke had separate apartments, and that when she coughed she brought up blood. Anita said the Duke was permanently angry and that he shouted at her a lot. Maria pretended not to want to listen to gossip, but she only said this when Anita had finished telling her all about it.

Giuseppe asked to see the Duke. He put his proposition before Antonio in the office at the side of the *palazzo* where the Duke interviewed such people as himself. Tenants, labourers, servants, builders, all came to see their Lord and Master here.

'Your father used to say how great estates eat up money,' Giuseppe said in opening. His little monkey face comical in its intensity. Giuseppe's great strength was that it was impossible to be angry with him. He was a tactful

24

man and chose his words carefully. 'That was what your father said.' Giuseppe reiterated, and added, 'Perhaps things have changed?' Then, without waiting for a reply he added, 'If not, there is a way that might fill your coffers and give me something I badly need.'

The room was lined with books to be read not for pleasure but rather for information. There were books about fishing and medicine, veterinary science and architecture, books about gardening and the land, books about butterflies and insects both pestilential and harmless, books about trees, books about guns, about game, and a hundred other matters. Often in the following years Giuseppe yearned to be able to get his hands on them, but he never had the nerve to ask.

There was a fire in the room and to Giuseppe the atmosphere was stifling, but the Duke sat there in a coat, puffing on a cigar. He had the lean sharp face of an eagle, a long nose and a haughty expression. He looked at Giuseppe keenly.

'What do you mean?'

'I mean, sir, with the greatest respect, I would like to buy some land off you.'

The Duke stared a moment at him then burst into mirthless laughter. Suddenly he stopped.

'Getting greedy, Palucci?' he asked. 'Getting ideas above your station?'

Giuseppe did not answer but remained still, waiting.

'Where would you get the money, Palucci? You are a labourer after all.'

'I worked, sir. I will give you a fair price, I promise.'

'But how do I know that the money was not stolen?' The Duke's eyes narrowed and a sly expression crossed his face. 'After all, you stole my father's trees.'

Giuseppe was stung into replying, 'But you gave your permission, sir! Those trees were superfluous and you know it. The wood needed thinning and clearing.' He

25

stopped, realizing he was protesting too much. 'I have not touched a tree since your father died, sir,' he said. 'You are aware of that, I am sure.' He could not keep the sarcasm out of his voice. Then, realizing that this approach would not further his cause, he cleared his throat and continued, 'However, sir, that is not the point. The money was worked hard for, and you can check that if you please.'

The Duke shook his head and laughed, a harsh derisive bark. 'Don't be touchy, Giuseppe,' he said.

'I am, sir, when it has to do with my honour which I guard jealously.'

The Duke made a face. 'Oh, your precious honour is safe. Checking where you got the money will not be necessary. I believe you.'

He seemed to have forgotten that they had ever played together when they were boys. Giuseppe thought how strange it was, but kept his speech formal.

'You will find that my money was earned honourably,' he said.

'I am sure you speak the truth, Palucci. So, what land do you wish to buy?'

Giuseppe was honest with the Duke. He told him what he wanted and why, even though, as he knew, his idea might be purloined by the Duke and used as his own. However, Giuseppe was banking on Antonio's lack of funds, the fact that if the Duke decided to adopt Giuseppe's ideas he would have to pay workers while Giuseppe knew he could accomplish the task with Maria's help.

'I want to buy the hillside upon which my house stands. I will give you in cash a fair and honest price for it. There are olive trees there; I want to clear the land and harvest the olives, then I would plant a vineyard in among the olives. Will you sell?'

The Duke hemmed and hawed, dithered and procrastinated over the forthcoming weeks, but Giuseppe knew he would eventually agree to sell the land. Anita Demarro

26

said that money was so tight in the *palazzo* that the Duchess could not buy any new clothes this year which made her very bad-tempered. Maria rolled up her eyes to heaven and shook her head and asked who on earth could want more than one dress for work and one for best? Giuseppe laughed and said that some day she would have one for every day of the week, and that the aristocracy were strange and stupid people if the d'Abrizzios were anything to go by.

'If they survived Garibaldi, they are not that stupid,' Giuseppe's father remarked, remembering those far-off heady days when he had marched through the streets in a red shirt. The villages of Sicily ran with blood in those days of the fight for the reunification of Italy.

'But we will never be Italians,' he added, shaking his head.

'No. We are Sicilian.'

The Duke finally parted with the hillside. It was land he never saw, never walked over, never cultivated. They struck a hard bargain. At first Antonio asked a price so unrealistic that Giuseppe's heart sank. However, he was stubborn and hung on tenaciously until the Duke lowered his price, then lowered it again. The amount agreed was still more than the market value but to Giuseppe the land was priceless. He was glad to pay even though the purchase left him with nothing at all, his only resource his strength.

The day he signed the papers was the happiest of his life for Maria had told him that day she was pregnant. He felt like a king walking up the hill to the grand *palazzo*.

Antonio d'Abrizzio was in a hurry to get his hands on the money and be rid of the little peasant, but Giuseppe did not mind that.

'You haven't brought Notary Gitano? You trust me, Palucci?' Antonio asked.

Giuseppe nodded. 'Yes, I trust you. Why pay the notary when I am quite capable of reading for myself?'

Antonio nodded and passed him the papers. 'Here,' he said. 'Read them.'

Giuseppe sat before the fire, sweat running off his face, and studied the documents. It took him some time to go through them all for he was not used to reading much. At one point the Duke pulled a bell-cord and a servant came in. The Duke asked for coffee and the man shuffled away, returning with a steaming cup on a silver salver. It did not seem to occur to him that Giuseppe might like some refreshment.

Giuseppe plodded on and, finally satisfied, signed the documents, took his copy, handed over the big bag of money.

The Duke was elated to receive it. Giuseppe noticed how his eyes lit up, his voice became animated and there was new excitement and energy in his movements. It was as if he had received a transfusion.

Giuseppe left, thinking how strange it was that the Duke should be pleased. If their roles had been reversed Giuseppe knew he would have thought this a day of mourning. Giuseppe knew the Duke would spend that money not on the house or the land but on travel and entertainment and the upkeep of an outmoded and outdated position.

He walked around to the rear of the *palazzo* and looked down the hill which he now owned. Oh, not right up to the driveway but near enough. There were unkempt gardens there before the land sloped away. Where the first gentle curve commenced, that was where Giuseppe's land began. It was his now. The breast of the hill which he would tend and cultivate and nourish with his bare hands, his heart, and all his energy. It was difficult to contain his joy.

He felt a surge of excitement so strong that he shook. He held the documents in his hands and executed a little caper on the gravel outside the shuttered windows of the *palazzo*, and the Duke d'Abrizzio standing at the ground-floor window saw him and smiled.

Chapter Two

Twenty years later Giuseppe Palucci's pledge and prophecy had come true. He had become a man of property. He owned the land as far as the eye could see.

The land was verdant and fruitful, thick with crop-producing trees. Vine and olive grew together down the terraced side of the hill, the ancient marriage of oil and wine. The lemon groves slumbered in the sun. The Paluccis grew their own vegetables, produced their own dairy products and slaughtered their own animals for meat. Entirely self-sufficient they lived well, and the farmhouse which had begun so humbly had been added to over the years until it was now a large sprawling building, white-painted and pink-roofed, its walls prettily covered in ivy and clematis, wistaria and bougainvillea. The house was shaded by a huge eucalyptus and four cypresses spearing the Madonna-blue sky.

When Giuseppe walked the uplands on moonlit nights he could see the *palazzo* on its hill, windows ablaze, watch the guests arrive, hear their laughter, see the finely dressed couples dancing. All mindless self-gratification, in his opinion. He often heard music floating over the valley as he and his family picked lemons, or, in winter, beat the ripe olives from the gnarled trees, old as time. Francesca, his daughter, would raise her head like a bird, listening intently. Giuseppe loved music but only on a Sunday as a reward. The rest of the week was for work.

29

Sometimes he saw the Duke galloping on his black steed, swift as the wind across the rocky landscape, and as Giuseppe clicked his teeth in disapproval and shook his head, he did it out of the sense of waste he felt was being encouraged by the Duke's distaste for honest labour, or perhaps his total ignorance of how to go about it, and not out of jealousy. Giuseppe felt himself the luckier of the two for he had purchased more and more land from the estate and his holding increased as the Duke's dwindled.

The d'Abruzzios, however, would not countenance a lowering of their standards to accommodate a less grandiose way of life, even if it did mean the sale of more of their property.

'Pride!' Giuseppe would say to his wife Maria as he undressed of a night, scratching the mat of hair on his chest and yawning. 'It's misplaced pride. If I lived up there, which thank the Madonna I don't, I'd soon lick the place into shape and not be forced to sell my land. I'd not be too proud to work it.' He would shake his head at the stupidity of others, feeling all the while the serene confidence and satisfaction his own diligence had bestowed on him. 'It's all pride. Soon they'll have nothing. Nothing but that great heap of stones on the hill, scorching in the summer and freezing in the winter, at the mercy of each wanton wind that chooses to whistle through the hills outside Palermo. Hasn't anyone ever told them how precious the land is? Not heaps of stones, not buildings, but land?'

Maria, lying in bed in her white cotton nightdress, with her hair unbound and falling over the counterpane in waves, would agree with her husband as was her wont. She agreed with him in all things. It was, after all, a wife's duty.

Giuseppe also thanked the Lord for Maria, though he did not tell her that. It was not good for a woman to feel she had power over a man. He was head of the household, and wife and family should go in fear of him. It was the right and proper thing in the ordinance of the good God. So he did not tell Maria how much he loved her, how much he enjoyed her, but she knew it anyway.

He liked to watch her as she moved about her work. Her beauty and grace astonished him even after all these years and eight children surviving. She had lost two, but that again was in the nature of things. Her hair was streaked with grey now and she still dressed it in a tight bun at the nape of her neck except in the dark of the night when it lay across Giuseppe's lips in wanton disarray.

He delighted in her inherent dignity, her equable temperament, her self-containment. He revelled too in her always willing and passionate body, in her fertility and her happy health. He rejoiced and was grateful for her competence. Her housewifery was superb and she was frugal. She cooked and kept house, managing everything with her daughter's help and with the recent addition of a servant. There was always well-cooked food for the table, fresh linen on the beds, clothes to wear, which were clean and pressed, meats cured and hung, cheeses maturing and bread rising. The farmhouse always shone like a new pin.

She had kept her word to him and had worked side by side with him during those years of struggle, when the success of the olive and lemon groves and the vineyard was an uphill battle and still hung in the balance. Her faith in him had never wavered and she had laboured alongside Giuseppe, giving him not only the encouragement a wife should but her physical support as well. He would always be grateful for that.

He had seen his family grow and prosper. He had had his children properly educated in Palermo; the girls in a convent of impeccable reputation and the boys with the Jesuits.

All this, the land, the vineyards, the lemon and olive groves, would be theirs some day; some distant, unimaginable day when Giuseppe Palucci was old and crooked like his father who now sat in his chair all day under the eucalyptus tree and ruminated on past pleasures and vanished virility.

But that was a long way off. Giuseppe's juices flowed, his energy sometimes exceeded that of his sons, his zest for life, and for his wife's generous body was undiminished. His enthusiasm for the land and his family was unabated in this his forty-fifth year, and Giuseppe praised the Madonna for smiling on the Palucci family.

He was still a sinewy man, neat and iron-boned, and did not look as strong as he actually was. His brown eyes were set in a criss-cross of walnut wrinkles from years of labouring in the sun and from laughter. He was a simple man, and a good one. He believed that there was right and wrong and nothing in between. It was as easy as that. It was wrong to kill, to hate, to covet, to be greedy, to lie, to cheat, to steal, or to boast about his acquisition of land which might invite envy and arouse resentment in his neighbours. He kept to these rules and felt he had nothing to be ashamed of before God. He went to confession monthly and told Fra Bartholomeo humbly that he had done his best and committed no wrong that he knew of and Fra Bartholomeo made the sign of the cross over him and told him to say a Pater Noster and an Ave Maria.

Giuseppe had worked hard and long all his life. He loved the land and had always been upright and honourable. People knew this and respected him. They knew too, though nothing was said, that he was acquiring the Duke's land and were glad for his prosperity. He did not talk about it to them, or brag about it which they appreciated, and it was one in the eye for the Duke whom they hated as a matter of course.

Giuseppe had four sons and four daughters. It had been a great day, a day that Giuseppe treasured, that day three years after the wedding when Maria had given birth to twin sons. Not one but two! Giuseppe's heart had overflowed with pride and joy and love. It was the only time in his life he had got drunk; the celebrations had gone on for two days. The boys had been christened by Fra Bartholomeo in the village church: Guido and Marcello. Guido was older than his twin by four minutes. These two were followed by Gina, the eldest girl, then Paulo and Mario, two more boys to help their father. Then, perfectly in Giuseppe's opinion, three girls for their mother: Francesca, Cecilia and Serena. The children followed each other at yearly intervals from the twins' twenty-two years down to Serena's sixteen.

Gina, Francesca, Serena and Cecilia helped their mother, and the two eldest, Maria told her husband, were ripe now to marry, God willing, if she could bear to lose them. Giuseppe said they were *all* ripe to marry, except little Serena who was delicate, a fragile child compared to the robust rest. She had been followed by the last two of the Palucci children who had died, one a week after birth, one at birth. People said then that the healthy Palucci strain had run out.

Gina had long been affianced to Lombardo Demarro who worked for Giuseppe, and all that delayed their wedding was a reluctance on her part to leave the loving Palucci nest. Maria had cast her eye upon the doctor's son for Francesca, her most beautiful daughter. The doctor's son intended to follow in his father's footsteps, and Maria, whose only fault in her husband's eyes was a driving ambition for her children to better themselves, desperately wanted the *cachet* such a match would give her in the community. To be the mother-in-law of the *dottore*! It was a position she coveted, and what Maria wanted, Maria usually got.

The house was always full of the sound of feminine voices, singing or laughing or chattering together, calling to each other through the rooms. Maria's voice was the

33

loudest and she could be heard across the groves issuing commands. 'Like a Sergeant-Major,' Giuseppe would laugh. Maria's voice always gave him a good feeling inside.

Guido and Marcello, Paulo and Mario, helped their father on the land. Paulo wanted to be a priest, much to his mother's delight and pride. Guido, Marcello and Mario never discussed their future, perhaps because it would have been futile. Giuseppe had carved this prosperous corner of the earth out of neglect and chaos and it never occurred to him that his sons might not see the beauty of it, and its enormous value, and be as grateful as he.

'Everything we can learn is here in nature,' he would say. 'Oh, I'm pleased that my children can read and write, can speak foreign languages, can understand great ideas. But Nature is the greatest teacher when all's said and done. All passion is there – love, tenderness, cruelty, injustice, beauty and death, birth – and most of all preparation. Nature teaches you patience. You have to wait. It's all there, you need look no further. And we learn from Nature its most essential lesson: that life is not fair. When you accept that, you can be happy.'

His sons listened and remained silent. They were used to listening respectfully to their father's dissertations. Maria insisted on respect. Giuseppe did not see the rebellious glances his sons sometimes exchanged, their restlessness when he philosophised. When they expressed a desire to go into Palermo, or complained that the village was dead, old-fashioned, and that nothing ever happened there, that the girls were unexciting and the community locked in the last century, Giuseppe was angry. Maria calmed him.

'They are stubborn like you. Like your father,' she told him. 'They take after you, stubborn and determined, virile and strong.' And her husband would grunt low in his throat. He delighted in her flattering accusations, enjoyed her teasing him. She made him feel so masterful, which

34

was precisely her purpose: to make him feel powerful and to pour oil on troubled waters, keeping the peace in her family. She turned him constantly into a figure of authority who wielded his power wisely.

'You are a tyrant,' she would affirm, 'but a kindly one. Like the great Emirs that once ruled in Palermo.' And he writhed in delight beneath her blandishments. 'A king, Giuseppi *mio*, a wise and firm king, and the good Lord will bless you for it.'

They loved their children and were exasperated by them. The young, Giuseppi was fond of saying, had gone to the devil. The boys caused more trouble than the girls, who were on the whole bidable.

'It's as it should be,' Maria said tranquilly. 'And you would despise your sons if they showed no mettle. They are trying to measure up to you, as you once did to your father.' And she would glance at the aged grandfather rocking to and fro in his rocking-chair under the eucalyptus tree just outside the kitchen door where she could keep an eye on him.

Giuseppe walked to church on Sundays in his navy blue suit, his arm through Maria's. They were followed by the Palucci crocodile: Guido and Gina, Marcello and Francesca, Paulo and Cecilia, Serena and Mario. Maria wore her best black dress and covered her head with her black lace *sciarpa*. The boys and girls behind them wore their Sunday best.

Giuseppe was peacock-proud at the head of his handsome family and nodded to left and to right, accepting compliments on the beauty of his fine sons and daughters.

In the church he knelt proudly in his pew. The Duke and his family sat separated from the congregation by the altar rails. They sat in high carved wooden seats at the side of the altar. The candles cast a hazy amber glow that blurred their faces and Giuseppe, bending his head in

35

prayer, did not see the exchange of glances between his daughter Francesca and Luciano, the Duke's twenty-year-old son and heir. The whole Palucci family missed the burning glances Mirella d'Abruzzio directed towards Marcello where he sat below her, his attention wandering while Fra Bartholomeo murmured his Latin and blessed them all. If Giuseppe thought of the Duke's family at all it was to pray for their lack, for how pathetic it was to have only two children to carry on your name.

In the first rows, just outside the altar-rails, sat the *dottore* and his family, the attorney and his family, and other professional members of the congregation. Next just behind and in pride of place among the farming community, sat Giuseppe Palucci and his family. This great honour, this immense distinction, delighted him. It had been a complicated and delicate promotion. He did not know how it was decided or arranged for no words were spoken. It seemed to happen by the mutual consent of the villagers that he was projected further and further forward in the hierarchical scheme of things until he had come to rest in this spot, as near the front of the church as a man in his position could hope to aspire to.

He had every reason to be gratified.

After church he would join the men in the square, have a small *grappa* and play *bocce* for a while before lunch which his wife and daughters were preparing at home. After an exchange of reassuring platitudes with his neighbours, Giuseppe would return home for the meal. After lunch he would bring out his gramophone, his only relaxation and favourite toy, and play the records of Benjamino Gigli singing arias from *La Boheme, Aida,* and *La Traviata.* Giuseppe sat beside his father in the shade of the tree. The glorious voice soared across the valley full of pain and love, a bit scratchy now for the record had been played so often, and Giuseppe would listen as the tears rolled down his cheeks at the beauty of the music.

His twin sons became old enough to remain behind in the piazza with their father and have a *grappa* with the men. Giuseppe was very proud of them. He was so small and they so tall. He would point to them. 'My sons,' he would say in a choked voice, as if everyone did not know who they were. The lads would stand about with their elders, pretending to be adult, preening themselves in their Sunday best. They would loiter for the requisite twenty minutes then separate from their father, the young men grouping together to ogle the girls and lounge about flexing their muscles, testing their mostly untried technique on any available female they could see. The girls would collapse in giggles at their horseplay and peacock-proud strutting.

It was usually dusty underfoot. The girls' boots were always covered with a fine film of sand. There was a cloud on the road where the people walked and a cloud billowed up from the men when they ran with the *boule* in their hands.

The men's faces were tanned. They showed white teeth when they grinned, and they smiled a lot and kept their hats on in the sun.

But Mario Palucci did not smile unless he wanted something. He was the only member of the Palucci family without the Palucci grin. He was serious, people said, and it was hopeless to try to work out who he took after, Giuseppe or Maria. Mario's face was not so much serious as sulky and he grumbled about the village and how boring it was.

He was certainly good-looking. The women shivered as he walked past for he aroused in them feelings they would have preferred not to entertain. They were good women and did not like to be troubled by the involuntary thoughts and desires that Mario Palucci put in their heads. The young girls found him irresistible and were drawn to him, heedless of danger, blind to his arrogance and the lack of tenderness in his hot gaze. He fascinated them in spite of, or perhaps because of, the fact that they dimly realized he would probably treat them badly.

Not so Guido. There was no danger attached to Guido. Good-looking, sweet-tempered, gentle, everyone loved Guido. He inspired confidence, had his father's reassuring air, and in his company one felt safe. He had a slow wisdom, his decisions the result of long contemplation. He never acted hastily and loved his family, particularly his twin, with a deep abiding passion.

Gina, the eldest daughter, was a tall and pretty woman but she was serious and acted as old as her mother, concerning herself with the management of the house and worrying all the time. She liked things perfect, everything neat and tidy and just so, and was frustrated because in the rough and tumble of the Palucci farmhouse things rarely were. She mothered her brothers and sisters just as Guido felt himself to be responsible for them next to their mother and father.

Francesca was the beauty. Everyone loved her and Marcello best. Guido's authority and Gina's maturity could not compete with the lively charm of these two. They attracted everyone both by their good looks and also by that indefinable magic that only a few possess. All the boys were in love with Francesca. It was not only the doctor's son who was enamoured of the Paluccis' lovely second daughter. She was the ideal of almost every young man in the area. 'Bella,' 'Bellissima,' followed her everywhere she walked with her native grace and modesty.

Gina did not resent her sister's popularity. She had had an understanding with Lombardo Demarro ever since she could remember. Anita Demarro was her mother's best friend, and Lombardo, her son, a few years older than Gina, had been a childhood friend who became her sweetheart and now her fiancé. This gave Gina a great sense of security. She liked the way her life was planned out. She was fearful of change and loved Lombardo, if not passionately, then sensibly and comfortably. She knew him inside out, knew what their lives would be like, what she could expect. Life with Lombardo would not be exciting, but it would be predictable. Gina hated the unexpected. She disliked surprises and loathed emotional confrontations or any kind of tension. They made her feel ill. She desired most of all to be placid and tranquil. She was not forever dreaming fairy-tales like Francesca, coveting wealth like Mario, ambitious like Marcello, or able to cope with change and challenge, deal with unexpected crises, like Guido. She kept her feet firmly on the ground and was happy to do so.

Cecilia was a jealous cat and resented Francesca's beauty. Unfortunately she had inherited her father's looks which was unkind of the gods who had bestowed Maria's beauty on the rest of the family. She spent her time desperately trying to attract the boys away from her sister, to little avail. Francesca had a natural magnetism her sister lacked.

Paulo's intensity worried his mother. He was so good that she felt the rigours of the priesthood would most likely ruin his faith, for he was not and never would be prepared for the fraility of human nature. Yet that was all he dreamed of, dedicating his life to the Church. Yet he could not leave his fellow men alone. He criticized, he judged, he was fanatical in his beliefs.

'If we really believe that by following the Commandments we will see God, how can anyone possibly break them?' he would ask.

Guido would shrug. 'We're human, Paulo,' he would reply. 'Jesus always forgave. He spent his time forgiving.'

'I think that God who made such beauty,' Giuseppe would say, sweeping his hand around to encompass the amber hills and the tall dark cypresses, the verdant groves and splashes of vivid flowers, 'I think that God would want

39

me to enjoy this, His creation.'

'God!' Mario would snort. 'Who believes in such children's stories nowadays?'

And Paulo quickly crossed himself, his thin lips drawn back in horror at the blasphemy.

'You'll suffer for that, Mario,' he said bitterly. 'You're flaying the Saviour with your words.' And Mario would laugh derisively.

Serena was weak, a gentle frail creature whom the others sometimes forgot about. She was only secure near Maria and that was where she was always to be found, in her mother's shadow.

Marcello, handsome, charming, with his devilish grin and good manners, was also self-contained. Maria never knew what he was thinking. He would rock his chair on to its back legs and survey the family with an indefinable expression on his face, as if he was apart from them, as if he could predict what they would say. He was selfish but no one ever minded as his gratitude for what he invariably received was so delightful.

Giuseppe did not see the flaws in his children. Oh, he complained about them, was irritated by their ingratitude, as he saw it, for they knew nothing of poverty, of discomfort and hardship. But he was blind to Mario's discontent, Serena's frailty, Cecilia's jealousy, Marcello's ambition, Paulo's fanaticism, Gina's premature gravity, Francesca's fastidiousness and Guido's unremitting sense of responsibility. He did not see their individual character traits, good or ill. To him they were perfect.

Giuseppe was fond of telling his friends that there was not a happier family in the whole of Sicily. Little did he guess that fate, or God, or life, had decided in an arbitary way to smash all that he loved most.

Chapter Three

Giuseppe loved his land. He loved to watch the fruit ripen, to hear the voices of the men as they beat the olives down with the long poles they used, or their laughter as the grapes were gathered. He loved the colour of the lemons. He loved the hot, dusty earth and the sharp green of the cypresses. He loved the ancient twisted bark of his olive trees and the smell of the land itself. He loved the delicate shifting shadows under the eucalyptus tree. He loved to stand outside his farmhouse on a summer night and watch the sun set, an orange ball touching the *palazzo* on the hill and the mountains in the distance with a fiery radiance. He loved the simple face of his father rocking in his chair under the eucalyptus, ending his days peacefully in the harmony of his son's house. He loved Maria and his children and was deeply content with their life. Please God don't let it end, he prayed, but this time God did not listen to his prayer.

The men were up and out first that fatal day that saw the beginning of the Palucci family misfortunes. Maria and her daughters yawned and braided their long hair and laid out their Sunday best.

It was a glorious day. The sun shone on the steep hillside, flooding the land with a golden haze dappled with purple shadows. The grapes were purple too, like bruises. Giuseppe, his sons and Lombardo were working in the groves. They all wore white collarless shirts, open at the neck to the waist, black trousers, and sandals on their feet.

It was Sunday but they worked nevertheless. Fra Bartholomeo had quoted Scripture when someone had asked if it was against the teaching of the Catholic Church to work on the Lord's Day. After all, it said in the Commandments, 'Thou shalt keep holy the Sabbath Day.' Fra Bartholomeo asked, 'Which one of you whose ox or ass falls down a well on the Sabbath will leave it there?' According to him Christ had answered that when asked the same question. It was a loose quotation, but it sufficed. Fra Bartholomeo was a countryman, he had grown up in these parts and understood that nature did not wait.

The thick mat of hair on Giuseppe's chest was revealed as he sweated with his sons and Lombardo. It was more grey than black now. Maria's voice, carried on the wind, made him chortle to Guido beside him.

'She's complaining that Gina has used too much garlic. Ay, ay, I like garlic.' And he slapped his knee and laughed loudly, full of the joy that sometimes surged through him, the gratitude for so much bounty, so much good fortune.

'Father, you laugh at nothing. Nothing at all,' Mario said.

'You call this nothing?' Giuseppe swept his hand around in a circle, then shook his head. 'You don't understand, do you?'

Mario did not reply. In the hair on his father's chest a golden disc nestled. It hung on a thick gold chain around his neck. The air on the hillside was aromatic, flower-scented, mint-laden, jasmine-sweet. But Mario did not find any pleasure in the fragrant scents as he looked at the golden disc on his father's chest. He wanted gold. Gold was power. Gold was freedom. Gold meant America. And his father had a lot of gold.

Collected painfully and carefully over the years, Giuseppe's gold had been hard won. As he had promised Maria, he had sweated and slaved to earn her a house and land, and then with his crops showing a healthy profit, had come the time to save, to accumulate, to put aside his pile of shining coins.

He hid his gold. No one knew where. Except perhaps Maria. He did not trust banks. The Duke had put some of his money in a bank that had lost it all. Giuseppe did not understand how. It seemed inconceivable to him that a bank could take a man's hard-earned money and lose it, just like that. It was the only time he had felt sorry for the Duke. Loss of his gold must be a terrible thing. The Duke had had to sell him more land and Giuseppe's conviction that the best place to keep your money was close by you was reinforced. But where? Mario had watched and waited. He had spent sick years wondering in vain where his father's money could be hidden. His soul thirsted for it. He ached for it more than he ever ached for a woman.

Then he had found out, quite by accident, and could not believe his luck.

The night before he had had Amelia in the doorway of the kitchen-cum-living-room. She was the girl who helped his mother with the heavy work, milked the goats, and generally laboured about the place. Everyone was in bed. At least, Mario thought so. Amelia needed little *finesse*, and less encouragement. She was as easy as sin and always ready. Mario did not need *finesse* either. He liked his pleasure fierce and fast with no time wasted. The door to the kitchen was open. Moonlight fell into the room, slanting across the floor. The clock ticked and an owl hooted. Mario's trousers were about his ankles and his breathing became faster. The girl pressed herself against him eagerly. He was working up to a climax when out of the corner of his eye he saw something move on the stairs opposite the kitchen door.

There was someone there. One of the family was coming down the stairs. The shadow lengthened. The movement made Mario freeze. Amelia opened her mouth to ask him why he had stopped but he clamped his hand over it and put his finger to his lips.

He peered into the dark shadows on the stairs. He did not want anyone to find him in this condition, with his pants around his ankles, so he pulled the door over very, very slowly, enough for them to hide behind. He was in awe of Giuseppe and even more so of his mother. If Maria or one of her daughters happened upon him having sex with Amelia in this way, like animals in a field, then he would be in real trouble. If it was one of his brothers he would not care. He would brag and shock the foolishly virtuous Paulo. It would show them what a man Mario was. How stupid it was not to take what you wanted when you could, and be damned to the consequences. His father and mother spoke only of honour and keeping the Commandments. How pathetic it was to listen to them and Paulo going on and on about morality. No one got anywhere, least of all out of this goddamned village, by keeping the Commandments. He pretended to listen, to be obedient. He did not want anyone to see through him, to realize what he was really like, what he really wanted. And that was his father's gold.

But he could not be sure who was in the shadows on the stairs. He shook his head at Amelia, pointed and pushed her towards the rocking-chair his grandfather spent his days in. It was empty now, the old man in bed. Obediently if sulkily she went and sat in it, throwing one leg over the arm. She was palpitating, wanting him to finish to her satisfaction what he had started, angry at the interruption.

He peered through the doorway, pulling his trousers up. All desire had left him and he was filled with a different kind of excitement.

A shadow had detached itself from the others, taken shape and revealed itself to be his father. Something about the stealthy way he came downstairs, the way he peered about as if to make sure he was alone, and particularly the

44

cautious way he moved about his own kitchen, caused Mario to pay attention. He could feel his excitement rising. He watched, eyes glittering, as his father took the wine-skin and poured some liquor down his throat.

Amelia chose that moment to move. Fed up with waiting for him, she stood up suddenly. The chair creaked. Mario saw his father become instantly alert. Amelia was looking towards him, pulling her skirts up and spreading her legs. Mario waved her away in a gesture of sharp dismissal. He saw his father cross the kitchen floor, open the door and peer out into the moonlight. Mario flattened himself against the wall. Amelia turned and ran away, the starlight catching the white of her petticoats, the sturdy legs and narrow ankles as she picked up her heels and ran. Giuseppe must have seen her for he grinned and muttered something Mario could not hear, then closed the door and latched it. He did not often do that. There was no need in this part of the world. The community was closely knit and it was in the interests of them all to be honest. Those who broke the rules were dealt with very severely for the village had its own rough justice. So Mario felt the tension rise in his body at his father's action. He knew what was going to happen. What he had waited so long to see.

Giuseppe was going to check his gold. Mario knew it with absolute certainty.

He peered in through the window. He could see his father, who had lit the table lamp. It cast a golden glow over the room and for a split second Mario thought how dear and familiar, how reassuring, it looked: Maria's pots and pans shining, the table scrubbed, the sausages and cured hams hanging from the rafters, the bunches of herbs and the bowls of fruit, his mother's apron hanging on the back of the door. It was that that moved him most. And the grizzled little man who was his father seemed a figure of majesty, a rock to lean on, a strong figurehead who had always been there to help and guide the family.

45

But it was only for a moment and then all such feelings vanished to be replaced by a thrilling curiosity.

Giuseppe stood up. He wore long johns and any air of majesty his son had briefly imagined seemed contradicted by the sight of this middle-aged little man in his underwear. He moved to the range. Casting another glance about him he turned to the wall and to Mario's intense interest began to move one of the bricks.

It was the hiding-place. Mario knew it unerringly. His father would not be so cautious about anything else. He had no other secrets. Mario watched, fascinated, as his father turned, holding a small leather pouch in his hands, and returned to the table where he emptied the contents.

Mario drew in a sharp breath. There was more, so much more than he had reckoned upon. Notes in rolls. Gold coins. A lot of money. The old man must be worth a great deal, he thought, then grinned to himself. Not for long. Not for long.

His father was counting the notes in the lamplight. The gold sat piled in neat little stacks. It glittered, sending incandescent splinters of light shivering into the corners of the room. The son watched his father finger the gold. There was nothing miserly about his touch, only a kind of wonder and delight. He flicked through the rolls of notes and his expression seemed to say. 'Is this really mine? How lucky I am.'

Mario watched for a long time until Giuseppe returned the gold to the leather pouch and put it in the hollow in the wall beside the range, replacing the brick. When he had done so Mario sighed in relief and exultation.

There! It had been under his nose, all his life. He had never thought to look behind the brick wall that he had taken for granted was solid.

He could have entered the kitchen and stolen it then and there that night, but he did not. He wanted to have everything arranged for his escape. He wanted the timing to be right. He did not want to be caught. If he was, the consequences would be horrendous. There was no court in the land as pitiless as the village if its unwritten laws were broken, and the most sacred law was loyalty to the family first, to the village second. It would be better to die than to be caught stealing his father's money.

It was Sunday tomorrow. He would act then. The sooner the better. But he would have to find a way to throw the family into confusion; something that would take attention away from him. The young men often went courting on a Sunday, so if he took the cart and was seen on the road to Palermo no one would think it odd. They would nod and wink and say Mario Palucci had a new girl. It would be tricky and he would need luck on his side. He felt full of a fierce exhilaration as he thought of what he was about to do. He felt no guilt. Of what use was the money to his father? He had enough land now to satisfy anyone and a bumper harvest coming in. He was old in his son's eyes, too old to feel the thwarted ambitions of youth. True, some of the money was for Mario's brothers and his sisters' dowries, but the boys could work extra hard and make up the balance in a few years, and the girls would marry without gold, they were pretty enough. Mario needed it more.

He hated the village. He would die if he stayed. Now, on this sunny morning he looked at his father with a blend of contempt and amusement and planned to leave for Palermo some time that day. Giuseppe felt his son's gaze upon him and turned and looked at him, his eyes squinting in the sun. He smiled at Mario and his son smiled back.

How stupid he was, the old man, Mario thought, with his simple trust and faith. Well, after today, Mario would not have to see him any more. The thought made his heart beat fast. Never again this endless scratching and toiling. Never again would he live in the country, but in an

47

American city. The buildings would be high and the air filled with excitement, and there would be rich pickings for a handsome young man with ambition.

He glanced over his shoulder impatiently. The first bell for Mass, the long warning tone, should sound any minute. He wanted to be on his way, to create his disturbance, whatever it would be, he had not decided yet, then leave, go, get out. His eyes met Paulo's. His brother was looking at him curiously.

'Why do you stare at me?' Mario asked sharply.

'We've all been watching you, Mario,' his brother Marcello said, smiling sweetly at him from the foot of the tree. Mario tore his gaze from Paulo's intense stare and glanced down in surprise at his young brother. He had not noticed him there. Marcello's eyes were dancing with laughter and a kind of malice that surprised Mario.

'We saw you last night,' he whispered from the foot of the tree.

Mario looked down on his brother's handsome face and for a moment his heart stopped and he felt his flesh chill in the sun.

'What do you mean?' he asked as innocently as he could.

Marcello laughed and looked over at Paulo who said contemptuously, 'You know,' then turned and went on with his work.

Giuseppe called, 'Marcello, come over here,' and the twin ran to his father. What did they mean? Mario's brain whirled. Had they seen him watch Giuseppe? Did they know or suspect what he was up to? If so, he had lost. But surely if they had glimpsed even a tiny part of what he had in mind, they would have been far more angry. But wait! His heart rose. Had they perhaps meant Amelia? Perhaps that was all. They had seen him with the servant. It would explain their innuendoes and leers. Oh, God, make it be that! If they told Giuseppe about his spying he dared not contemplate the consequences. He shuddered.

48

The church bell rang out over the fields, valleys and hills, loudly demanding, summoning them. It was time to leave. Mario shrugged off his fear. He was sure now that they had seen him with Amelia, that was all. He took a deep breath. For the last time, and without a second's regret, Mario looked about him, shouldered his basket and walked towards the home he had lived in all his life and that he could not wait to quit.

~~~~~~

Gina could hear the church bell toll, echoing across the countryside. She could see, from the kitchen window, the villagers on their way to church. In their Sunday best they walked stiffly, uncomfortable in the unaccustomed constraint of corsets, tight waist-bands, heels on their shoes and laced boots.

Gina sighed. She wished she could go now to their parents' room and help her mother to hook up the back of her dress. Maria could not reach around that far any more and was always glad of assistance. Francesca would have to do it.

Gina did not go to her mother because she had not finished preparing the ingredients for the preparation of the meal on their return from church. She knew no one would care if she left the task until they came back from mass, but she could not allow herself to do that. It would nag at her during the service and until she got home if she didn't finish it now. She could not leave anything unfinished. It would be like a buzz in her head, irritating her. So she sighed and bustled about the kitchen completing her task. The pasta had to be made and left ready. The mint cut and rinsed. The meat diced. The garlic peeled.

Amelia helped her. Gina did not like her. There was something about the girl, a look in her eye, that embarrassed Gina. She seemed somehow impertinent. It

49

was her mother's fault, Gina decided. Maria refused to call her a servant. She insisted on telling the girl that she was part of the family.

But Giuseppe had no such reluctance. He loved the sound of the word 'servant'. The power it gave him. It was a sign of how far he had travelled on the road of life, from penniless labourer to prosperous landowning farmer and fruit grower. The fact that he could employ Lombardo and Amelia gave him great satisfaction. To give his wife someone to take the burden off her shoulders increased his standing in the community and had contributed to his elevation to the front pews in the church. Maria, however, felt a certain shame in asking Amelia to perform the tasks she herself disliked doing so much. She felt embarrassed to ask her servant to do the very things she was employed to do and often ended up doing them herself. And Amelia took advantage.

Gina, when she heard the church bell, called out to the girl, 'Have you put the towels out for the men?'

'Yes,' she answered and turned to look out of the window at the men walking up from the olive groves. Mario was out in front. He walked energetically and looked as if he was in a hurry. Amelia's eyes, watching him, were full of desire.

'Well, then, go and see if Mama needs anything done,' Gina called quite sharply. She guessed what was in Amelia's mind. The girl reluctantly tore her gaze from the men and went upstairs.

Gina could hear her mother's voice admonishing Cecilia. She shook her head. Her sister worried Gina. She was difficult. Full of resentment about Francesca's popularity. Well, she'd have to learn. Their mother should be firmer with her. Mario and Cecilia, thought Gina, belonged to another family. She clicked her tongue against her teeth and shook her head. She glanced out of the kitchen window to see that the old man was all right. He lay, a heap of bones loosely held together with age-old sinew, quite content in his chair, constantly moving his toothless gums against each other.

The men stood in turns under the pump behind the house. They shouted to each other and Marcello was singing in a clear pure voice. It was a joyous sound but Gina did not smile.

'They'll be late if they don't hurry,' she said aloud as she did every Sunday. The song Marcello sang was ribald but Gina did not know that.

~~~~~~

The church bell rang again. It was the second warning. Everyone hurried out, buttoning the last button, putting on a hat, patting a stray curl, smoothing a skirt. Giuseppe arrived to check them like a benevolent Sergeant-Major. He strutted up and down the crocodile; Maria at its head, waiting for him to join her, Gina and Mario, Paulo and Francesca, Guido and Marcello, Serena and Cecilia. Giuseppe loved this moment, his family so good-looking, so healthy, so prosperous, all together, couple behind couple, dressed in their Sunday best.

Gina fidgeted at the thought that if he took much longer they might be late. She thought this every Sunday, felt her anxiety nag, but they were never late.

Mario felt a wave of irritation. It was the same every week, Giuseppe's inspection. And there was never anything to correct except maybe Paulo's shoes which he always forgot to clean and which would be covered in white dust anyway by the time they reached the church.

Giuseppe nodded in satisfaction. They were all perfect, he thought. Marcello and Guido particularly gave him pride. If I am a king, then they are princes, the little man thought as he looked at his tall handsome sons. He did not notice that Mario was watching him and could see the admiration in his eyes.

They went by, two by two, up and on to the road. Francesca looked back and waved to the old man who nodded and smiled fondly at her.

The dust rose in clouds. They walked in the bright light of the sun, their heads high, Serena giggling to Paulo who paid her no heed. He suffered from headaches and was starting one now. Tension seemed to build and build in him until his head would explode into pain. Only Maria could help him then. Her cool firm hands massaging his temples with camomile oil, the softness of her bosom when he laid his head to rest upon it, only she could allay the throbbing in his head. Now, squinting his eyes against the glare of the sun, he hoped the headache would go. He did not want to worry his mother. He did not want to have to admit to his weakness.

Francesca's heart beat fiercely. She would see him soon. Luciano. Luciano. Luciano. She whispered his name to herself, hugging her secret closely. Luciano. Love. No one knew about their love. It had been a natural thing. They had always known each other, played together secretly when they were children in the wood behind the *palazzo*. She used to pick flowers there although it was forbidden, loving the privacy, the green gloom. Peeping around a tree one day, her arms full of poppies, she had come upon the Duke's son Luciano, her own age. They had stared solemnly at each other, liked each other at once and become firm friends. They met every Sunday after that, neither of them telling anyone about their meetings, keeping them secret by tacit consent. Then Luciano was sent away to school. She missed him but lived in certainty of his return. She thought of him as part of her life. Luciano would like this, Luciano would like that, she thought possessively. Or, I'll tell Luciano when he comes home. And she went to the wood each Sunday and thought about him, waiting patiently for his return. Then every Sunday in the holidays after lunch she would hurry to meet him.

52

She liked to be there, in the woods, alone, silent. The house was always full of noise. Here there was a cathedral-calm that stilled her soul and allowed her love to blossom. He would arrive, often on horseback, and greet her like an old friend. They would talk or be silent as the mood struck them, supremely content in each other's company. It was he who talked most, she listening intent and rapt, hanging on his every word as he spoke of Sicily, its history, the Emirs, the grandeur and decay. He was bright as a star, a man to worship. She never examined her feelings, living from one meeting the next. It did not occur to either of them that they were in love until one Sunday a month ago she had been sitting, back against a tree, thinking of him, knowing that at any moment he would arrive, breathless, his eyes seeking her out from the shadows in the green gloom of the forest.

She had heard the hoofbeats on the forest path and had felt her heart race so fast it scared her. So she jumped up to greet him, her sudden movement causing his nervous mare to rear and throw him. He had landed at her feet, rolling over unhurt to look at her. She had been frightened. Her hands flew to her mouth and her eyes were wide.

'All right, Francesca, I'm yours,' he laughed, and tears of relief spilled down her face.

'I thought you were hurt,' she whispered.

He was appalled to see her cry. She seemed fragile and in need of his strength, so he jumped up, pulled out his handkerchief and dabbed her tears away.

They looked into each other's eyes. Hers were shining beneath the tears. Luciano trembled, knees giving beneath him. He sank to the ground and pressed his forehead to her slight form. She shivered, her body shaking as if a storm overwhelmed her, and laid a timid hand on his dark hair. He raised his face to look at her and they sprang apart, shocked. He got to his feet, blushing and stammering, brushing leaves from his coat and breeches. They were embarrassed in each other's company for the first time.

They met every day after that. They did not touch each other often, they were afraid to. But every now and then he kissed her. The magnitude of their feelings, their poetic, romantic ideals and youthful lust, made each moment they spent together overwhelming and dangerous.

He held her hand and counted her fingers, bending them back a little, flexing his own, marvelling at how small her hand was. They gazed at each other, unembarrassed by the stare, as if to memorize each feature. He laid his lips against her cheek, feeling the texture of her skin, its fragrance.

They were frightened of the passion they felt for each other, drowning in each other's eyes and dreaming in wonderment about each other. Each detail of the loved one's face, each pore, each tiny mark, was cherished, became precious. They were euphoric, half-awakened, expectant and indifferent to the future which could not treat them kindly. They could not see beyond the next caress. They had not faced up to their positions in life, the insurmountable differences between them, and were not in any condition to do so. Reality was suspended and they spent their days and nights drugged by passion.

However, the irrefutable fact was that Luciano was the Duke's only son and heir. He had been brought up to be aware of his responsibilities. His father expected him to marry an aristocratic heiress. Precisely that. He had a list of suitable candidates. He expected his son, by an advantageous marriage, to rescue the estate from the inevitable bankruptcy the family faced if something was not done within the next few years. Luciano was aware of his duties, aware of the great name he bore, aware of what was expected of him. His invalid mother and beautiful

54

wayward sister depended on him. Most of all he was the repository of his father's hopes. But so great were his feelings for Francesca that he had forgotten all that, and had not given a thought to duty since he had fallen from his horse at her feet.

Neither had it occurred to her that their stations in life were so divergent as to make marriage between them impossible. Unlike Romeo and Juliet who were instantly aware of the impossibility of their love, Francesca and Luciano remained in unthinking blindness.

She walked behind her brothers to the church on light feet. Soon, soon, she would see him. Every minute away from him she spent thinking of their next meeting. When she could see his face all she wanted was to gaze upon it, to drink it in, and when she could not see it she dreamed of it. She was not sure sometimes what was reality and what was a dream.

She did not hear Cecilia behind her, being cruel at her expense.

'Francesca thinks she is better than we are. Look how proudly she walks. She sticks her nose in the air and ...'

'Shut up, Cecilia, do. I will not listen to a word against Francesca,' Guido hissed over his shoulder.

Francesca was oblivious of his championship of her. In her head the words sang like music. I love you, Luciano. I love you. I love you. And her little feet went faster and faster until Guido cried, 'Stop it, Francesca. Don't hurry so. We can't keep up.'

'She's hurrying because she cannot wait to get to the church to see the Duke's son,' Cecilia whispered. She dared not say it too loudly for she was afraid of the consequences of her words. If her father heard her there would be trouble. But no one paid any attention to what she said. They did not believe her. She ground her teeth together in annoyance. She hated her sister but she was much more frightened of their father. Who knew how he would react to the news that his daughter was exchanging amorous glances with the Duke's son? For all Cecilia knew he might take Francesca's side against her. It often happened that way. She would report something patently wrong that someone else was doing and get into trouble herself for her pains. She pouted sulkily. It wasn't fair. She had told her father that Mario was making free with the maid Amelia and instead of being angry Giuseppe had laughed, and told her to mind her own business, and said his son was a man and that she did not understand such situations. It was always, always like that. And the boys she wanted followed Francesca like sheep, and she had eyes for no one but the Duke's son. Cecilia smiled. That was bound to end in trouble. Francesca could not have him, that was sure. She sighed. Today in church she would pray that somehow her sister would go away. It was an unlikely event but she would pray for it anyway. She had the medal of St Jude in her pocket. He was the patron of hopeless cases and she would pray to him. With Francesca out of the way, everything would be different.

But Francesca would never leave. Father doted on her, Mother had decided that she would marry the doctor's son and Fosca was no reluctant suitor. Bumbling, certainly, but not reluctant. He worshipped Francesca like a saint. Well, Cecilia wished he could see her sometimes at home when she was being teased. How she lost her temper then, Fosca would not believe! In his eyes she was the Madonna, no less. And Mama was pleased as punch about it. He was all set to take over the practice from his father and that would put him in a very prominent and important position in the village.

There remained only Luciano d'Abrizzio. Luciano who loved Francesca passionately. There was a pretty kettle of fish and it must end in trouble. Cecilia knew her sister. She was romantic and would be fiercely loyal to her, refusing to be sensible like Gina. There was no way a Palucci could

56

marry a d'Abrizzio. Even Father would not want that. She sighed again and looked at Francesca's ardent profile as she hurried along. Oh, she was headed for a fall, Cecilia mused. Reality was going to break into the dream-world she was living in and then there would be tears, as Maria was fond of saying.

Marcello was humming to himself and his shoelace was trailing in the dust of the road. Guido started laughing at his twin.

'Shoelace,' he said, 'as usual. You'll trip.'

But it was impossible to disturb Marcello's good humour. He smiled his enchanting smile and looked at his sister. Serena bent at once and tied it up for him. Guido shook his head.

'You'll have to learn to do them yourself. Aren't you ashamed?'

Marcello shook his head. 'I can do them myself as well you know.' He shrugged. 'But why bother when sweet little Serena will always do it for me?'

He looked over the valley at the high red hills. He loved this land. Like his father he loved each tree, each rill and valley, each curve and mountain, but unlike Giuseppe he wanted to enjoy it in a different way. He wanted to enjoy it without having to toil for his place in the sun. He wanted money and power. He did not envy the d'Abrizzios. Like his father he despised their profligate ways. But he wanted what they had. He wanted the *palazzo* on the hill. He would plant trees from the Lebanon there to bring shade. He would clear the land, the forest, and create flower gardens that would be the envy of the world.

Somehow he would get what he wanted. Not by working his guts out though. He had always had things handed to him on a plate. He got what he wanted simply by asking and a good deal of luck. And women adored him. His mother and sisters lavished all creature comforts on him and he had come to take those for granted. He had found

57

the girls in the village ready to assuage his every need. They asked for nothing in return and he gave them precisely that. Even the women in Palermo who were used to being cossetted by men seemed perfectly happy to give Marcello Palucci anything he wanted, anything he desired, for nothing more than the pleasure of his company. Elizabetta Celli summed it up when she smiled her luscious smile at him.

'You are a formidable lover, *caro*. You are beautiful. You are entertaining. To have all this, what more could a woman want?'

He grinned at her. 'Money,' he said, biting into a peach.

Elizabetta licked the juice from his mouth. 'I can get that easily enough,' she said, 'from the pigs. I am not greedy. From you it would be asking too much. To have your body, such a body! Your smile! Ah, *caro*, what a smile! And money too. It would be too much.'

'Nevertheless, I'll have it some day.'

'Then look out, women of the world,' she laughed. 'It is from the old or the ugly we usually get the money. From the beautiful like you we get pleasure. Men so handsome do not need to pay.'

He smiled now at the memory of the voluptuous Elizabetta. He would wait and see and take what opportunities came his way, keeping his friends, not offending people, but in the end getting what he wanted. He looked over towards his father and saw that Tomaso Canona, a farmer from further down the valley, was greeting Giuseppe. They exchanged a few words then the Paluccis went into church, all except for Mario who lingered outside. Marcello grinned again as he thought of his brother. 'Too impatient,' he mumured.

Serena glanced up at him as they entered the gloom of the little church. 'Did you say something?' she asked. He shook his head. 'No, sweet sister. Nothing.'

'Still with us, Mario?' Tomaso Canona was asking,

looking at him quizically.

'Not for long.' Mario could have bitten out his tongue. It was stupid to make Tomaso suspicious.

The farmer looked at him intently. He was a silver-haired man with a deeply tanned face, black eyes and bushy eyebrows. He had connections, everyone knew. Anyone who left the village asked Tomaso for names and addresses of people who would help them.

'You will go, I know,' he said sagely, 'one day soon. Nothing will keep you here.' He smiled at Mario. 'Oh, don't worry. I'll not say anything to your father, but any fool can see how restless you are. Look at you now, can't keep still, can you? But before you go, come to me and talk, *a quotro occhi*. There are names I can give you …'

'What names?' Mario pretended ignorance, but he was pretty sure he knew who the men were, and what they represented. They would be immensely useful to him. He tried to keep the eagerness out of his face.

'What names?' he repeated.

Tomaso Canona smiled again as if something amused him. 'So, you go soon?' he asked. 'I get that feeling from you.'

Mario shook his head vehemently and squinted up at the sun. 'No,' he said. 'One day, perhaps, who can say? But how can I go? I have no money.'

Tomaso tapped the side of his nose with his forefinger. 'Ay, ay, you will, Mario, you know you will. But I will not speak of it except to say …' he looked around him '… that if you do go to Palermo, see Sandro Brancusi. He is the one who will help you.'

Mario leaned forward to hear the whispered name. Now he snorted in derision.

'Palermo? Who wants to go to Palermo?' he laughed, then realizing what he was saying, shook his head disparagingly. 'When I go, *if* I go, I will go to America,' he said, his eyes glittering.

59

'America?' Tomaso raised his hands in the air in a gesture of astonishment. 'Well, well, America. Big dreams. I underestimated you, Mario. But I can help you nevertheless. In New York you see Luigi Stroza. And in Chicago you see Salvatore Lucca. Mention my name, they all know me.' He was watching Mario closely.

'And in Rome?' Mario asked.

'In Rome, Enrico Domini. He is the man to see in Rome. But how do you expect to get the money to take you to America?' he asked curiously, his eyes narrowing. 'It is an expensive journey.'

'Oh, it is just a dream,' Mario said lightly, and Tomaso laughed, knowing it was no such thing. Mario Palucci would escape, and soon, he was sure of that.

A tinkle of altar bells heralded the arrival of the priest and the commencement of Mass. Giuseppe's face appeared at the door of the church. He called out, 'Mario! Come on, you're late.' Then he disappeared.

Tomaso clapped his hand on Mario's shoulder.

'Good luck,' he said, and the two men went in out of the sun.

~~~~~~

She could see Luciano's face in profile. Francesca was so full of love for him that it overflowed into her prayers. The ardent yearning in her daughter's expression as she knelt in church caused Maria's heart to skip a beat. She was so beautiful, so pure. She had no notion that the direction of her daughter's gaze had any other target than the priest and the altar. But Mario knew precisely where Francesca looked with such passion.

A sudden thought struck him. He gasped and put his hand over his mouth, bowing low. Giuseppe glanced at him, surprised at his son's fervour. Mario was not usually so demonstrative in his worship.

Mario kept his head in his hands and his face covered.

Of course, of course! Francesca and Luciano. It was the way out for him. A tremor shook his body. He had thought and thought until his head ached for a way to distract his family's attention, to get them out of the house and concerned with other matters, firmly away from him and his activities. But how? The Palucci household was peaceful. They all led placid and predictable lives. Someone was always in the kitchen, except in the dead of night. He thought he could probably get the money then, that would be easy now that he knew where it was, but how would he escape? Giuseppe would discover the loss and his absence and in a trice everyone would be alerted and all stations covered, all escape routes blocked. All he could do was to try to escape by day. Then he could be on a train before they knew the money was gone and before they missed him. He needed at least a six to eight hour daylight start.

So, he thought, what if the family were in turmoil over their beloved Francesca, the light of her mother's eyes, the *dottore's* son's intended? Their innocent little dove who went into the woods each Sunday to meet Luciano d'Abrizzio?

Mario honed and perfected his plan as he knelt there. He did not care if, in the process, he caused heartbreak and shame, dishonour and despair. All he cared about was the success of his escape with his father's nest egg. If to accomplish that he had to wreak havoc in his family, too bad. With one throw of the dice he planned to gain his heart's desire and he was prepared to sacrifice anyone who stood in his way.

He rubbed his eyes, looked up and smiled. Fra Bartholomeo was chanting the *Gloria*. Mario sneaked a glance at his sister. Her face rapt, her attention riveted altarwards. He followed her gaze. The Duke's son turned his head as if in boredom every five minutes or so, and his hooded glance met hers. No one else saw, no one noticed

61

except Cecilia, the heat of their exchange, the ardour that was almost palpable in the crowded church. Mario shook his head. To be so blind, to be so unobservant, seemed to him almost unbelievable. He glanced to where, a little ahead and to his right, knelt the Doctor, his wife and son. The young man, whey-faced from his constant studies indoors, feverish in his desire, covetous in his intent, looked at Francesca with such greed that Mario almost crowed for joy. It all lay there, his means of escape, in that triangle of glances. In that exchange, Francesca to Luciano, Luciano to Francesca, Fosca to Francesca. Couldn't he see, the doctor's son, who she looked at and how? Was he so blind that he thought her ardour was directed towards the Blessed Sacrament and not the flesh and blood aristocrat who must be forever outside her grasp? The candles flickered and the smell of incense filled the church. Francesca's head drooped, overcome by an excess of emotion, her limbs melting under her beloved's passionate gaze.

When Mass was over they left the church and stood about on the yellow sandy road. Fosca hurried up to Francesca who hung on Gina's arm. Mario watched closely. Fosca said something to her and she shook her head. He's asking her to walk with him this afternoon and she has refused, Mario thought. That means that she is meeting Luciano for sure.

Francesca was glancing over her shoulder now to where the Ducal party was leaving the church by their private side-entrance. Luciano looked over to Francesca. He mouthed something that Mario could not decipher, then followed his father and sister into the carriage. Mario caught Mirella's eye. The Duke's daughter had the boldest eyes he had ever seen. They looked right through you. He thought she could read what he was thinking and blushed under her gaze, but in a moment she had disappeared into the carriage which rolled away from the church in a cloud of dust.

There were two spots of pink on Francesca's cheeks. She saw Mario looking at her and waved to him, unguarded and innocent. Her eyes were bright, like the stars at night. No, not at night, he amended, for they blazed with a passion that was close to ecstasy. Sun-stars. Stars of the brilliance and golden heat of the sun, not shimmering satellites of the cool silver moon. Those eyes of hers were full of hope and expectancy and for a moment he felt a worm of unease crawl in his belly, and had a sudden urge not to hurt her or to damage her joy. But it was only a fleeting impulse. He drew a breath and looked over towards Fosca who stood beside Francesca, still trying to get her attention. The doctor's wife called to her son. She was a hypochondriac and constantly on the verge of collapse. Her husband was holding her arm while he conversed with Notary Gitano.

'Fosca! Fosca!' she called, and the doctor said, 'Leave him *cara*, leave him.'

Her cry and the doctor's command had been heard by everyone. They all looked to where Francesca stood with her arm in Gina's, Fosca standing beside her like a dog, Mario thought, slavering over a bone. The community looked on them fondly. It would be good if they married. Good for Maria and Giuseppe who would thus be raised even higher. Good for the *dottore* and his wife for Francesca would bring a rich dowry. Good for Francesca for she would have position in the world as the wife of a doctor, and good for Fosca for he would get himself a jewel of a wife and one of the most beautiful girls in Sicily.

Again Francesca shook her head at Fosca. He shrugged and turned away. As he walked towards his mother and father, Mario fell into step beside him.

'What's the matter, Fosca?' he asked gently.

The young man stopped and stood beneath the ancient fig tree that grew beside the church. 'Nothing,' he said, then unable to contain his worry, 'Oh, it's Francesca! I try to get her to walk out with me each Sunday evening but she always refuses. I don't know why.' He looked at Mario

63

with an expression of hopelessness in his eyes. 'She dismisses me as if I was a fly. She hardly listens. It's as if she's not thinking about what I'm saying. Do you know why?'

Mario thought, the fool! He does not deserve her. He is too stupid. Too dense.

'I love her, you see,' Fosca continued. 'Look at her now,' he added hopelessly.

Gina had gone over to Lombardo, who was talking with her father, and Francesca had been cornered by two youths, one of whom was Filipo Canona, Tomaso's son. The boys were preening themselves in front of her and she was laughing, her cheeks flushed, her eyes sparkling. Filipo took a comb out of his top pocket and combed his thick hair with a flourish.

'Everyone is in love with her but she seems to be serious about no one. Yet I have spoken to your father, Mario, and he has given me permission to walk out with her. Your mother was very encouraging.' The boy looked earnestly at him. 'But how can I get anywhere with her unless I can talk to her, and how can I talk to her if she will not walk out with me?' He sighed, and taking out a white handkerchief, mopped his brow.

'Why won't she walk with me, Mario?'

Mario looked at Fosca. Now was the time to put his plan into action. He stared at the boy with an expression of feigned surprise on his face.

'You don't know?' he asked in astonishment.

Fosco looked at him. 'What do you mean?' he asked, perplexed.

Mario shrugged and turned away. 'Oh, Fosca, it's not my place ... I thought everyone knew ... but no. Of course they don't. If they did they ...'

'Know what? Everyone knows what? For God's sake, Mario, what are you talking about?'

Fosca plucked the sleeve of Mario's jacket, almost

64

jumping up and down with impatience and anxiety, and Mario marvelled at how easy it was to plant the seeds of doubt and curiosity.

'No, no, Fosca. If you have not guessed I have no right to destroy your trust. My father certainly does not know … he would commit murder otherwise. Though how you both cannot see is beyond me.'

'Mario, you will drive me mad! See what? Guess what?'

'Look, Fosca, are you sure you really want to know?'

'Know what?' His voice was high-pitched with exasperation. Mario felt like shaking him.

'Why Francesca will not walk out with you on Sundays?'

'Of course. That is what I keep asking you.'

The sun was sharply overhead. It blazed strongly, turning the whole sky primrose and ruby. People were dispersing, the men strolling to the *osteria* to order a *strega*, the women walking down the road in groups, gossiping then waving goodbye as they went in their various directions to their homes to prepare the Sunday meal.

'Go now. Go! Your parents are waiting,' Mario said, moving away. Fosca followed him. He was feverish in his disquiet, the suspense making him hysterical.

'Do you know why Francesca will not walk out with me?' he cried.

'I'll meet you later, about three. Siesta time. Behind our house.'

'Why? What for?'

'*Mamma mia*, give me patience.' Mario looked into Fosca's innocent, anxious eyes. 'So that you can find out why Francesca will not walk out with you on Sundays,' he said as calmly as he could. Or any other day, he added to himself. What an idiot!

'I don't want to do anything that's … that's …' the doctor's son's voice petered out as he looked at Mario doubtfully. His parents were beckoning to him. His

65

mother had her black umbrella up against the sun and was waving a handkerchief in front of her face.

'That's what?' Mario stared at the boy, his eyes narrowed as if daring him to continue.

'What? I don't know. I ...'

Mario shrugged and turned away. 'If you think there's something wrong, then forget it.' He made as if to go but Fosca grabbed his arm, curiosity overcoming his sense of honour.

'All right. I'll see you at three, wherever you say.'

'The old barn.' The barn was on Palucci property but just on the verge of the Duke's woods where Francesca and Luciano met.

'The old barn then,' Fosca said and left Mario, running to join his parents who had begun to walk towards the doctor's house.

Mario turned, trying to still the elation in his heart. He walked to where the men were gathered. Guido shouted to him, waving him to join them, pleasure writ large on his face. Mario smiled. It was not something he normally did and Guido wondered why his brother was so happy today.

Mario looked back after Fosca. He saw Tomaso Canona watching him speculatively and his face lost its smile. It became blank and no one could have seen how joyful he felt behind that serious mask.

~~~~~~

The women prepared the meal under Maria's guidance. Serena and Cecilia shook out the fresh cloths and laid them on the trestle tables under the eucalyptus tree. They kissed their old grandfather as they passed him and he chortled delightedly at their caresses, patting their cheeks. Gina was in the kitchen seeing to the pasta and the roasting meat, and helping Maria with the cooking. Her mother's face was hot and red with the heat from the range. Flies droned and Maria shooed them away as she tucked an escaped lock of hair tidily back in place. Amelia was mixing the ingredients for the sauces that Gina had left ready; she had only to add the perishables. She looked sulky. She had not laid eyes on Mario since last night when he had so suddenly lost interest in her and was plagued with doubts about him, so she threw resentful glances here and there as she worked. Maria decided to ignore her. There was nothing to be done with Amelia when she was in one of her moods.

Francesca was cutting herbs, making the salad, chopping tomatoes and fennel, and mixing the dressing.

Cecilia put the cutlery out, giving each fork and spoon and knife an extra polish on her apron, and Serena took little glass vases off the dresser in the kitchen, filled them with water, then put a single marigold into each receptacle and left one in front of every place at table. Francesca then arranged the fruit in a huge central bowl – peaches, apricots, plums and grapes. She added laurel leaves to the bowl and placed a glass dish full of water beside it for rinsing. The girls and their mother laughed and gossiped as they worked. This morning they were teasing Francesca because outside the church Filipo Canona had given her a rose wrapped in silver paper, and so had Bernado Genaro.

'Two of them! Two!' Serena squealed in delight.

'It's because you are so pretty,' Gina said.

'And good-tempered. Don't forget that. That's what draws the men. Much more valued than good looks is a sweet temperament,' Maria said, looking at Amelia.

'It's a disgrace,' Cecilia cried bitterly.

'Oh, shut up, Cecilia! I think it's wonderful,' Gina called tartly, as she left the kitchen. She went to the door of the house and stared out over the fields. She was watching for Lombardo and the return of the men.

'Well, she draws attention to herself, the way she walks, and the way she looks up from under her eyelashes at the men. Butter wouldn't melt …'

'No, I don't!' Francesca was stung to reply. 'Mama, tell her she's lying! I don't.'

'Oh, that's unfair,' Serena's gentle voice affirmed. 'Francesca, you need not worry. You do not draw attention ...'

'She's just jealous. Don't listen to her, Francesca.'

Gina was shading her eyes, searching the horizon. Lombardo was always first home together with Giuseppe. She watched for him calmly. There was no excitement in her heart, just a steady pleasant expectation. She was a realist. She knew Francesca was the beauty of the family, the one that had that intangible mysterious hold over the opposite sex. Marcello had it for women. Mario too to some extent though in his case she could not think why. There was absolutely nothing anyone could do about it. It was the unfairness of life that her father always talked about.

'The men are coming,' she called, and the women hurried to put the finishing touches to the meal.

Maria patted her cheeks with her apron, then removed it. She would re-don it each time she and Amelia served.

They sat around the table in their accustomed places. Amelia, at the end of the table beside Maria, could not even see Mario so had to make do with casting him expressive glances while she was serving, to which he did not respond. She wondered if he was sick. He had been too preoccupied even to notice her presence since last night. Grandfather sat in his rocking chair beside Giuseppe. Gina cut up his food for him. Giuseppe poured the wine, and Marcello and Guido made them all laugh with a description of the doctor's wife having the vapours in church. Francesca was animated and excited and the conversation was carefree. They laughed a lot, teased each other, and the old man smiled benevolently at the family, glad to be alive for one more day and to suck the soft meat and drink the gravy, surrounded by such a loving family.

The girls' faces seemed so young to him and the boys so handsome and virile. He wished them joy and prosperity as he sipped a little wine.

They ate pasta and salad, followed by succulent roast mutton, and finished up with fruit, choosing carefully from the laurel-decorated bowl and dipping their choice in the water before they bit into it. They took their time, relaxing and lapsing into contented silences between courses. All except Mario who was alert and tense. The girls did not notice but Marcello watched from under half-closed eyelids and Paulo watched Marcello watching Mario.

They were cool under the tree and the drone of insects was the only accompaniment to their laughter and conversation. When they had finished, Mario sprang to his feet.

'Date, Mario?' Marcello asked, smiling at his brother. Giuseppe laughed lasciviously under his breath and drew a frown from Maria. Mario shrugged and did not answer.

'Mama?' he asked.

'Go, son, go,' she replied. 'Although you should rest. And you'll miss Papa's music.'

'Yes, go, and good luck to you, son.' Giuseppe tapped his nose and gave a conspiratorial laugh as if to applaud his son's virility. He had opened the top button of his trousers and he patted his belly contentedly as he drank the last of the wine.

Mario went. Marcello watched him leave. Then he went inside and brought out the gramophone and put it on the table. It had a curved horn that he turned towards his father.

'*Aida* first,' Giuseppe said, a rapturous expression on his face.

This was the peak of his week, his date with Gigli. The music exploded over them where they sat and flowed beyond the quiet hills. Giuseppe closed his eyes in ecstacy.

69

Here he was, surrounded by his family, the woman he loved passionately, his beautiful children, his dear old father sucking his teeth in the shade of the tree, outside his own comfortable house, full of good food cooked for him with love by his daughters and servant. Who ever would have thought he would have a servant? And his beautiful wife whose body he would enjoy a little later between the cool sheets of their bed. He was a truly blessed man. Here he was listening to Gigli while he surveyed his fertile acres. Ah, at such a moment a man could die of joy.

Chapter Four

The twins sat together under the eucalyptus tree. The women were clearing the table after the meal, shaking the cloths free of crumbs. Guiseppe, his head full of music, had gone up to the bedroom for his *siesta* and had been followed by Paulo who liked to kneel and pray in the quiet time after lunch.

'As if he hadn't done enough praying in church today,' Cecilia said acidly as she watched him go.

'I think I can still hear Father's music,' Guido said softly. Marcello did not reply. The twins often did not have to answer each other. Although they did not know precisely what went on in the other's head they had a rare communication and didn't need cumbersome speech.

'Papa is very happy today,' Guido continued after a pause.

Again Marcello simply nodded. 'I hope nothing happens to spoil his content,' he remarked finally.

'I hope so too, Marcello.'

'I've been feeling uneasy of late,' Marcello continued.

Guido nodded. He too had felt an alien undercurrent of unease pervading the atmosphere.

'I would kill anyone who hurt Father,' he said, surprising his twin.

'Would you, Guido?' he asked incredulously. Guido looked at his brother.

'Yes. Wouldn't you?'

'Who would hurt him?' Marcello asked, parrying the question.

'I don't know. Why have you been feeling uneasy? I've felt it in you.'

'It's just a feeling I have. Everything has been so good all these years. None of us ever even ill. What luck! Except perhaps Serena.'

'Oh, she's just a little delicate,' Guido said. 'She'll be all right with Mama.'

'What I mean … we're all of us all right if everything goes on exactly as before.' He frowned. 'But it can't, Guido, can it? It has to change.'

'It will get better provided no one rocks the boat.'

Marcello blinked. 'What do you mean by that?'

'Provided no one does something stupid. Gets greedy. Or violent.'

Marcello stood and stretched. 'Oh, you're being fanciful, Guido. What can happen?'

'I don't know. Perhaps I *am* being stupid.' He followed his brother's example and stood up, stretching.

'I think I'll go upstairs,' he said, then slapped Marcello on the back. 'I'm tired.'

'I'll follow you in a minute.' Marcello stood and looked up at the *palazzo* above him, sizzling in the orange heat.

Guido loved him. It saddened him to realize that his brother, although intuitive about his moods and impulses, did not really know him. He believed Marcello to be content here, with what he had in their father's house. He would never understand why Marcello wanted more. Wanted it all. The castle, the land, position, wealth, power, everything.

Marcello stretched again and grinned, his lips parting to reveal fine white teeth. He'd have it, too. He had always got everything he wanted. How he would do it he had no idea at all, but he would, some day. Smiling to himself, he followed his brother upstairs.

~~~~~~

Mario had sloped off towards the back of the house as if he were going to the village. He glanced back over his shoulder but no one was paying any attention to him. The girls and Amelia had begun to clear away. Having made sure no one was looking, he doubled back and walked in the opposite direction, away from the village until he came to the barn. He had to hurry to conceal himself inside before Francesca came. She would pass any moment now, making her way to the woods as she did every Sunday. He wanted to be in place before Fosca arrived. He had only been in the dim interior of the barn a moment when, to his horror, he heard the doctor's son calling to him loudly.

'Mario, Mario, where are you? I'm here.'

Mario pounced on him as he reached the barn and pulled him inside unceremoniously.

'Shut up, you fool,' he whispered. 'Someone might hear.'

'Does that matter?' Fosca asked innocently.

Idiot! Mario thought, but said nothing.

They stood inside the barn, Mario peering through a crack in the door. Once or twice Fosca began to speak but Mario hushed him violently. They had not long to wait.

Francesca came into view, making her way past the lemon trees towards the wood beyond. She was singing to herself and stopped every now and then to pick a flower. Mario gestured to Fosca.

'There she is. Follow her. Follow quietly then you'll see,' he said softly.

'No, I don't like to …' Fosca sounded uncertain.

Christ, Mario thought, he's going to muck up the whole thing if I'm not careful.

'Shut up and do as I say,' he hissed, then added reasonably, 'Fosca, do you or do you not want to marry my sister?'

The boy nodded eagerly.

'Then your only chance is to do what I tell you. All right?'

73

Fosca nodded. 'Listen, follow her but don't let her know you are after her. Keep out of sight, do you hear?'

Again Fosca nodded.

'Now go. Go!'

'Aren't you coming too?'

'I'll follow presently.'

Francesca was disappearing into the woods, a blur of white against the green density of the trees.

'Hurry or you'll miss her,' Mario urged. 'And whatever you do, keep quiet. No matter what you see, don't *do* anything.'

Mario felt sure he could rely on Fosca not to do anything rash. He was thick, Mario decided, and came to his decisions slowly and uncertainly. God help his patients if he ever had to do an operation, Mario thought ruefully.

He pushed the young man forward and watched in irritation his hesitant pursuit of Francesca. Then Mario turned and hurried back to his home.

It took only a moment. All was quiet. The house and household slumbered in peaceful content beneath the shade of the trees. Mario ran in through the kitchen door, calling out as he entered: 'Papa! Papa! Francesca is in the woods with the Duke's son, Luciano. Fosca's gone to find her. There will be trouble. Hurry!'

His father took longer coming to the head of the stairs than Mario had anticipated. He was not used to alarming summonses. In an agony of tension, Mario kept shouting all the time.

'Mama, Papa, hurry! It's Francesca. In the woods. who knows what will happen. She is with Luciano. Fosca has gone to find them. Hurry! Oh, hurry!'

Guiseppe appeared, pulling on his trousers, his eyes full of sleep. 'What? The woods? Francesca? What?'

He scratched his chest and yawned and Mario wanted to scream. Maria appeared behind her husband. She was pulling a shawl over her ample bosom and her hair was unbound.

74

'Mama, Francesca is in danger. She is in the woods with the Duke's son. Oh, God! Fosca has gone to find them.'

Maria paled. 'Jesu Christo,' she murmured as Guido and Paulo came out on the landing followed by the rest of the family, Marcello last. They were all in various stages of undress. Gina was the only one missing. She had gone out walking in the village with Lombardo.

Giuseppe cried, 'Where is Francesca?'

Mario struggled with his impatience, 'I've told you, Father. In the woods, the clearing. In danger.'

Mario decided that the news must have sunk in by now and left the farmhouse pretty certain what would happen next. His father and mother followed by the rest of the family would go into the woods looking for Francesca. Even if the full import of what he had told them did not penetrate, the message to go into the forest would take them there. As there was only one path, and that one led to the clearing, they would find her. There would be confusion all around, he was banking on that.

The next part was the most difficult for him. He could predict his own family's reactions but he could not be sure how the d'Abrizzios would behave.

He grabbed the old bicycle from outside the farmhouse. Giuseppe called after him, 'Mario, Mario, wait for us,' thinking he was going into the woods ahead of them. But he mounted the bicycle and pedalled up the dirt road towards the castle. Glancing over his shoulder a few times he almost despaired, for the farmhouse remained quiet, no activity visible. It was as if he had never dropped his bombshell.

Suppose they thought he was joking? Suppose they did not take him seriously and went back to bed? He fretted and fumed as he pedalled along. Could they have treated such alarming news with indifference?

But no. As he turned a sharp bend around the steep hill that led to the *palazzo*, he could just make out the figures, black silhouettes against the sun, of his mother and father emerging from the house, followed a few paces behind by the rest of the family. They hurried across to the woods, one behind the other. He noticed that his father carried his hunting rifle and put a spurt on, bicycling up the incline as fast as he could.

He had to walk up the gravel drive. The great pillared building rose before him, shimmering in a golden heat haze. On a wide square terrace on the first floor above him he saw the black-gowned figure of the Duchess. There was a table in front of her with a bowl of figs on it and her legs were covered in a light fringed shawl. She was drinking out of a fine Venetian glass half full of ruby wine. The Duke stood behind her and facing away. His hawk-like profile stared into the sun. His back was ram-rod straight and he stood with one hand behind his back, the other resting lightly on the stone balustrade. They were both unmoving, except when the Duchess raised the glass to her lips. The silence was profound, the heat intense.

At last the Duchess looked down and stared at the intruder beneath her. He might have come from Mars the way she scrutinized him. The Duke had his back to Mario. Nevertheless it was he who spoke. Without turning around, he said, 'What do you want?'

The voice was cool and pure, the language spoken in an unfamiliar way. Mario's bravado deserted him. All at once his plan seemed crazy and ridiculous. This world was so remote, the Duke and Duchess so daunting in their dignity, their arrogant assumption of superiority, that he found himself speechless for a moment.

The Duke turned suddenly and looked down at Mario, his eyes fierce as an eagle's.

'Well, speak up, young man. What is your business here?'

Mario realized that the Duke did not know who he was.

76

Everyone knew the Duke. He was instantly recognizable. But to the great man Mario was nothing, a nobody. One of the peasants. An indistinguishable member of the community he cared little about. Mario felt a surge of rage. The anger was the spur he needed.

'Sir, I want to tell you … it is because my sister … my sister's honour …'

'What does he say?' The Duchess's voice was querulous. 'I don't understand his speech.'

'He says something about his sister's honour. Though what that has to do with us …'

'Why is he bothering us?' The Duchess sounded exasperated. 'Please tell him to go away,' she ordered the Duke as if it was beneath her dignity to address him herself, Mario thought, sweating below them in the heat.

The Duke raised his voice a little, leaning over the balustrade. 'Alfonso! Alfonso!' he called and a uniformed servant emerged from the house. He came and stood behind Mario.

'Escort this intruder off my property,' the Duke ordered. The servant started forward and laid a hand on Mario's arm, but he interrupted.

'Listen, sir, please. It's your son Luciano. He's in the woods with my sister Francesca. My father is Giuseppe Palucci. He has gone after them. He has a gun.'

The Duke had pricked up his ears at the name Palucci. The servant almost lifted Mario off his feet and it took all the latter's self-control not to hit him. The Duke raised a hand to stop the servant who relinquished his grip.

The Duke stood, hand raised, immobile for a moment in the scorching sunlight. A girl had appeared at the French windows above on the terrace. She seemed like a mirage or a ghost, pale in her white dress. Slight, beautiful, her thick brown hair caught at her neck by a satin bow, she was about the same age as Mario.

'Well, Father? Not going to defend the family honour?

77

Or do you think it's all right for the Duke's son to debauch the village maidens?'

The Duke paid no attention to his daughter. 'Where are they?' he asked.

Mario pointed. 'Below. In the clearing in the forest nearest us. They go there every Sunday.'

'So that is where he goes!' The words seemed to escape the Duchess's lips involuntarily. 'Ah, God,' she moaned, 'my son!'

'Quiet, Antonella! Be still. You too, Mirella.' The Duke looked down at Mario. 'You will lead us.'

Mario shook his head. 'No' he said, 'they'd kill me. I only told you because ...' He could not think of a reason.

'You are despicable,' Mirella d'Abrizzio said in disgust. Mario squirmed.

'You want something?' the Duke asked. Mario shook his head. 'Oh, but you do. You want something all right. Just like your father. Greedy lot! I don't know what you're after but it will do you no good, boy. You'll get nothing from me.'

He looked down in contempt but Mario did not care. It was all going exactly as he had planned.

The Duke seemed suddenly galvanized.

'Come, Alfonso,' he said. He strode across the terrace and disappeared into the house. The servant looked at Mario with disdain.

'Don't let me see you here no more,' he said softly. 'Sneakin' on your own sister. Dirt is all you are.' He gave Mario a push then turned and went into the house.

Mario walked the bicycle to the end of the drive. He was trembling and his knees felt weak as if he had Amelia against the doorway again. He pulled himself together. It was nearly over. He mounted the bicycle. He looked around him, noting the buzzing of the bees in the tangled undergrowth, the bright splashes of poppies, the heat of the sun. Soon now I can leave all this, he thought. His heart was singing as he free-wheeled down the slope, his long legs stuck out before him. He laughed out loud, then pedalled home as quickly as he could.

When he got to the farmhouse it was deserted and silent. It was extraordinary. He had never known the kitchen of their home completely empty before.

'Hello? Hello?' he called, just in case, but there was no reply. Curiosity, he decided, was one of the world's great weapons. It would have impelled everyone to follow Giuseppe to the woods just as he had hoped.

Satisfied that he was alone, he went to the wall beside the range. Now that he knew the brick was loose, it was easy to see its slight difference to the others. Whistling softly between his teeth, he removed it.

Nothing! There was nothing there. He pushed his hand in but his fingers met only emptiness. Panic filled him. He groped about but to no avail. Nothing.

He had to find the money. He had gone to such lengths with his elaborate plan that he would have no choice now but to leave the house. He could not face what would be in store for him when his father realized the full extent of his meddling. And he would. Giuseppe was nobody's fool.

Sick with anxiety he pulled at the other bricks. They remained fixed and stable. He was sweating now, his fingers slippery. Then he paused, frozen, with his hand in the empty hollow.

Someone had laughed. He had heard it distinctly. He cocked his ear, listening intently, every nerve alert.

Silence.

He waited. Again silence.

He must be getting jumpy. He must have imagined it. He began to grope in the hollow again. Nothing there.

He was dripping with sweat now, moisture running down his face in rivulets, '*Jesu Christo, Jesu Christo*, help me, please.'

He was in too much of a state to realize the irony of his

79

prayer, but it paid off. Almost immediately a brick on the row above moved under his touch. He cast it aside and felt within.

The pouch! It was there. Jesu Christo, *grazie*, it was there. Relief flooded him. He carefully took out the bag and put it into his pocket. It weighed heavily and he smiled. He put the brick back carefully into the hollow. He picked up the other brick and replaced it too.

He took the stairs two at a time and went to his room where he had stowed a parcel beneath his bed. It held the bare essentials, his papers, his razor, some soap, a change of shirt. He picked it up and put the pouch inside.

He closed the bedroom door behind him, went down the stairs, checked that everything was in its accustomed place, that all was neat and tidy. It was all perfect. No one would know that anything was amiss. With all the excitement going on they would not miss him until supper, or the money until … who knew when? The fracas in the woods would keep them busy.

Whistling under his breath he went outside and mounted his bicycle. He began cycling towards Palermo. It would be a long ride. Later he hoped to cadge a lift. But he was on his way. He was free.

He did not hear the laughter that floated after him on the wind, nor did he see the face at the window, the eyes that watched him out of sight.

~~~~~~

'I adore you, Francesca.'

'I adore you, Luciano.'

The light flickered through the meshed leaves. Green shadows moved as if the wood was underwater. It was cool in here out of the sun. The grass smelled sweeter than the flowers she carried. The moss was soft as velvet.

Luciano looked at the girl's face turned up to him. It was luminous with love. The depths of her eyes were cloudy and dense with desire. Their hands sought each other continually.

Luciano gathered her in his arms and held her fiercely to him. She clung to him, murmuring endearments, aching to melt further, deeper into his embrace. He smoothed the hair from her forehead, kissed it again and again, then looked at the warm generous mouth. Her lips were full and red and slightly parted. He bent his head and kissed them. Beneath his her mouth opened, and he moaned a little as they kissed. They had never kissed so fully before and he did not think he could bear the sweetness of it. He could feel her hip against his body and the long line of her thigh against his leg.

They slid to the ground and again he ran his hands over her face, pushing back her hair. 'Francesca *mia*, Francesca *mia*,' he almost sobbed.

'Luciano, Luciano,' she breathed in his ear. Her cheeks were hot, her skin soft beneath his palm.

'Oh, darling, darling girl, I love you so.'

'I know,' she whispered. 'And I love you.'

There was no choice for her. It did not occur to her to stop him as he unbuttoned the top of her dress. It seemed natural and beautiful that in this cool and dappled place he should claim her body for his own. She had always been his. For as long as she could remember she had loved him. So now when his lips sought her she arched her body to his, aiding him, guiding his mouth to her warm breasts springing free as she slipped out of her bodice. She smiled and closed her arms about his head.

'Oh, you are beautiful. Beautiful!' he said, kissing her face, her body.

'Let us be naked together, Luciano *mio*,' she whispered. 'We never have before.' He nodded, pulling off his shirt and riding breeches, and she took off her clothes slowly and laid them on the earth beside his. They stood naked, breath held, their bodies pearly against the verdant background.

81

They shivered but not from cold.

'You are beautiful too,' she sighed, and slowly, calmly they lay down together on the pile of their tangled clothes, indifferent to the prickles of twigs and stones and broken branches, only aware of the softness and hardness of each other's bodies. They looked at each other shyly, and touched each other gently, their breath quickening.

'I think I could die, you are so beautiful,' he said.

'Ah God, Luciano, so could I. Oh, hold me, hold me close.' And with a sigh of delight, he wrapped her in his arms.

At first they did not hear the roar that Giuseppe let out. They were so deep in their embrace, their pleasure.

'You bastard! You beast! Defiler! *Jesu Maria*, take your filthy hands off my daughter.'

The bull-like bellow was followed by a torrent of abuse and Francesca turned from her lover to see the agonized face of her father at the farther side of the clearing. It was full of shock and shame and anger.

'Jesu Maria, I'll kill you, you little beast, you shit, you loathsome animal!'

His voice was shaking and tears were running down his face. Fury and grief were at war in Giuseppe and the pain in his heart nearly overpowered him. The gun shook in his hands.

Francesca suddenly became conscious of her nakedness. She shook her hair over her shoulders in an instinctive and vain attempt to conceal her nudity. Luciano divined her sudden awareness and shielded her with his body, one arm across her shoulders.

'Luciano, you fool! Idiot! What the devil do you do?'

Everyone looked across the clearing to where the Duke had suddenly appeared.

Francesca moaned. 'Ah, God, no!' And shrank against the tree. Luciano, ignoring his father, picked up her dress and handed it to her, still protecting her with his body.

The two older men faced each other across the clearing; the Duke with Alfonso behind him and three or four miscellaneous servants, and Giuseppe with the Palucci family. Fosca had joined them from behind his tree, lasciviously ogling Francesca, unable yet fully to comprehend the exact nature of what was happening. Maria kept blessing herself and murmuring *Ave Marias*, her face white and quivering with shock. Francesca and Luciano stood frozen to the spot, staring at each other like Adam and Eve after the Fall.

'Put your clothes on, Luciano. Leave that whore and come home at once.' The Duke's voice was cool, his words old-fashioned and insulting. 'What delusions do you have, Giuseppe Palucci, that you set your wanton daughter to seduce my son? Is my land not enough? Do you want to bleed me dry?'

'Shut your dirty mouth,' Giuseppe screamed in anguished tones. 'It is my daughter you speak of. Your son has defiled her, my innocent, my dove.' He clutched his chest, agony splitting him.

'I did not defile her, Signore. She is precious to me. I love her.' Luciano's voice startled them all. It was as if a statue had spoken. Luciano and Francesca had been still as a painting. The focus of the scene, but not taking part in it, they stood there dappled in green shadows, unreal as a romantic fresco.

'Don't be stupid, boy. Leave the girl. Come here.'

'No, Father. With respect, no.'

Francesca stood looking at Luciano, her dress in her hand. She seemed to have lost any consciousness of her nakedness, indifferent to their stares, hanging on the words of her lover.

'Will someone cover my daughter?' Giuseppe cried out, and Maria suddenly galvanized by the tone of his voice, rushed to Francesca's side.

'Shame! Shame!'

It was Fosca's voice, the invective screamed at Francesca across the clearing. They all glanced over at him, surprised by his vehemence.

The full meaning of the scene had gradually dawned on him. Now, his face contorted in fury, hatred and disgust, he screamed again and again: 'Shame! Shame! Shame!' He twisted his hands together, wringing them like a peasant woman over a dead body, his face screwed up.

'Shame! Shame! Shame!' He ran away from them, through the woods, pushing Paulo and Marcello aside as he passed, leaving his words hanging on the air behind him.

Paulo recovered his balance and looked at Marcello. 'I did not see you there, brother,' he said. 'Where have you been?'

Marcello looked at him with innocent eyes.

'Why here, Paulo. Here all the time. But you look ill. You are shocked.'

Paulo's face was filled with disgust.

'I cannot see anything but her.' He pointed to Francesca. 'In her disgrace, I wish I had been struck down dead rather than see what I see now.'

'Oh, be Christ-like,' Marcello said coolly. 'Isn't that what they try to teach you?'

'Don't be blasphemous,' Paulo said, eyes feverish. 'That my sister could … that she would … oh, shame!' he echoed Fosca.

'Christ forgave the woman taken in adultery,' Marcello said smoothly. 'Isn't that so?'

'Oh, shut up. Just shut up!' Paulo cried vehemently and went over to where Cecilia stood.

'Disgusting,' she was murmuring, but there was a look of triumph on her face that she could not quite conceal. 'I'm glad you agreed with me,' Paulo said and nodded, satisfied.

Maria was trying to pull Francesca's dress on her but her daughter stood inert and seemed in no hurry now to cover herself. Indifferent to her mother, she stared at Luciano,

84

shrugging Maria away. Her lover took the dress gently from Maria who looked at him dumbly and allowed him to remove it from her hands. She watched as he pulled the sleeve over Francesca's arm in a gesture of infinite tenderness. All of them watched breathlessly as he helped her put her arm through the other sleeve and knelt and held her skirt so that she could step into it. He ignored his father's shouted strictures.

'Come here at once, Luciano. At once, do you hear?'

Luciano lifted Francesca's hair gently from under her bodice at the back, and arranged it over her shoulders, then fastened up the little row of buttons at the front. She watched him gravely all the time.

The onlookers were embarrased by the intimacy of the private little scene. Luciano excluded them. He and Francesca were isolated and protected by his loving gestures, by the reverence he showed her. The trees sighed in the soft breeze that stirred the leaves and sent pale shadows rippling across their intent faces.

Then the calm was suddenly and violently splintered.

'Leave that whore alone, Luciano. Remember who you are and who *they* are. Come here at once.' The Duke's voice was harsh and insulting. He gestured to his servant, Alfonso, and the man began to walk towards the couple who were absorbed in each other. Luciano was still naked, his slim young body marble-white in the green shade.

Overwhelmed and humiliated, the tears running down his cheeks and his breath coming in short ragged gasps, Giuseppe heard the Duke's words. A mighty anger shook him and he shouted: 'Do not speak like that!' He almost pleaded, breathing heavily through his nostrils, 'You speak like that at your own peril. Your son has defiled my daughter, my precious ...'

'Your daughter is a whore who is trying to bewitch my son,' the Duke cried, 'and it will not work. Your strategem will fail.'

85

'Come away from here, Francesca,' Maria said softly, taking her daughter's arm. Giuseppe raised the gun.

'No! No, Father, no,' Serena cried, her eyes wide.

'Don't!' Guido ran to Giuseppe and Maria put out her hands and screamed silently, No. No.

'There is blood in my heart,' Giuseppe shouted, and pulled the trigger.

The shot echoed through the woods. A flurry of startled birds soared out of the trees. Luciano had been pushed aside out of the bullet's path by the servant Alfonso who lay now at Francesca's feet with half his head blown away. She stared down at him in horror, unable to comprehend what had happened. Serena screamed. Guido paused in mid-action, stunned at the speed of the disaster. One moment the man stood there, breathing, moving, the next he lay inert and faceless, a thing on the forest floor.

The Duke grabbed his son by the arm and began pulling him away. The servants closed in between him and Francesca, forcing the boy along, firmly propelling him out of the clearing. He stretched a hand out to Francesca but she could not reach. It was rudely wrenched back by his father. A tall footman walked to where the lovers had been standing and picked up Luciano's clothes. He stood for a moment then spat on the ground, looking with contempt at the Palucci family who now had closed ranks around Francesca.

Maria took her daughter's arm and drew her in the opposite direction, the family in a circle about them. Francesca had stretched out her hand to Luciano but in the end as they were drawn inexorably apart she let it fall. Looking back over her shoulder to try and see him she could see only the Duke's men picking up the body of the dead servant and carrying him out of the clearing. One of the servants had taken off his shirt and covered Alfonso's face with it. She saw her father's tragic eyes and her mother's bewilderment and felt nothing.

The clearing was empty now. The birds had returned and settled on their branches. The only sign in the sweet stillness to show that anything unusual had happened was a bloody mess on the ground beneath the trees where two of the Duke's hunting dogs sniffed and licked their lips.

~~~~~~

Giuseppe sat in his chair, his shoulders slack, his body curved over in despair. His head hung down, nearly touching his knees.

They would come for him soon. He had killed a man, the Duke's servant.

The light slanted lower through the open window, the shadows lengthened. There was absolute quiet in the room except for the occasional moan that escaped his lips. Serena and Guido sat at the table, their faces tense and worried. They waited, they did not know for what.

Giuseppe moaned again as the awful reality of the situation became clearer in his mind. His daughter had been grossly insulted, destroyed. That ripe and beautiful body that he had seen sinfully exposed was condemned by that revelation to dire disgrace in the community. No one would want her now. Maria would never be the mother-in-law of the *dottore's* son. Fosca would tell everyone. He was a fool and incapable of discretion.

Giuseppe gave a snort. He had always tried to be discreet. It was a virtue he admired. Much good it would do him now. He groaned again, squiriming in his seat. He knew the community. He knew how their collective minds worked. They changed sides quickly in situations like this. His daughter had been found naked in the woods with the Duke's son. His family was dishonoured thereby. In one fell swoop he had lost his standing. Oh, they would feel sympathy for him, would understand his pain; but they would pity him, a man who could not keep his daughter in order. He could no longer be respected, looked up to. But

87

much worse than what would happen to him was Francesca's fate. She would no longer be eligible, no longer have the pick of the men in the village. She was damaged goods. Oh, *Jesu Maria*, he thought, my daughter, my beautiful Francesca, the light of my eyes, what will happen to you my pretty one?

He would be demoted in the community, he knew and accepted that. They would move him back down the church. When he went to mass he would find the pew they had promoted him to occupied by someone else, perhaps by Tomaso Canona and his family. Tomaso's ambitious wife would be in Maria's place. It was not to be borne. If he had never been promoted, if he had never been elevated, it would not have been so bad. But they had lifted him up to be cast down. He would be punished, he and his whole family, silently, with no right of reply. Oh God!

And he had killed a man. He had taken a father perhaps, someone's husband, someone's lover. He had extinguished the light. His only hope was a plea that it was a crime of passion. His daughter was being defiled, it was a matter of honour. Surely the judges would see that and sympathize? Surely they would not condemn him completely.

But he had killed the Duke's servant. And the Duke was very powerful. Who had ever pitted himself against the Duke and won? Perhaps God was punishing Giuseppe for the acquisition of the land? Perhaps it was wrong to try to better oneself? Perhaps he had committed the sin of pride, the sin of covetousness, without even being aware of it? Or greed? The Duke had called him greedy. Perhaps he had climbed too high above his station?

He had killed the Duke's servant. A sob escaped him. A cry of horror followed it and he buried his face in his hands. He who had never raised a hand in anger to anyone in his life, he who had never been able physically to

88

chastise his children, he who could never bring himself to lay a hand on them except to caress or to embrace, he had taken a life. In a blood-red rage, in a moment of madness, he had murdered. The horror of it overwhelmed him.

He tried to think. As he saw it he had two choices. One was to take the family lock, stock and barrel and move. The village would give him time to do that. To leave. Go. Run away. He had the money to do it. He could afford to run, build up a new life outside Sicily.

He did not want to behave in such a way; it smacked of cowardice. He did not want to run away. He did not want to do anything dishonourable. He had never done anything dishonourable in his entire life and he did not want to begin now. Compounding the crime. He had lived his life on strictly moral lines and he was too old to change. And where would he go? It would be terrible to leave. Where did he know but here? He wanted to stay but from now on life would be unbearable. He had only been to Palermo twice and both times, though he would never admit it, he had been scared by the big town. He would die away from his home. He loved every blade of grass, every tree, every handful of dust.

He would have to stay. Stay and face the consequences of his crime and his daughter's disgrace.

But what of his family? Could he sentence them to the punishment he richly deserved but they did not? Innocent, they would suffer cruelly. His children's lives were before them. They would transplant without too much pain. Maria would be behind him whatever he decided. Staunch and true, she would be like his right arm.

Well, at least he had the money. If he decided to stay he could afford the best attorney, the best defence lawyer in Palermo. If he left he could afford to set them up in style. He thought he would stay. He did not seem to be able to summon up enough energy to run. He consoled himself with the thought that they would probably give him a short sentence, because of the circumstances. It would be terrible, a nightmare, but Maria and the family would be looked after. His wife was strong. He had the money.

Giuseppe sighed. He stood up. He went to the wall beside the range. He did not care that Guido and Serena were in the kitchen with him. Secrecy did not matter any more.

He pulled out the brick.

There was nothing there. He could not believe it. He rubbed his eyes. No, this could not be happening? He repeated his son's action in reverse and pulled out the lower brick. Perhaps he had put it there by mistake. He knew he had not but he searched nevertheless.

Nothing. He gave a strangled cry, as if he were choking.

'What is it, Papa?' Serena asked him, her voice trembling.

She could not understand what had happened now, kept visualizing the blood, the mess on the forest floor, trying to control the hysteria that threatened to engulf her if she let go, even for a minute. Her mother, looking after Francesca upstairs, refused for the first time in her life to allow Serena to stay by her side and the youngest member of the Palucci family was terrified. Violent images had disrupted the tranquil set of her mind and she was held powerless under their onslaught. Only her mother could soothe these nightmare visions away. But her mother refused to see her. Her father gestured to her angrily, as if to push her away violently with his waving hand; her father who had always held out his arms to her, who was constant in his devotion. Everything was upside down. Everything in her world had turned around, become ugly and frightening. Serena lapsed into a nervous silence, sitting subdued at the table, staring at her hands. Guido patted her shoulders but she pulled away from him. She wanted Mama.

Guido sat waiting to be of help. He had realized that it

was his savings Giuseppe was searching for in the hollows in the wall by the range. He guessed what had happened, saw that there was nothing where he knew there must have been a treasure-trove, saw his father slump empty-handed back into his chair.

Something had been nagging at the edge of Giuseppe's thoughts. It had been there, slipping in and out of the deepest reaches of himself and he had not been able to grasp it. It floated around just out of reach. Now he knew.

Mario! Mario telling them about Francesca in the woods with the Duke's son, alarming them. Why? Mario never did anything for anyone except himself. Giuseppe knew that but rarely acknowledged the fact. He faced it now. What was in it for Mario? Nothing. What could he gain by revealing to them Francesca's shame? Nothing, nothing, nothing. There would have been more chance of profit if he had kept quiet about it, Giuseppe thought bitterly.

And he had not stayed with them. His son had not been with them in the woods to see what happened. Again, why? It was abnormal not to bother about the consequences of his warning if it was sincerely delivered. No, he had been up to something else, diverting attention. Why?

So that he could thieve his father's money, to take what rightfully belonged to his family. To all of them. His son was a thief.

Giuseppe had thought himself crushed and despairing, he had seen himself brought low and humiliated by the day's events. He had not known that there were deeper chasms of agony yet to plumb. The pit of despair he now found himself in was bottomless.

He covered his head with his arms and hands as if to obliterate his presence from the room. The sound that came from him was like the mewling of a cat, little whines and wails of pain that pierced Guido's heart and frightened him.

'Papa.' He half rose at the table but his father shook his head from side to side, tearing at his hair with his hands, as if he would wrench his head off, as if he would tear it from his neck.

'Leave me. No! *Jesu Maria*, no! Leave me alone,' he wept, and Guido sat down obediently as he had always done when his father commanded. They sat for a long time. The silence was broken only by Giuseppe's tormented grieving. The light lengthened, shadows fell across the land. Then suddenly, without warning, Giuseppe stood and rushed out of the room, leaving his children staring after him.

~~~~~~

'Is Mama coming down soon?' Serena asked, knotting her fingers and looking at her brother with anxious eyes.

'Soon, Serena, soon. She'll be here soon,' he said in soothing tones.

'What will happen, Guido?' she asked nervously.

He shook his head. He had no idea. He wished he knew. He wished he was a little boy again, confident in the knowledge that his mama and papa were all powerful and could fix anything. He shivered. It was frightening to see your whole world collapse. It was terrible to see the father you adored, a rock of a man, disintegrate in front of your eyes.

He looked around the familiar kitchen. Would it ever echo to their laughter again? He thought of his father's monkey face grinning as he unbuttoned the top of his trousers after a good meal. He visualized Giuseppe's kindly, loved-filled gaze travelling over the faces of his wife and children. A cold fear clutched his heart. Where had his father gone? Where was he now?

'Mama!' he called out, a child again wanting to be reassured. And Serena, sitting at the table beside him echoed him.

'Mama! Mama!'

But neither of them moved. They were sitting like that half an hour later when Gina and Lombardo burst into the kitchen.

'My God, what has happened?' Gina pulled off her hat and looked at her brother and sister who stared back at her as if she were a visitor from another land.

'Fosca comes running into the piazza talking some nonsense about Francesca and the Duke's son. What is happening here? I thought it was a mistake or that he had taken leave of his senses, what there are of them.' She paused and looked around. 'But I can see from your faces that something is very wrong. What happened?'

Serena ran to her sister and clung to her. Next to Maria, she was most comfortable with Gina.

'Oh Gina, Gina, it's awful! Oh, Madonna, it is shameful. Oh, we are ruined.'

'Serena, my dear, keep calm. Just tell me slowly, everything.'

'It's Francesca, naked she was, in the woods. Oh, the shame, the shame ...' Serena's words were interrupted by Gina who was amazed.

'That is what Fosca said. But it can't be true! I don't understand. How could Francesca ...?'

'Don't talk like that, Serena. It's not nice,' Lombardo said. 'Francesca is a virtuous girl. She would never ...'

'But I *saw* her,' Serena cried, stung. 'I saw her with my own eyes. Naked as the day she was born.'

Gina turned to Guido, sighing. 'Perhaps you better tell me. Serena is not making any sense. Please, from the beginning.'

So Guido told her, calmly and explicitly. When he had finished there was a stunned silence, then Serena said, 'Just as I told you, naked in the wood. Now do you believe me?'

'This is stupid, crazy.' Lombardo found it difficult to absorb what he had just heard. He kept shaking his big head to and fro in disbelief. 'It's crazy. It couldn't have happened There must be some mistake.'

'Hush, Lombardo,' Gina said gently. 'We must think of the others. Where's Mama?'

'Upstairs with Francesca,' Serena answered her brightly. Now that Gina was here and in charge she felt much more secure. 'And Cecilia is with them, or in her room. I don't know where Paulo and Marcello are, but they went upstairs ages ago. Guido is here. Mario has gone.'

'And Papa?'

'He went out. He said, "Leave me alone," and went out,' Guido said, pointing to the door.

'That is not like him,' Gina said. 'Still, I suppose he is very upset and feels ...'

'Lombardo, go and find Papa. Bring him here.' Gina was decisive. 'We must decide what to do. I'll get Mama. We must not lose our heads now.'

Lombardo did what Gina asked. She sighed and went upstairs to the bedroom she shared with Francesca. When she opened the door she found the room in darkness, the shutters closed. Maria was sitting in a chair beside the bed. She put her finger to her lips when she saw Gina enter the room.

'She's asleep now, I think. She's exhausted,' Maria whispered.

'Mama, are you all right?' Gina asked anxiously, trying to see her mother's face in the dim light.

'Oh, Gina *mia*, will we ever be all right again?' Her mother's voice was flat and unemotional and that worried her eldest daughter more than if she had been in a state.

Maria sighed heavily, 'It was no one's fault, Gina. Poor Francesca! She was a romantic innocent. In love with the Duke's son – what folly! It would be ridiculous, a farce, were it not so sad. How could I think to warn her about that? I could not foresee such madness. And he, the bold young man, it seems he was as innocent as she. Poor babes, poor fools! And your father, Gina, what else could he do? He wanted only to protect her reputation. The Duke was shocked as well. You cannot blame him.' She frowned. 'But he should not have insulted your father. No, he should not have done that.'

Gina put her arm around her mother's shoulders. 'Come, Mama. We must go downstairs and decide what to do.'

'What can we do?' Her mother's face crumpled in pain as she faced the realization of what the future could hold. 'Except hope that the Duke will be merciful.'

They had not seen Serena follow Gina into the room. She cried out now in a panicked voice. 'Oh, Mama, Mama!'

Maria pulled herself up, drawing on her reserves of strength. 'But we will be all right, Serena, never fear. We will be all right. The good God will not fail us now in our hour of need. We must go to the Duke. Throw ourselves on his mercy. He'll see reason. He is a good Catholic after all, a just man ...'

And fiercely to herself, she muttered under her breath, 'He's got to be. Please, Madonna, he's got to be!'

Maria touched the cheek of her sleeping child, Francesca murmured, 'Luciano. Luciano *mio*,' in her sleep.

'That's something you'll have to give up,' Maria said, but her daughter did not hear her, did not wake up. Her lashes lay on her flushed cheeks and the hair rested damp on her forehead. She babbled in a troubled fashion and Maria soothed her.

'There now, Francesca. Sleep ... sleep.'

'Come along. Let's go down,' she said then to Gina and with a last glance behind her left the room on tiptoe, motioning the others to follow.

When they reached the kitchen Lombardo had just arrived back. He was breathless.

'I can't find him. I can't find him anywhere.'

With one swift glance around the room Maria

95

established that it was Giuseppe of whom Lombardo spoke. An icy hand gripped her heart. She stumbled and nearly fell. Guido leapt to his feet and helped her.

'Where are Marcello, Paulo and Cecilia?' he asked.

'I sent Cecilia to her room,' his mother said.

'Here I am, Mother.' Cecilia came slowly down the stairs. Guido called. 'Marcello, Paulo!'

Paulo and Marcello came out on to the landing.

'Help me to search for Papa, quick,' Guido said. 'Hurry now.'

He turned to Maria. His mother was looking at the wall, at the two hollows left by the missing bricks. Empty hollows. She pointed at them, unable to speak.

Paulo and Marcello came down the stairs. They too saw what she saw.

'He took it?' she said incredulously to Guido. 'He took it?'

Guido shook his head. 'No, Mama. He could not find it. He searched and searched but he could not find it.'

'You knew?' Maria asked.

He shook his head again. 'No. I guessed when I saw what Papa was doing. It was not hard to figure out. It was the money.'

She nodded. 'It was gone?' she asked in disbelief. 'Are you sure?'

'Yes, Mama.'

'Yes, Mama,' Serena said, full of importance, 'I saw him too. I did not think of the money, but I saw him search and search. Then he moaned and moaned, such a terrible sound, and held his head and pulled his hair. It was awful. Like he was losing his mind.'

Maria looked puzzled. 'Then who ... who ...' She bent her head, then looked up at Guido as the truth dawned slowly.

'Mario,' she hissed, her eyes blazing. 'Mario!' she said, certainty in her voice. 'Oh, *Jesu Maria*, my son, my son.'

96

She grabbed Guido's arm. 'Giuseppe guessed,' she cried. 'He guessed. Then he would …' She stopped, all colour draining from her face. 'Oh, my God, there would be nothing left for him. Nothing! Oh, *Jesu Christo*.' Her voice rose and she rushed from the room.

She ran as she had not run since she was seventeen, across the field to the barn. The day was slipping away and the land was covered with darkness. An early dew had fallen. It wet her feet but she did not feel it. She only knew she had to get to Giuseppe before … Her mind did not dare to continue. Lips trembling, heart pounding, she reached the barn, pushed open the heavy door, the door that Mario had hidden behind earlier in the day.

She was not surprised when she saw the dark shadow swinging from the beam across the roof. She was not surprised at the hideous awkwardness of the body suspended thus, hanging between roof and floor. She was surprised at the terrible face. She had known. Her body and soul and mind, so in tune with his through twenty-five years of marriage, had known long before she reached the barn door.

She felt her heart being torn out of her body. The pain was like none she had ever known before.

'Cut him down,' she said calmly.

The light had gone out in her life. There would be only dimness from now on.

'Cut him down,' she screamed this time. Her voice reverberated throughout the barn and Lombardo moved to do her bidding.

Chapter Five

Fra Bartholomeo said he could not bury Giuseppe in hallowed ground. He had committed suicide and therefore had died in mortal sin. So Giuseppe was laid to rest in a grave among the lemon groves beside the woods. They erected a stone statue of Mary of Mercy over his burial place and planted a cypress and some flowers there. It was a peaceful spot and almost at once a family of birds came to nest beneath the young tree and filled the air with their song.

The family had not expected anyone to attend the funeral. They sat in the kitchen with the casket, just themselves, believing that Giuseppe would have only the family to mourn him. A knock on the door surprised them. It was the priest.

'I come unofficially,' he said, touching the shoulder of the weeping widow. He was surprised at her appearance. He had seen the face of grief often but Maria was blasted by anguish. She had lost all her warm plumpness and looked saggy and crumpled. Her face was skin and bone with flesh hanging down in folds under her eyes, at her jaws, where her apple-firm cheeks had once been.

'Maria, do not weep so. He is …' Fra Bartholomeo was going to say 'with God' but he stopped himself in time. Giuseppe was not with God. He had committed the unpardonable sin of taking his own life. The priest looked at her speechlessly.

'I know what you were going to say,' she cried, 'and you were right. He *is* with God. Do you hear me? Giuseppe is with God.'

'Mama, Mama.' Gina bent to take her mother's hand but Maria pushed her away and looked at the priest, challenging him.

'Did Jesus say that?' she asked him. 'Did Jesus ever actually *say* that? That if you … do what Giuseppe did, under such provocation, you will not see the face of the Divine Master?' She looked at Fra Bartholomeo piteously and begged, 'Did he?'

The priest shook his head. 'Only the Church,' he said. 'But you have to follow the Church's teaching.'

Maria was not listening. 'Ha! There, you see.' She turned triumphantly to Gina. 'Jesus did not say it himself. Only the Church. The Church are men. Men can make mistakes. My Giuseppe was a good man. All his life, good. He kept the Commandments. Did he not, Father?'

'He did, Maria. He did.'

'Then he is with God,' she said firmly.

Francesca, pale as the lilies on the casket, stood beside Guido at the kitchen table. Her brother held her hand. Her face was expressionless. She knew that if she cried she would never stop. It was all her fault, she knew that. And the Duke's. The rest of the family blamed Mario but if it had not been for her none of this would have happened.

'Papa was all right until he found Mario had gone with his money,' Guido had told her. 'It was not your fault, Francesca, it was Mario's. I will kill him.'

She smiled. Gentle Guido trying to look fierce. Francesca blamed Luciano's father and herself. She did not blame Luciano. He had not made her do anything she had not fully wanted to do. But the Duke had no right to speak of her as if she were a loose woman. He should not have insulted her father. She would pay the Duke back. Somehow. Some day. In the meantime she would have to learn to live with herself, with the turmoil that was within her. She would have to harden her heart, learn to dominate her emotions and find a way to avenge her father's shame and death.

She could not stay here now. She would have to go away. Fosca had told everyone. He had come to the farmhouse to bring condolences to Maria. Francesca had been feeding the chickens in her black mourning clothes when he went into the kitchen to speak with her mother. He had come out after a short while and stood staring at her. Then he had come over to her and looked her up and down as if she had no clothes on.

'Whore!' he hissed at her, and all she could do was continue scattering the grain for the chickens, her chin trembling, her eyes blurred with tears of rage and shame.

'This is all your fault. Your father's death, the disgrace of your family, all your fault. You are a whore, Francesca Palucci. You are not fit to be any man's wife.' And he left her, her body shaking with sobs she could not release. So she stood trembling as if she had the palsy while the chickens gobbled and scratched at her feet.

She would have to leave, she thought now in the darkened kitchen where the body of her father lay in its cedar-wood casket on his own table.

Voices were lowered and Gina poured coffee for the women and *grappa* for the men.

Francesca took a drink to her grandfather. He sat huddled in his rocking-chair. It had been brought into the kitchen, and was destined never to leave it. 'It's not winter yet,' he said, for they only brought the chair in when it was cold. Then they told him about his son. Now he sat in the chair and rocked, staring at the coffin, an old, old man in shock, his last days on earth blighted by tragedy.

'Why?' he murmured. 'Why? He was my *son*. It is not right. *I* should go first. It is in the nature of things. It should have been me.'

Francesca knew it would not be long before he followed Giuseppe. She sighed a long desolate sigh and turned to Cecilia. They looked at each other wordlessly, then in an access of shame and sympathy Cecilia put her arms around her sister.

'Oh, Francesca, I was so jealous of you! It all seems so silly and pointless now. I'm sorry. Can you forgive me? I didn't mean all those nasty things I said to you.'

Francesca patted her sisters cheek. Cecilia's face was swollen with weeping, but Francesca did not cry. She felt curiously detached and emotionless, as if she had already left the place.

'It's all right, Cecilia. It doesn't matter now,' she said.

Paulo wasn't there for the funeral. He had asked Fra Bartholomeo to send him to the seminary immediately instead of in the winter as previously planned. He wanted to run away. He could not face his father's death or his mother's grief, he said; he had to go. He stood before the priest, his face set, the premature lines running from his nose to his jaw, dark circles beneath his tormented eyes. His headaches had started again, cleaving his skull with a white-hot agony. Fra Bartholomeo explained that you could not run away from life to God, that God *was* life. Life and Death. But Paulo would not listen and insisted he wanted to go to a monastery now. There was something very wrong there, the good priest thought, as Paulo looked at him with burning eyes.

'You do not know, Father. My thoughts torment me. You do not know the hell in my head.'

Fra Bartholomeo was perplexed by Paulo's vehemence but said nothing. It was not his business. The man could be a saint or a lunatic. How could he, a simple country priest, know? No, the church ruled that it was the business of the instructors to watch, sort out the cranks and freaks from those with genuine vocations. The brothers would sort it all out. They were adept at that kind of thing.

So Fra Bartholomeo shrugged and asked Maria's permission for her son's departure. She gave her consent absentmindedly, still too shocked by the loss of her husband to take in what was happening, too numb to really care. So Paulo was sent to Rome, to the Little Brothers of St Anthony. Let them sort it all out, Fra Bartholomeo thought, and wished him well.

Serena clung to her mother's skirts. She seemed lost and terrified but could not claim her mother's attention as before. Maria virtually ignored her, behaving as if she were a troublesome little dog at her feet. Marcello sat in the corner, his face closed, unsmiling. He had hardly spoken since the terrible day their lives had been shattered. Occasionally Guido took his brother's shoulder in a fierce grip and the twins stared dumbly at each other.

Lombardo had been a tower of strength. He had looked after all the funeral arrangements, for Maria had been incapable of managing anything. She who had once held so firm a reign on the running of the household was now unable to make a cup of coffee. With quiet strength Lombardo organized it all, right down to the statue and the plot of land where Giuseppe would be laid to rest.

~~~~~~

It had been a surprise to see Fra Bartholomeo arrive at the farmhouse for the funeral. The family sat around the coffin, the room full of their grief. 'We are alone now,' Maria said. 'Alone.' And the priest patted her shoulder.

There was a knock on the door. They all looked at it, startled. Lombardo strode across and opened it.

'May we come in?'

It was Tomaso Canona, his mother Anica, his wife and his son Filipo. They were followed by Beno Mutti, Notary Gitano, the storekeeper and his wife, the doctor and his wife (though not Fosca), other workers and farmers. One by one they tiptoed into the Palucci kitchen and reverently

102

paid their last respects. The whole village had come to bid farewell to Giuseppe Palucci.

'Your husband was a fine man, Maria,' Tomaso Canona said, his hand on her shoulder. 'You have nothing to be ashamed of.' Nothing could have touched Maria more than this display of loyalty and love by her neighbours. She drew a shuddering breath that tore through her body and, shivering, broke down in a storm of weeping. Giuseppe could be laid to rest with his friends and the community about him, paying tribute.

When it was time they took the coffin on their shoulders; his sons, Marcello and Guido. No one remarked on the absence of Mario or Paulo. Tomaso Canona and Beno Mutti helped them. Fra Bartholomeo led the procession, followed by the men bearing the casket. Maria was supported by Gina on one side and Lombardo on the other. Francesca walked alone after them. There was a space around her. No one seemed to want to get too close to her and the community cast curious glances in her direction. The looks were furtive, under lowered eyelids, cast sideways. They had heard the stories, exaggerated now, and could not resist conjecture. And Francesca felt every covert look; every speculation pierced her. She stood a little straighter, her resolve to leave becoming stronger.

They crossed the field in blazing sunshine and the birds sang as if nothing had happened, as if everything was normal. The villagers fanned out around the grave and Fra Bartholomeo murmured prayers he was not supposed to say. They came to his lips involuntarily. He found he was not able to keep silent even though he knew the Church was quite specific about such matters. A suicide could not receive a Christian burial. Well, it did not seem relevant now, that rule.

As the coffin was lowered into the grave Tomaso Canona was heard to whisper and point and they all looked up. The Duke was standing at the edge of his

103

forest, the forbidden woods where Francesca and Luciano used to meet in the cool green gloom. He stood there, tall, dressed in black, and leaning on his silver cane. As they watched they saw him take off his hat and bow his head. They all saw the Duke's mark of respect for Giuseppe Palucci. All except Maria who was in a state of collapse, and Francesca who kept her eyes closed throughout the ceremony at the graveside.

When the brief ceremony was over the people raised their bowed heads and saw that the Duke was gone.

~~~~~~

The funeral party went back to the farmhouse but the villagers would not come in again. They dispersed in quiet little groups to their homes, the men to the *trattoria* for a *grappa* or *strega* to celebrate the fact that they were still lustily alive, thankful that their hearts beat strongly and that they were not like poor Giuseppe, six foot under in the cold earth with worms for company.

In the farmhouse Gina took Maria upstairs to her bed. She was in a state of collapse. All life seemed to have drained from her. She curled up in a foetal ball in the bed she had so joyously shared with Giuseppe, and lay there inert.

'Mama? Mama? Is there anything I can get you?' Gina asked when she had pulled the curtains but there was no reply from the bed. Maria lay, eyes open, staring into a pit of loneliness.

'Oh, Mama.' Gina's voice broke on a sob. She kissed her mother's forehead and dampened it with her tears but there was no response. She went out, closing the door behind her. On the stairs she wiped her tears away with the back of her hand and took a deep breath. Then she went down into the kitchen.

'Everyone listen,' she said to the family, 'we can't let things drift. There's work to be done. Papa has been dead for days now. The harvest cannot, will not, wait. Today we buried him, God rest his soul. Now we have to face facts.' She sighed and frowned. 'Mama is not well. She cannot do anything ... she is incapable at the moment. I will take on her duties.' She faltered and Lombardo put his large hand reassuringly on her shoulder. 'I wish I did not have to talk like this but the work must go on.' She gulped and continued, 'Francesca will help me and Serena and Cecilia. Lombardo and Guido and Marcello will organize the work force ...'

'No, Gina, I cannot stay here now. You must see that. I cannot live here any more, I must go.' Francesca's troubled face was turned towards her sister, her eyes pleading for understanding. 'Oh, I *want* to help you, I don't want to desert you, but you must see how impossible it would be for me here.'

Gina went to her sister and folded her in her arms. 'Stay, dearest. We love you so. They will forget, the village. Tomorrow, next week, it will be something or someone else.'

But Francesca shook her head. 'No, I must go. I cannot remain. I would die. You saw them today, peering at me, looking at me as if I were a whore.'

'Where will you go? How will you go?' her sister asked.

Francesca shrugged. 'I don't know. I just know I have to.'

'I will go with her,' Guido said.

'Oh, no!' Gina cried. 'Not you too. There will be no one left.'

'It is what Papa would have wanted. I am the eldest, and there is something you all forget: there is a task to be done before any of us can rest. I mean to find Mario.'

Everyone looked at him, silently, understanding dawning.

'Mario,' Cecilia spat out the name, then looked at Guido. 'Kill him for me.'

'Kill him for all of us,' Gina said.

105

Guido nodded. 'It is vendetta, I promise.'

He walked around the table, looking at each member of his family and then Lombardo in the eye. He shook their hands solemnly. 'I will come back some day,' he promised. 'When it is done. One day, I promise.'

They had lowered their voices, as if someone might be listening. They drew together closely around the table.

'Papa must be avenged,' Guido said firmly. 'That is why I must go. We will both go, Francesca and I. Lombardo, you must look after the farm. Papa would want it.'

Cecilia shook her head. 'Papa was so proud of his sons. Yet look what has happened. Mario and Paulo ...' Her voice broke.

'Marcello?' Guido looked at his twin who shook his head.

'No,' he said, 'I couldn't make a decision now. I'm not capable.'

'You are always capable, Marcello. You are the strongest one.' Marcello shook his head. 'Not now,' he said, softly. 'Not now.'

Gina stood up. 'Do you realize what you are saying?' she asked.

'Lombardo, they do not mean ...'

Lombardo cleared his throat. 'It is the shock. Cecilia is right. Giuseppe would have liked his sons to continue his work. But they are not here, except for Marcello. Will you run the place, Marcello?'

'I've said no, I meant no,' Marcello answered, his voice steady. 'Lombardo must take over. You are right, Gina. Mario will not come back. Neither, I think, will Paulo.' He looked at his twin sadly. 'Guido will have to journey very far, and who knows what will happen to him during that time. It is always hard to come back to the home of your childhood. Gina is right. Life must go on. Lombardo, do not let us down now.'

'I want Papa back,' Serena cried, her voice strangled. 'I want my mama and papa!'

'Hush there, child. Hush,' Gina soothed her.

'I won't let you down. I'll stay as long as I am needed. Gina knows that. And if any of the Palucci men want to take things over, I'll gladly bow out,' promised Lombardo. He gripped Gina's hand firmly in his own.

Guido smiled. 'That would not be fair,' he said. 'You'll be marrying Gina soon?'

They nodded. 'I don't think we should wait long now that all this has happened,' said Gina.

'It's not respectable for me to be here. So we will marry soon,' said Lombardo.

'Then if you do, you'll want some security. It would not be right if one of us suddenly marched home and decided to take over. Marcello, you understand?'

He nodded.

'Then that's settled. Gina, you must take care of the family, and Mama until she is better. Serena and Cecilia will help you.' Guido heaved a sigh of relief. 'Good. It is all decided. Gina, can you make us some coffee, please, and we will discuss how to get the money for our journey.'

~~~~~~

A few days later the Duke sent for Guido and Francesca. The summons came, delivered by one of the servants who had been in the clearing that day. He was ice-cold with hostility and seemed barely able to get the words out. Gina thanked him and said her brother and sister would be honoured.

'I doubt it!' the servant dared. The Duke, after all, was not there. 'There is no welcome there for your family.'

Gina did not repeat his words to the others but her heart sank to remember them

Francesca was overjoyed when she received the summons. 'It is Luciano!' she said to Gina. 'He has explained how he feels about me to his father. That is why he has sent for me.'

107

Gina shook her head, looking at her sister with sympathetic eyes. 'Don't spin dreams, Francesca. I don't think the Duke could or would allow such a liaison.'

'Oh, Gina, don't! Don't try to depress me. If you knew how I ache for him, long for him. And I know he feels the same way about me. You'll see, Luciano has got around his father. That is why he has sent for me.'

Gina shook her head again and said nothing.

Guido walked beside Francesca on their way to the *palazzo*. He was determined to stay close to her all the time. Unlike Francesca, he did not think their visit would be a happy one. He looked at his sister. He could see how vulnerable she was. She had put on her best clothes, a skirt and a blouse made by Maria. Her eyes were full of hope.

They walked up to the great pillared mansion hand-in-hand. Francesca squinted her eyes against the sun and stared at the vast building before her. The white pillars shimmered in the golden light like a mirage or a fairy-tale; a palace suspended in dazzling mid-air. The road was hot and dusty. Francesca's boots were white by the time they arrived and for the first time reality overwhelmed her. Since her father's death she had put her feelings on ice, frozen them, afraid to explore her emotions, afraid she would go mad. She felt lost in time, waiting. And all the time Luciano was there in her heart, cherished. Just as when he was away at school she knew he would return, so she waited for him patiently to send for her, to let her know when to come to him. She had marked time since the tragedy, certain he would act, would contact her. As she made plans to go away with Guido she was subconsciously expecting to change them. She would receive a summons to meet him here, or in Palermo, or Rome, or Paris. She was confident of that. And now the message had come. Her brother was asked to accompany her as a chaperon. It would all be settled today.

But now, for the first time, she saw the great house

clearly, through different eyes, and shuddered. To be mistress of this? An overwhelming realization of Luciano's position forced her to face the situation realistically. Suddenly, in one brief moment of time, she knew how hopeless her position was. She saw through the tall windows white-jacketed servants and chandeliers hanging diamond-bright in vast tapestried rooms. She shivered, felt the world come to a stop. She grabbed Guido's arm for support for she thought she might fall, then summoning all her courage she drew herself up to her full height, took a deep breath and prepared to face an interview she both desired and dreaded.

'Here they are.' It was a girl's voice, and for a moment Guido thought it came from the sky. But, looking up, he saw a white-clad figure leaning over the balustrade of a terrace on the first floor. The girl had long bronze hair full of amber lights. It cascaded over the warm stone as she spoke. 'You are the Paluccis? The ones my father sells the land to?' She folded her bare arms on the balustrade and stared at them. 'And you are the one my brother Luciano was mad about?' She gazed down at Francesca, then stood up. 'Yes, well, he wants to see you.'

Francesca put her hand to her heart. 'Luciano?' she asked.

The girl laughed. 'Oh, no! Papa. It is he who wants to see you. Luciano has been sent away.'

'I don't believe you. He must be here somewhere.'

'He's not, I'm afraid.'

'Mirella, come here at once.' It was the Duke's voice. 'Bring the Paluccis to me.' Then, irritably, 'I'm lost without Alfonso.'

Guido shivered. Alfonso, he remembered, was the servant his father had killed in the woods.

They could not see the Duke. The girl withdrew abruptly and Guido looked around for the way in. The lower floor of the *palazzo* was shuttered firmly. They were about to circle the building to find an entrance when Francesca saw a small stone stairway leading up to the terrace.

When they reached the top there was no sign of the girl but the Duke stood at the open french windows, his back to them. He was a strangely sombre figure dressed in black, tall and hook-nosed. He raised one hand, motioning them to follow him, and as he did so he disappeared inside the building.

Francesca glanced at Guido who shrugged. They followed him, stepping out of the golden-white dazzle into a room of such splendour that Francesca gasped and faltered to a stop. There were countless gilt-framed mirrors. Portraits hung on crimson silk damask-covered walls. The furniture was gilded and upholstered in thick satin; opulent chandeliers hung from the decorated ceilings. Rooms led one into the next. The Duke led them ever onward. He was always at the exit of the room they entered and beckoned them on from majestic doorway to doorway, a tall black figure who disappeared when they stopped, open-mouthed, to look at the magnificence around them. So they hurried to follow, constantly drawn on by the long-fingered gesturing hand.

Why he led them so far was a mystery, at least then. Afterwards Francesca realized that there was no better way of showing her Luciano's inheritance, and of intimidating them, than by making them follow him through the overpowering grandeur of his home. Through splendid room after splendid room he led them, until entering a hall of mirrors they discovered him, sitting at the far end upon a throne before them.

They stopped, speechless. They were overawed, stunned by the place they found themselves in. Francesca felt awkward and clumsy. She looked down at her boots, white with dust, then at the cheap material of her skirt. She groped for Guido's hand, found it and was grateful

110

for the gentle pressure of his fingers. They stood before the Duke as he sat, one elbow resting on the gilt and ormolu arm of the throne, his hand beneath his chin, gazing at them speculatively, looking very like the golden eagle that spread its wings above his head at the back of the dais. Francesca squirmed beneath his cool appraising gaze. She knew he could visualize her without her clothes and felt naked and ashamed before him, wanting to strike his face and rebuke him for the impertinence of his eyes. She had an overwhelming desire to cross her arms, as if by doing so she would protect herself from his frank stare, but she stood meekly still, suffering it, enduring it, praying for it to end.

At last he said, 'At least Luciano knows a beauty when he sees one.' He laughed to himself then, and closed his eyes. His face looked weary and old.

'You are not going to believe this,' he said after a moment, 'but I liked your father. I respected him.'

They did not answer. There was nothing to say.

'I am sorry he died,' the Duke continued.

'Are you apologizing?' Francesca tried to imitate the formal idiom of his speech. The Duke's eyebrows shot up. He was like his son, Francesca thought, surprised. Luciano would look like this in forty years.

'Apologizing? What on earth do you mean?' he asked in surprised tones. 'What have I to apologize for? I am simply saying that it is no cause for rejoicing, your father's death, even if he did get ideas above his station.'

He leaned forward. 'Tell me,' he asked, 'did he put you up to it?'

'Put me up to what?' Francesca was perplexed.

'Seducing my son.'

Her face flushed and her eyes snapped. Guido's grip on her hand tightened.

'How dare you, sir? We fell in love. My father had nothing to do with it. He did not approve of it any more

111

than you.' She felt tears prick the back of her lids.

'Don't speak to my sister like that, sir. Show her respect or we will leave.' Guido spoke quietly and the Duke transferred his gaze to the man.

'You may ask Luciano,' Francesca continued. 'Where is he?' She looked around as if the young man might pop out from behind the Gobelin tapestry that hung from ceiling to floor at the back of the glittering throne-room. It depicted an idyllic country scene and Francesca could not help thinking of herself and her lover in the forest. The Duke smiled to himself at the girl's insouciance.

'He is not here. I have sent him away.'

She gave a little sob. 'Then it's true?'

'Oh, yes. You will not see him here. Do you think I am a fool?'

'Then you knew he loved me!' she cried in triumph, 'else you would not send him away, not if you had nothing to fear.'

'Stupid girl. How could I have anything to fear from you?' The Duke said it mildly, as if speaking to a child, amused at her audacity. 'Every young gentleman falls for a servant, an older woman, or a whore. The first thing he sees that moves his manhood, he lusts after. But lust is soon and easily satisfied.' He glanced to where the sun blazed through the tall window, as if remembering something. He sighed heavily then turned his attention back to the couple standing before him, so shabby, so unfashionable, so uncouth. So young. Oh, so young.

'I have sent him out of harm's way till he forgets all about his passion for you. Which he will, very soon. You would be surprised my dear how quickly a young man forgets. And there are women to be bought in Rome who will help him drown his regrets; women a man would kill for.'

'Why did you bring my sister here? Not to tell her that surely,' Guido said, shifting from one foot to the other. He

112

was acutely uncomfortable under the Duke's eagle gaze in this stifling magnificent hall.

'To see her with her clothes on perhaps? I was curious …'

'How dare you, sir! Come, Francesca.'

They turned to walk out but the Duke's laughter stopped them. 'Don't be stupid,' he said. 'Such dignity. Such pride. I wanted to say that I respected your father. I needed to make that clear. Also I wanted you, my dear, to see for yourself how impossible any liaison between you and my son would be.' He spread his hands and once more Francesca looked around the tall mirrored room.

'You are the head of the family now?' he enquired of Guido who nodded. 'I heard your brother has run away with all your father's money?'

Guido looked startled. 'How did you know that?'

'There is little that goes on here I do not know about.' The Duke smiled.

'You did not know about your son's affair,' Guido retaliated quietly.

'Ah, Guido, no.' Francesca was reproachful, laying her hand on her brother's arm.

'You are right, I did not know. About the most important thing, I was ignorant.' The Duke shrugged. 'But it is true about your brother?'

Guido was forced to nod.

'Ah, how terrible! Nevertheless, he simply copied your father. Don't you see? All this is a direct result of your father's greed.'

Francesca drew in a sharp breath and the Duke held up a hand to silence her.

'Please, child, listen to me. There was a time when your father would not have presumed. For a peasant to aim so high …' He tutted reprovingly. 'I remember as boys, what friends we were. I never realized when I gave him permission to steal my father's trees that he would develop

113

such grandiose ideas. In those days the people belonged to the castle. All the land was my father's, and all the cottages and farms on it. Everything and everybody was his. He was their master, their overlord. Your grandfather was one of his people. The peasants worked the land. My father organized it all. At harvest time he fed them, down there, in the derelict remains of a huge barn. It was a time of laughter and joking. The people were happy, or if they were not then they were certainly very fine actors. They gave the impression of being very content. They loved him. It was an ordered life and everyone knew their place.'

Guido snorted. 'Spare us, sir. You really believe that?'

But the Duke continued, his brooding profile sharp as a falcon's turned from them. 'Then the peasants became greedy. Garibaldi!' He spat the name out. 'They got greedy, wanted more. They got what they wanted.' He turned to them. 'They got wages and rights; they found they could buy land.' His eyes narrowed and he stuck his head forward on its scrawny neck. 'They found also that they could go. Leave. Now the young men desert the land. There is no one left to work it. What do you think will happen next, eh?' He looked at them, his eyes sharp. 'I will tell you. All the youth will go, looking for better things. They will leave the land and it will die. The cities will become larger and larger. We will make a concrete world, a hell, an arid place not fit for animals. I travel. I know. It has begun already. Because people get above their station. Because people get greedy.'

There was silence. Guido and Francesca waited. They did not understand what he was talking about. The Duke stared unblinking into the light. Eventually he turned back to them. 'The land your father bought from me reverts back on his death.'

He said it softly and at first Guido did not register the meaning.

'What? I don't understand.'

114

'The land I sold your father reverts back to me when he dies.'

'Is that true, Father? If it is you have added fraud to your long list of crimes.'

Francesca and Guido looked behind them. They saw the girl in the white dress standing there. She had lace at her throat and wrists and an apple in her hand. Her mane of amber hair was touched with light and she stared at her father with undisguised hostility.

The Duke stood. 'Go to your room,' he ordered. 'At once.'

'No, Father, I will not. I am not a child to be ordered about. It will not wash. You cannot cheat these people.'

She turned to Guido and Francesca. 'He talks constantly of honour but he himself does not know the meaning of the word.' Her voice was contemptuous and Francesca looked at her with startled eyes, amazed that she dared to speak to the Duke so, admiring her courage and her championship of them.

Guido cleared his throat. 'I know that my father bought his property from you, and from your father. He told us so often. The sale was witnessed by a notary.'

The Duke nodded. 'That was the house, and the acres around it. Some three, I think. But the vineyards and olive groves revert to me. Everything else reverts to me. It is now mine.'

There was silence.

'I don't believe you,' Guido said eventually.

The Duke smiled. 'He trusted me,' he said.

'And you tricked him?' Francesca said. He nodded.

'You are a destroyer!' Mirella cried. 'You have ruined my mother. My poor beloved mother.' She glared at her father. 'Your excesses will drive her to her grave.' There was a feverish note to her voice. Her eyes were very fierce, like his own.

'You are beautiful,' she said to Francesca. 'Luciano loves

115

you. He is devastated to lose you but my father will never allow you to see him, so his happiness is to be sacrificed too. We all bow to our non-existent honour. Something my father has very conveniently buried unless it suits him to brandish it at us like a weapon.' She looked closely at Francesca. 'Do you know Papa had to manacle Luciano to Gianfranco to get him away from you? To get him away from here. Luciano cried like a baby.'

A fierce joy stabbed Francesca's heart. She would go to Rome; she knew his whereabouts now. She would find Luciano. Somehow she would find him.

'Get out of here! Get out of here, both of you,' the Duke shouted. 'You are intruding.'

'A moment, sir,' Guido said quietly. 'You are wrong. We are the very people you need now. Without the likes of my father, you and your kind are doomed. You talk of greed. You accuse us of overstepping the mark. But we pay for everything we possess. We work for it. What we take we give back a hundredfold while you are a parasite. You feed and feed and suck the source dry. You leave the land empty. Never, I repeat, never, lecture me or mine again.'

There was the sound of clapping from the girl standing behind them. Guido turned to his sister.

'Come, Francesca, this is no fit place for you,' he said and they walked away from the Duke.

Mirella caught up with them in a room shimmering with golden statues and ornaments, paintings and tapestries. She called out their names and they stopped and waited till she caught them up.

'I have never heard anyone talk like that to my father,' she said, breathless and pink-cheeked. 'You were magnificent.'

'I told him the truth,' Guido replied with dignity.

'How will you manage?' she asked. 'Have you any money?'

'No,' Francesca said. 'None at all.'

116

'We have no money either. I would give you some if I had any. We live on credit. This place is mortgaged. The paintings disappear. The chandeliers vanish. My mother's specialist will not see her until his bill is paid. Sometimes we do not eat. In this land of milk and honey, we have nothing to eat.' She laughed, pushing back her amber hair, looking at them with wide eyes. 'Isn't it funny to think that we, up here at the top of the world, are hungry, while you, the peasants feed off plenty?' She shrugged. 'Ah, it's strange and no mistake.' She turned and walked away but before she reached the door she said, 'Why don't you borrow some money from your friends in the village? They are more likely to have some than we are. It's a thought.' Then she was gone.

Francesca pictured the Duke. She had always thought of him as a leader, a proud example of breeding and position. Yet, seeing him in this grand palace, she realized that he could not measure up to her father in nobility. Giuseppe had more dignity in his little finger than this man had in his whole body. Her father had been honourable. This man was not. Her father had killed himself. This man would not. This man would live with his shame.

She touched Guido's sleeve. He was staring after Mirella. Francesca was desperate to escape the place. They walked out through room after room until finally they emerged into the burning sunlight. When they got outside Guido punched his fist into the palm of his other hand.

'Jesu Christo, I want to kill him,' he whispered. He leaned against the wall of the *palazzo*, feeling weak and angry.

'Don't talk about it now, Guido,' Francesca said. 'We will get our own back some day, you'll see.'

'I should have strangled him then and there!' Guido cried. A servant was watching them from the doorway. He leaned against it casually, picking his teeth with a toothpick. But he was alert. Waiting.

'Come along, Guido. Doing anything like that now would only land you in jail. Come along.'

117

Her brother pulled himself together. 'I suppose you are right,' he said. 'Then come home and let us decide what to do about this mess.'

~~~~~~

The family took the news of the Duke's dishonesty philosophically. Guido and Francesca were surprised. They had expected anger, exasperation, resentment; anything rather than this almost tired acceptance of the Duke's duplicity. The only one who was really upset was Lombardo. 'It's so unfair,' he said. 'So terribly unfair! A man's whole life gone with nothing left to show for it'.

Gina said, 'Father always told us that life was not fair. In any case, there is nothing we can do, is there?'

Mirella d'Abrizzio's idea had lodged in Guido's mind. It was a good one. Their father had helped many of his neighbours financially. They had to raise enough money to leave Sicily, enough money to keep them until they located their brother. It might take a long time, they could not be sure how long, and to do the job properly they needed funds.

'You cannot be suspect wherever you go,' Lombardo said. 'You must dress decently, look respectable, or they'll put you in jail.'

'Tomaso Canona will be the man to help,' Gina said. 'He knows people. He has connections.'

'I am not happy about some of his connections, Gina,' Lombardo said, but she shrugged.

'Oh, in this case it is all right. It is father's interests we pursue. It is vendetta, not our own advancement.'

'A debt is a debt,' Lombardo said heavily. 'I would rather we did not owe his friends anything.'

'Well, that is just not possible,' Gina said reasonably. 'Where can these two babes go on their own without help? They will be doomed to failure. The world is a big place, Lombardo. They'll need all the help they can get.

118

Otherwise, as you said yourself, they'll end up in jail.'

'I suppose you're right.' He sighed. 'So, use Canona's friends, but only to find Mario, OK?'

The brother and sister nodded. They were not concerned about who they sought help from, so long as it was forthcoming. They had examined the deed of sale and found that what the Duke had said was true. There it was: 'On the decease of the purchaser, the abovementioned Signore Giuseppe Palucci, the aforesaid land will revert in toto to the Duke d'Abrizzio and all entitlement will cease …'

'I would understand if you did not want me any longer,' Gina said quietly to Lombardo. The big man pulled her fiercely to him and held her in his strong embrace.

'Never say that, *mio amore*. Never! I love you. With nothing, I love you.'

'What will we do?'

'Begin again.'

'All that Papa worked for, everything, gone.'

'Not our home, Gina. We have the house. And soon we will have more. A leopard does not change its spots. The Duke will have to sell again. He'll need money. We will buy back the land. You know we will.'

'Suppose … he will not sell to us. Suppose he sells to someone else?' she asked fearfully.

'Hush, dearest. We'll face that when we come to it. *If* we come to it.'

They talked in the kitchen in the evenings of Mirella d'Abrizzio's suggestion, and it was Tomaso Canona who finally gave them the money, swearing he was happy to do so.

'We may not be able to pay you back for a long time,' Guido said. 'Go to Enrico Domini in Roma,' Tomaso said, paying no attention. 'Here is his address. He too will help you. He will give you funds. Find you a place to live.'

He smiled at Guido and Francesca, flashing his white

teeth. 'And whatever else you need, just ask. He will find Mario for you. I have addresses everywhere. In case. Sicilians have powerful friends everywhere. You are content?' Guido nodded. 'So, everyone is happy.'

They left soon after that. They kissed their mother goodbye. Maria hardly noticed their going. Her grief had made her turn in on herself. Everything and everyone was outside her loss of Giuseppe. It absorbed her to the exclusion of all else. Nothing that happened in the farmhouse held any importance for her. She stayed in her darkened room, holding Giuseppe's jacket in her arms, her eyes vacant, not seeing or hearing anything.

Gina and Lombardo wished them well. Gina wept, holding her favourite sister close to her.

'I'll miss you, little one,' she said. 'I'll miss you so.' The lump in her throat made her voice sound harsh.

'I'll be back, Gina,' Francesca said.

Lombardo embraced Guido, kissing him on both cheeks and calling him brother.

'You'll be married when we return,' Guido said, 'and then you will really be my brother.'

The big man nodded. 'Fra Bartholomeo will marry us after the harvest. Though there won't be one for us now, will there?'

'You need Lombardo,' Guido said to his sister. 'You need his strength, Gina.' He kissed her then turned to Marcello. The brothers held each other close for a long silent moment. There were tears on Marcello's cheeks when they finally broke the embrace and Guido wiped them away with his thumb. They spoke no words. They did not need to.

The girls and Marcello and Lombardo waved them goodbye, and Tomaso Canona drove them in his old beaten-up jalopy to Palermo. Each mile they travelled both broke Francesca's heart and filled her with hope. She watched the farmhouse become a dot on the horizon, then disappear. It was the only home she had ever known. The wrench was brutal, hurting her deeply, pulling her up by her roots. Yet she was glad to quit what others had told her was the scene of her shame.

Luciano was not there any more. Neither was her father. Paulo and Mario were gone too, and everything had changed. Her mother spent her days in bed and the routines of a lifetime were out of kilter. The times were uncertain. Yet, though she ached to remain in the warm familiarity of her home, at the last she had been eager to escape and rush towards another destiny.

Tomaso Canona left them on the outskirts of Palermo. 'Be careful now. And use the address I have given you. These people will look after you.'

They watched him disappear back down the dusty road. With apprehensive hearts, they turned their faces towards the town.

PART II

Chapter Six

Minouche Aubin stood, half in shadow, staring across to where the Seine, swollen by rain, lapped the greasy cobblestones with a soothing, hypnotic sush-sush sound.

It had almost mesmerised her and she had forgotten to light the cigarette which dangled on her bottom lip.

She was very wet. The rain had saturated her yet she seemed quite oblivious of it. She was a slight boyish figure dressed in trousers, jersey and velvet jacket. Her straw-coloured hair was plastered to her skull. The hair looked as if it had been chopped off with shears. Her eyes, dark and solemn, were faraway, looking to another place.

When the footsteps sounded behind her it took her a moment to recall her thoughts and bring them back to where she actually was – in the night, in the alley, in the rain.

When she heard the sound she did not seem to register it. She did not move but stood still, leaning against the wall. No one could have guessed that her senses were alert and that her hand had closed on the knife she always carried in her pocket.

'Minouche?'

'Oh!' She turned in relief *'Mon Dieu*, it's you, Pierre. You frightened me.'

Pierre was her best friend, as dear to her as a brother. He was a bouncer in La Vie en Rose, a giant of a man with a broken nose and kind eyes.

'Yves is back,' he said. 'I hurried to tell you.'

She swore, then spat on the ground, but she did not feel so brave and Pierre knew it. Instead she felt paralysed by fear. She was terrified of Yves. She told herself to calm down, to fight the growing tide of panic his name always brought with it. Pierre remained silent at her side, waiting for her to speak.

'Do you know where Scarlatti is?' she asked him at last, her large black eyes revealing her fear.

He shook his head and looked at her. She seemed so helpless to him, so small, like a trusting child. Yet he knew she wasn't. She was, as the Americans said, 'a tough cookie', or at least appeared to be. Except when it came to Yves.

'We'll have to find Scarlatti then,' she said. 'He's the only one who can deal with Yves.'

Her mouth was tight, as if she had sucked something bitter, and she shivered in the rain.

'Here, let me,' Pierre said, and draped his old mackintosh over her shoulders. She shrugged it off.

'No,' she said, then; 'Give me a light, Pierre.'

He snapped his lighter and the flame flickered under her face, casting shadows on her cheeks. She drew on the cigarette but it was damp. She turned to him as she threw it in a puddle where it hissed and died.

'What can I do to help?' he asked in a whisper.

'Find Scarlatti for me.'

'He won't do anything for me. You'll have to come too,' he said. He was nervous of Scarlatti. Everyone was. Everyone except Minouche.

Scarlatti ran their Quarter. He ran drugs and gambling, he ran a stable of prostitutes, and he liked everyone to obey him. He had told Yves not to come on to his patch again. He would not be pleased to find he had been ignored. Minouche was not afraid of Scarlatti and he sensed it. She eluded him, but then she eluded everyone. She was hard to reach.

No one knew how old she was, she did not know herself. Born in the slums, she had never wanted to leave them. She liked the feel and smell of the back streets she had inhabited all her life, and when she needed privacy, away from the teeming overcrowded existence she led, then she went down to the river. The flowing, lapping waters soothed her spirit, sustained her. She would walk along its banks, smoking, her mind a blank. She felt part of the slate-coloured river, like it was her mother, the mother she had never known. Madame Lefranche said it was because her star-sign was Pisces. 'You'll never be happy away from water,' she said, and Minouche believed her. The river brought her peace.

She had never aspired to a better way of life. Unlike the other girls she did not yearn to enter Fouquet's or Maxim's in diamonds and pearls with a rich lover on her arm.

'*Mon Dieu*, I would feel a fool,' she would say, shrugging her shoulders. She liked the *bistros*, the little cafés and smokey bars she frequented. She lived most of her life in them or on the streets. They were her territory. she was like a fish out of water elsewhere.

She had been born in the Quarter, in the tiny box-room she still inhabited. Her mother died there giving birth to her. In the place where they lived there were only the barest amenities. Her father, Yves Aubin, never bothered with her. He was a brutal ne'er-do-well who drank himself to insensibility most nights in the cafés around about the area. He left her to survive as best she could with no help from him. The women in the neighbourhood helped when and where they could but little Minouche learned the hard way to become independent while she was still very young.

Yves Aubin was the only person she feared. Scarlatti had saved her from him once. All she could do was trust that he would do so again.

When Minouche had been about fourteen, her father

had come home one night from the bar where he had been drinking heavily. He had found her in her chemise, just about to get into her bed.

She had been afraid of no one then. Fear had not yet entered her life. Oh, yes, Yves was often drunk but she could deal with that. Usually he came home and passed out on his bed on the other side of the room without even removing his clothes. She was so used to it that she thought all men were the same. She did not trust any of them, but neither did she fear them. Life was tough, sure, but if your expectations were minimal and all you wanted or needed was a cup of coffee and a brioche for breakfast, one meal some time during the day and a couple of cognacs in the evening, well, it was not too difficult. She spent her days in petty crime. She was into scams and cons, living by her wits. She filched what she needed from the shops and markets and sold the surplus. She survived. Somehow, against all odds, she survived.

That fateful night when Yves came into the attic-room and stared at her in her scanty attire she felt terror for the first time. Suddenly, this strange and monstrous feeling invaded her being, disturbed her nerves, shattered her peace of mind.

He had lumbered across the room, big-bellied from the booze, pulling his shirt off, stumbling a bit but not too drunk, smiling but in an ugly mood.

She had not tried to stop him. It would have been useless to do so. He was too big, she was too tiny, and he probably would have killed her. She had endured the ordeal silently and hatred was born in her. Hatred and fear. The twins. After that, once a week, he raped her. For two days after the attack she could not go out; she could not even walk. Bruised, violated, vandalized, her fragile body could not sustain the cruel punishment it had received. She became sick and weak. Everyone noticed but she said nothing. The neighbours asked but she lied. She thought people would reject her, be horrified, blame her. She thought it must be her fault, that in some way she was beneath contempt.

Madame Lefranche, the butcher's wife, finally forced the truth out of her. A fat jolly woman with frizzed red hair, she was deeply concerned by the change in her little neighbour.

One day she stopped the girl outside the shop with a tap on her shoulder. Minouche jumped like a scalded cat when Madame Lefranche touched her, and then the woman knew something terrible was wrong. She had never known the girl's nerves so jagged. She steered her into the back of the shop and coaxed the story out of her.

Minouche, a bundle of bones and screaming nerves, gaunt-eyed and guilty, sobbed her heart out on the woman's shoulder. Madame Lefranche realized sadly that there was nothing she could do about it. Not in practical terms.

'If we accuse Yves Aubin who is, begging your pardon, a vicious brute, he will deny it,' her husband said when she told him. 'I am sorry for Minouche, so sorry. The man is a beast. But what can we do? *Pauvre petite*,' he said and sighed.

'I comforted her as best I could. I promised nothing,' Madame Lefranche said, putting her hair into curlers carefully, to get the frizz uniform all the way around her head. But we cannot allow it to go on.'

'Well, what can we do?' Monsieur Lefranche asked reasonably, scratching his belly under his long-johns. 'Yves Aubin is legally her guardian.'

'Much guarding he has done! Left her to fend for herself since she was a babe. And now this.' Her pendulous cheeks shook with rage. 'Oh, it vexes me so. Men!' she said, glaring at her husband who sat peaceably on the bed in his underwear.

'What have I done?' he asked mildly, catching her glance.

She could not sleep. She cudgelled her brains to think of a way out for the little waif. Her husband snored beside her.

She sighed in his direction a couple of times, then suddenly, in the middle of the night, sat up, making the springs creak and waking Monsieur Lefranche with a start.

'I will go to Scarlatti,' she said.

Her husband thought she had taken leave of her senses. 'What? That crook? We'd best keep away from him. He's destroying the neighbourhood. He is giving the Quarter a bad name. He's a scoundrel, a dog. What do you want with him?'

'He will help the child. I will go to him,' she said with determination, lying back down and heaving a sigh of relief. She knew she would never rest until this thing was resolved to her satisfaction for the little face of Minouche haunted her, and the thought of the girl being at the mercy of such a brute made her very angry.

She was as good as her word. She went to see the Sicilian in his apartment in Rue de Sfax in the Fourteenth Arondissement. She was amazed at the luxury she found there.

'I could not believe it, *chérie*. It is a palace! I thought crime was not supposed to pay, but it does. It does!' she said to her husband afterwards, full of excitement at what she had seen.

At first Scarlatti was not interested in the fate of Minouche. 'He screws her, so what?' he asked indifferently.

'But he is her father!' Madame Lefranche said.

'All women are whores,' Scarlatti said. 'She'll get used to it.' He looked at Madame Lefranche with velvet eyes, black as sin, whose depths were as cold as pebbles in an icy stream. He sat on a white leather sofa. How did he keep it clean? she wondered. His bodyguard, an Algerian dark as night, had a face as inscrutable as a cat's. He never left the Sicilian's side. Scarlatti wore a suit of pale grey silk and a lace cravat at his throat. He had gold rings on his fingers.

Madame Lefranche persisted. 'What does she look like, this fourteen year old?' asked Scarlatti.

The butcher's wife bristled. 'If you think I'm going to deliver her to you so you can …' she remembered the word he had used, 'screw her like her father, then you're mistaken!' she said indignantly.

He shook his head, laughing at her. 'I have as many women to screw as I need. But someone else might like her.'

He caught Madame Lefranche's eye. 'Jeez, you're just like my mama in Sicily. Hey, don't look at me like that! I'll only put her out if she's agreeable.'

'You promise?' she asked anxiously. 'You won't go back on your word?'

His eyes glittered like black coal. 'I *never* go back on my word.'

'Only if she wants to?' Madame Lefranche repeated.

He seemed to find her persistence amusing. 'OK, bring her here,' he said.

The next day she took Minouche to Rue de Sfax. The girl wore trousers and an old sweater. She had chopped off her hair. It stuck out every which way and Madame Lefranche did not have much hope of her making a good impression.

To her surprise, Scarlatti seemed pleased with Minouche. 'Good. Good. Good,' he kept repeating. 'She can be of use to me.'

He was a man who made up his mind quickly. He had been looking for a child with enough intelligence to climb through small windows, act as look-out in places where an adult would be suspect, and eavesdrop in places where the average person was too large to conceal themselves successfully. He had used a couple of children and they had nearly landed him in jail. They either gave themselves away, fell asleep or blabbed.

He looked into Minouche's alert eyes. She was not afraid of him, he could see, but every time her father was mentioned those dark eyes became fixed and shocked. He

131

was pleased with her. She was tiny enough to be useful, and her fear of her father would be the stick he would use to keep her in line.

'What will you do with … with Yves?' she asked, eyes wide and staring at him. She had stopped calling Yves 'Father' after he had started to rape her.

'I'll tell him to leave my patch,' Scarlatti said mildly.

'He'll never go,' she said firmly.

'Oh, yes, he will,' he replied softly, smiling his ice-cold smile.

Yves went. He disappeared the next day and Minouche breathed a sigh of relief and began to work for Scarlatti. She never forgot what she owed him, and if sometimes she saw and heard things that made her uncomfortable, she gave no sign. She did not judge people and was indifferent to the judgement of others upon her. Life was life. There were good and bad things in it and one had to survive. She had a philisophical acceptance of the ups and downs of existence and saw no point in expending energy worrying about the morality of others. She had a firm sense of what was right and what was wrong for herself. She would never betray a friend, was loyal to a fanatical degree, but saw nothing immoral in stealing, cheating, or lying to the punters. After all, how else would she live? And if people were foolish enough to fall for a scam, well, they deserved what they got.

Scarlatti trusted her. Sometimes he took her to places he would take no one else. She got to know everyone. She said little. She never blabbed. She was, in her own way, content.

She liked to know everyone and everyone to know her. She liked the paperseller saying 'Bonjour, Minouche' each morning when she came down to get her breakfast in the Deux Pigeons. She liked it that René there knew her name and had her order ready without her needing to ask. She liked it that Madame Lefranche shouted 'Bonjour, Minouche' when she passed the butcher's shop, and

Evangeline Dupont from the Pâtisserie and Monsieur Rouden from the greengrocer's cried, '*Ça va, Minouche?*' to her as she went by. At the end of the street where the lights flashed on and off, the all-night staffs of the girlie shows on their way home in the morning, called, '*Bonjour, Minouche*' as they went by. She liked it that all the girls, if not in the Moulin Rouge at least in the Petit Moulin beside it and the Vie en Rose round the corner, knew her name and who she was. They called '*Bonsoir*' as they went to work. She was acquainted with all the stage-hands from the shows and often sat with them, sharing a smoke on a pile of flats and scenery from the theatres.

Faces were cut, acid was thrown, people were knifed, maimed, shot even, if they did not toe the line and obey the rules. Sometimes there was an accident and the wrong person met his or her end. Well, tough. *C'est la vie.* It was a fact of existence. Sudden death was something she had to learn to accept. Minouche sauntered along the Quarter's streets, hands deep in pockets, knowing who she was and where she was, and that it was here she wanted to be.

Four years had passed since Yves had disappeared. Now, on this dark wet night, the reflection of the street-lamps shimmering in the murky puddles, Pierre had told her that her father was back.

'Let's have a cognac?' he said. 'You look frozen. Terrible.'

She smiled at him. Her face changed when she smiled. It became radiant.

'Terrible? Am I so bad?'

He shook his head and put his raincoat around her shoulders again. This time she did not resist.

'After all,' she said, 'he can't hurt me now.'

Pierre looked down at her. She did not reach his shoulder. She still had the body of a child.

'I don't like it, Minouche. Yves is dangerous.'

He remembered all the fights in the bars, the skirmishes with broken bottles. Yves' ugly face flushed with drink.

133

'Leave it all to Scarlatti,' she said. 'He'll fix it.'

Pierre shrugged, 'Come, we'll have that cognac then look for him,' he said, turning up the collar of his jacket.

He put his arm around her and together they walked up the alley away from the river.

~~~~~~

When they reached 'civilisation', as Pierre called the Quarter, they ducked into their favourite café – bar, the Deux Pigeons. The air was thick with smoke and steam was rising from the customers' camp clothes. Waiters rushed about and the clink of glasses and the roar of conversation assailed their ears. Minouche loved it. *'Bonsoir, Minouche,'* someone called, and she waved to them and laughed.

'René, two cognacs,' Pierre said breezily, relaxing in the warm familiarity of the place.

'René, what is it?' Minouche had seen the look on the waiter's plump face as he glanced at her. He was worried.

'Your papa has been here, Minouche. He is looking for you. Monsieur Picard does not want any trouble. He said to say Yves Aubin means trouble. He hopes you can keep it away from the Deux Pigeons.'

The waiter wiped a damp cloth across the marble top of their table as he spoke. They glanced over to the bar and saw Monsieur Picard looking at them through the mirror that ran its length.

'All right, René,' Pierre said soothingly, 'we don't want trouble either. You know that. Scarlatti will see to it.'

René wiped his face with his apron. 'That is what I mean. We don't want Scarlatti here either. Who knows what ideas will come into his mind when he sees the place? We do not want to be on his list of convenient bars to use.'

Minouche said nothing. René looked from one to the other. 'Who knows what Scarlatti will think or do?' he continued. 'If Scarlatti becomes fond of a place, a lot of the customers prefer to go elsewhere.' René appealed to Pierre. 'You know Scarlatti's presence makes people uncomfortable. Being near him is dangerous.' He shrugged. 'One never knows what he will ask and there is no way to refuse, you know that.' The waiter's eyes were uneasy. 'It is better not to attract his attention at all.'

They drank their cognac then ordered coffee. Gradually, in the warmth of the café, Minouche's confidence returned. After all, as she had said, what could Yves do to her? But even as she thought it, she shivered. Pierre stood up.

'Come on, let's find Scarlatti.'

René and Monsieur Picard heaved sighs of relief as the pair went back out into the driving rain. 'Shit!' Pierre said, looking at the sky and turning up his collar again. 'Let's try Dino's.'

Dino's was a little Italian restaurant in Rue de Fonce. It was not far and they hurried down the side streets that were shortcuts until they reached it, the rain hitting their faces sharply, bouncing off the puddles on the pavements, flowing in a stream of filthy sludge in the gutter.

Dino's had red-checked curtains covering the lower half of its glass door, and Minouche was not tall enough to see over them. 'Is he there?' she asked hopefully.

Pierre peered in then shook his head. No Scarlatti. They trudged up to the Moulin Rouge where Scarlatti sometimes had a table. Benny, the English ASM, checked for them but said no, the Sicilian had not been in that night.

By now Minouche was saturated. The legs of her trousers flapped wetly as she walked.

'We'll have to go to his apartment,' she said.

She had not been there since Madame Lefranche had taken her four years ago.

'He won't like it.' Pierre was reluctant.

'Well, too bad! *Mon Dieu*, what can I do? We have tried everything else. Besides, I'm drowning.'

They took a tram. They did not pay. Minouche never

paid on principal. She did not carry money. She did not need to. The restauranteurs knew of her connection with Scarlatti and fed her free. They did not mind. She kept him off their backs and her appetite was small.

Minouche remembered little about her first visit to Scarlatti's. She had been too frightened and apprehensive at the time to bother about her surroundings. Now she looked curiously at the home of the man who had saved her life.

The huge front doors had shiny black iron mesh shielding them. The hall floor was marble of a shade like the black sausage in Lefranche's. There was another wrought iron grille in front of the lift which had red carpet on the floor and a mirror at the back.

The rain ran down Minouche's face and the water from her slacks and shoes left a puddle on the rug.

'You could live in here,' she said, grinning up at Pierre. 'Comfortably,' she added. He was always teasing her about her indifference to comfort.

'I don't like this, Minouche,' he said. His face was red and uncomfortable. He was uneasy in the grandeur of these surroundings.

The lift stopped and they got out. Scarlatti's door was opposite. The corridor was carpeted, this time in beige. Pierre's shoes squelched as they crossed to the door and rang the bell.

The Algerian opened the door, his black face impassive, eyes expressionless. He had his right hand inside his jacket. Minouche thought it probably held a gun.

'Wha' ye want?' he asked, holding the door open only a crack.

'I want to see Scarlatti.' Minouche said firmly.

'Who I say?' the Algerian inquired.

'Come on, you know me, Ali. Stop being an imbecile.'

'Who I say?' he asked again, his face empty.

'I think he's high,' Pierre whispered behind her.

'It's Minouche,' she said loudly.

136

'You know you supposed to wait for Scarlatti to get in touch wi' you.' Ali sounded remote and made as if to shut the door in their faces.

'Tell Scarlatti Yves is back in town. So much for his authority! Everyone is laughing, saying Yves pays no attention to Scarlatti.'

'Come in. Come in.' The voice came from inside the apartment.

The Algerian went on standing in the doorway, not moving. Minouche pushed the door further ajar and went in, Pierre following.

'Take off your shoes at the door. I don't like my carpet dirty,' Scarlatti said. They obeyed.

Scarlatti sat in his silk suit on the white sofa. It was a wine-coloured suit this time. He had a drink in his hand, a light pink rosé in a cut-glass. His simian profile was to them. He did not look round as they walked into the room. When they reached the centre he suddenly turned his face to them. His eyes were reptilian, milky and inhuman.

'*Mon Dieu*, you look awful. Ay, ay! Stay there. Oh, for God's sake, Minouche, you look like a sewer rat.' He threw back his head and laughed, but there was no humour in it. 'I never thought of that before – a sewer rat. It's what you are, Minouche. Ali, listen, she's a sewer rat. Goes places no one else will go. Crawls down slimy holes. For me, eh?'

The Algerian was leaning against the wall by the door. He did not move or laugh or seem to be listening. As Minouche came towards him, Scarlatti put up his hand.

'Don' come any nearer. Stay there and don' sit down. I don' wan' my furniture fucked up.'

He wore a ruby on his little finger. It matched his suit. 'So now you wan' my help again?' he asked, eyes narrowed.

Minouche knew he liked opportunities to put people in his debt. 'I've done you enough favours,' she said, shrugging. 'Anyhow, you don't want it to get about that Yves just walked back in the territory? Without your permission?'

'No. We don' want that, do we?' The Sicilian looked at her, his face amused and derisive. 'Oh, no, no, no, that would never do, eh, Ali?

The Algerian smiled.

'You'd think he was out of it, wouldn't you?' Scarlatti asked. 'You move suddenly, you get a knife in your heart.'

Minouche thought, it wasn't a gun, it was a knife. She used a knife. Pierre was an expert with them. He had taught her. Now she was as expert as he.

'Well, that's what they're saying,' she repeated, a little apprehensive. Things were not going the way she had envisaged.

'I'll fix it for you, OK?' He was smiling to himself and nodding to her. She wanted to thank him but his face was closed, as if he was someplace else. Suddenly he looked up at her, milky black eyes full of ridicule.

'God, you're ugly, Minouche,' he said. 'Why don't you do something with yourself? Fix yourself up? Clean yourself a bit? God, you're a mess.'

Minouche looked at him, feeling her lips tremble at the unexpected slight. She looked around at the white room, the chandelier, the jade pieces on the glass-topped table, and made a face, sticking her fingers in the air in an obscene gesture. Still he watched her, pebble eyes expressionless, so she said, 'I don't want to get all elegant and tidy. I might attract attention. This way, no one notices me.'

Scarlatti nodded, suddenly grinning.

'Yeah, I never thought of that. So you could be Theda Bara if you tried, eh?' He chortled to himself as if he found the thought unbearably funny. 'Well,' he said eventually, straightening up, 'you're not so stupid. But I tell you, Minouche, you'd find it a hard job, to look good.' He turned away. 'Go on. Get out,' he said coldly. 'You're dripping on my carpet.'

They put their shoes back on at the door and had to let themselves out. The Algerian still leaned, glassy-eyed, against the wall.

~~~~~~

It was still raining but not so heavily. Water flowed in little rivulets down the gutters and gushed into the drains.

'*Mon Dieu*, it's cold.' Minouche shivered. 'I gotta get out of these clothes, Pierre. I'll catch cold, see if I don't. Pneumonia, maybe.'

She took his arm, rubbing her cheek against the wet sleeve of his coat.

'Oh, you're such a consolation to me. I don't know what I'd do without you.'

He glanced down at her little heart-shaped face. How Scarlatti could miss her beauty, Pierre didn't know. His heart twisted with love for her and he gave her a quick hug.

'Come home with me, Pierre,' she said. 'Make sure he's not there.'

He knew who she was talking about. He could hear the fear in her voice. 'I have to get to the Rose,' he said, and added hastily as he felt her arm pulled away, 'but I'll go with you first, Minouche, see you safely in. OK?'

She nodded and tucked her arm back into his.

They walked back in silence in the rain. There were few people about in the inclement weather. Lights shone from houses, their reflection glimmering in the damp darkness. The families inside looked cosy and tidy, Minouche thought, as if they had life all organized; a time and a place for everything. Mother in the kitchen cooking, Father reading the paper, children working at their books, a dog, a cat. She did not envy them. She valued her freedom, her vagabond life. She did not want to be inside one of those glowing spot-lit homes; she liked to be outside, looking in.

Her nose felt cold and there was a drip on the end of it, she could feel it. She sniffed and wiped the sleeve of her jacket across it. It did not help. The jacket wet her whole

139

face. But she felt safer now. Scarlatti had promised and he did not break his word. Besides, he insisted on being obeyed. Otherwise he'd lose control and there was a queue waiting to take his place at the first show of weakness. And Pierre was with her. That gave her a nice feeling of security. He would make sure Yves had not come to her room while she was out. The thought that he might be there, waiting for her, made the back of her neck tingle. The bitch of it was, Scarlatti would want something in return. Maybe something in the drug delivery line. He was heavily into traffic in opium from China. Shit! she thought. Shit. I'm getting in deeper than I want.

Well, she could worry about that later. Since when was life easy?

When they reached the house she lived in, Pierre went ahead of her. The wooden stairs were uncarpeted and worn down in the middle where a million feet had trodden over the centuries. When he reached her door on the second floor, he flung it open, waited, and then leapt in, hands out, knife at the ready. He looked around, alert and wary, but there was no one there.

'OK, Minouche, all safe. Christ, I don't know how you live here! It's freezing. It's like the Gâre du Nord.'

'I'm OK,' she said.

'Well, lock the door behind me when I leave.'

She nodded. 'Thanks, Pierre.' She touched his arm. 'You are good to me.'

He was embarrassed. He shrugged and said, 'See you tomorrow. I'd better get to the Rose.'

'Maybe I'll come in later.'

'That'd be good. '*voir*.'

She'd meant to lock the door at once. She never could remember why she didn't. It stood to reason. She had been nervous, no, terrified of Yves. Pierre had told her to lock it. Yet she left it for those vital five minutes. No, three. It couldn't have been more than three.

140

He must have been in the shadows below and come up when he saw Pierre leave. Or he could have been at the top of the next flight of stairs that led to the attic. He could have been there all the time. Heard them even. In any event, she went to the stove to light it and the lamp before she locked the door, and by the time she had done that it was too late.

Yves stood in the doorway looking at her. He had not changed in four years, except perhaps to become more dew-lapped at the jaw and baggy around the eyes, and his belly hung out a little further over the top of his pants.

'Hello, Minouche.'

She stared at him. 'What do you want?' she asked stupidly.

'To come home,' he said. His face had the self-pitying, smarmy, pathetic expression he always had when he had been drinking.

'Don't be stupid,' she said, and noticed how his eyes suddenly flashed anger. 'Scarlatti knows you're here,' she continued, and to her surprise he showed no fear. 'So?' He shrugged, swaying ever so slightly nearer the door, her only escape route. She wanted to scream, call out to Pierre, but it was too late, and yelling would do no good here. God knows in the past she had done enough of it to no avail.

He took a few steps forward.

'Don't come near me,' she said, panic rising like bile within her.

'Aw, Minouche, have pity on your poor old father. Didn't I care for you when your mother died?'

'You killed her! With your bestial ways and drinking all the money. And you never cared for me in your life. Never did one fucking thing for me.' Her voice was higher than she meant it to be and she was jittery with nerves. She told herself to keep calm.

The rain pattering on the window gave the room an underwater feeling. Watery shadows rippled over the surface of her bed.

141

'Aw, Minouche, c'mon. I did my best. You know how difficult it is. Your poor old father has been having a hard time recently. It's been tough. You don't know. Things have not been good for me.'

That was why he was not frightened of Scarlatti, she thought.

'Think I care?' she cried out defiantly. She was horrified to find she was near to tears.

'I wanna move back here,' he continued as if she had not spoken. 'See, there was a misunderstanding between you and me. That's what it was, a misunderstanding.'

So that was what he had persuaded himself that his brutality to her had been – a misunderstanding. The heavy mass of him lying on her, grunting, heaving obscenely, relieving himself into her, tearing her apart, was a misunderstanding! She shivered and he took two places towards her.

'Don't move!' she shouted. 'Don't come near me.' Her voice was suddenly authoritative and he stopped. She had never spoken to him like that before. He had not seen her since she was fourteen. She had grown, not so much physically but she had been on her own for those four years, had been her own mistress, lived her own life, and acquired an indefinable air of independence.

He smiled at her, a foolish vacuous smile, and moved forwards again.

'I said, don't come near me.'

But he went on moving, and as he did he began to unbutton the top of his trousers.

'I'll teach you, my girl.' She could see he was trembling with rage. 'Speak to me like that, would you? I'm your father. Law says so. You'll learn who's master here.'

He kept advancing slowly, as if facing a wild animal he meant to curb, anger white around his mouth.

'I'm warning you,' she cried, frightened and cornered. He paid no attention, moving inexorably forward.

She closed her fingers around the knife in her pocket,

glad she had not had time to take off her velvet jacket. He was a big man, a heavy man, but he was a little unsteady. She was quite calm about what she was going to do, and prayed she would do it efficiently.

'Please stop.' She tried one last time, a pleading note in her voice. He recognized it and took it as a sign of weakness. Paying no attention to her command he moved again until he was close enough for her to smell him. He made her sick to her stomach.

'You'll see who's boss,' he snarled, his breath foul with stale beer. 'You little whore! I'll show you.'

He lunged to grab her and force her on to the bed behind her. In one clean motion, she took out the knife and drove it up into his throat. Swiftly and efficiently, as Pierre had showed her, she buried it deep.

Yves, her father, stood with eyes bulging like a gargoyle on Notre Dame. Then a scarlet fountain gushed from his throat, leaping out, a crimson cataract, splattering her as he fell across her bed. Minouche stared at him. She had stopped shaking. She felt calm, peaceful, watching his blood flow, his life dribble away. She smiled. She felt no guilt. She felt only relief. She would never have to worry about him again. She would never glance over her shoulder and be frightened that she would see him. She would never enter this room apprehensively, scared that he might be lying in wait for her.

She did not hear Pierre come into the room but stood staring at the body of the man she hated, the man who had been her father.

'I was worried, Minouche. I don't know why. I got to the end of the street and I began to feel these prickles down my spine and I was frightened for you. So I came back and … *Mon Dieu*, what …?'

'I killed him, Pierre.' She said it simply, on a sigh.

'I can see that.'

'I did it as you said. One swift thrust. It was quick.'

'It must have been. I've only just left you. *Mon Dieu!*' He stared at her then at the body on the bed.

'Minouche, we have to get out of here. You don't want to end up in prison.'

'I'm not sorry, Pierre. He threatened me again. He was going to rape me. He was a beast. He did not deserve to live.'

He saw she was calm and unemotional. He took her shoulders. She still wore her damp clothes but that could not be helped. There was no time to change now. He shook her gently.

'Listen, Minouche, listen. *You* know he was a beast. *I* know he was a beast. But the *gendarmes* do not know that. The law may not see things your way. We must go. Get out of here. Now.'

She came to life slowly. She stretched like a cat in the sun, raising her arms above her head so he could see her bare midriff. She smiled at him, a grin of calm content.

'OK, let's go,' she said as if it was an ordinary day, as if nothing had happened and they were going for a coffee in the Deux Pigeons.

When they reached the street, he asked, 'Where? Where are we going?' She laughed. 'Back to Scarlatti,' she said. 'Where else?'

~~~~~~

Scarlatti and the Algerian did not seem to have moved since Minouche and Pierre had left them over two hours ago.

The Algerian let them in, then stood with his back to the wall beside the door. Scarlatti sighed when he saw them.

'Oh God, what have I done to deserve this? My home a railway station. Riff-raff in and out. Jesus!' He did not seem surprised to see them.

He still sat on the white sofa, but now he wore black satin pyjamas. He smoked a Balkan Sobranie, exhaling through his nostrils. He listened as they explained.

'So you fixed the bastard for me, saved me the trouble?'

he said when they had finished, then looked up at them with milky eyes half concealed by his lids.

'Yes,' Pierre said. Then added, 'The *gendarmes* will find him. They'll want to talk to Minouche.' Pierre knew that Scarlatti would not want that. The *gendarmes* might ask some awkward questions. Pierre knew that Minouche would die rather than tell them anything, but she might inadvertently give something away and Scarlatti did not know her as well as Pierre did. Scarlatti could not be sure she would not be indiscreet and let something slip.

Pierre was full of conflicting emotions. He loved Minouche, had always loved her. Now, if he saved her, he would lose her for she would have to leave the Quarter. He could not bear that. Minouche made life for him bearable. Pierre did not find his existence in the Quarter such fun. He did not enjoy it as Minouche did. He had a pessimistic personality, dour and laconic. Life seemed a tough relentless struggle for the likes of him. Most of the things he wanted – a little house, enough money to pay for a few luxuries – were and always would be outside his grasp. He knew things would never get better for him. No miracle would happen. He would remain a bouncer in La Vie en Rose until he was too old, or not strong enough to do the job any more, or got sick. Then they would let him go without so much as a thank you and he would be on the scrap heap. He had no illusions.

Neither had Minouche, but the difference between them was that she liked things the way they were. For God's sake she liked that grim little room she lived in, the dirty streets, the steamy cafés, the ugly people. She liked her life exactly as it was and some of her content rubbed off on him. When he was with her he saw things through her eyes and the world took on a new and shinier patina, and became a much more hopeful place to live in.

He did not think he could survive without her. Depression would eat him up like a cancer, destroy him. In

145

that sleazy joint with its tawdry decor and fifth-class dancers, rejects from the Moulin, he was desperately aware of the hopelessness of the life he lived. He felt acute pain in the face of the misplaced determination and optimism around him. It physically hurt him. He ached with despairing compassion at the dancers' certainty that they were one step away from 'the big time'. They were full of cock-eyed expectancy. A producer would walk in and snap them up. Then the Moulin. Hollywood even. What did they see in the mirror? he wondered. Did they not notice the bags under their eyes, their flabby breasts, their fat thighs? They strutted the little stage, walked the catwalk between tables awash in beer and wine, with hope and confidence. And sitting at those tables were the lust-filled apologies for men to whom sex was a shameful and dirty act. Men who hated women. Men who did not even like themselves very much. Men who screamed 'Get them off! Get them off!' with glassy-eyed intensity.

Pierre's life was made bearable by Minouche's acceptance. She saw the reality, dwelt happily on it but luxuriated in the dreams of others and wished them well in the fulfilment of their desires. When Fifi Le Bon stuck tassels on her U-shaped boobs and said, 'Look, *chérie*, some day I won't have to do this any more. In through that door Mr Griffith will walk. D.J. himself, looking for a Frenchie. He'll see me and – snap! I'll be off to Philadelphia in the morning. Or should I say Hollywood?' Minouche would say, 'Sure, Fifi, sure you will,' believing it might happen, that there was that possibility. And when Suzette, called Sauce Piquante in the Rose, insisted that one day the producer of the Comédie Française would come to La Vie en Rose and take her out of the dump and put her in Molière and Racine, Minouche would nod eagerly and say, 'I'll bet he comes soon, Suzette. I'll bet he does.'

No, Pierre did not want to lose Minouche. He did not think he could live without her.

'So what do you want me to do about it?' Scarlatti asked, and shrugged.

'Nothin',' Pierre said. 'Thought you should know, that's all. We'll go.'

He turned, but not before he caught the gleam in the Sicilian's eyes.

'No,' Scarlatti murmured. 'Listen.' He paused, looking at them closely. 'You two look weird,' he remarked. 'You're still in the same dripping clothes.'

'Well, we didn't wait to change, Scarlatti,' Pierre said sarcastically. 'Dead body on the bed, you don't hang around getting into suitable clothes to visit you.'

Scarlatti nodded. 'I can see that,' he said seriously. 'Still, makes me uneasy. You two drippin' on my carpet.'

Pierre said, 'Where'll we go tonight? *Gendarmes*'ll be lookin' for Minouche.'

Scarlatti's eyes flickered. 'And you. Coulda been you, Pierre, eh?'

Pierre felt his stomach lurch. Of course! He hadn't thought of that. Then a smile lit his face. He could stay with her! Of course they would be looking for him as well. He had not realized it before. He had thought only of protecting her. But he would be wanted as well, and that meant he could stay with her. Fate had lumped them together. He had dreaded separation from her and now he realized that there was no need. The Quarter was full of informers and someone would have seen him go into the house Minouche lived in. The police might choose to think he had killed Yves Aubin. Looking at how tiny Minouche was, it would seem more likely that Pierre had done the murder. It was his style. Shit, he had taught her that thrust! The thought made him feel colder than he already was.

He said so to Scarlatti. He felt good about it. It bound them together, Minouche and Pierre. He could share her fate whatever it was. Look after her. Take care of her. Give himself a purpose in life.

147

'Well, you can't stay here, that's for sure.' Scarlatti stood and for the first time that night Minouche saw him off his white sofa, in motion. He was small and slim, moving with feline grace and contained energy.

'I have an idea,' he said, looking over his shoulder at them. 'How would you like to go to America?'

'I wouldn't,' Minouche said promptly.

'Oh? Why not?' Scarlatti was always calm, but Pierre did not like his tone. He reckoned they were on their way to America whether they liked it or not.

'I like it here. I'd never want to leave. It's my home. It's where I belong,' Minouche continued vehemently.

'Well, you can't stay here now,' Scarlatti said, amused. 'God, girl, you've murdered your own father. Jeez!' He looked up to the ceiling, 'You can't stay in the Quarter now. Some people.' He shook his head. 'Shit-silly!'

Minouche had not realized that she could not stay in Paris. She had visualized being hidden, perhaps here in Scarlatti's apartment, then after a week or two returning to her old life in the Quarter. Madame Lefranche, Monsieur Rouden, Evangeline Dupont; *'Bonjour, Minouche'*; the Deux Pigeons, the Vie en Rose, the girls at the Petit Moulin; *'Bonsoir, Minouche'* over the streets, slate-grey in the rain, the neon lights flashing over the river. She realized how stupid she had been. She could never return to that life again, not while she was wanted for murder. She felt a great black cloud blanket her heart and soul. She could almost feel the past slipping away from her, out of her grasp. All the familiar ties she held so dear, that filled her with confidence and gave her her security, were suddenly, abruptly, taken. She was alone in a strange and unfriendly world. She sighed and shrugged.

'OK, America,' she said. If she couldn't live in the Quarter then it didn't matter to her where she ended up.

Scarlatti was pouring himself some wine. 'That what you say?' he mimicked. "OK, America"? Half the population of

148

the Quarter would sell their souls to go to America and that's all you got to say?'

'I said OK, Scarlatti. What do you want? Don't expect me to celebrate. I like it here.' Tears threatened. She blinked rapidly.

'So, why do you want to send us to America? I know you have a reason. You never do anything for nothing, do you? You want me to do something for you, eh?'

'Want you to act as courier. No one'll suspect you … you look like a child.'

'But I might not get into the country. I think they're choosy now. America, I mean.'

He nodded, amused, smiling in a superior way. '*I* arrange it, you'll get in. What you think I am? An imbecile?'

He sipped his drink, looking at her through half-closed eyes. 'Pierre goes with you. Your big brother, hey, Pierre? Only you'll travel as Pierre Dejeune. We have it all arranged. The papers and everything.'

There was silence in the room.

'You mean you were going to send me anyway?' Minouche asked breathlessly. She felt as if she were choking; she could not get enough air. '*Mon Dieu*, I would not have gone!'

Her thoughts tumbled over each other. Scarlatti with the papers ready. How did he know she would need to leave the Quarter? How did he know unless …

Pierre looked at the smiling basilisk face, the hooded eyes, almost in awe. He admired winners like Scarlatti, their flair, their devious minds, their lack of conscience or any morals. How comfortable it would be to have no scruples.

'You sent for Yves, didn't you?' he asked, but it was more a statement than a question. 'That was why he came back, no sweat. Yves was a coward, a craven bunch of shit, yet he returned.' Pierre shook his head to and fro and

149

Scarlatti stared at him, eyes cold as ice. 'You sent for him so Minouche would have to leave. One way or another, she'd have to go. Jesus Christ.'

'Is that true?' Minouche asked in disbelief that rapidly changed to amazed acceptance. 'That was why he wasn't afraid! I wondered. Yves was always shit-scared of you yet he wasn't tonight. Pierre's right. I threatened him with you, Scarlatti, and he didn't bat an eyelid. He just laughed. Jesus!'

She was stunned. Then she looked at the Sicilian. 'You did, didn't you? Send for him to shift me?'

Scarlatti shrugged. 'Whatever it takes,' he said calmly.

'Did you know where he was all these years?' she asked, but the question was rhetorical, she did not need an answer. Of course he did. Yves was probably in his pay, or else Scarlatti had something on him. Screwing his daughter would not get him into any real trouble.

'Did you know I'd kill him? Did you anticipate that?' she asked.

Scarlatti grimaced. 'I didn't plan on it,' he said, 'though something was bound to happen. He was getting greedy. He had to go. If not you, someone else would have got rid of the – what you call him? – bag of shit. He won't be missed.' He was smiling at Pierre, the dead dark stones of his eyes fixed on the giant's face. '*Mon Dieu*,' Minouche breathed. '*Mon Dieu*.'

'Did you plan to send me too?' Pierre asked. Scarlatti shook his head.

'Someone had to turn up. Someone called Pierre Dejeune. You did. Very convenient. How much the Rose pay you? Shit, man, you'll make in a day more'n you make there in a week.'

'Doing what? I have my standards.'

'Not any more.' Scarlatti's voice was cold. 'Not with a murder inquiry hanging over you. No, standards tend to be dropped when your freedom is threatened, eh? You're going to America with her.'

'Maybe they won't let me in?' Pierre said, echoing Minouche, but he knew the answer he would receive.

'It's arranged.' Scarlatti was unperturbed. 'All taken care of.'

They stared at him, stunned, as he walked to the white sofa, sipping his wine. There was silence.

'Doing what?' Pierre asked after a moment. 'That's what I want to know.'

'Don't worry your head about that,' Scarlatti said tranquilly.

'Oh, but I do,' Pierre said acidly. 'I don't want to be arrested on arrival and sent to the electric chair.'

Scarlatti looked offended. 'Do you think I am so stupid?'

Put like that, Pierre thought, OK, maybe I don't have to worry. His fears were somewhat mollified. Scarlatti was certainly not stupid.

'You will act as ... er ... messengers to a guy called Salvatore Lucca in Chicago. You'll deal with his second-in-command, next to his son, a guy called Palucci. Guy I deal with. We need to open a passageway from here, or rather Marseilles, to there, Chicago. It has to be arranged. You leave day after tomorrow. Your papers are in order.' He glanced up. 'Except a photograph of you, Pierre.' He grinned. 'We left that open,' he said. 'Ali will take you to Lotte.' Lotte had a whore-house that Scarlatti ran on Rue du Bac. 'You go on the boat from Marseille. Ali will take care of you until you leave.'

'How do we find this guy, Palucci?'

'He'll meet you. No sweat. No problems. You'll get all the instructions as you need them. Just relax and enjoy the trip. Don't worry. It's a piece of cake.'

He toasted them, raising his glass filled with ruby wine, but didn't offer them anything.

'To America, eh?' he said, eyes glittering through half-closed lids. Minouche wondered if he noticed that

151

they had nothing to drink, then decided that he was very well aware of the fact.

'To America,' she echoed him, her heart heavy as a stone within her.

'To America,' Pierre said breathlessly, amazed at his luck, hardly able to believe it. Miracles could happen after all.

'Now get the hell out. I *hate* people drippin' on my carpet.'

Chapter Seven

When Guido and Francesca arrived in Rome they chose a hotel to stay in that was not too expensive. It was grander, however, than anything they had ever seen, even in Palermo.

'We'll stay here until we find a cheaper place to move to,' Guido said, putting his arm about his sister's shoulders, feeling her nervousness. 'We'll check out Tomaso Canona's addresses and ask Paulo if he knows anywhere more suitable.' He gave his sister a little reassuring shake, kissing her pale cheek. 'I do not want to have to worry about you, Francesca, every time we go out. You are very beautiful. We'll stay here, but I don't intend to remain here in Rome long. Unless Mario is here. We still have to find out where he is.'

'It will take time, you know,' Francesca said, looking at him doubtfully. He was going to have to kill his brother and the full realization had only just begun to dawn on him. She could feel his anxiety, just as he could sense hers.

She was going to try and find Luciano. She did not tell Guido that and whether he guessed her intent or not, she did not know. Each time she thought of her lover, desolation engulfed her. It was like drowning in a sea of darkness. Yet she felt secure in the knowledge that Luciano loved her. He had not left her willingly, he had not deserted her. What had Mirella said? 'Papa had to manacle Luciano to Gianfranco to get him away from you,

153

from here. Luciano cried like a baby.'

They were desperately nervous in Rome at first. It was as well they were together otherwise neither of them would have budged from the hotel room. The traffic frightened them, the crowds, the density of the buildings, the rush and bustle of the big city.

But Guido would not let Francesca see how reluctant he was to go out into the busy streets, and Francesca went with him because she did not like to remain alone in the impersonal room.

She bought flowers from the street-seller in the Piazza de Spagna and tried to make the room look pretty.

As soon as possible they went to see Paulo. He was in a seminary well down the Appia Antica, an old and peaceful monastery with a bell-tower and a view of Rome that was quite breathtaking. But the tranquillity and beauty of the monastery did not appear to have calmed Paulo's soul. He seemed taciturn and gloomy to his brother and sister, full of frustration and uncertainty and a terrible restlessness.

'What is it Paulo?' Francesca asked. 'Are you getting headaches again?'

'You are like Etna,' Guido added, 'a volcano ready to erupt.'

The monastery cloisters had a peaceful atmosphere. A covered shaded walk ran around the four sides of a grassy square wherein a fountain splashed with a cool sound and four rose bushes bloomed, filling the air with their sweet scent. There were birds bathing and fluttering in the fountains' waters, and frescoes decorated the warm stone walls where the monks walked as they read matins, compline in the evening and lauds at break of day.

Francesca looked at her brother's narrow, troubled face. The simple stuff robe of the novice hung on him like a sack and his eyes darted constantly around, finding no resting place.

'They say my vocation is suspect,' he said, twisting his

hands together as if he were wringing out a cloth.

'Fra Bartholomeo said much the same thing,' Francesca reminded him gently.

He glanced at her sharply. 'Well, he's wrong,' he said fiercely. 'They are all wrong. "Lord I believe. Help thou my unbelief," ' he quoted, then shrugged and looked about with nervous, fevered glances. 'It's normal to feel as I do. I'm being tested, that's all.'

They said nothing but walked together under the arches of the peaceful cloisters.

'How was Papa's funeral?' Paulo asked after a pause.

'It was fine. Just fine,' Francesca answered.

'How can you say that?' He turned on her, face contorted. 'How? Peaceful? What was peaceful about our father's death, eh?'

'Well, his funeral was, Paulo.' Francesca faced him, speaking firmly. 'Everyone came. That was a surprise. The whole village.' Her lips trembled and she struggled to remain calm.

'Fra Bartholomeo said that he was not allowed to pray over Papa, but he did,' Guido said. 'It was a lovely address, calling for hope and God's mercy.'

'But he should *not*!' Paulo banged his right fist into the palm of his left hand. 'He should not break the rules of our Holy Mother Church like that. It is forbidden. It is against the Church's teaching.'

Francesca touched his sleeve.

'But, Paulo, it helped Mama. What does it matter if he bends the rules a little?'

'It matters. Can't you see? That is the whole point. You cannot bend or break the rules of God and the Church.'

'Your God is very fierce, Paulo,' Francesca said. He said nothing in reply but stared unseeing to where the birds, feathers fluttering, dipped in and out of the sparkling drops of water, then shook themselves and fluttered their wings, heading away into the sun. 'He made them,' she

155

said, pointing. 'He must be kind,' she added uncertainly. She looked up at her brother but he had not heard her, locked as he was within his internal struggle.

'We missed you,' Guido said. 'Only you and . . . Mario were missing.'

A terrible shudder shook Paulo's frame. 'Don't say that name.'

'Papa is buried beneath the trees.' Francesca's voice was soothing.

'I know. Lombardo told me. He and Gina write to me,' Paulo said. 'They said Marcello's gone?'

Francesca nodded. 'Yes,' she said. 'He left a note saying he couldn't stand it. Couldn't remain without Papa and Guido. Especially Guido.' The chorus of the birdsong was loud and joyous but Paulo, looking off into the distance with narrowed eyes, did not hear it.

'You'll never bring yourself to kill him,' he said calmly.

'Of course I will.' Guido was firm. 'I have to.'

'But you won't,' said Paulo.

'He has broken up the family. He has dishonoured us. I will kill him.'

Walking between her brothers, Francesca thought how alike they were physically. But whereas Guido's face radiated vitality and good humour, Paulo's intensity burned with a nervous flame, glimmering and igniting, then dying and nearly going out in despair.

'Where are you staying?' he asked.

'In a very grand hotel near the Termini,' Francesca replied. 'We can't afford it really, even though we have money. It has to last us though, so we'll have to find somewhere else soon.'

'Signora Merciano's on the Via Lombardia near the Trinita dei Monti. She puts up relatives and friends coming to visit the brothers here,' Paulo said, suddenly practical, smiling at them. 'I'll give you her full address. It would be a good place to go for the brothers would only

156

recommend a Godfearing house.' Then he drifted away from them into himself, into the hell he lived with.

'You will do something about Mario, won't you, Guido?' he said at last.

Guido nodded.

'And the Duke?' he persisted.

'We'll take our time, Paulo,' Guido said. 'We need time. This must not be bungled. *Piano, pianissimo*. I have to see Enrico Domini. Tomaso Canona told me to go to him. But I will deal with Mario, trust me.' He clasped his brother's hand, his grip firm and reassuring.

'Gina said in her letter that the Duke has taken Luciano and Mirella off. To marry them safely, she says, keep them away from peasants.' Paulo glanced at Francesca who lowered her head.

'I'm so sorry Francesca,' he said, embracing her. 'But I sincerely hope you have quite recovered from that madness.' He kissed her head but Francesca remained silent. What was there to say? Paulo would never understand. To him the world was black and white. Choices were clear-cut.

'We won't talk about that,' Guido said sharply. 'She's over it now. She hates the whole family as much as we do.'

'No, I don't,' Francesca said calmly. 'Luciano gave me only happiness.'

Paulo looked at her incredulously. 'You call this happiness?' he asked.

'Luciano only gave me love,' she insisted. 'He did me no harm. And I don't want him hurt. Only the Duke.'

Paulo shook his head. 'Women! I don't understand you. Carnal creatures. Creatures of the flesh.' There was great distaste in his voice. 'The temptation of man. What if you had become pregnant, hey? Had you thought of that? Would he honour you then? Of course not! You would be like every other harlot in history. He would cast you aside without thought or pity. Oh, Francesca, grow up.'

157

'Paulo. Oh, Paulo, what do you know of love?' There were tears in her eyes but her brother did not see them.

'Mario is the most important,' he said.

Francesca looked at him intently, tears on her cheeks. 'How can you square that with God?' she asked curiously. '*I* know it is wrong but I am not going to be a nun. Jesus told us to forgive our enemies, didn't he? So how can you square it with God, Paulo?'

'It is family. It is not the same thing,' he said. His face was a battleground. His body seemed too frail to contain the terrible conflict within him.

'It's revenge, Paulo,' Guido said. 'That's not approved of, is it? What about "turn the other cheek", eh, Paulo?'

'Shut up!' Paulo screamed, looking for a moment quite mad. Then he recovered himself. 'Oh, damn. It's difficult,' he said. He seemed near to tears. 'I'm all mixed up. Oh, why did this have to happen? Everything was so simple before.'

'Well, it has happened,' Francesca said. 'And Lombardo says that that . . .' she faltered, '. . . Mama is going to die.'

'Don't say that, Francesca, please. It's a terrible thought. That Mario could have brought about all this pain. It is terrible.' Guido kept shaking his head as he spoke. Paulo looked into the distance where the hills rose velvet-green. 'Sometimes I cannot bear it,' he said, and there was such horror in his voice that his sister shivered.

The little fat monk who had brought them to Paulo came to show them out. They embraced their brother, kissing him on cheeks and lips. They turned once to look back at him and wave. He stood in the shadows of the cloisters, a tall gaunt figure with a face full of suffering.

'I hope he'll be all right,' Francesca said.

The little brother looked at her curiously. 'He grinds his teeth at night and keeps the others awake,' he said. 'I don't know what is the matter with him. He's haunted. It frightens me sometimes.'

158

Guido looked into his guiless eyes. 'A great wrong was done his family. Our brother betrayed us.' The monk's eyes widened. 'Oh, not Paulo,' Guido hastened to add. 'Another brother. He brought about the ruin of our lives. I'm afraid Paulo cannot rid himself of the horror we have been through.'

'But then he must forgive this brother,' the tubby little man said simply. 'It is the only way he'll find peace.'

'Up to that time Paulo believed that all men were either good or bad. He is shaken to discover that this is not so.'

'God help him then,' the little brother said, and made the sign of the Cross. 'May God help him.'

~~~~~~

They moved to Signora Merciano's the following week. The location of the boarding-house was delightful, at the end of the Via Lombardia overlooking the Piazza di Spagna. Although the amenities were basic, it was comfortable.

The Signora would not tolerate any 'hanky-panky', she told them, looking at them severely.

'I don't put up with it. I am a respectable lady, a widow. It's why I have to have people here, in my house. I don't like to, but unfortunately it is necessary if I want to eat.' She pursed her lips. 'My sainted husband is not here to take care of me any more.' She looked as if she begrudged him his freedom, felt a deep resentment that he had chosen to die and leave her to fend for herself. 'Now I have to manage on my own. Men!' She looked at Guido with distaste. 'I will not have people in my house who do not behave properly, who take liberties. I expect you to behave like nuns and priests. That is why I like to have the religious and their families boarding here. They behave themselves. No hanky-panky.'

She scrutinized them closely. 'You are sure you are brother and sister?' she asked suspiciously.

Guido and Francesca nodded. She had a bunch of hairs sprouting out of her chin and Francesca watched fascinated as the little tuft bobbed up and down as the landlady spoke. 'You may verify that at the Monastery of the Little Brothers of St Anthony,' Guido informed her.

'Umm,' she said. 'You *are* alike, I must admit.'

She put them in rooms at opposite ends of the building; Francesca at the front, Guido at the back.

The week after they had moved into Signora Merciano's, Guido went to see Enrico Domini. He had been postponing the visit, nervously putting off the evil day when action would be required of him. Whenever he thought of Mario he felt as if a giant hand was squeezing his heart. His breath became short and a vice gripped his temples. Hatred and fear filled him in equal proportions and he had to sit down a moment, trying to calm the storm within.

He was surprised at the grandeur in which Enrico Domini lived. It was nearly as impressive as the d'Abrizzio *palazzo*. Set off the Via Flaminia, bordering the Borghese Gardens, it was an elegant and beautifully proportioned white stone house.

A servant answered his ring. Guido found himself in a courtyard where a statue of Neptune raised a triton in the air, stone nymphs sported, a fountain splashed and ivy grew on the walls. He followed the servant up three steps into a cool interior; a grand circular hall with curving staircases to either side.

'I'll see to it, Stefano. Thank you.'

Someone leaned over the wrought-iron banister that ran across the landing and curved down the stairs. Guido looked up, his eyes not accustomed to the gloom.

'You want my father?' The voice was female, cool and light, with a hint of laughter in it.

As he stared up, trying to see her, she turned and stared to descend the stairs.

160

First he saw her legs. He had never seen so much of a girl's legs revealed. They seemed to be encased in a pearly gossamer-fine mesh. She wore leaf-green shoes that matched the belt on her white linen dress. The legs were long and slim, as was the girl.

She walked down the stairs, hand lightly resting on the banister, then across the marble hall, her heels clattering. She came and stood beside him. She was nearly as tall as he, so tall that her eyes were level with his. They were a startling blue and she had bobbed blonde hair.

She took Guido's breath away, she was so very strange to him. He was not a man who noticed what people wore or how a woman's hair was dressed, used as he was to the women in the village, his sisters and his mother. They had a natural style, wore their hair long and untrimmed when young or pleated behind their head. Their clothes were unstructured, flowed in unsophisticated lines, were long and simple. This girl was all artifice. Her lips were rouged, her nails painted a bright red, clothes cunningly tailored.

He had never seen anyone like her in his life. The colour of her eyes! How light they were, like water in a lake. Her skin was white. He had never seen skin as white as a pearl before, and her eyelashes and eyebrows were silky-blonde like wheat in a field. She was all the golds of the sun from platinum to warm yellow. And she was so tall and slim, unlike his rounded sisters.

He stood looking at her with his mouth open. She laughed. She had taken in every detail of his appearance as she crossed the hall, appraising him as his father would have an animal he wished to buy. A hot flush rose in Guido's cheeks and anger surged through him as he became aware of the candour of her gaze, but he did not know how to extricate himself from the situation without sounding crass. It was outside his experience.

'Lost your voice?' she asked, laughing.

'Enrico Domini. I have an appointment with him.'

161

'My father, yes,' she said. 'Of course. Follow me.'

She walked across the hall and knocked at a door. There was an answer from within and she opened it.

'Father, it's . . .' She turned and her bobbed hair swung like golden silk. She looked at Guido, her eyes dancing. He had not noticed that there were tiny flecks of green in the blue. It made her eyes seem liquid and deep. As she moved closer to him he could smell a jasmine scent that rose from her body's warmth.

'Your name?' She looked at him as if she read his thoughts and again he blushed.

'Guido Palucci,' he said. His voice had become husky and he cleared his throat. She turned her head and looked back into the room.

'Guido Palucci, Father,' she said. Then, turning to him again, she whispered: 'I'll wait for you,' and gave him a little push into the room, closing the door behind him.

It was vast. The walls were wine-red and hung with paintings. The chairs were gilt-edged and stood against the wall like sentinels. An enormous chandelier hung from the ceiling.

At the opposite end of the room, sitting behind an imposing desk, his back to the long windows behind him, sat a man with a mane of silver hair, smooth olive skin, heavy black brows and a welcoming smile.

'Greetings to a brother.' He leaned forward and, without rising, extended his hand. Guido shook it and sat in the chair Enrico Domini indicated. It was a leather chair, a match to the one Domini himself was sitting in and not at all like the ones around the walls of the room.

'Tomaso Canona told me you were coming.'

'Yes, sir?'

'Yes. He told me some of the circumstances. Tragic, tragic.' The man shook his head. 'To have a brother like that who dishonours the family. It is not to be borne.'

He picked up a cigar, snipped the end with a gold

162

cutter, then lit it. He shot his cuffs as he did so. He wore gold cuff-links and his shirt was silk with the same subtle patina or sheen that encased his daughter's legs. He had a heavy gold ring on his index finger and a gold bracelet around his wrist as well as a watch. Guido had never seen this before. The Duke did not dress so grandly, nor did he wear gold. 'Family loyalty, it is the most important thing,' he said.

While puffing clouds of grey smoke that wreathed his head, his large brown eyes studied Guido. How had he sired such a blonde daughter? Guido was wondering.

'So what can I do for you?' Enrico Domini asked benignly, spreading his hands. 'Anything. Just ask. A favour from a brother.'

'Find out for me where my brother Mario is,' Guido said, his voice suddenly firm and positive. 'So that the family can deal with him and right the dishonour he brought upon us.'

The man nodded. 'Yes I thought you might want that. I can do it for you. But, remember, it will take time. I have contacts all over the world. He could be anywhere. Tomaso seems to think America.'

'America?' Guido was nomplussed. America had not figured in his speculation. America was very far away. The man nodded. He is smooth as cream, Guido, thought, and repressed a sudden and surely unreasonable dislike of the man. Was it jealousy? he wondered. Did he envy the man's affluence? The luxury in which he obviously lived? Guido could not answer truly. He simply knew he felt uncomfortable in Domini's presence.

'America?' he said again, finding the prospect daunting.

'Yes, America,' Enrico Domini repeated, puffing at his cigar. 'But he may not have gone that far. We simply don't know. However, you understand, if I suddenly start asking questions he will be alerted. It will not do to let him know you are looking for him. I cannot say, "Do you know Mario

163

Palucci? Where is he?" Someone then will say to him, "They are looking for you." He would run away. No, I have to be discreet. I cannot ask outright. I have to be subtle. Ask who is new here, who is new there. Eventually we will find him.'

Guido nodded. The man smiled.

'Good. Then leave it to me. It will be taken care of.'

There was a pause. He smiled speculatively at Guido. At last he said, 'Now I have a little favour to ask of you.' Guido's heart sank. 'It's really quite a pleasant task.' Domini leaned back in his chair and put his finger tips together, then pressed them to his lips.

'Guido, I'll be honest with you,' he said as if he had suddenly made up his mind. 'I have some money . . . the Government will insist on checking, as if a man's money was theirs by right. Ah, it is a problem.'

Guido nodded but didn't know what the man was talking about.

'Now this money I have needs a home for a while. I want you to go to the Banco di Roma Commerciale, any branch, and open an account for yourself in your name and put the money in. You will use some of it for expenses while you are in Rome, and from time to time I will give you further sums to deposit. You will bring me an accounting when I ask for it. I will tell you what is a reasonable amount for you to spend. It will be generous, I do assure you.'

Guido thought the request seemed reasonable. But a thought struck him.

'You trust me?' he asked. 'What's to stop me, if I was dishonest, from stealing all your money? If the account is in my name?'

Enrico Domini shook his head and laughed as if he found the idea very amusing.

'You won't do that,' he said, then added, his eyes suddenly blades, so sharp that Guido drew in his breath.

164

'There would be no hiding place. Remember, I have contacts all over the world. If you did that, you would never live to spend the money.'

There was menace in the man's statement that froze the blood. Guido shivered. Enrico Domini spread his hands again and became genial, as if he had never been otherwise.

'But you are an honourable man. You will not steal. Never. I would not believe it of you. If someone came in here now and accused you of dishonourable acts, I would not believe them. I would know they were lying. I am a good judge of character, believe me. Now to pleasanter things. You are staying at Signora Merciano's in the Via Lombardia. When I need you, I will contact you there. When I have news. Give you your spending money, eh?' he grinned.

How did he know where I am staying? Guido wondered. He knew he had not told the man or his daughter, so how did he know? He took the proffered hand and shook it. He knew he was dismissed but felt the meeting had been inconclusive, as if there had not been sufficient explanation. However, he walked away from the desk and when he reached the door, glanced back over his shoulder. Enrico Domini had his head down and was busy writing. He did not look up as Guido opened the door and left.

~~~~~~

The girl was waiting for him in the hall. She was smoking, something else he had never seen a woman do. He stood looking at her. This time she blushed under his scrutiny.

'I have never seen anyone like you before,' he said. She bit her lip, then came towards him and put her hand on his arm.

'Guido,' she said softly, 'Guido, where do you come from? Sicily?'

He nodded.

'Be careful of my father,' she said.

165

He looked startled. 'Why?' he asked, but she changed the conversation.

'Would you like some coffee?'

'Very much.'

'Then follow me.'

She led him through another door into a walled courtyard, overwhelmingly green, shaded by lime and magnolia trees. There was a marble table on wrought-iron legs and white wrought-iron chairs. She indicated one.

'Sit down.'

The servant, Stefano, appeared.

'Bring some coffee, Stefano,' she said and the man bowed and disappeared. There was silence. The girl drummed her fingers on the white blue-veined marble table top. Her hands, he could see, had never done hard work. Long fingers, long scarlet nails.

'What is your name?' he asked.

'Eleanor.' She smiled at him. Her smile was intimate, drawing him into her warmth and approval. 'Eleanor, after a Queen. My mother was English.'

That explained a lot. The milk-white skin and golden hair. Was?

'Is she dead then, your mother?' he asked gently, afraid to hurt.

She gave him a quick look.

'You are sensitive,' she remarked. 'That's why I told you to be careful of Father. You're a kind person. You are sad for me that she is dead?'

'Of course,' he said, looking at her curiously.

'Most people in Rome, my father's . . . er . . . friends, they don't care. It is a closed society. They never accepted her, a foreigner. Now they don't like me.' She shrugged. 'But you don't want to hear all this.'

'Oh, but I do. I want to know every little thing about you.'

She fascinated him. He stared at the pale golden lashes,

the fine wheaten brows, in wonder. She seemed to him infinitely exotic and lovely.

The coffee came on a huge silver tray in a silver coffee-pot. He watched her as she poured. She handled the heavy pot and the delicate china competently, her gestures graceful but firm.

'Some of my father's friends are dangerous,' she said. Then asked, 'You're not going to work for him, are you?'

He shook his head, a little annoyed.

'No. But why shouldn't I, if I want to? Don't you think I can take care of myself?'

She smiled at him again, that curiously intimate smile. 'You are very innocent,' she said. He was disconcerted. He felt she was belittling him.

'Perhaps you think I am,' he said. 'Don't judge by appearances.'

She looked contrite. 'I didn't mean to offend,' she said.

'Well, I'm not working for him,' he said, and closed his lips and turned his head away. He was not going to tell her his business. It was, after all, a family matter.

'Are you going to stay in Rome?' she asked after a moment.

'For a time, yes.'

'To work?'

He shook his head. He could see her confusion. Suddenly she looked like Francesca, bewildered and curious. He threw back his head and laughed, and she looked at him in surprise and delight.

'I'm glad you can laugh,' she said. 'No one here does.'

'I can see what is puzzling you, and you are a woman and curious. You have to find out.'

She pouted, made a face. 'So?'

'It is obvious I am not a gentleman, that I am from the country. Yes?' She nodded. 'So why have I not to work? That is what you are asking?'

She laughed then at his frankness and lack of pretension.

'See,' he said, 'my sister Francesca and I have come here on a family matter. Your father is helping me to clear it up. And I will leave Rome when that is done.'

'Will it be a short time or a long time?' she asked. He shrugged. 'I don't know. That depends on your father.'

She sighed deeply. 'Have you seen Rome since you came?'

He shook his head. 'We have seen a little,' he said. 'The Trinita dei Monte. The Via Lombardia where we live. The monastery where my brother is. The little trattoria where we eat.' He made a face. 'The food there is no good. Aye, yi, yi!'

She laughed and looked at him. 'Will you let me show you . . . you and your sister, a little of Rome? It would give me such pleasure. Please?'

She coaxed him like a child, but he did not need to be coaxed. 'Of course,' he cried, delighted to accept, enchanted at the prospect of seeing her again.

'Good. Then it is decided. Rome is a beautiful city. There is much to see. It is also corrupt and greedy.' She shrugged. 'I think Rome, and my father of course, killed my mother,' she said. Before he could say anything, she laid her hand on his arm. 'I like you. I like you very much.' Her eyes were steady, the look she gave him intimate. He felt his heart leap. She got to her feet.

'I'll see you then. Tomorrow. Ten o'clock. At the foot of the Piazza di Spagna. Yes?'

He stood up. He had not touched his coffee. He picked up the delicate cup and gulped it down. It scalded his throat but it was delicious.

'Stefano will show you out. Till tomorrow then.' She waved at him and was gone.

Chapter Eight

The lights shone like a diamond necklace strung across Lake Shore Drive. Mario sat back in the car's plush interior and puffed on his cigar, content with the night's work. He only wished The Ape, with his bad breath, would not sit so close. The Ape was his bodyguard. Six feet tall, with the squashed face of an ex-contender and the scrambled egg brains of a dum-dum who took more punishment than he gave. Still, he frightened people and Mario liked that. In the Ape's shadow, no one dared touch him.

Salvatore Lucca had touched him tonight. He was pleased with Mario. He had clapped him on the shoulder. Touched him. Sign of affection. Approval.

Lucca, unlike most of his fellow countrymen, did not like to be touched. It was English, that, not liking to be touched. Latins were tactile. But not Salvatore Lucca. Yet tonight he had put his hand on Mario's shoulder and said, 'You do good, Mario. Very good. You run the territory OK. Unlike some who get too big for their boots and end up in the bottom of the lake, weeds growin' outa their ears.'

Mario smiled to himself in the warm dark of the car. Let the old man think that; that he, Mario was safe, loyal. Let him speculate on Mario's affiliation.

He had no intention of remaining Lucca's arse-licker. Fucking old Napoleon! Wanted everyone to bow and scrape. Well, he, Mario, would kow-tow until he could knock Lucca down. Push him off.

Mario grinned. Fucking old man. He tapped the dividing glass and the driver pulled it across, not taking his eyes off the road.

'We near?'

'Sho', suh.' The driver was Moses. Stoopid dumb nigger Mario muttered. Had to spell things out for him.

'How long?'

'Five minutes, suh.'

Moses looked through the driving mirror at Mario. He knew what his boss was thinking. Man, *he* was stupid! Thought he couldn't speak American. Thought Moses dumb, deaf and blind. Moses missed nuthin'. He kept his counsel. He was doing overtime in his head. Head'd bust with all he had in it. Facts. Dates. Disappearances. Deliveries. All there. Up there. and he'd use it some day. Trouble was, who to sell it to? The Feds? The Chicago Police? Lucca? Lucca's rival Tony Moriano across the tracks? The O'Brien gang who were jostling for position on the fringes of the territories, Lucca's and Moriano's. There were many potential buyers and it gave Moses a comfortable feeling to be sitting on the information, having a hard time making up his mind who to trade it to. He would have to wait and see. Time would tell. He wasn't in a hurry. But he had to be careful. Couldn't be premature. If he was caught, even suspected, he would end up in the morgue. Meanwhile he drove for whitey, pretended to be dumb and chalked it all up on that little blackboard in his head.

There he went again: tap, tap, on the window. Impassively he drew it back again. Said, *so* polite, 'Yes, suh?'

'We near?'

'Yes, suh.'

'How long?'

''Bout three minutes, suh.'

He glanced in the rear-view mirror again. Man sure

170

didn't see the irony. Frettin', he was. Impatient. Couldn't control it. That was bad. Patience paid off. Moses smiled to himself, but inwardly. Nothing showed on his face.

Mario was on his way to pick up these two Frenchies at Union Station, ten o'clock. He didn't want to. He squirmed under the orders Lucca had given him as if he were some two-bit messenger boy. Girl was called something unpro- nounceable, Min . . . somethin', and a guy called Pierre. Pete it would have to be. No one went around this town calling himself Pierre. Faggot's name. Guy might be a fairy. Jeez! Mario reflected impatiently, what was he supposed to do with them? Lucca said to put them up. He had no intention of doing so. Marylyn was in his bed on the black satin sheets. Jeez! Not fuckin' likely. This Frenchie pair would have to find someplace else. Marylyn on those sheets drove all else from his mind. Waitin' for him, she was. Said things to him to make him harder 'n a steel rod.

The black car swung to a halt.

'Right on time, suh.' Mario jumped out.

'Wait here.'

'Suppose they move me on, suh?' Moses knew no one would but he liked to play dumb and aggravate Mario.

'Be here when I come back or I'll have your fuckin' black hide.'

Mario jabbed the cigar within an inch of Moses's face then turned and walked up the steps to the station. The Ape at his side.

He paced the platform, waiting. Stoopid voice with a clothes-peg on its nostrils said the train was delayed. Mario walked up and down, up and down, seeing no one, engrossed in his own thoughts.

Things had gone well for him since he left Sicily. He had landed in New York, gravitated to Chicago where it was all happening, used his contacts, introductions given to him by Tomaso Canona, and ended up working for Salvatore Lucca.

171

Lucca was eighty if he was a day and Mario, who quickly adopted an American accent, wore American clothes, drove an American car, ate American food which suited his impatient disposition, and cultivated all things American, came to despise and loathe the little man who still spoke to him in Italian and reminded Mario of Giuseppe. He hated the little man in the same way that he had hated his father. He chaffed under Lucca's command, his authority irked him, and he determined to take over, unseat Salvatore Lucca as soon as he could.

The man was old. Mario was young. But Mario was impatient, too impatient to wait. He burrowed deeper into his camel coat and pulled his hat low over his eyes.

There it came. Fuckin' late! He couldn't keep still. Tapped his foot. Took off his hat. Smoothed his brilliantined hair. Put his hat on. Stared down the platform.

Jeez, there they were! He thought he'd choke on the cigar. Man was a giant! Fuckin' colossus. Made The Ape look like a retarded dwarf. Man looked nobody's fool. Shit! Mario would have to get him. Have to. Otherwise he'd lose face. Must have this Froggy giant workin' for him.

Then there was the girl. She had somethin'. Big eyes. Never seen such big eyes, lookin' like butter on a waffle. The guy was big, the girl small. Tiny. Fit her in your pocket. Make a man feel like Tarzan. Some hell of a guy.

Mario shook hands with them. Their English was not too bad. It sounded cute from the girl. He was not too happy at the way the giant looked him over. Looked right into him. Scrutinized him like he was a specimen in a laboratory. Mario shifted beneath his gaze. Who'd he think he was anyway? He'd have to learn. Learn who Mario Palucci was.

'Lucca sent me here te meet ya,' he said, pumping the giant's hand with an enthusiasm he did not feel.

Then he smiled at the girl. Cute little hat on the side of

172

her head, cute little dimples in her cheeks. He was enchanted.

'Sure are welcome,' he said. 'Journey OK?' looking into her eyes, changing his mind about having them to stay at his place. Have to get Marylyn out. Marylyn was a dime a dozen.

This guy could be a great help. Look at the Ape, bumbling around, looking for cases, tripping over them. Stoopid fuckin' animal! Look at this guy. Muscles bulging, arms like oaks, bright intelligent eyes that missed nothin'. Je-sus!

And her. Cute little bundle. Accent gave her class. Yes, he could put them up all right.

Fuck Marylyn.

~~~~~~

'Ees big . . . your car,' the girl said, settling back in the limousine, holding on to the small attaché case she carried.

'Yeah. Everythin's big in America,' Mario said casually. He was looking where her black silk stocking ended. He could catch a glimpse of white skin and black panties. She had crossed her legs to reveal a sexy glimpse of flesh, the satin trimmed with fine lace.

When he looked up, he saw that the giant Pierre ("Call you Pete, OK?" "My name is Pierre.") was watching him. Mario gave him a wide smile, showing his even white teeth, making his eyes twinkle a little to soften his expression. He had found his film star smile worked on people and he used it to great advantage. Not on this guy though. Pierre stared back at him, cold as ice.

'Have a cigarette?' Mario took out a gold cigarette case with his entwined initials, M and P, embossed on it.

The girl took one, and he lit it with his matching gold cigarette lighter. She dragged on the cigarette, then blew the smoke out through her nostrils. She looked out of the window of the car.

173

'Cute houses,' he said, and she smiled. He could not tell what she was thinking. She had a self-contained look and her huge brown eyes revealed nothing.

'You come from New York?' he asked, more for the sake of something to say than because he was interested.

She shook her head. 'No. We went from Paris to Canada. There are a lot of French there. We stayed a little while then we came here. With stops, of course. It was all very simple.'

He smiled at her again, exerting his charm. He wanted this girl to like him. She was not like the others, the two-bit floozies with platinum curls and false eyelashes who teetered on high heels and acted sexy, and who in bed "ooh'd," and "ah'd" in all the right places, doing what they thought he wanted them to do, not knowing he knew bad acting when he saw it. Afterwards they acted ecstatic and he knew they had done it so many times that the whole thing was mechanical.

"Jeez, you were great, Mario. Never seen one like yours. No wonder they call you Big Boy." As if he didn't know what they were doin'. This girl was not like that at all.

'Hey, I bet you're hungry?' he asked, wide-eyed and eager, looking at her, hoping she appreciated him. She nodded, catching his mood.

'Listen –' He tried to sound spontaneous, get the right inflection, then caught Moses's glance in the rear-view mirror and decided to sack him, then remembered he couldn't. Lucca gave him the car and Moses went with it. Mario was sure Moses spied for Lucca but it didn't unduly perturb him. Lucca was getting old, past it. Given time, Mario would sack Moses if he wanted to.

'Listen,' he said, 'why don't we stop off at the deli and get some supplies?'

The girl was laughing. She had little white teeth, like a child's. Her tongue looked pink in her mouth and he wanted it in his.

'Deli? What is "deli"?'

174

'Oh, a store.'

'What is a store?' she asked, choking with laughter.

It was OK. She was flirting with him. She must like him. She had her hand over her mouth, trying to stifle the giggles.

'Jeez . . . don't you know nuthin?' He clapped his hand to his forehead in mock dismay. She chuckled with him, playing the game.

'*C'est une épicerie fine,*' the giant said in their lingo, not joining in.

'Ah, *oui, je comprend.* I see.' She flashed Mario a grin. 'Yes, it's a good idea. It would be nice,' she added in the halting English he found so sexy.

'First I thought we'd go to see the man, Lucca.'

It was Pierre who spoke, looking at Mario levelly. The giant saw through him, Mario realized. He understood all the little games he was playing. He made Mario uneasy.

Mario knew, too, that he was right about Lucca. They would have to go to him first. He hated that. He wanted to be the one in charge. Mario decided he would go on working on the guy. Patience, that's all it needed, and a little time. He wanted this guy on his team and he had discovered that you could get anyone on your side eventually. All it needed was to be relentlessly nice and friendly to them. People found it hard to resist unmitigated concern and interest. In the meantime, although he would have given anything to be alone with Minouche, keeping the banter going, he realized he would have to put up with the French guy and make him feel welcome.

'Sure. You're a right.' Sometimes, to Mario's horror, his American slipped and a couple of unwanted a's stuck themselves on to his words. The giant glanced at him sharply.

'Listena me. We go to Lucca. He's the boss-man. Still.' He let the 'still' hang around a while, then continued,

'*Then* we'll go to the deli, grab us some food, then back to the apartment.' He directed his grin all around. Moses, glancing in the mirror, thought to himself, Jeez! Who's he trying to impress? Knowing all the time. He's hot for the girl, he thought, and smiled to himself. Ice-prick Mario, as Marylyn called him, was like a college kid with his first date; out to come over big. Asshole, thought Moses.

The girl seemed delighted. In fact, Minouche thought Mario a weird and wonderful bird of prey. She sensed the air of danger about him and it attracted her. She liked the ruthless undertow of his personality and thought him the best-looking male she had ever seen. With his brilliantined black hair, his big brown eyes, the crooked grin and snazzy clothes, she was bemused by him.

When they reached the brownstone on North Southport where Lucca had lived ever since his arrival in Chicago some forty years previously, Moses brought the car to the curb and parked it.

There were kids playing around a fire hydrant and a man sat on a porch down the street, puffing on a pipe. It was a warm day but Mario kept his camel coat on. A couple of women were gossiping, drawing apart, step by step, sentence by sentence, as if they had not enough time to say to each other all that needed to be said and could not bear to stop. They ended up shouting goodbye to each other from houses five numbers away.

It was a domestic scene; people living ordinary lives, going about their daily routine. A woman came out of the bakery with a loaf under her arm. A man rode by on a bike; a couple of teenagers stood shyly together, not touching, giving off waves of desire. Mario and his party looked strange among them.

He led the way up the steps to the front door. Minouche was still carrying the case. The door had coloured glass panels on both sides. Mario rang the bell and they waited.

At last a square, tough-looking woman answered it. A

smile broke the severity of her face when she saw who it was.

'Mario, Mario, nicea to see you. Youa handsome boy! Come in. Come in.'

She led them into a front room. It was large, full of red plush and mahogany furniture and Tiffany lampshades, a little sombre but comfortable. There were sliding doors at the end opposite the window. A large bull-like man stood there twitching the lace curtains back and forth, peering out. He rested one foot on the seat of a chair and nodded to Mario.

One side of the doors slid open and a slick young man with a patent-leather look hairstyle, a pimply skin and a cigarette between his teeth, appeared. Mario glanced at him indifferently and walked over to him as if to pass him and go into the other room. But the young man put up his hand. There was a malicious smile on his face that curved his lips down so that the cigarette seemed to be suspended in mid-air.

'Not you, Palucci. Just the Froggies.'

Mario, to his fury, had to move away from the sliding door and allow Minouche and Pierre to pass by him into the inner room. Pierre glanced at him in passing and Mario felt furious and humiliated.

~~~~~~

They were greeted by Salvatore Lucca, a little wizened man, shrewd of eye and wrinkled of face.

'Dear children, nice to meet you. Your journey went all right?' They nodded. 'Good. Good. It was carefully planned. For your safety.'

He shook hands with them formally, then asked them to sit in the two chairs facing him, smiling at them like a benevolent grandfather. He sat in his huge winged chair in front of a crackling fire. The heat in the room was tropical.

'I like it,' he said, divining their thoughts instantly and gesturing to the glowing coals. 'Cold blood at eighty, you see. You wait. It won't be too long. Time flies.' He leaned forward and patted Minouche on the knee. 'Want some advice?' he asked. Then, without waiting for a reply, he continued, 'Enjoy it while you can. Grab it all now. Only thing I regret, the ones that got away.'

He chuckled. 'You staying with Mario?' he asked, and Minouche nodded. 'Good, good. Watch him. I don't trust him.' His currant eyes darted a glance at Pierre. 'He's transparent, Mario Palucci. Ambitious as hell. Hungry for power. And impatient.' He clicked his teeth, shaking his head. 'Can't wait.' He leaned forward. 'See, you've got to find out if the doors are locked before you break them down. Stands to reason. Mario just crashes in like a stampeding buffalo. Know what I mean? Before he knows.' The fishy eyes caught Minouche's and she sensed for the first time the steely core of the boss-man.

'Don't get me wrong, I like the guy, but he needs watchin'.' He stared at her, his small eyes running over her body, and she tried not to let him see her shiver. He leaned over again and ran his hand up and down her thigh. There was silence in the room. He gave her a grin, false teeth moving perceptibly in his mouth. Then, abruptly, he sat back and she pulled her skirt down over her knees.

'Nearly gave me an erection then. You could name your price if you could achieve that. I give all the money I got, an' it's a fortune, I swear, everythin' I got for one erection. Jeez, it'd be good! Trouble with old age . . . no pleasure no more. Remember what I said: enjoy it while you can.' He looked at Minouche. 'Jeez, you're pretty,' he said lasciviously. 'But you're safe with me, eh?' He chuckled and glanced at Pierre, noting the whiteness of his knuckles, the glassiness of his eyes.

The woman who had let them in came into the room. Lucca looked at her with distaste.

'Some wine, Florinda, for the lady. And you?' He looked at Pierre. He seemed amused by the giant.

'Wine is OK,' said Pierre.

'For me, a tea, Florinda, a fuckin' tasteless tea that's good for me. Keeps me alive another few hours, eh?' He looked at Minouche. 'My wife.' He gestured at the large woman. 'Fuckin' herbal tea,' he muttered, looking up at the ceiling and clicking his uneasy false teeth.

When she had left the room, he turned to Minouche and Pierre. 'Women get old. Loose their juices,' he said regretfully, then sighed. 'So do men, but not until later, much later. An' men don't get so ugly. Men can be father to three generations of children. Not women. Once they're past bearing, they get ugly. Best to trade them in for a new model.'

Florinda came back with the wine. 'It's good,' she said, her big plain face wreathed in smiles. 'The best Sicilian wine.'

Minouche sipped the ruby liquid and felt the glow as it hit her stomach, bathing it in fire. She was empty so the effect of the alcohol was more noticeable. It calmed her. Made her feel good. Florinda waited expectantly.

'It's very good,' Minouche said, nodding, and the woman smiled in satisfaction, then left. She returned a moment later with the tea. Lucca looked at it, pushed it away with bony impatient hands, then ignored it for the rest of the interview. He waited patiently for his wife to leave. She refilled their glasses, tucked the rug around her husband's knees, piled some logs on the fire and finally departed. Lucca simmered with impatience beneath her ministrations and visibly relaxed when she left.

'Scarlatti? How's Scarlatti?' he asked.

'Very well, when we last saw him.' Minouche thought of Scarlatti, his simian face and snake-like eyes. 'Very well' seemed a pallid description of him.

'He's OK,' Lucca said. 'Not like Palucci. He knows his

territory, doesn't try to expand without permission.'

It was unbearably hot in the room. The red velvet curtains were tightly drawn. There was no air. Lucca's chin fell on his chest and Minouche could see his gums beneath the false teeth. They were pink as a baby's. He seemed asleep or lost in dreams and she thought, yes, he is an old man. An old, old man. Suddenly he looked up and his small watery eyes, like fish in a tank, focused on her. She shivered. They were ruthless and indifferent as the eyes of a killer shark.

'Now,' he said, 'have you brought me my present?'

She knew at once what he meant; the battered old case she carried. It had made itself at home among their luggage all the way from Scarlatti and Paris. No one had shown any interest in it, least of all the customs officials. Scarlatti had told them Lucca would know immediately if it had been opened, but Minouche and Pierre had not wanted to pry. Rather the reverse. They were terrified that it might contain something that they would not want to carry. In the event, they both felt ignorance was bliss.

Now Minouche put it on the old man's lap. He passed it to the young man with the patent-leather hair and pimply skin who all the while had lounged in the doorway.

'Take it upstairs, Pino. Lock it in the safe. Here!' He threw the young man a bunch of keys which Pino deftly caught in one hand, then grinned at his own prowess, revealing bad teeth.

'Come right back,' Lucca said. 'Pino's my son,' he added. 'I trust him.' He smiled a yellow smile at Minouche. 'As much as I trust anyone.'

She was thinking that bad teeth must run in the family when he leaned over towards her and she could see how dry his skin was. Like the case she had brought from France, toughened by time. His breath smelled stale.

'You are wanted there? In Paris, France? For murder?' he whispered.

Minouche felt her stomach sink. She nodded.

180

'Well, you'll be safe here.' He winked and patted her knee again. 'We will look after you. I'm pleased with you. Lucca is pleased. Long as you don't get outa line, you'll be OK.'

He nodded and smiled. Pino came back into the room. They exchanged glances, father and son. He threw the keys back to his father but they fell wide and Minouche saw the irritation in the old man's eyes. She bent to retrieve them and pass them back to him. That wasn't wise of Pino, she thought. She didn't like him. Didn't like the way he looked her over, the sneer constantly on his lips. She didn't like him or his father but there was nothing she could do about it.

'Now go, I'm tired,' Lucca said, pulling the rug closer about him and waving them away. *'Buona sera. Buona sera.'*

They went back into the other room, Pino bringing up the rear and closing the sliding door behind them. He was smiling, endlessly smiling. Mario was waiting, pacing up and down, up and down. Minouche was overcome with relief at seeing him there. The Ape was asleep in a chair, his hands clasped across his belly, his mouth open. He looked very peaceful.

'OK, I see Lucca now,' Mario said. Once more Pino blocked his way.

'He don' wanna see you,' Pino said, his fingers almost touching Mario's chest. Almost, but not quite.

'I got somethin' t' say t'him.' Mario was blustering now, hating to be made to look like a lackey, an unimportant minion, in front of the girl.

Pino sighed elaborately. 'Well, he don' wanna hear it. Lucca says he don' wanna see you, he don' wanna see you, OK? You go home now. Fix up these two Froggies wi' rooms an' feed them like Lucca tells you, servant-boy. OK?'

Pino had not stopped smiling, but his black eyes were cold. Mario was white with rage but there was nothing he

181

could do. But, goaded beyond endurance, he could not resist one taunt: 'Your old man isn't gonna live forever, Pino. Watch out then!' he said. He instantly regretted it. Pino shook his head and tutted loudly.

'Rash!' he said, still smiling. 'Very rash.'

Minouche looked back as they drove away. Pino stood at the front door watching them, the cigarette dangling from his bottom lip. She saw he was still smiling.

~~~~~~~

Mario's apartment was on Lincoln Avenue. It was on the second floor over a speakeasy he ran for Lucca. It had two entrances; one up a flight of wooden steps from the street, the other down a hidden back stairway. It was spacious, untidy, furnished with only the basics. Mario was obviously not a homemaker. Few personal effects seemed to have been added since his arrival. But to Minouche it was lovely. Used as she was to a gipsy existence, it seemed luxurious. She would be at home here, she decided, ecstatic over the hot and cold running water, the drinks cabinet and mirrored bar in the living-room, the pale beige couch.

Mario seemed to have recovered his good humour. Full of suppressed excitement in the presence of Minouche Aubin, he was well into his stride; showing her the separate entrance of the night club, preening over the apartment and its appointments which she seemed so impressed by, boasting a little, letting drop names that she did not recognize to impress her. He was, it seemed, on nodding terms with everyone who was anyone in Chicago, from the Mayor on down.

Mario mixed them a highball when they had put their cases in the room he had given them. They were off the gallery that ran around the next floor. The rooms were functional, small, simply furnished. Mario hoped Minouche would not stay long in hers. He had definite plans to install her in the master-bedroom that was his.

Marylyn was there, looking cheaper in his eyes than usual. He told her to scram, to vamoose to the club below, then to get lost and not bother him any more. With indifference she eyed her rival, shrugged, put a few flimsies in a case and left.

He mixed the drinks strong and with a flourish that asked to be admired. Minouche hoped they would eat soon, she was very hungry and did not want to drink any more alcohol on an empty stomach. However she said nothing, glancing at Pierre who, she noticed, did not touch his drink. He stood in the living-room, arms crossed, leaning against the wall.

'Tonight I'll take ya to the Blue Lady.' Mario said. He seemed full of nervous energy, constantly clicking his fingers, smoothing back his hair, moving about the apartment. 'It's Lucca's. It's fun. Got an evening dress, baby?' he asked Minouche, winking.

She smiled at him. Suddenly she was very tired. The journey had been long and she had been anxious. The relief she felt at getting rid of the attaché case and its unknown contents had relaxed her. All she wanted to do was sleep.

'I think Minouche is tired,' Pierre said quietly. 'I think a little food would be good. Build up her energy. What about the deli?'

For a moment it seemed as if Mario wanted to hit him. His eyes blazed fiercely and he glared at the giant who looked coolly back at him. But he quickly recovered. Years of concealing his resentment from his father had given him the ability to control himself.

'Sure,' he said breezily. 'Sure. What time is it?' He clicked his fingers. 'I know. Great idea. Getcha something from downstairs, from the Blue Lady. Hell, no. Now I think, you get gussied up, baby, an' I'll take ya down. Be quicker. All of us down, yeah. We'll eat down there. Great food. You'll love it.'

183

Minouche couldn't keep her eyes open. She kept falling asleep in the bath as she tried to wash away the exhaustion she was feeling. She wanted to enjoy the experience. It was all so luxurious here; lots of water, soaps, soft towels. Scarlatti had given her and Pierre money to purchase evening clothes before they left Paris, telling them that it was *de riguer*. 'In America you wear evening clothes alla the time,' he said. 'Women dress up for breakfast. I seen it in the movies.' She had bought a beaded affair on the Boulevard Faubourg St Honoré. She had never been in that street before and had not enjoyed the experience, worrying in case she was recognized by a passing *gendarme* and arrested. But she loved the dress. The base was flesh-coloured chiffon and on to it, in cunning design, to conceal and reveal but not to shock, were sewn mother-of-pearl sequins and seed pearls and little crystal beads that sparkled and shimmered in the light. It was the only dress she had ever possessed and she put it on now, for the first time, wishing she could go to bed, aching for sleep.

Mario and Pierre were waiting for her. Mario whistled when he saw her and she felt better. She liked him, with his good looks and charm, and wanted very much to impress him.

Pierre looked uncomfortable in his new evening clothes which were not the best fit in the world and in which he felt ill-at-ease.

They went down the back way. A concealed door in the living-room slid open smoothly to Mario's touch and they found themselves in a carpeted corridor. As they walked down it, they passed the men's and women's toilets.

'There's an entrance outside. Leads to the coffee bar. Innocent. Then you use another sliding door to get you . . . here.'

A burst of sound, smoke, music and excitement greeted them as they entered, like a huge wave breaking over the shore. Minouche's adrenaline started pumping. The Ape greeted them. He seemed touchingly glad to see Minouche and she gave him a special smile.

The room they found themselves in was foggy with cigarette smoke. It was jam-packed. Voices were pitched just below a shout and the roar of the smartly dressed crowd was only just topped by a jazz-band playing the wildest music Minouche had ever heard. She turned to Mario, her eyes bright as lights that had just been turned on.

'*Mon Dieu*, it is wonderful, the music,' she said.

Mario, looking into those bright eyes, felt a surge of protective affection for the tiny French girl.

'Oh, yeah. The joint's jumpin',' he said. 'It's great. The greatest. Here, lemme take your arm.'

Putting a hand under her elbow he guided her across the room, around the raised dais where the orchestra played to the table at the front just below the band.

'How's that?' he asked and held her chair for her. She flashed him a grateful look which made him feel masterful. He clicked his fingers to summon a waiter. One instantly appeared.

'What'll you have?' Then, without waiting for a reply, 'Champagne. Got to be champagne.'

'I didn't think we could get alcohol here?' she said, wide-eyed, staring at the drinks being served.

'Oh, sure. Lucca says the law is unpopular, the people unwilling . . . so,' Mario shrugged, 'we supply. We're makin' it and they're lappin' it up. That's part of our racket. Here, taste it. It's swell.'

Minouche gave up the idea of food. The music had got to her, set her feet tapping and her body moving. It made you happy, that music, made you excited. Made you want to drink and dance and live.

Whatever it was they drank, out of a bottle with a French label, it was not champagne, but it raised her spirits and for the first time in a long time she felt happy.

Mario introduced her to a guy called Jake who played piano in the club and a huge black woman called Ella Mae who sang the blues. She had all the pain in the world in her voice.

Minouche never did get any food that night. She was pleasantly relaxed, on the point of being drunk, when at last she returned to her room.

Mario said goodnight to her in the living-room. He seemed suddenly shy. It made her like him even more than she already did, if that were possible.

'I gotta get back. See ya in the morning.' And he left her there with Pierre.

Pierre looked at her when they were at last alone.

'You're drunk,' he said, smiling.

'I know,' she said, smiling back.

'He's got the hots for you.' Pierre looked at her, one eyebrow raised.

She nodded. 'I know.' Then, defiantly, 'And I like him.'

He did not let her see how that hurt. He was adept at concealing his feelings for her.

'Be careful of him.'

Again she nodded. 'I will.'

'He destroys,' Pierre said. 'Mario Palucci destroys.'

'Oh, Pierre, don't be silly. I believe you're jealous. He's OK.'

'Well, don't say I didn't warn you,' he said grumpily.

'I still love you, Pierre,' she said softly.

He knew what she meant. He knew she loved him as a brother. She really cared for him, but not in the way he wanted, not in the way he craved.

'I know,' he said, and kissed her cheek. 'Now get some sleep. Sleep off the booze. *Bonsoir, ma chérie.*'

'*Bonsoir*, Pierre,' she said and went to bed.

Chapter Nine

Gina and Lombardo sat at opposite ends of the table in the kitchen, staring wordlessly at each other.

'I'm glad Papa did not live to see this day,' she said.

'Your father would know what to do,' Lombardo said humbly, bowing his shoulders.

Gina shook her head. 'No, no, Lombardo. Do not blame yourself. We are getting along fine.'

She looked at Grandfather. The old man now sat near a window, rocking in his chair, constant tears drenching his face. He had refused to sit under the eucalyptus tree he had so loved and had been weeping silently since Giuseppe's death six months ago. They had got used to his tears.

Gina and Lombardo did their best. They still had a grove of olive trees and with that and the animals they had survived. But it was a sad comedown.

Giuseppe had been wrong about the community. Gina and Lombardo were not demoted to a back pew. The villagers had ushered them, that first Sunday after their father's funeral, into their usual places, high up in the little church.

Maria did not see. She did not go with them. She went nowhere these days.

Gina had grieved sorely that her favourite, Marcello, had followed his brother's example and left. They had not heard from him and had no idea where he could be. She wrote to Guido and Francesca in Rome.

> We don't know why he went. He simply left. We came
> down one morning and found a note saying, "I cannot
> stand it here any longer. Forgive me dearest Gina." He did
> not have to go and all I can say is that he seemed very
> preoccupied and quiet since Papa died. I think perhaps he
> realized that he was Papa's favourite and was lonely for
> him. He was always the gifted one. We miss him and with
> you all gone things are sadly lonely. Oh, how did we offend
> God to bring such disasters upon ourselves? Give our love
> to Paulo. We love you and wish you success.

They had married six months after Giuseppe's death and
Lombardo promptly moved into the farmhouse. Gina had
become very much like her mother. Marriage had filled
her out, given her dignity and authority, put a sparkle in
her eyes and a sway in her walk, a sort of swinging of the
hips that told everyone more than words could say that she
was enjoying her husband. It made Lombardo ache to
make love to her.

The absence of the Duke from the *palazzo* above helped
on the farm. Nothing was happening. Since the news of
the loss of their land everyone speculated about what
would happen to the carefully tended vineyards and
groves that would shrivel and die without constant water
and attention. Who would look after them? Would the
Duke employ labourers or casual help? Would he let them
go to rack and ruin? No one knew. All they knew was that
he had gone away and all around the land, staves had been
driven into the ground and an ugly barbed-wire fence had
been erected, disfiguring the earth. It marked the Duke's
property, defacing the landscape, making it look like a
battlefield.

Lombardo got Signore Gitano to check the authenticity
of the Duke's claim and that it was indeed valid.

'I said at the time, I told Giuseppe not to sign anything

188

without me examining it first. Ah, but it is a scandal! He would not listen. He would insist on trusting the Duke. He believed the *Signeur*, the *Padrone*, would behave properly. That he could behave so dishonourably, so deviously, is shocking. A man in his position!'

Everyone agreed the Duke was indeed a scoundrel. They were glad he had gone to Rome or Paris or London with his children, it kept him out of the way. They sniggered over their *grappa*, making lewd jokes about his fear that his children would fall in love with farmers and peasants.

'He will find them nice boring mates, no passion, no fire,' they agreed.

Everyone was worried about Maria.

'She is dying, Lombardo,' Gina said, looking at her husband across the table. 'What am I to do?' she frowned and leaned across, arms outstretched, palms turned upwards, asking his advice as she always did. His heart leapt within him at the joy she constantly gave him, at her deferment to him. She could so easily have assumed leadership; after all, the farm was her father's and now belonged to her and her family. But even when they were alone, and particularly in public, she turned to him as the final authority, the master, and never allowed anyone to forget or show him less respect than they would have shown Giuseppe.

'Should I let her go? Die? She wants to, I know. Or should I send her to the hospital in Palermo where they will try to keep her alive? What will I do?'

He reached out and laid his hands flat on hers. 'Let her go *mi amore*. Let her go.'

'But I don't want to,' she said fiercely, her eyes filling with tears. 'I love her so. I cannot bear to lose her.'

'You have to let her go,' he repeated firmly, confident that she would take his advice.

He glanced over at Grandfather, surprised that the old

189

man's damp face was turned towards them. He usually seemed oblivious of the activity and conversations in the kitchen but now he was watching them intently.

'Let her go,' he said, looking at Lombardo and nodding. 'Let her go to Giuseppe.'

'Listen, Gina,' Lombardo said, 'what do you think life is like for her, eh? Without the husband she loved? He was the light of her life. Now the light has gone out. She lies there in bed, day after day, staring at the wall, bereft of the man she adored, a picture of the horror of the last time she saw him etched on her brain.'

'I would have liked to go to Simona,' the old man said, staring out of the window at the shifting shadows the leaves made as the breeze stirred them. 'It's not that I haven't been happy – I've been incomplete, that's it. And I've been waiting. All these years, waiting to join her. I sat out there under the eucalyptus tree and watched your lives pass me by like a spectator.' He looked at Lombardo. 'Simona was my wife,' he said. Lombardo knew that but he let the old man finish. 'She died when Giuseppe was born. I miss her each day of my life.' His chin sank on his chest and he lapsed into silence.

'If I died,' Lombardo said, then seeing her face hurried on, 'oh, I know you'd miss me . . . Hush, listen! You could make a new life for yourself. You're young enough. But your mother? She lived with Giuseppe for twenty-five years. She loved him. He died in such a terrible way. She wants only one thing – to join him.' He paused and bent his head, uncertain whether to go on, then raised it and closed his hands over hers, holding them tightly in his huge fist.

'Listen, Gina, the other morning when you were feeding the chickens I found her on the stairs.'

Gina looked surprised. 'Out of bed?' she asked. Lombardo nodded. 'What was she doing?'

'She was looking for the gun,' he replied. Gina jumped, her eyes opening wide, but Lombardo held her hands

190

tightly and continued. I said to her, "What do you want Maria?" She said, "Giuseppe's gun, Lombardo. For God's sake, give me his gun." "What do you want with it?" I asked. I knew, but I asked anyway. "I want to join him." And she sat down on the stairs in her nightgown as if her legs wouldn't hold her up any more. "I know what I want is terrible, Lombardo," she whispered. "Gina will think I betrayed her. Serena and Cecilia will break their hearts. And you know, Lombardo, that is not important to me any more. My heart is so cold. What is important is that I join him. He will be so lonely." And still I did not quite understand.'

Gina watched him wide-eyed. 'I don't understand either.'

She could hear the song of the birds outside. The sun slanted in through the open door in a golden haze. In the valley the workers called to each other, their laughter echoing, and out at the back a cock crowed. All the everyday sounds and sights. The old man seemed to have fallen asleep in his chair by the window, his chin on his chest, his eyes closed, his cheeks wet. Gina listened to her husband intently.

'Your mother is afraid that if she dies naturally she will go to Heaven,' he explained. 'She looked at me with an expression of pain and horror in her eyes that frightened me. "Don't you understand, Lombardo?" she said. "Giuseppe committed suicide. He has gone to Hell. I do not want to go to Heaven if Giuseppe is in Hell. Don't you see?" I said, "You cannot be sure." She shook her head, "No, no. Fra Bartholomeo says you cannot go to Heaven if you die in mortal sin, and he says that if you commit suicide you are in the worst kind of sin for you have taken away God's most precious gift – life. The Church says so too. No Lombardo, my husband is in Hell and I must go to him. And if I do the same thing, commit the same sin, then I'll be with him wherever he is. Don't you see?" She

191

clutched my arm but she was very calm, very determined. "You must understand. I have to be with him. I am part of him. He is part of me. We were joined together forever. I have to share the afterlife with him, care for him there. The Church says he is in Hell so I want to go there too." '

Lombardo looked down at their locked hands. 'As you know Gina,' he said, 'I don't believe that. A good man like Giuseppe, who led a blameless life, no, I don't believe he has gone to Hell. But Maria does. "How do you know you will find him in Hell?" I asked her, "Don't be stupid," she says angrily to me, "If he is there I'll find him." '

Lombardo shrugged his wide shoulders and shook his head. 'It's no use arguing with her. She has this fixed idea, Gina, and nothing will shift it. So you must let her do what she wishes. It's the only way she'll find peace.'

'Mario has a lot to answer for,' Gina said bitterly. 'He must be made to suffer. He must die.'

When she spoke like that he did not recognize her. This was not the soft pretty woman whose eyes darkened in passionate love each night and who smiled at him all day. This was an angry woman who controlled a virulent hatred that required vengeance.

'Don't, *mi amore*, don't!' he cried, distressed. 'I cannot bear it when you speak like that.'

'It is vendetta, *caro*.' There were two bright spots of colour on her cheeks and she banged the table with her fist as she spoke. 'Vendetta. You are not of our blood. You don't understand. Guido and Francesca have taken on the responsibility. It will be done. As for Mama, I do not know. How do you expect me to do this unnatural thing? Allow my own mother to commit suicide because she wants to join my father in Hell? Ah, God, Lombardo, how can I agree to a thing like that?'

They left it like that. Later Cecilia brought Filipo Canona to the house. She was holding his hand and had a blush in her cheeks.

Gina served up the food and Filipo and Lombardo ate heartily. Lombardo poured the wine and they talked and drank, laughing a little. Serena was quiet as usual, a shadow, pale and withdrawn. Gina watched her go up the stairs when supper was finished. She is going to Mama, she thought, and sighed. Serena was always to be found beside Maria.

'Filipo wants to talk to Lombardo,' Cecilia said, lowering her head and rolling her eyes. Things had changed since Francesca had left the village. All her sister's suitors were now Cecilia's.

'Aha!' Gina nodded her head. 'I'm glad, Cecilia. Tell him to talk to Lombardo as soon as he wishes.'

She grinned at her sister then pinched her cheek. 'I'm glad for you,' she repeated, and Cecilia laughed. It would be a good match, joining the two families, and the Canonas were rich.

A scream tore the air and the warm chatter ceased suddenly in the drowsy kitchen.

Lombardo leapt to his feet. 'It's Maria,' he cried with certainty. 'Gina, stay there.'

Serena stood at the top of the stairs, her face wild, her hands brushing frantically at the bloodstains on her skirt. Gina ran after Lombardo who took the stairs two at at time. He tried to stop her entering the room her mother had shared with Giuseppe for twenty-five years, the room where she and her brothers and sisters had been born, but Gina had followed too closely and was already there.

Maria was dead. Her face looked young, like a girl's, and her eyes were open. Lombardo gently closed them. Black hair lay over the white sheet and her mouth was fixed in a smile. What had she been thinking when she died? Gina wondered.

She had cut her wrists. There was blood everywhere on the lower half of the bed.

At first Serena had thought Maria lay there, quietly

thinking or sleeping. She had not noticed the blood. She had knelt at the bedside and put her hand on to her mother's body and felt the sticky mess. Giuseppe's razor lay on the floor beside the bed. Lombardo turned Gina's face away from the sight but she removed his hand.

'So, she got what she wished,' she murmured, and he nodded.

'You better see to Serena,' he said. 'She'll take this hard.'

'Another score to settle,' Gina murmured, and went out onto the landing and took the weeping girl in her arms.

~~~~~~

'If you play your cards right, you could catch the eye of the Conte de Ville. They say he is rich as Croesus.' Eleanor laughed, waving her hand towards the box across the theatre.

The Rome Opera House was crowded. Bejewelled women smiled and flirted with men in evening dress. Gigli and Melba were singing *La Traviata*. Truly a night to remember, glamorous and heavenly. Eleanor had a box, her father's box, and had invited Guido and his sister. It was the interval. People were promenading in the hope that the great tenor would put in an appearance. Sometimes he did that, came out to the foyer of the Dress Circle and held court for a quarter of an hour. People gazed at him, touched his costume reverently, spoke a few words of admiration and congratulation, and the great tenor accepted the tributes then returned backstage to husband his energies for the next act.

Guido had gone for ice cream. Francesca looked at her new friend.

'I don't want to catch anyone's eye,' she said tartly, 'all I want is to hear the music. It brings back such happy memories. I told you, Eleanor, about Papa each Sunday, sitting under the shade of the eucalyptus tree, looking out over the valley.'

194

Eleanor sighed enviously. 'Oh, it sounds so happy. Tranquil. Father says he loves Opera, he has this box, but he never comes. I would love him to come with me but he never has time. He's always too busy.'

Guido returned with the ices.

'Oh, how wonderful!' Francesca cried, clapping her hands. 'Strawberry ices!'

'Have you seen Father recently?' Eleanor asked as lightly as she could.

Guido shook his head. 'No, not for weeks. He'd said he'd let me know but I think I will call on him tomorrow. I've asked him and asked him but the answer is always the same.'

He was becoming impatient. Waiting did not suit him. It relaxed his energies, took his anger off the boil. The life they were leading was pleasurable but idle and purposeless. Day drifted into day and nothing was accomplished. Guido wanted to get the matter of Mario cleared up. Finished and over. But Enrico Domini would not see him. The phone calls once a week always conveyed the same message: no news yet, be patient. Eleanor was beguiling his time away and he felt sunk in inertia.

'He must see me soon,' he said. 'Family matters are of the first importance. I must deal with it, settle it, get it out of the way.'

What would Eleanor think of him if he found out that the matter he talked of, the family situation he had to clear up, was murder? he wondered. Would she turn away from him in horror? He dared not ask himself the question.

Francesca took her brother's hand in hers, and Eleanor hoped her father would forget all about this "family matter" that would send the brother and sister away.

She had fallen in love not only with Guido but with his sister as well. She was madly, romantically, in love with the tall, handsome Sicilian. She ached to touch him and only managed to keep her hands off him with the greatest

195

difficulty. Her heart beat twice as fast as normal when he looked at her. She was off her food, sang all day, had alternate fits of violent weeping and sublime euphoria, was emotional and only came fully alive in the presence of the man she loved.

She also adored Francesca. She was the friend Eleanor had never had. From the first moment, when Guido's beautiful sister cried, 'Oh, you are lovely! Guido did not exaggerate,' to this evening at the Opera, Francesca had endeared herself to the lonely half-English, half-Italian girl.

They had gone shopping together. 'You cannot be seen in those clothes,' Eleanor had told them firmly. 'Neither of you. They are fine for the country but here in the city they just won't do.'

Guido sulked for half a day, his male pride badly bruised. Francesca felt humiliated but realized their reactions were stupid and that they had better listen to the expert, for Eleanor was certainly dressed in the height of fashion. Guido and Francesca had to admit to themselves, albeit reluctantly, that they looked like a pair of rustics, country bumpkins in the stylish metropolis. Their honesty got the better of them and they admitted to Eleanor that their clothes were sadly provincial.

So they went shopping. The clothes were very expensive but they had received a large float from Enrico Domini and still had a considerable sum left from what Tomaso Canona had lent them. Francesca needed no prompting to shorten her dresses, and with Eleanor's help she bought a lovely new outfit and some silk stockings. Francesca felt free as air in her new clothes.

Eleanor bought them some accessories. She insisted on giving presents.

'The clothes are so light,' Francesca said, 'I feel I could fly. No petticoats. What bliss!'

The Roman girl smiled, beguiled by Francesca's

lightheartedness. She trusted these people as she had never been able to trust anyone in the Italian capital. In England with her aunt it was different.

'I am not interested in men like the Conte de Ville,' Francesca was saying again. 'You know that, Eleanor.'

She nodded. 'Because of Luciano d'Abrizzio? Oh, Francesca, do you still think of him?'

'How can you ask that?' Francesca looked at her friend with reproachful eyes. 'I will never forget him. Never!' she said vehemently.

She broke off, took Eleanor's hand in hers and pressed it. 'It was so painful. So painful. But it was the most wonderful thing.'

Eleanor glanced at Guido. His face, full of concern, was turned towards his sister.

'Are you still intent on finding him?' Eleanor asked. They had searched Rome with Eleanor's help but there was no sign of the d'Abrizzios. Eleanor knew the society in which they would move and felt anxious for her friend, for if the aristocrats did not accept her after all these years, how would they treat a newcomer so obviously working class, no matter how sweet she was? How would the young man react if they succeeded in catching up with him? Would he be as glad to see Francesca as the Palucci girl seemed sure he would? Eleanor was filled with foreboding when she asked herself these questions.

Francesca's eyes were full of tears.

'Yes,' she said nodding, 'I am. I love him more than my life. It keeps me going. So you see, I am not interested in anyone else.'

'I think you are crazy! I think you will find him and say, "Oh, my God, what did I ever see in him?" I think you will find him married to another. I think he will do as his father asks. I think you are wasting valuable time and energy and emotion on someone who does not deserve you. It is he who should be looking for you, not the other way around.'

197

'How do we know he can?' Francesca shook her head. Her eyes were full of pain. 'Do not hurt me, *cara*. I do not like to think about it. I hope you are wrong,' she said simply and a tear splashed on to her cheek. Eleanor pulled out her handkerchief and dabbed it away. She hated to see her friend distressed.

'Forgive me,' she said, and put her arm around Francesca, 'I don't mean to be hurtful. It's just that I hate to see you suffer. If he was the kind of man that you deserve then he would have crossed oceans, slain dragons, defied his father to get you. Nothing could have stopped him.'

'That happens in fairy tales, Eleanor. Not real life,' Francesca said.

'Exactly!' Eleanor retorted, and feeling her point was made she turned to Guido.

'Why not let bygones be bygones and simply enjoy life a day at a time?'

Francesca and Guido exchanged glances. If only she knew, Guido thought.

'Our family feels things very deeply. We harbour things. They do not go away . . . pouf . . . like that.' Francesca took Eleanor's lighter and snapped it alive, then blew out the flame. 'Though we appear to recover and lead normal happy lives, the pain remains deep inside. It smoulders and at night it glows in the dark. Like this!' She snapped the lighter again and the flame sprang up, vital, burning. Francesca looked quizzically at her friend and Eleanor shook her head.

'I think that's sad. It eats you then. Consumes.'

'No one can know how terrible my pain was, how deeply I suffered. Still do. The night is long and filled with memories. But I plan, I plan. In the meantime the day is for pleasure, I agree. I will not allow this thing to ruin my life. I will not allow this pain to destroy me, no matter what happens. Do you understand?'

Eleanor shrugged.

198

The orchestra was tuning up. People were returning to their seats. Guido held one of Francesca's hands, Eleanor the other.

She held the two hands in hers and pressed them.

'You are both close to my heart.' She released the hands and laughed. 'Now let us listen to the music.'

~~~~~~

The next day Guido went to see Enrico Domini. He had phoned him regularly but a servant or a secretary always answered and said, 'Signore Domini says to tell you there have been no developments and he asks you to be patient.'

Now Guido determined to beard the lion in his den. He wondered if Enrico Domini knew of his daughter's close friendship with Francesca and himself. On consideration he decided that Signore Domini probably did. A man like that, powerful, knowing what was happening in places like America and France – Eleanor had told them he even had contacts in the South Sea Islands and Malaysia – it seemed inconceivable that such a man should not know what went on in his own backyard. Obviously then, he did not disapprove. Or perhaps he had some other reason not to put a stop to his daughter's friendship with them? Perhaps he simply did not care.

Guido had not been to the house since that first day. It seemed such a long time ago now. Eleanor had made the time vanish. They had drifted through such pleasant days and evenings. Picnics in the Borghese Gardens, exploring the Roman ruins, gaping at the Pantheon, the Collosseum, the Caracalla Baths, and all the other amazing sights Rome had to offer visitors. They drove up into the hills, stopping at little trattorias on the way, eating salami and pasta and drinking the wine of the area. They visited the Opera or dined out under the stars in the Piazza Navona, exchanging ideas, talking about life. Most of all, for Guido, there was the joy of looking at Eleanor, appreciating her

199

beauty, her many-faceted loveliness.

To touch her scorched him. He did not dare to get close to her more than once or twice a day or his heart might stop or burst out of his breast. But he could look. All day. All evening. Study the fine blonde down on her cheeks and just above her top lip. The curve of her eyebrow, its golden hairs smooth as a bird's wing. The tip of her nose where there was a minuscule dent. The mole on her neck, just under her ear. It was unbearably sweet to watch her. Sometimes she bit into an apple then gave it to him to take a bite and he could taste her on it. Sometimes she leant forward and he felt the silk of her hair against his cheek. Sometimes her leg touched his and his knees went weak.

And always there were the messages from her eyes; that she found his presence as exciting as he did hers. Her blue eyes sometimes widened and those green flecks in their depths expanded and became pools of desire.

He shivered now as he remembered her eyes last night at the Opera, and wondered how much longer he could hold out without making a move. He had not, simply because he had wanted to get the whole business of Mario out of the way before he did or said anything. In any event it had been easy. Francesca was always with them. She would have left them alone together if either of them had even hinted that they wished it. Up to now they had not, Guido because he was committed to the vendetta. And Eleanor? He did not have any idea why she chose to avoid being alone with him. Perhaps, he told himself, she did not want to rush things. Perhaps she wanted him to be the one to make all the moves. Whatever the reason, their feelings for each other were implicit in their every look.

So Guido decided he had to see Enrico Domini, try to get his task moving, because he did not think he could hold this tide of passion he felt for Eleanor at bay much longer. Once unleashed he was afraid that he might drown in it. He could so easily forget his duty to his family, could put aside the dishonour they had suffered.

Enrico received him in the same room. He was sitting exactly as Guido had left him that first time, nearly a year ago.

'Come in, my boy. Come in. This is an unexpected pleasure,' he cried, holding out his hand which Guido shook.

'Sit down. Sit down.' Guido obeyed. 'What can I do for you?'

Guido cleared his throat. He knew that Signore Domini had, while greeting him, noted the improvement in his dress and his expression was approving. But he said nothing, waiting, eyes narrowed.

'I wanted to know, Signore, if there has been any news of my brother Mario?'

The dark eyes were suddenly slits. 'No. I said to wait.'

'If you'll forgive me, Signore, I have waited a long time.'

'These things take a long time.' The voice was cold. 'I sent you clear messages. Easy to understand.'

Undaunted, Guido insisted, 'With the greatest respect, Signore, the time is passing.' Sweet, sweet time, happily spent. Why was he bothering this man, hurrying him, when to leave Rome was the last thing he really wanted? Why did he find it so difficult to admit? But no, Mario always came between him and his plans for the future. Nothing could be decided until the matter was dealt with. Until it was Guido was not a free agent. Until it was he could not devote himself to his own happiness. He thought of Giuseppe and bit his lip.

'With the greatest respect, Signore, the time is passing,' he repeated firmly. 'And I have to, er, settle with my brother as soon as possible. It is difficult for me to believe you cannot find his whereabouts more quickly, you so powerful, with so many contacts.'

Enrico's eyes had all but disappeared. 'Is it now?' he said. It was not a question. His voice was harsh. 'And why do you

201

think I would not tell you if I knew?'

A thrill of fear coursed through Guido. He remembered Eleanor's words 'My father is dangerous' and believed them now.

'I don't know,' he said truthfully.

'Well, son, don't speculate. Don't even try.'

Guido was suddenly absolutely certain that Enrico Domini knew where Mario was, but that for some reason he did not want to tell him just yet. He would inform Guido when he was ready and not before. Certainly not now.

Guido smiled at the man behind his desk, his sudden disarming smile. The hell with it! He did not mind waiting. It meant time with Eleanor. He would not have to leave her just yet.

As if he felt Guido's acquiescence, Enrico relaxed and smiled too.

'You and your sister have become friends with my daughter,' he said. Again it was a statement. Guido nodded.

'Yes, Signore,' he said. 'She has been very kind. She has shown us this beautiful city.'

Enrico Domini nodded. 'Yes, I know.' He looked intently at Guido. 'I guard my daughter well. She does not know it, of course, and you will not tell her, but she is on a long lead. The lead is made of steel.'

His eyes were glittering in his handsome face. Again Guido felt fear.

'Be proper with her, eh? I expect your behaviour to be impeccable. You must never overstep the barrier between peasant and lady.'

He nodded in dismissal and Guido got up. Now he knew he did not like Enrico Domini.

'Wait until I get in touch with you,' Domini said. 'Patience, son, patience.'

Guido took the proffered hand, shook it and left the room, this time without looking back.

~~~~~~

The following week Francesca fell ill with a slight fever and an upset stomach. Guido, alarmed, telephoned Eleanor who sent along a doctor. He diagnosed a touch of influenza and recommended milk and dry biscuits, egg-nog with nutmeg, and rest. These minor illnesses could become serious if neglected.

Through her window Francesca could see the flower-decked Spanish Steps and her room was full of scent and colour, for Eleanor had filled it with blossoms. Eleanor and Guido sat with her, steadfast in their determination not to neglect her and filled with a kind of excited terror at what would happen if they were left alone together. They clung to the sick girl for protection from themselves.

All Francesca wanted was that they should leave her alone. They made her self-conscious and restless and she urged them to go out without her and leave her in peace. She said she could not sleep with them there and would be cooler and calmer if they left her by herself. She felt sleepy and it was their misguided kindness that kept her awake. They gave in, kissed her, and left the house.

So they were alone together for the first time. They walked out into the sunshine, following the Via di Trinita di Moniti to the Villa Medici and into the Borghese Gardens, not touching, not even looking at each other. There was a smell of fresh-cut grass and an old woman was feeding the birds, cooing as she scattered crumbs.

Guido took Eleanor's hand. It shocked him that his skin against hers could be such an extraordinary sensation. She moved her thumb against the pulse in his wrist and felt it leap.

They had not spoken. There was an atmosphere between them that made speech impossible. She turned to him and looked at him. With a little moan he pulled her to him, his lips clumsily searching for hers. When they found what they sought they clung to each other, mouth to mouth, drinking each other in. People passed them by, unnoticed. They were oblivious of the outside world.

They parted, breathlessly, greedy for more, yet anxious for a moment to recall themselves to reality. Then she said, looking at him, panting a little, her eyes dark with desire. 'Let's go back to your room now, Guido. Now.'

'Are you sure?' He did not want her to be hasty, to rush into something she was not ready for. At the same time he desired her so much he could not think rationally. Now, his body urged, now. And that was what she had said. Now.

They walked back blindly. They saw nothing. The sun dazzled their eyes and they looked into its glory unblinking. They reached the lodging-house. His room was at the back. It was not as nice as Francesca's, darker, less airy. But they did not care.

They undressed each other slowly. They kissed soft naked flesh, they massaged and touched each other breathlessly, each astonished at the beauty of the other, amazed at the tingling excitement of each new encounter of hands and mouths. When he entered her he was surprised to find her still a virgin. But he could not stop now, to ask, to reaffirm her acquiescence. Besides, though she cried out, her pain turned in seconds to passionate response and she pushed his legs further apart with hers and raised herself to him in abandon. He held on for her a moment, and then they reached their climax together, clinging close, shuddering in spasms of ecstacy.

For a long time they did not stir.

'I could not imagine anything so beautiful,' she said at last, and there were tears on her cheeks.

'You were a virgin,' he said.

'Of course. What did you think?'

He said nothing, realizing how it would sound if he told her the truth. He lifted himself on his elbow to look at her. He drew his finger over the wing of one eybrow.

'You are so beautiful,' he said. 'You are a miracle, Eleanor.'

She laughed warmly, basking in his love, her body content. 'I know.' She smiled. 'But so are you.'

He sat up suddenly. 'Your father! He'll kill me if he ever finds out.'

'I'll deal with Father. Don't worry about him. He could never refuse me anything.'

Guido shook his head and looked at her with serious eyes. 'No,' he said, 'I don't think he wants me for you. He made it plain. "There is a dividing line between peasants and ladies" – something like that. "Don't cross it," that's what he told me.'

'Did he?' She sounded very surprised, then threw back her head and laughed. 'He can talk!' she said. Then added, 'It doesn't sound like him.'

'Well, it's what he said to me. He warned me, "Hands off".' Guido frowned. 'You once told me your father was dangerous. What did you mean?'

'Why do you ask?'

She sat with the sheet over her legs, her small breasts and creamy torso dappled in sunlight from the window.

'Because I get the feeling that he is playing with me.' He shrugged. 'I don't know.'

'No, what I meant was . . .' she hesitated. 'Men do . . . errands for my father. I think they are dangerous. I wanted to make sure you were not one of those men.'

He thought of the bank account. He shook his head.

'No. He's finding out something for me. That's all.'

'Those men carry guns, Guido. I can see the bulge under their jackets.'

'But why? What would they be doing to carry guns?'

'I don't know. Something for Father.' Then she pulled him to her. 'Look, Guido, let's not talk about it now. Let's just be together. I don't know what goes on in my father's life and I don't want to know. I only know that it killed my mother.'

205

She looked suddenly very sad and pulled the sheet up to cover her breasts.

Guido said, 'All right, my darling, let's not think about him now. Let's just concentrate on ourselves.'

He pulled the sheet down again and folded her in his arms. She gave a little sigh of contentment.

'I love you, Guido. So much.'

'I love you too, Eleanor,' he replied and began to kiss her.

~~~~~~

They went to his room each day after that. Eleanor came to see Francesca, her arms full of flowers, fruit and English books, for she was teaching them to become more fluent in the language they had learned from the nuns and the Jesuits in Palermo. Eleanor would laugh and kiss the invalid, chat with her until Francesca told them to leave her, that she felt weak and unsociable and that they were too full of vitality to suit her indisposition. Then Eleanor and Guido would go out, walk around the Piazza di Spagna or stroll through the Borghese Gardens, then creep back up Signora Merciano's stairs, furtive as criminals, giggling to each other, fingers on lips. Guido did not forget the Signora's stricture that she would not tolerate any hanky-panky in her house. He did not wish to upset her or the good brothers who had recommended them.

By now she trusted them. Her beady eye was fixed instead on the couple to whom she had rented the large apartment on the ground floor. They also said they were brother and sister but she had her doubts and had lost interest in the Paluccis while consumed with curiosity about the newcomers. In any event she hardly ever saw the Paluccis, which was just as well for she would surely have sensed something if she had been on the alert.

Eleanor and Guido made love all afternoon in the

206

shadowed room. Besotted with each other, they submerged themselves mentally and physically and thought no one noticed, while even the flower-seller on the Via Condotti where Eleanor and Guido bought sweet-peas and violets was aware of their liaison. Their bodies gave off the heat of passion, requited, satisfied, and their eyes heralded exactly how they felt.

'Be careful, Guido.'

He had come to kiss his sister goodnight. He left the door of her room open when he was there so that anyone passing could see in. Signora Merciano walked past on her way to the upper floor.

'*Buona sera, Signora,*' they called out together, and she replied in kind.

Guido turned to his sister. Her face was no longer flushed but pale, her eyes larger than normal and circled by dark shadows.

'What do you mean, be careful?'

'With Eleanor,' she whispered. She did not want to upset him but he said angrily, 'What do you mean, be careful with Eleanor?'

He was embarrassed, awkward that she seemed to know something, seemed to be aware of what he had been sure was concealed.

'Please, Guido, don't be angry. You know how I love you both. It's just that . . .'

'What is all this about? Are you jealous I go out with Eleanor, is that it?'

'That is not worthy of you, Guido.'

He saw he had upset her, that there were tears in her eyes. He knew she was right. What he had implied was despicable, an insult to her generous nature. He immediately felt ashamed and fell on his knees beside the bed.

'Francesca *mia*, beloved sister, forgive me. I had no right to speak to you like that. It's just that I thought . . .'

'I know.' She touched his hair. 'You thought no one knew. But, Guido, you cannot hide such things. All you have to do is catch two people in love exchanging glances and everything they try to hide is obvious to all. I know about these things. Mario saw me and Luciano and he knew, that was how. You cannot hide that kind of love.'

He bowed his head. Her hand played with his hair, combing it with restless fingers.

'Listen, Guido, all I'm saying is, be careful. There's something . . .' she wrinkled her brow, thinking, searching for the right words. 'Something not right there.'

'What do you mean?' he was puzzled.

'Have you noticed that Eleanor has no friends?'

Guido felt his anger rise again and Francesca, sensing it, quickly reassured him. 'This is not because of herself, I think, but because of who she is. She is a beautiful person, inside and out. There is not an unkind or nasty bone in her body. No, Eleanor is lovely. So why has she no friends at all?'

She was looking at him intently. 'Until we came along, there seems to have been no one. She has never taken time off from seeing us to have a chat with girlfriends, which would be normal. Neither are there parties she has to go to or meetings with childhood friends or friends of her parents. Two strangers arrive out of the blue and she can spend all her time with us. It's very odd, you must agree.'

He knew she was right. It was odd. Eleanor lived all her life in Rome except for the summer holidays in England. Yet she had never mentioned another person she was fond of there or visited. She had no girlfriends, no ex-boyfriends, never mentioned family friends.

'I think it has something to do with her father, Guido,' Francesca said.

He nodded. 'Yes. She says he is dangerous. But she doesn't say why.'

Francesca leaned forward. 'Then you must be very

careful. It takes a very grave danger to isolate them so. Have you noticed how people look at her, Guido? At the Opera? In restaurants? Places where the affluent Romans meet? I thought it was admiration at first. People looking at her, women particularly, from jealousy maybe. She is very beautiful. But it is not that. It's something much harder to define. Fear? As if she were contagious?'

'You exaggerate, Francesca!' he exploded. 'Ah, come now, it's not like that.'

But he knew she was right. Knew without a doubt that with her usual sensitivity she had put her finger on it, identified something that he had been subconsciously aware of all along but had not wanted to acknowledge.

They heard Signora Merciano returning down the stairs so he kissed his sister's forehead.

'You're very precious to me,' he said. 'Get better soon.'

She nodded. 'I miss Luciano,' she said with a little sigh. 'I try not to be self-pitying, but I miss him. I don't think anyone realizes how much.'

He gave her a quick hug. 'I know you do, sweet sister. I'm not as crass as I seem sometimes.' He went to the door just as Signora Merciano reached the landing outside.

'You still here?' she asked suspiciously.

'Just going now,' he replied, winking at Francesca.

'Be careful though,' she called after him as he left.

'I will,' he said. 'Don't worry, I will.'

~~~~~~

Eleanor ran her hand over Guido's chest, then bent and kissed him. They had made love slowly, taking their time, their mutual climax prolonged and prolonged until they thought they would die. They had slept, their bodies tangled, and now, wakening in the shaded room, Eleanor had propped herself on her elbow to gaze at Guido and marvel at her lover.

'I love you so,' she said. He thought of what Francesca

and he had talked about a few days before. It seemed disloyal to think of it at a time like this, and in any event what could he say? He could hardly ask Eleanor why she had no friends. So he said nothing.

But later, when they had dressed and he had led her out into a twilight full of stars, tiptoeing out of the house, careful not to make a noise but laughing silently all the while, over dinner he asked her.

'What does your father do exactly, Eleanor?'

She looked at him, surprised. 'Business,' she said, shrugging.

They ate in the Piazza Navona. Opposite them the great Bernini fountain splashed and the air was fresh and cool. Eleanor laughed at a group of barefooted children who were playing at the fountain's edge, shouting to each other in high voices.

Guido poured some wine. 'What kind of business?' he persisted.

A closed look shuttered her face. 'I don't know,' she said, and looked to where a beggar-woman was holding out a dirty hand, trying to reach the diners over the railing that cordoned off the restaurant.

Guido grabbed Eleanor's wrist. 'You must,' he said, surprised at his own vehemence. 'Come on, don't act the innocent with me. You must know something.'

She looked at him with startled, hurt eyes.

'Guido,' she pleaded and he let her go.

She rubbed her wrist. The beggar-woman put her hand under his face and he snarled at her. 'Go away, will you?'

The beggar-woman smiled, showing one large yellow tooth.

'You are angry,' she said to him, 'anger is all around you. There is hatred in your heart. It fights love. It will kill if you don't take care.'

He found he was shaking. Eleanor was staring with fascinated horror at the beggar-woman. He reached into his pocket and took out a handful of coins, scattering them over the cobblestones at the other side of the rail.

'*Grazie, Signore! Grazie, grazie,*' the beggar-woman chanted, gathering them up in greedy haste as the group of barefooted children ran over from the fountain to join her in grovelling for the coins.

'What is the matter, Guido?' Eleanor asked him gently. 'I've never seen you like this before.'

He shook his head. 'I'm sorry. So sorry. You know I would not hurt you for the world.'

She sighed. 'Often we do what we don't want to do,' she said. 'My father is in everything illegal.'

'Like what?'

'For God's sake, Guido, do I have to spell it out? What do you want, absolution?' She turned away from him, lighting a cigarette with trembling fingers. 'I truly don't know exactly,' she said, looking sadly now to where two of the boys were punching and kicking each other for possession of a coin.

'But you must have some idea,' he persisted. He did not know why he was doing this. Like pressing on a wound, he knew it would hurt but he had to go on.

'Yes,' she said wearily. 'He is part of the Organization.' She shrugged.

'I know that,' he said. 'That was why Tomaso Canona sent me to him. But that was good. We help each other in the Organization. It's OK. We hurt only those who deserve it. Vendetta.'

She looked at him, amazed. 'Is that what they told you in Sicily?' she asked. He nodded.

'They said nothing of gambling? Prostitution? Smuggling? Gang wars? Drugs?'

He shook his head. 'No,' he said. His throat was dry. 'No. The Organization may be involved in America like that, but not here. And in America only because it is necessary. For protection.'

211

She snorted. 'You are naive,' she said.

'Why?'

'I don't know about America,' she said, 'only what I hear of Italy. You are not only naive, you are blind or foolish.'

He felt the blood rise to his face. The rage the beggar-woman had spoken of rose in an overwhelming tide within him. Shaken to the core by an anger he could not control, humiliated and embarrassed, he stood up, threw some *lire* on the table, stumbled over the leg of his chair and stalked out into the square, leaving her alone.

She called to him, a desolate cry, 'Guido!' But he did not look back. She stared after him until he vanished into the Corso Rinascimento. Then, feeling lonelier than she had ever felt before, she ordered a coffee and drank it in the waning light.

~~~~~~

When Eleanor arrived home she was surprised to find her father in the hall. He was a small man reaching only as high as her shoulder. He did not like to stand. He preferred to be found seated, or to leave before others rose to their feet. He had become adept over the years in stage-managing his life so that he need not be dwarfed by other taller men or his daughter. She could not remember a time when they had stood thus, face to face in the hall.

'Eleanor,' he said, 'just in time. You are on the midnight train. Luigi and Bernadetto are waiting in the car outside.'

She had not seen them. She had noticed little on the journey home. Eyes blinded by tears, hurt, her heart desolate, feelings of despair and emptiness within her, she had been preoccupied, wondering how it had happened, how such communion of mind and body could turn so suddenly and conclusively into coldness and anger. Bewildered by the turn of events, she said to Enrico, 'Please, Father, I'm not in the mood for joking.'

Even as she spoke she knew it was no joke. Her father

212

never joked. She suddenly became aware of the activity in the hall. Stefano was carrying her bags down the stairs and Lucetta her maid stood with hat and coat on, gloved fingers laced together, supervising.

'Father, what is this?' she asked, panic rising.

'Why, my dear, you are going to England. Now. Tonight. I had a letter from Helen. She is so sad that you have not been at all this year.' He smiled at her and she could see a trace of malice in his expression. 'I said there was nothing to keep you here at the moment. They are expecting you at Elm Court. It is all arranged. Lucetta will stay with you as usual. She has done all your packing. Luigi and Bernadetto will accompany you.'

'But why, Father? What have I done?'

She knew he was punishing her. His tone indicated disapproval, but she was surprised at his coldness. He had little time for her, it was true, but in general he had been a kindly and indulgent father.

'Why, Father? What have I done?' she repeated.

'I'll tell you what you have done, slut!' He spat the word at her and she realized that he was truly angry. He was trembling like a leaf. She remembered fleetingly that Guido had been shaking too when he had stubbed his cigarette out at the table in the Piazza Navona. She had never seen either of them in such a state before.

She was tired and worn out by the emotional turmoil that had held her in its grip all the way home. She was too confused at first to understand the harshness of her father's tone.

'Slut, you have been fucking that Sicilian peasant.'

She gasped, drawing in her breath as if he had hit her. She had not thought how her affair with Guido would look to others. She could only see the beauty in their relationship. What her father's reaction would be if he found out had not crossed her mind. That he could speak to her as he just had, shocked and humiliated her.

White-faced, she stared at him as if she had never seen him before.

'I will go nowhere, Father. I am eighteen years of age. I love Guido and he loves me.'

Enrico Domini looked at her as if she had lost her reason. It was the look you give a mad person babbling insanities at you in a language you do not understand.

'Love? What do you know of love? Love with that . . . but no. I will not speak about him or I would have him killed for daring . . .'

'Father, I love him, I told you.' She was weeping now. 'Pity me, Father. I love him so. You must have loved my mother once. Don't you remember what it was like? How it felt?' She was wringing her hands, tears spilling down her face on to her silk blouse, sobs tearing her chest.

Enrico Domini guffawed in a furious angry laugh.

'Your mother! Ice-cold English bitch. I hated her, do you hear me? I hated her!'

'Oh, Papa, please,' she sobbed. 'Ah, God, don't! Don't speak like that. I do not know you.'

'You will do as I say.' He spoke quietly and the soft tone of his voice frightened her now in earnest. The light in his eyes was fanatical. With a great effort he collected himself and continued, 'You are going to England. That should please you. You love Elm Court so. Christopher will be there. You like him, I know. I see no reason why you should not marry him. That is the plan. That has always been the plan.'

She drew in a sharp breath, looking at him now as if he were a lunatic.

'It is all arranged,' he reiterated. 'Even before I found out what you were doing, like a bitch on heat with that peasant, it was arranged.'

'How did you find out, Father?' she asked quietly, trying to gain control of herself, think what she was going to do.

'I had you followed,' he said, almost absentmindedly.

214

'You have always been followed. I know the date and time you first let that bastard screw you.'

She suddenly became very angry. Her tears stopped and she drew herself up and looked down at him.

'How dare you?' she cried, and he laughed up into her face. 'I will not go, Father. You cannot force me, do you hear? This is the most ridiculous thing I have ever heard of. We are not living in the time of the Medicis. Even the great Lorenzo would not force his daughter to marry against her will.'

He looked up at her. His eyes scared her. They stared at her with insane scorn.

'I am not Lorenzo di Medici,' he whispered, 'I have much more power than the great Lorenzo ever dreamed of.'

'Well, you cannot force me, Father. Not even you can do that.'

At that moment there were sounds of a scuffle and the front door burst open to admit a wild-eyed Guido, struggling between two men.

'Darling!' she screamed.

'Eleanor, what the hell's happening? Let me go!'

'We found him, Signore, outside. He was trying to get in.'

'I walked down the street and was going to ring the bell when these two gorillas seized me as if I were a criminal.'

'Guido, *mi amore.*'

She had run across the hall and flung herself at her lover, her arms about his waist, her cheek on his chest.

'What is it, my darling? What is all this?' he cried, bewildered. Luigi held one of his arms in a hammer-lock, Bernadetto the other. Eleanor covered his body with hers.

He stared at her ravaged face, repeating, 'What the hell is all this?'

Luigi and Bernadetto looked at Enrico for instructions, silently asking what to do next. Enrico walked slowly towards the little tableau.

'Get off him,' he hissed at his daughter, and in a

215

movement that hurt and made her cry out and was stronger than Eleanor could have believed possible, he dragged her away from Guido and flung her across the hall. She skidded across the marble, ricocheted against the banisters and fell to the floor. Her maid caught her, lifted her up instantly and steadied her.

'Leave her alone. What are you doing?' Guido, shocked beyond belief, unable to believe the evidence of his own eyes, struggled like a man possessed. Eleanor smoothed her skirt, and, trembling, tried to regain her composure.

'Have you gone mad?'

Guido could not understand what was happening. He hardly recognized this wild-eyed little man, roughly manhandling his own daughter, as the urbane and self-possessed businessman who had interviewed him. Bewildered by the turn of events he looked at Enrico as if an explanation might be forthcoming; as if there could be a rational explanation for this barbaric behaviour.

Enrico stood before him, bristling with anger, a little man crackling with uncontrollable frenzy.

'You fucked my daughter,' he said. 'For that I could have you castrated.'

'Ah, Father, no! Stop it now,' Eleanor pleaded. Lucetta held her back or she would have run to where her lover stood pinioned, confronting her father. Enrico did not seem to hear her. His voice was calm and deadly and he prowled around the hall like a hungry tiger in a cage.

'And I would have you castrated, don't think I wouldn't, except that I have work for you.' He drew a deep breath, then turned to face Guido.

'We have found your brother. Come here tomorrow after lunch, about three, and you will get your instructions.' A shudder shook his stocky frame. He turned to his henchmen. 'Now throw him out,' he said. 'It makes me sick to look at him.'

The men did as they were told, dragging Guido

struggling and protesting to the front door. He heard Eleanor cry out something after him but he did not hear what she said.

'He is trying to separate us. He is trying to send me away.'

But he did not understand her words. She watched him go. She looked at her father then turned to follow Guido. Stefano barred her way.

'Let me pass,' she cried, but suddenly from behind something was pressed over her nose and mouth, a cloth or cotton wool smelling sickly-sweet. She drew a deep breath to give the impetus to brace herself, to struggle, to fight. And lost consciousness.

Chapter Ten

There was a ringing in his ears as if his head was going to burst. Anger shook him, humiliation overwhelmed him. He wanted to destroy, to smash, to annihilate. There was a red mist before his eyes and his whole body ached.

Luigi and Bernadetto dragged him out into the street and flung him to the pavement with force. Luigi hit him with his fist closed. Bernadetto kicked him. They gave him a professional going-over, almost casually, a little grunt accompanying each blow, each punch, nothing more. No unnecessary effort was expended. Then they left him, palming their hands together as if to brush off dirt.

As pain took over from anger he found himself on his hands and knees like an animal, blood pouring from his nose or mouth, he was not sure which, his body gripped by agony, his only concern to manage to stand and get himself home to Via Lombardia.

He tested his legs. They felt like rubber. They doubled under him as he tried to stand and the pain was excruciating. He crawled over to the railings and pulled himself up using them as a support. He took deep gulps of air even though the action seemed to split his skull in half.

Shakily he stood up. He concentrated his mind on each painful movement, willing himself to rise and walk when his body screamed to lie down, to curl up and remain immobile. With supreme effort he managed to put one foot in front of the other, legs trembling, until he found a cab.

The driver looked at him sceptically but he said, 'Been attacked and robbed,' through stiff, blood-caked lips.

Luckily for Guido the state of security in Rome was the driver's hobby-horse. He was instantly sympathetic. It was his pet theory that Rome was going to the dogs, that the streets were not safe for man or beast any more. He made sure though that Guido had enough money to pay him. 'They did not rifle my trouser pockets,' he said. After that the driver kept up a cheerful monologue about how the youth of today were thugs and layabouts, reminding Guido suddenly and clearly of Giuseppe.

It was for a moment as if his father was with him in the taxi. He could almost feel him, smell him. He felt like a child again, breathing the scent of hay and grass and earth, and a sense of loss overwhelmed him. He shivered and wrapped his arms about his body as if to hold himself together, trying not to pass out from the white-hot agony that rent him every time the cab jolted over the cobbled streets.

At last they reached the Via Lombardia. The drive had seemed an eternity to Guido, whereas in fact it only took ten minutes.

'I think I should take you to the hospital, Signore,' the driver said, and Guido opened his eyes painfully and looked at him. He had kind eyes, a fatherly man Guido thought, and nodded. He opened the taxi door and found he could not move. When he did a searing pain ripped open his chest and the world receded from his consciousness, a pall of black closing his eyes.

'I think they broke something,' he said through stiff lips.

'Let me help.' The driver went around to his side then tutted and shook his head.

'You're in no condition to go home, Signore,' he said firmly.

Guido suddenly realized that he could not get to the front door, never mind his room.

219

He felt in his pocket and got out some money. He pressed the notes into the driver's hand.

'Take me to the nearest doctor,' he said, 'I think I'm going to pass out . . .' And he did.

~~~~~~

When he came to he was in his bed in the lodging house. Francesca was beside him. She was holding his hand, weeping. He tried to lift his head but it throbbed unbearably. He felt no pain though his body seemed to be floating.

He was worried by her crying. She seemed shaken by sobs, and he could see that she had been crying for a long time. He wanted to reassure her. There was nothing so badly wrong with him that warranted that helpless, hopeless sobbing.

'Lie still, Guido.' Francesca's voice was soft and full of concern.

He was suddenly overwhelmingly grateful for her presence. 'I'm all right,' he said. 'Bit woozy. As if I was drunk.'

'You're full of morphine. You broke two ribs.' She pressed a cold damp cloth to his brow. 'How did you do it?' she asked. 'It wasn't an accident, was it?'

'No. Enrico Domini's men did it to me. He found out about Eleanor and me.'

'I told you to be careful.' she whispered.

'He's mad, I think,' Guido said. 'Certainly dangerous. He wants to see me today.'

'Well, you can't go. You're too badly hurt. He'll have to wait.'

A little moan escaped her and she turned away from him.

He caught her wrist. 'What is it, Francesca? Shouldn't you be in bed? Are you all right?'

'Mama is dead,' she said.

'What?'

'Mama is dead.'

There was silence in the little room where he had made

love to Eleanor. The pillow was still impregnated with her scent, the view from the window reminded him of her. Everything in this room was Eleanor, Eleanor, Eleanor. Why did he have to learn of his mother's death here? Now the room would always be hated, always intrinsically mixed up with the hateful news.

'How?' he asked through lips that pained him now.

Francesca lifted Gina's letter from her lap. 'It's all here. It doesn't make pleasant reading.'

He took the letter from her, struggling to rise. His torso, he realized, was strapped, bound up, and his head was spinning. He fell back on the pillows, groaning, so Francesca took the letter back and read it to him.

'Serena is distraught,' she said when she had finished. 'Poor, gentle Serena. She is not strong enough to bear these tragedies. Poor, poor, Serena.'

Guido's face was turned from her. She knew he was crying. 'The pity of it all!' she said. 'Oh, the pity of it all.'

'Well, I have no more excuses now. I must find Mario at once. I have to get this thing done.' Then he asked, 'What about the funeral?'

'It is over. Gina said that she did not expect us and they did not want to hold things up. She says . . . where is it? Oh, here: "Mama is laid beside Papa. She wanted so much to be with him. She could not live without him. So be happy she is at peace." The letter was delayed, Guido. We have to accept that Mama has gone.'

He stretched out his arms and Francesca went into them. Brother and sister held each other tightly. They were family. They knew without speaking how the other felt, the waves of loneliness that overwhelmed them, the aching sense of loss.

At last, at the same instant, they released each other. 'I'm going to keep you here all day,' Francesca said, 'Then tomorrow you can do what you have to do.'

'No. I must get things rolling,' he said.

221

'I'll go and see Signore Domini, Guido.'

He sat up again, biting back a cry of pain.

'No, you must not go there. I forbid it. Sweetest sister, he is a truly dangerous man. I am worried for Eleanor. She was in a terrible state last night. Please wait until I can go.'

'All right, Guido. Don't distress yourself. All right,' she soothed him.

'Promise?' he asked. 'I won't rest until you do.'

'Promise.'

She brought him broth to drink. Signora Merciano was angry about the disturbance and only grudgingly allowed Francesca to prepare the soup in her kitchen.

'First *you* are sick,' she complained, 'then your brother comes home covered in blood and the house is turned upside down. In the middle of the night too,' she grumbled on as Francesca stirred the liquid she had prepared. Mama's recipe.

'He was very quiet, Signora,' she said. 'He had been brutally attacked. You are a good Catholic and go to mass each Sunday, no? And Jesus tells us to look after the sick.'

'Well, yes, it is my duty. and I am doing it,' she said, lips pursed. 'But I do not like all this sickness in my house.' She looked at Francesca with narrowed eyes, and waved a finger at her. 'And that is not all.' She clicked her tongue against her teeth. 'He has had visitors in his room, your brother, in the afternoons. Lady visitors. Signor Ferri heard them above him.'

Francesca busied herself with the stirring and turned her face away from the landlady in case she saw the blush that darkened her cheeks. 'And there are two men out there watching our house,' the landlady continued relentlessly. 'It cannot be the Ferris they are watching. They only came to see their daughter who is in the Convent of the Immaculate Conception. They often come. They are quiet and respectable. So it is not them, is it? Oh, no. It is you those men are watching. Well, any more disturbance and you must leave. I cannot have you here. I do not like what I do not understand.'

'Excuse me, Signora, the soup is ready. Thank you. Thank you very much for the use of your kitchen,' Francesca cried, and left the landlady standing muttering in the centre of the room.

She looked out of the window of her front-facing room. You could not see the street from Guido's room.

Yes, Signora Merciano was right. Two men lounged opposite, trying unsuccessfully to appear as if they were a part of the normal street life. But they were totally at odds with their surroundings. They would be at odds with any background, she thought. Their clothes were so flashy. They sported two-tone shoes and silky suits, brilliantly coloured ties, padded shoulders, and over all this wore imitation camel hair coats draped over their shoulders, even though the day was warm. They had fedoras tilted over their eyes and their appearance would have made Francesca giggle except for the menace inherent in their nervy pacing, the furtive glances they cast at the windows of the Merciano house, and the curious bulges under their jackets that they kept touching as if for reassurance. She guessed those bulges were guns.

She shivered. She did not want to trouble Guido about the men. She had a nasty feeling that they were the same ones who had beaten him up: Enrico Domini's men.

Guido drank his soup. As the day ticked by he improved by leaps and bounds. The doctors had done a good job. But Francesca could see a terrible anger building in him.

At three o'clock the doorbell rang and an irate Signora Merciano came panting up the stairs to the door of Guido's room.

'Those men, the ones I told you about, they want him.' She pointed at Guido, her face a mask of disapproval.

'What men? Francesca, what men? What is she talking about?'

'It's all right, Guido. Calm down. Signora, you're upsetting him.'

'Upsetting him! Upsetting him! He is upsetting *me*!'

'Stay there, Guido. I'll take care of it.'

He was trying to get out of bed but Francesca pushed him
back and, gently guiding the protesting Signora Merciano
out of the room closed the door behind them.

The two natty dressers stood at the door, uneasy, constantly shifting about.

'Signor Domini wants to see Guido Palucci,' the smaller of
the two said. He raised his hat to Francesca and she saw that
his black hair was parted in the centre and greased back into
two points at his neck. The bigger one behind him had a
cigarette hanging from his bottom lip. His mouth seemed to
be permanently half-open. He had a broken nose and
breathed noisily through it, as if he suffered from tonsils
and adenoids.

'Well, he can't see Guido today,' she said briskly. 'He's too
ill. Some thugs beat him up and broke two ribs.' The big one
sniggered. She stared at him levelly, 'Funny how stupid
some people are,' she said, her gaze going from one to the
other till they became embarrassed and their lids drooped
protectively over their eyes.

'Can you believe anyone being so brutal? Animals would
not behave like that.' She continued staring at them.

She turned to close the door when the smaller one's
attention was caught by a movement behind her.

'Wait, Signorina. I think Guido Palucci may have other
ideas.'

Guido stood there, trousers and shirt half on, jacket over
one shoulder, painfully decending the stairs.

'I'll go, Francesca,' he said, silencing her protests. She
looked into his face and saw the pain and anger there, the
need to act, to do something. She shrugged and stepped
back.

'I'll go,' he repeated. 'I need to find some answers.'

~~~~~~

The man behind the desk seemed to bear no relation to the sputtering tyrant who had shrieked at him in the hall the previous night. It was the Enrico Domini Guido had met on the two previous occasions: calm, courteous, urbane. He even looked tall sitting behind his desk.

'Guido,' he began as if last night had never happened. 'it's good to see you. I know you will be glad to hear that we have located your brother Mario. I knew it would please you.'

Guido was about to say something but Enrico held up his hand. 'Don't thank me, my dear boy. It was a pleasure. I'm only sorry it took so long. These things are not as easy as they first seem. But your patience is at last rewarded.' He leaned forward and Guido, looking into his smiling eyes and bland face thought for a moment he must have dreamed the screaming, red-faced little man of the previous evening. Then he felt the ache in his chest and knew he had not.

'Your brother Mario Palucci is in the United States of America, in Chicago, Illinois. He lives on Lincoln Avenue, drives a Ford convertible, has a French girlfriend, Minouche Aubin, and runs the Blue Lady nightclub where he sells bootleg booze.' He smiled at Guido. 'How can a nation that bans alcohol call itself civilized?' he asked and spread his palms upward. 'You'll find him at number 1046, corner of Lincoln and Clark. He lives over the club. Doing well for himself, your brother.' He looked at Guido quizzically. 'That comprehensive enough for you?'

He opened his mouth to reply but was forestalled. Enrico Domini reached into a drawer and took out an envelope which he pushed over to Guido.

'Your tickets and money for expenses,' he was saying. 'See you all right until you get there.' He stood up and put the envelope in Guido's hand, hustling him out of the room.

'Good luck, Signore Palucci. Goodbye. I expect you'll

225

want to get to America and the, er, conclusion of your business with your brother as soon as possible. If you need anything, feel free to ask me. You have the names in New York and Chicago? Tomaso Canona gave you the contacts?' Without waiting for a reply: 'Good, good. And good luck. Goodbye, Guido.'

He realized he was going to be outside the door in a minute. It was difficult to turn against the tide of their movement, his body aching, Enrico Domini firmly guiding him out of the room, but just as the door was about to close on his back Guido pushed against the impetus outward, turned and stepped back into the room. The unexpected movement threw Enrico Domini off his balance and he staggered back in confusion, at an immediate disadvantage. "Where is Eleanor?"

Enrico Domini's face reddened. He tried to control himself. The Palucci boy refused to be steamrollered out of the room and stood now, towering over him, demanding to know about Eleanor. How dare he?

For a moment Enrico glowered in impotent rage, then he thought better of physical retaliation and walked slowly back to his desk, seating himself and looking steadily at Guido.

'You seem determined to try my patience,' he said calmly. 'My daughter's whereabouts are really none of your business. However, as you appear to be intent on finding out, I intend to be honest with you.' He looked at his watch. 'At this moment, Eleanor is at sea. The ship will take her to her – er – intended.' He raised his eyebrows at Guido. 'Her betrothed. Her fiancé. I really don't know what you would call him today, but he is the man she will marry.'

Guido looked at the little man in disgust.

'You don't know her,' he said contemptuously. 'Do you?'

'I know human nature,' Enrico Domini said. 'After a while she will forget you. Romeo and Juliet would have

226

forgotten about each other if they had not been so precipitate and rushed headlong into drama and death, quite unnecessarily. They were really not suited to each other. As unsuited as you and Eleanor. She is young. She is ready.' His eyes narrowed and he looked up at Guido with contempt. 'How you ever dared . . .' He stopped a moment in order to control the tide of rage that threatened to overwhelm him, then continued, 'Now get out! Remember that what I said last night still goes. I can make you wish you had never been born.' He picked up the telephone. 'Go on. Get out. I have work to do.'

This time he did not get up to show Guido out but watched the young man leave the room, the telephone slippery within his grasp. He replaced it when the door closed behind Guido, took a handkerchief out of his breast pocket and wiped his hands on it.

He tried to calm himself. Why was he so upset? Why did that young man have such an effect on him? If he was honest he knew why, only he did not want to think about it.

He walked to the window. It made him sick to his guts to think of those two together, Eleanor and Guido. Eleanor was so like her mother. Tall, cool, blonde. Like champagne in a delicate glass.

He thought of Eleanor's mother, Alice. Alice Huntington. Ice cold Alice whom he had loved hotly with a passion to melt an iceberg. Only it had not. Alice had married him for his money, and on the rebound, and had frankly admitted in her cultured English accent, in tones of contempt. "Did you think I loved you, you fat little man? Did you really think that?" On their wedding night she had informed him bluntly that she had no intention of sleeping with him.

'Then I'll divorce you,' he had said, humiliated and hurt.

'Do,' she said coolly. 'You could try. You forget I took

instruction for you and we were married in the Holy Roman Catholic Church in bloody Rome. Why else did you think I married you here? Think I like the place? I did it, *amigo*, in case of just such a contingency.'

She had looked so seductive – graceful, well-bred, a challenge to his manhood.

'And,' she had continued, '*think* of what Society here will say. Do you suppose I have not noticed how you are ostracized? I imagine one of the reasons you married me was to get into the more exclusive circles. Think what your enemies will say when I tell them why you are divorcing me.'

'What do you mean?' he had asked, perplexed.

'We got a divorce, my darling, because you could not get it up! That is what I should say. If you divorce me, I will make you the laughing stock of Rome.'

He had been shocked that she could have talked so dirty. He had thought her a great lady. He was appalled, too, to find that it excited him. She had laughed at him. He could hear her laugh now as if it was yesterday. Nothing could ever heal that wound.

'My flesh crawls when you touch me, Enrico, so you never shall. Is that quite understood?'

He stood at the window now thinking of Guido Palucci and Eleanor. Oh, yes, he knew very well why he hated to think of them together. His daughter, the very image of her mother, enjoying that peasant!

Usually the sight of his garden outside calmed him. His office looked out on the courtyard and it was his favourite place, full of old stone statuary and greenery. He liked to have an expresso there about this time every day and sit in his chair staring at the exquisite delicate grouping of Orpheus leading Eurydice out of Hades. He loved the classic lines of the group, the calming play of water from the fountain. He opened the French window behind his desk and went out into the courtyard. The coffee waited for him. Stefano must have brought it. He noticed that his hand trembled when he lifted the cup.

Oh yes, if he were honest he knew what was wrong. He had loved her. He had fallen head over heels, madly adoring Alice Huntington. She had played her game well. Flirting with him, teasing him, until he did not know what he was doing.

Their marriage contract had stipulated that she should become a Catholic and that he would settle her family's debts and pay them a considerable annuity for the rest of his life towards the upkeep of Elm Court, one of the stately homes of England. The agreement also said, at his insistence, for he was a jealous man, that if ever Alice was unfaithful to him, all payments to her family and to her would cease. On his death she would inherit all his money and property.

He had told himself that her behaviour on their wedding night had been the result of nerves. He refused to accept her contempt, her ridicule, as genuine. Sure that if he were patient she would relent, get over her reluctance, he waited. But she never relented, never got over her reluctance. The honeymoon period came to an end. She behaved to him with impeccable politeness in public, with distaste in private. She acted as if she could not bear to be alone in the same room with him.

He was frustrated, almost mad with desire. He knew he was not repulsive; many women had found him attractive. He looked in the mirror and saw a good-looking man. True, his legs were short for the size of his body, but in bed what did that matter? Napoleon also was short. Enrico could not understand her.

He tried to rape her. After all, to possess her was his right, she was his wife. He went into her room one night to find himself face to face with the steel nozzle of a gun.

'I keep it under my pillow, *amigo*, in case you get any ideas,' she whispered, smiling. She called him '*amigo*'

229

deliberately, knowing it was Spanish, knowing it infuriated him.

It was that night, facing the gun she held, that he realized finally that she meant what she said. She really meant it.

What Alice could not know about her husband, although she should have guessed, was that he was quite ruthless. It was common knowledge that what he wanted, he usually got. She thought she had him all tied up. She did not know her opponent. In her English way she expected that although she broke the rules, which after all was a woman's prerogative, he would not do anything that was totally unacceptable. She should have known better. She should have realized by this time that nobody got to the position of power her husband was in by adhering to the Marquis of Queensbury rules, and that by denying a man like him something he wanted badly would goad him into a determination to possess it at all costs.

One night, three weeks later, her door burst open. Instead of Enrico she saw his two bodyguards, his two thugs. The gun was whipped from her hand, her arms pinioned, and horrified she saw her husband standing in the open door. There were another two men behind him.

'You see, my dear, my men are willing to die for me,' he said. Two of the men held her arms. The other two took an ankle each and opened her legs. One of the thugs lifted up her satin nightdress with rough hands, holding her spread-eagled on the bed like a human sacrifice.

She screamed but there was no one to care. The servants were his. Their loyalty to their master was absolute. They had been chosen carefully for their jobs.

He took his time with her. The bodyguards looked on. They could vouch for the fact that he could get it up. He enjoyed himself, paying her back for every humiliation, every frustration, every cruelty.

230

He took her three times in front of his men, then he left and she was never the same again.

Eleanor was the fruit of that night.

Enrico always thought of Alice with unease. He could never forgive her. He had not wanted to do what he had done to her. He had simply wanted her to love him. She had made him lose face. She had wounded his pride. She had forced him to act like a beast. He had wanted so much a reciprocal passion but she had forced him into a situation that made him behave like a satyr. For that he never forgave her.

Eleanor he loved, but she too made him uneasy. She was so like her mother. The realization that his daughter was sleeping with Palucci disturbed him more than he had believed possible. It was as if someone had achieved easily what he had failed to do. He reminded himself that Eleanor was his daughter, she was not Alice though she looked so like her. Nevertheless Guido Palucci had hopped into bed with her, obviously with her consent. It irked him and he could not but compare her ardour with her mother's coldness. The thought of the lovers together made him furiously angry.

He stood up, knocking over the coffee cup. Fuck Palucci! His card was marked. His days were numbered. Eleanor would forget him in England. She loved Elm Court. She would love Christopher. Eleanor was happier, he thought bitterly, where blood was thinner and the climate more temperate.

And Palucci went to his own execution ... Enrico Domini smiled. The young man was marching to the electric chair, did he but know it.

Brother Mario had grown too big for his boots in Chicago, the city where men knocked each other down like skittles. Mario Palucci was fucking things up for Salvatore Lucca. Like Alice he had insured his life, taken precautions, thought he was safe, but Mario had

231

underestimated Lucca just as Alice had underestimated him.

Well, he was about to find out his mistake. Guido was intent on vendetta. The police would be waiting for him. He would be watched from the moment he landed in Chicago until he killed his brother. Then he would be arrested. Two birds with one stone. Lucca had said. Mario and Guido Palucci. They did not understand in the USA about vendetta. Guido would be arrested and convicted of first degree murder. There would be witnesses, Lucca would see to that. Even if he escaped, they would catch him eventually. Mario's so-called friends would be watching. So would Lucca. So would the police. They would watch him walk into the trap. There was not a hole small enough for Guido to crawl into. With all those people tailing him, keeping him under surveillance, he had a one-way ticket to the death chamber.

Enrico Domini smiled and nodded to himself, satisfied that events had been set in motion. There was no stopping now. He could relax.

He looked at his watch. He decided to visit his mistress that evening. She would relax him. He'd bring her a little trinket. Fuck Palucci. Fuck Eleanor. Fuck anyone who tried to cross him and didn't understand how powerful a man he was. They learned eventually. Like Alice.

Chapter Eleven

Mario grunted contentedly to himself as Moses drove the car across the bridge, up Michigan Avenue and along Lakeshore Drive. He would live here some day. Lucca was a cheapskate, hanging out in a dump in the German Quarter, North Southport. Jeez! What was the point havin' money if you didn't spend? The lights twinkled in the de luxe apartments along the lake. He knew of some of the toffee-nosed inhabitants. They were his clients. He could frighten fat-cat men and render them sleepless. Mosta those guys could be corrupted, easy as anything. Parade a young and sexy doll in front of their greedy eyes, promise a blow-job, offer a little sex *à trois*, mix a little cocaine in interesting places, and their mouths began to water.

See, these guys felt they owned the world, that they deserved it all. Anything. They never seemed to realize until it was too late that there was always a sting in the tail. They made the mistake of believing that they could do anything they liked. Mario knew there was always a price to pay. Always. In the end you had to pick up the tab. These guys in their high sparkling towers, looking out over the lake, forgot that. They dived into lust, booze, drugs, all the forbidden sensations, did their thing, the thing that made them weak. Then they were trapped. Taste some, try some, you got hooked. Couldn't do without it. That dame made you feel something you never felt before. You kept harking back to it. It got under your skin. The same with booze. Drugs too. You had to have it once more. Just once more, honest. Then you'd give it up for good.

Mario grunted again, looked up and caught Moses's eye. He had to get rid of Moses. Guy was always lookin' at him, staring. Christ!

'Keep yer eyes on the road,' he rasped at the black man who cried,

'Yes, sir,' quickly back at him, military style, taking the mickey. Jeez, the impudence!

The car drew to a halt and Mario got out. They were on Clark, three blocks from the Blue Lady and his apartment. He looked around. The Ape should be here. He felt the adrenelin pumping. He was about to throw weight. Show who would soon be boss. Take over from the old man. He moved his shoulders around beneath his coat, pulled his hat down.

Tommy Doyle had to be taught a lesson. Shown exactly who to be afraid of.

The Ape emerged from the shadows. 'Here, Boss.'

'Yeah, well, where's the fuckin' shop? Let's deal with these punks quick.'

'Here, Boss.'

'Please, Ape, don't call me "Boss". Mister Palucci, OK?'

'OK. Here, Mister Palucci.' The Ape's simple face irritated Mario. He knew it and ached to please, be accepted, but nothing he did really satisfied the handsome Sicilian. Now Mr Lucca, he thought, Mr Lucca was different. Made the Ape feel special. Good. Made him feel important. But not *Mister* Palucci. Mister Palucci liked the Frog, Pierre. Couldn't he see that the Frog hated him?

The Ape didn't like these beating-up jobs. Mister Palucci did, you could see. He wasn't yellow, naw, nothin' like that. It was just that he preferred to *look* menacing. Usually it was enough to frighten people off. He'd no objection to

234

killing, but quickly, so they didn't have time to realize what was happening. But beating up? Mario liked to see a little blood. It was not necessary, Mr Lucca said, made men resentful.

'Ask nicely,' Mr Lucca said, 'stand over them. Always at least three per person. Just stand there an' ask nicely. Don' use violence except as a last resort. Then, if they don' see reason, blow 'em away. But, Christ, warnings don' have to be blood baths.'

But Mario didn't believe in violence as a last resort. He needed to see a little blood. It made him feel a man.

'Break open the door, Ape,' he said now, standing in the dark street.

'Couldn' we knock? Mebbe they're friendly.'

'Shit, do as I tell you,' Mario said, that dangerous look in his eye. 'Asshole!' he muttered.

The Ape took off his jacket. The freezing wind whipped in from the Lake, making him shiver. He wrapped his jacket around his fist and arm, then punched a hole in the glass door. Tommy Doyle's tasteful engraving in the glass read:

T. DOYLE, TAXIDERMIST
ALL KINDS OF ANIMALS STUFFED
YOU NEED NEVER SAY FAREWELL TO YOUR
LOVED ONES

It ended up in smithereens on the floor. Ape felt it was a shame. It was a nice sign, a friendly thought.

A man came running into the shop from upstairs. He was half undressed, wearing a singlet and pants.

'What the shit?' He stood still, staring at the wreckage of his glass door on the floor. 'What the fuck's goin' on here?'

He was a big man. Not as big as the Ape, but big and

well-built. His Irish face was wrinkled up in perplexed anger.

'What the hell's wrong?' He looked at Mario. 'You nuts or somethin'?'

'Shut up,' Mario said coldly.

'Hey, hey, I paid my dues,' Tommy Doyle cried. 'Holy Mother of God, you've decimated my door. I've paid my dues to Lucca. What else d'you want?'

'I hear you been selling privately, Tommy,' Mario said, dangerously quiet. Tommy's taxidermy took second place to supplying liquor to interested parties. He creamed off the profits but Lucca was not too grieved about it; Tommy's contribution to the Organization was considerable. Now this punk Palucci had started counting dimes and was doing his best to fuck up a perfectly good arrangement.

'You keepin' more'n your fair share, Tommy.'

'Hell, no, I never.' Tommy shook his head in fervent denial. ' 'Sides, I settled up wi' Lucca. whaddya doin' outa your territory?, eh? Lucca never said ye could come here. Lucca know about this, eh?'

'Soften him up for me, Ape,' Mario said.

This was what the Ape hated. Everything peaceful and you had to make jam of the man's face so Mario Palucci could deliver the *coup-de-grâce*. The Ape hit the man. It was half-hearted but the Ape's fist was sledge-hammer hard and Tommy Doyle was out of training.

'Again,' Mario said, and the Ape did as he was told.

'And again.' The punches hit Tommy like a ton of bricks. His nose was bleeding, his eyes had a glazed look, his jaw was swollen and he would have a shiner tomorrow. Mario, however, was only warming up. When the Ape had hit the man another half-dozen times Tommy lay on the ground among the broken pieces of glass from his smart doors, begging for mercy. Then Mario moved in. He had a gun in his hand. He bent down, squatting beside

236

the beaten man, shoving the gun down his throat. Tommy gagged on it. Wet his pants, the Ape saw. His eyes in his bloody face were wide with terror. Mario still sounded calm and mild. The Ape looked away.

'Listen, Mick, you never mention Lucca to me again, see? Lucca's old. Past it. I'm takin' over. You get my drift? You have me to deal with, understand? You pay me in full, see, you know what I'm talkin' about.' Mario pressed the gun further down the Irishman's throat. Tommy gagged again but managed to move his head to show he understood.

'Next time I'll pull the trigger,' Mario said, and removed the gun. He pulled out a handkerchief, wiped the gun on it, dropped the handkerchief on Tommy Doyle's chest and left the shop. 'Bloody stupid Mick!' he said.

There was a little group of spectators outside the store. They scattered into the shadows when Mario and the Ape appeared.

Mario got in the car and the Ape followed. Mario nodded to Moses. 'The Blue Lady', he said, then shouted at the driver, 'Don't forget to tell your fuckin' boss, will ya?'

Deed I will, punk. Deed I will, thought Moses, but he said nothing at all.

~~~~~~

Lucca felt the pain in his chest and wondered what it was. Could be the news about Palucci, could be a heart attack, could be his last hour. Trouble with being old, you never knew how serious a pain was.

He did not believe in doctors. 'Once they start fiddling with you, they never stop. Puts money in their pockets.' And he was terrified of hospitals. 'Only way you come outa there, feet first,' he was fond of saying.

The pain stabbed and he hoped it was Palucci. The alternatives were not very attractive.

Christ, Palucci was overstepping the mark. He had done

the rounds of six other associates, annexed them to his own territory, and if he was allowed to get away with it people might get the wrong idea and think that he, Lucca, was losing his grip. Mario Palucci was a threat.

Pino was to take over when Lucca died. The old man sighed. Pino was no Capone, had no real organizational flair, liked hurting people. Trouble with the modern generation, they had no *finesse*. Pino was ambitious, though. He was pretty ruthless and he understood the rules of the game. Palucci played as if there were no rules and that meant trouble. He was causing mayhem all over, stepping on people's feet. If he wasn't stopped he'd bring about a war. Bring down the wrath of the big men on his, Lucca's, space.

Lucca had lived in relative peace with the other Mob bosses and he did not want to change tactics now. God forbid. Everyone was getting jumpy. The FBI and America at large wanted to clean up the country. Eliot Ness was putting them away like a drunken Irishman. Public feeling was running heavily against the mobs and in Salvatore Lucca's opinion it was punks like Mario Palucci who were drawing attention to them. Unnecessary attention. Look at Dillinger gettin' shot right in front of the Biograph. It was too much. You'd think that Mario would take the hint. Why, the Biograph was just up the road from the Blue Lady. Round the fuckin' corner, for Chrissakes. If the Organization kept its quarrels quiet, secret, like in the old days, then all this attention would be directed elsewhere. Where it belonged, in Lucca's opinion. But, no. Power-hungry punks like Mario Palucci had to show the world what big guys they were and get their names splashed all over the papers. Had to go round breakin' down doors. Shit, why didn't he get Buster Keaton to film it?

Lucca listened until Moses had finished.

'You did good, Moses,' the old man said. 'Keep an eye on him.' He waved the black man out.

238

'His days are numbered,' he said softly to himself, and this time Moses's smile split his face as he left the room.

Well, Lucca thought when he was alone, the time had come. There was no way he could hand Mario over to the cops and too many people knew he worked for Lucca. Feds were making arrests left, right and centre and Lucca had no intention of spending his last days inside.

Mario would sing if he were taken in, that punk would do anything to save his own skin. So he had to be got rid of in a way that was clearly unconnected with Lucca or his friends.

So let his brother do it. Guido Palucci, according to Enrico Domini, was aching to find Mario. The vendetta Lucca understood. The family all seemed to be trouble-makers though. Enrico Domini in Rome was pissed off with the brother, Guido, who had been making trouble there. For whatever reason, Lucca did not know and did not want to know, Domini wanted Guido Palucci sacrificed. *Bene.* It suited perfectly. Guido could do the job and be handed over to the cops. Two birds with one stone, unconnected with Lucca. It was perfect.

Lucca hoped he would arrive soon, blow his brother away. He had everything ready. Half Chicago would be watching Guido.

'The curtain,' he said to himself, rubbing his hands together and grinning, 'is about to rise. Goodbye, Mario Palucci.' He smiled. 'Then there is Minouche.' Whenever he saw her he could feel a stirring in his loins, a definite sensation where there had been no activity for years. She triggered something in him, something past and regretted. He welcomed that sensation with the desperation of a man who could feel the breath of death on his cheek. It was like a return to youth and vigour.

He was in a dilemma as to what to do about it. He did not see her much. He could not imagine actually climbing on top of her. He remembered himself, the sap rising,

239

taking the women he wanted with the strength of virility. He could not do that now.

Well, he thought, there were other ways. He squeezed his eyes tight shut. To get that feeling again . . . he had meant it when he said he would give anything.

The most terrible thing about being old was when the sap stopped rising. It was not just sex, it was the joy of life, the feeling that you could move mountains, the vitality in your thighs, the life that stirred below the skin surface, that fed you energy and joy.

He would just have to force her. If there was any hope, he just had to have it.

He would frighten her. That worked best. Better than paying. But no one must find out. It could be used against him. Only Moses and Pino could be trusted.

He smiled, moving his teeth around his gums, getting relief, thinking of the past, knowing it would never be like that again. But hopeful, too, for this young French girl sure as hell had an effect on him. Yes, indeed.

~~~~~~

Mario found a message waiting for him with Mandy the hat-check girl at the club.

Lucca wanted to see him. Fuck Lucca, he thought, and went down the back stairs to where the noise was.

The place was crowded. He cruised between tables, casting greetings to right and left, slicking back his hair, the picture of debonair confidence. But inside he was acutely uneasy. He found he was unable to shrug off Lucca's summons that easily. Jake was playing some fancy piano behind Ella Mae in black sequins crooning "Man of my Dreams" deep into the mike on the apron-stage.

He crossed to his regular table where Minouche sat accompanied as usual by Pierre. Mario wished the guy would take a powder. Always fuckin' there. Never someplace else. Even making love to Minouche, Mario felt

240

the giant's unseen presence. The big guy never took his eyes off the girl. Far from getting him on his side, in the Palucci camp as it were, Mario could sense that the French giant hated him. There was nothing you could put your finger on, he was always polite, never argued or got out of line, but it was there, in his eyes, his white-hot hatred of Palucci.

Mario understood it. After all, Mario had stolen his girl, nicked her right out from under Pierre's nose. Gave Mario the creeps to be with him sometimes, depending on him, and all the time the hatred there, palpable on the air like a bad smell. The hell with him!

Mario kissed Minouche, putting a firm arm possessively around her. He was very proud of his ownership of her and wanted Pierre to see and understand this was *his* woman.

'Hi, sweetheart,' he said, then immediately the inner uneasiness overwhelmed him as he remembered. 'Lucca wants to see me.'

'Why didn't you go direct to him?' she asked, smiling, her little face full of love. She adored Mario. Every time she saw him she became enslaved anew. She touched his face with her fingers, but as usual he flinched from the intimate gesture in public. She had tried to teach him to show a little tenderness but it was no use. Even when they made love he would not bother with foreplay.

'Let's get on with it, sugar,' he would say. Sex for him was its climax. Time spent on arousal or prolonging the pleasure, a waste. So she gave up. It didn't matter. She worshipped him. He was her man.

She did not know the ins and outs of his activities, but she suspected that violence was part of him. It did not matter to her. She had grown up in a violent world and knew one had to be ruthless in that world to survive. She liked his dangerous side, felt it protected her. She bent happily to his will, accepting his air of urgency and brusqueness as assets rather than the reverse.

She often thought of Paris, of the crowded streets and

241

cafés, the Quarter, Madame Lefranche, the girls from the Petit Moulin. She missed her life there. But Mario was here and that was what was important. Chicago was different from Paris but at least it was a city. It had that same bustle and hum, that underlying excitement. And when she was homesick and thought of Paris with longing, she tried to remember Yves Aubin, the blood and the fear, and reminded herself how she had nearly gone to prison. She had told Mario about Yves. He had whistled in admiration.

'Jeez, baby, you got guts. That's the way to do it.'

'Still, I had to leave Paris, Mario. Me and Pierre.'

'Yeah, well, if you hadna youda never met me, sugar. We'da never become a number.'

She hung on his every word, gazing up at him with adoring eyes. As always, she was closely observed by Pierre. She wanted to be her lover's slave and thrived on his air of authority. She mistook his boasting for statements of fact. She was content to wait on him, his moods, his pleasures, to serve him, to allow him to be boss-man, owner, king.

He revelled in her elevation of him into a god. He basked in her adoration. It made him feel strong and invincible. Now, sitting at the table, the admiration in her eyes gave him the courage to meet with Lucca. After all, who was the guy? A washed-out old has-been.

'Pierre, will you come with me?' he asked. Then seeing the giant glance involuntarily down at Minouche, he added impatiently, 'She'll be OK here, Pierre. What can happen to her here?'

The Frenchman glanced at him through slitted eyes. There it was, the spark that irritated Mario. But he held his impatience in check. He could not afford to antagonize the Frenchman. The Ape was brute strength. An ox. A bull. Pierre was not only larger than the Ape, he was quick and sharp, a tiger, cunning as a hunter. No, he must

242

pretend he did not sense the man's feelings. But he was aware, and it was good that he was. He congratulated himself. He knew his enemy.

Well, he could not think of Pierre just now. It had been a good night's work and if Lucca didn't like it, that ass-hole could go jump in Lake Michigan.

Mario felt elated. Tommy Doyle was licked. A guy with influence in the Mick community. The news would spread. People would hear. Mario's reputation as a man not to be messed around with would spread.

They left the club. Moses was waiting at the wheel of the car in Clark Street. The Ape had naturally tagged along. He followed Mario everywhere, like a dog. Mario forgot he was there sometimes. Even when he was taking a leak, the Ape stood in attendance, in case Mario needed him. He felt good now, in the back of the car between the Ape and Pierre. It did his confidence no harm at all, big guys like that, one each side, having to do as he said. He cleared his throat and winked broadly at the Ape.

'You went straight over an' told him. You couldn't wait, Moses, could you? So, I'm not too popular with the big chief tonight, eh? Eh?' Mario smiled at the Ape, then at the black driver.

'No, suh.' Moses's eyes looked at him through the mirror, a sarcastic expression in their dark depths.

Trouble sure was brewing for the cocky little wop, if only he knew it. Moses smiled inwardly. Wouldn't trouble them much longer. Thought he was cock-o'-the-walk, struttin' like a world contender, like the cocks before the fight he used to go to in Alabama. Well, soon Mario Palucci would be out of it all. Zap! Moses deftly slid the car up Diversey and into North Southport. Pity he couldn't be there to hear what Lucca said to the jerk. Mario looked on Lucca as a meal-ticket, Moses thought, pushing his people around, thinking himself so tough. If only he knew he was the sucker. Lucca would get him in line.

Pino let them in. He jerked his head towards Lucca's room and motioned Mario in. Coulda greeted me. Costs nuthin', a good evening. Just that! thought Mario. But Pino was always economical with talk.

Lucca was in his chair, a rug over his knees, fire blazing. He leaned forward and spat out, 'What the fuck you think you doin'? Just who do you think you pushin' around, punk?'

Mario could see the bones of his face, yellow skin stretched tight, yellow teeth moving on his shrunken gums.

He didn't reply. Kept his eyes at a point slightly above Lucca's head, standing to attention like a recalcitrant schoolboy in front of the headmaster. He would have liked the Ape and Pierre standing by him, shoulder to shoulder, taking his side, but Lucca had roared at him to "Leave the goons outside". Lucca's face changed, lost its enraged expression.

'Look at me, Mario,' he said, spreading his hands, 'an old man. Can't you wait? Can you not wait till I die? You so greedy? So impatient? Won't be long now, boy, till I'm gone an' the position is up for grabs? Hey?' He squinted up at the Sicilian. 'An' has it occurred to you, Mastermind, how come I got to live so old, eh? That ever cross your mind? You go on the way you're doin', you'll end up in a pool of your own blood before you're thirty years old. *Mamma mia*, some people are in a hurry! Can't wait.'

The old man closed his eyes and sighed, then lapsed into silence. Mario didn't know if he was asleep or not. He looked at the old guy sitting there, slumped in his chair.

If I blew him away now, if I shot him now, it'd be great! he thought, get rid of the old devil. But I'd never walk outa here alive. Pino, Moses, the boys in the hall – Ricci, Beno the Bones, Forno, Gicci – all of them would stop me. They'd do it instinctively.

When they thought about it, really thought, they'd

244

prefer him to Pino, he knew that. But if he shot the old man now they wouldn't have time to realize that fact. They wouldn't have time to think. They'd just take him out, quick as a flash, come out blasting. They all thought they were wise guys but they were dumb. Regretfully Mario gave up the idea. Man was right. His time was nearly up. It would be wise to wait.

He glanced down at Lucca to find icy eyes staring at him, reading his thoughts,

'Yes, sirree, you're too impatient. Someone'll put a hole in your pump and you'll end up six-foot under while you're still in diapers,' he said, eyes glittering. 'Took me twenty years to make peace with the Micks. Twenty to make peace with the blacks. We all help each other now. In *my* territory we got mutual respect, savvy? Some of my contemporaries, some of the Capos, the big bosses, get greedy. They never last. Too greedy is dead. Or at best, prison. You hear me?'

Mario's attention was elsewhere. He turned his concentration back to the old man.

'Tommy Doyle was useful and profitable to me, Mario. Now he's turning to others.'

Mario gasped. 'Jeez, he can't . . .'

'Aha! Got your interest at last, have I? He's gone over to the Ellis brothers. Did a deal, got protection, half an hour after you left. Ellis is in with Capone. Heavy stuff. It'ud be a war we *havta* lose you asshole. You ask me why we gotta lose? I tell you. They got more help. They got more connections. It's strategically necessary we lose, got it? Or are you too dumb? Anyhow, war is always a waste of time. Waste of time, waste of energy, waste of manpower, waste of money.' He ticked them off on his fingers, glancing up contemptuously at Mario. 'You never think like that, Mario, you never qualify for leader. Now go. Get outa here. Leave me alone. And leave things alone. No more original ideas, you get my meanin'?'

245

Mario went into the hall. Beno the Bones and Ricci stared at him expressionless, hands near their jacket pockets. Yes, he thought, if they had heard anything from Lucca's room they would have shot him first, asked questions later.

He shivered, his confidence deserting him. He did not want to die. Maybe he should proceed more carefully. What Lucca said was true. Old man was lookin' at the end of his life here. He hadn't much further to go. Then, Mario thought, between himself and Pino there would be no contest. If he upset the other mobs now, antagonized them, he would bring unnecessary attention on himself before he was ready. Then who knew what might happen? Get attention when he was the big man. Not while he was a cog. No way.

Shit, he thought, the old man has something there. All he had to do was wait. Why hadn't he thought of that for himself?

PART III

Chapter Twelve

Lady Wylde sat at her desk chewing her pen. A stack of engraved invitations lay on the desk and with them were a bunch of letters, some to be answered, some to be sent. The replies were unsigned.

She held a letter in her hand, idly fiddling with the pages. It was from Enrico Domini.

She stared out of the window where the copper beeches splashed their russet glory across the green of chestnuts, limes, oaks, aspens, and most of all the elms. They had been growing on Elm Court land for more than five centuries, and when Helen Wylde was troubled, the sight of them never failed to give her solace.

In spring, bluebells spread themselves under the trees and the lawn rolled its smooth green carpet to the lake where lily-of-the-valley in their hundreds scented the air with a sweet and heavy perfume.

However, Lady Wylde's gaze was not focused on the view. Nor did she look at her family on the croquet-lawn, swinging their mallets and chattering, voices high as magpies. She was thinking of Eleanor Domini up in her room, refusing to eat.

She had missed the girl this summer and wondered what had kept her in Rome away from her beloved Elm Court. An expression of annoyance marred the beauty of her fine classic features.

'Damn!' she said under her breath. 'Damn, damn, damn!'

She had groaned for twenty years now under the yoke of their indebtedness to, and dependence upon, Enrico Domini. The upkeep of Elm Court and all the luxuries she and her family had come to take for granted were his gift, and though she was grateful she nevertheless chaffed under the weight of such an obligation.

When Enrico had married Alice Armstrong, Helen's first cousin and her father's ward (the Wyldes brought Alice up), Enrico had undertaken to finance the estate and give the Wyldes a more than generous allowance for its upkeep. At the time of their marriage Enrico, flushed with love, had been willing to be generous. The estate was in the direst straits and it was an offer that at the time was most heartily welcome.

But times had changed. Her uncompromising English truthfulness forced Helen to face the fact that she did not, in retrospect, think the bargain fair, and it irked her to be under this huge obligation to "that Italian crook" as she mentally called him. Alice as a wife was not worth the huge sums of money Enrico Domini was committed to paying out to the Wyldes, and now that she was dead it seemed doubly unfair. Yet how could she voluntarily return to the anxiety of unpaid bills, mortgages, leaking roofs and the decline of the beautiful house she loved so dearly. And without Domini's money, that is what would happen.

Each year Helen resolved to speak to Enrico, release him from this legally contracted obligation. Each year she put it off till the next.

She had never liked her cousin much. Alice had been a wilful beauty who wound Helen's father around her little finger, and was thoroughly spoiled. She had succeeded in getting her own way in everything except the one thing she wanted more than anything else: Hugh Wylde.

Helen had never understood why Hugh had fallen in love with her instead of the brilliant, bright and beautiful ward. As young people they lived on adjoining estates and

250

Hugh Wylde, who was soon to be Lord Wylde, was big brother to them both.

Then the big brother had turned into a handsome prince and both girls fell in love with him. Helen had been resigned to Hugh's choosing Alice. She thought of herself, her fine English beauty, as unremarkable whereas Alice's flamboyance was irresistible. But Hugh had fallen deeply in love with Helen. For a long time she could not believe her luck. He persuaded her, however, that he was not seduced by Alice's charms and that what he wanted in a wife, and what he loved in Helen, was her sense of humour, her courage, her innate dignity and serenity.

When Helen had married Hugh and become Lady Wylde, Alice had gone crazy. She went to London and began to show a streak of recklessness that alarmed Lord Huntington, Helen's father and Alice's guardian. He was getting old and the honour of the family was very important to him. Alice was gadding about London, associating with unsuitable people in unsuitable places, getting her name in the yellow press. She had at one point been using opium freely and openly, and consorting with poets, artists, bohemians and the like. All terribly worrying.

All Lord Huntington wanted was a peaceful life at Elm Court. He handed the place over to Hugh and the men were struggling to keep it going, but neither was much good at finance.

Then Alice had produced Enrico Domini as her prospective husband. Lord Huntington had identified the Italian at first glance as a crook. He pointed out to Alice their differences in upbringing and warned her of the man's ruthlessness which he had correctly sensed simmered very close beneath the surface. She would not listen. She flaunted Enrico under Hugh's nose, as if she expected some protest. But none came. Hugh was courteous, said that he and Helen hoped they would be happy.

Helen was convinced that Alice had married Enrico

251

Domini in a gesture of defiance. She guessed at the time that Alice had not married for love. Certainly she was luxury-loving and her husband was rich. Helen thought that Alice married Enrico Domini for several reasons. One, because she could not have Hugh and she thought her gesture would make him sorry. Two, because Enrico was much older than she and represented the father she had never had. Three, he could give her a very exciting life and Alice craved excitement. And four, he was the sort of man the family would not approve of and that gave her a perverse pleasure, for she blamed the family as much as Hugh that he had not chosen her. It was sad, a sorry tale, and all they could do was watch as Alice walked into the lion's den.

Her grandiose gesture had given them financial security. The marriage contract, drawn up at Alice's stipulation, required Enrico Domini to support the Court for the rest of his life and beyond. Why? They had asked themselves the question often. What had been in Alice's mind when she had insisted on that stipulation? Was she frightened to cut herself off from the home she loved? She cherished every tree and stream; each flower was dear to her. The house was certainly her home, the place where she had spent all her happy times. Did she know then that her marriage to Enrico would be a disaster? That she might need to return there? Was she worried that with Hugh and Helen ensconced as Lord and Lady of the Manor, she might not be welcome? That by making this agreement she was not only ensuring the future of the property but assuring herself a place within its walls? Sometimes Helen thought in the darkest corners of her mind that Alice's real reason had been to leave an avenue open to Hugh. That she intended to go on trying to coax him away from her cousin. She had put such thoughts aside as unworthy, but they had crept back. Whatever the gesture meant, it had bound them to Enrico Domini forever.

They had thought that Alice would soon tire of the Italian and leave him, get herself another, more suitable man. In the event this did not happen.

Alice believed erroneously that she could lead her pet Italian around by the nose. He worshipped her. He was, Helen could see, half out of his mind about her. Alice thought she could control him.

How idiotic! She had totally underestimated Enrico Domini: his pride, his power, his sadistic nature, his ruthlessness. And she had paid most horribly.

Helen remembered as if it were yesterday her cousin's return to England one year to the day after her wedding, that grand pretentious wedding in St James's. It had set all London whispering. A year later, she was shocked at Alice's appearance. She could not help but pity her. All the wildness gone, the sparkle dimmed, the spirit broken. Alice did not even notice Hugh. Pregnant, listless, she had turned in despair to Roger Huntington, a hurt child again. He had taken her to his heart and they consoled each other, forming a close friendship.

Eleanor had been born in Elm Court. A few months later her mother took her back to Italy. Alice had been forced by that clever agreement she had contracted with Enrico Domini to spend six months of each year with her husband. There was sadly no way out of it. And even in her depressed state she would not give up the advantages of wealth, risk losing all she had paid for so dearly.

When she returned to Rome she jumped at every sound, flinched at the slightest gesture of affection, and withdrew more and more into herself. A shadow of the vivid flame she had once been, she did her duty to her husband and child with no warmth or vitality, like an inscrutable oriental servant. And then she died. Quite quickly and suddenly.

In spring, returning from her six months in Rome, grieving at Lord Huntington's death, she was soaked in a shower at the funeral. She caught a cold. It became an infection, not serious they thought. It had gone to her chest, turned to pneumonia, and she was dead in a week. The doctors said she had no resistance, that she had not put up a fight. She had just died.

Since then, by mutual agreement, her daughter had spent spring and summer every year, with the Wyldes at Elm Court and the rest of the time in Rome with her father.

To do him justice, Helen mused, Enrico Domini had never reneged on his commitment. Sometimes she wished he would. Almost, but not quite. She loved the things his money bought, the comfort of the estate, the freedom from the financial worries that had tormented them in the years before Enrico had been married to Alice. She derived enormous joy from knowing they could afford to keep up and run Elm Court in a fitting manner.

It was accepting the money from Domini that irked Helen. She longed to be able to fling it back in his face, especially in the years just after Alice died. For all her faults, poor Alice did not deserve what the Italian had done to her.

The family loved Eleanor. She was bright and beautiful like her mother, but she was reserved and reflective while her mother had been butterfly-giddy. She was generous and kind and loving. She refused, however, to hear a word spoken against her mother or father. They respected her for that but it made intimacy with her impossible for there was so much that had to remain unsaid.

Helen sighed. She missed Hugh, missed him with an ache every day of her life. She had been happy to see him off to the war, proud of him in his uniform, stupidly ignorant of what it entailed. You waved your men off, certain of the rightness of their cause, confident of their invincible strength. No one warned you.

Enrico Domini's money had helped enormously after

Hugh had been killed. Uncomfortably aware that a lot of it came from the thriving black-market and other suspect sources, Helen was nevertheless dependent enough to take and be glad of it.

And now this! Helen focused her eyes which had been staring unseeingly. Through the window she could see Christopher teasing Sylvia. Her daughter and her son. She sighed. It was about Christopher that Enrico Domini had written. She picked up the letter again and ran her eyes over the second paragraph.

> . . . you'll agree that a match between them would be perfect. Eleanor and Christopher are so suited to each other. They are not too closely related, Alice was only your cousin. And an alliance between them will ensure the continued prosperity of Elm Court. You will undertand my desire to keep my interest in your home alive . . .

Oh, the iron fist in the velvet glove! The threat so soft as to be almost concealed.

Her eyes scanned further down the page:

> Eleanor seems to be very much her mother's daughter . . . fallen in love, a mere infatuation, with a Sicilian peasant, a farmer from the backwoods . . . after her money . . . cannot of course tolerate the situation so have sent her to you for safekeeping and in the confident knowledge that in your own, mine, and Eleanor's interests you will encourage a match between her and Christopher that will benefit us all.

'Encourage a match,' she murmured under her breath. 'Heavens, does he think we still live in the Middle Ages? How exactly am I supposed to do that?'

~~~~~~

Eleanor had arrived at Elm Court in much the same state as her mother twenty years previously. Helen suspected that the person who had caused the girl's collapse might be

255

the very same who had destroyed Alice. She also thought that the girl might have been drugged.

The two thugs who delivered her left without explanation. '*Non comprendiamo l'inglese*,' they repeated fervently. Helen was sure this was a lie.

Would they never be rid of Enrico Domini? She understood precisely what he was saying in the letter; Eleanor marries Christopher or the deal is off. No more money. No more protection. End of life as she knew and loved it. The graciousness of the lifestyle she led was becoming a thing of the past in her own circle. Sadly the great houses were becoming tourist domains. The great families found it difficult to continue in style, never mind try to keep their houses in good repair, without American money, husbands or wives taken from trade and industry, mortgages that were outrageously expensive. The first families were thinking of letting in visitors. Helen hoped that her home could remain her own private domain for as long as possible.

If Enrico stopped his allowance she would have no redress in law. He was the kind of man who would enjoy reducing them to poverty if she crossed him. Also he was the kind of man who would not be bound by court orders. And he was in Rome and she in England, and the English courts had no jurisdiction there and vice-versa.

She rubbed her forehead. Added to this was the fact that Christopher was in love with Eleanor. She wished heartily it was not so. Then she could have fought Enrico Domini and to hell with the consequences, for she would never encourage her son to marry someone he did not love. But he had been mad about Eleanor all his life. A repetition of herself and Hugh Wylde. She always smiled when she thought of Christopher, and reflected now how gentle he was, what a kind man. Eleanor brought out the knight in him.

She had to admit that marriage between those two

would considerably simplify things. Enrico would be doubly bound to the family and the upkeep of Elm Court, and she could stop worrying. Everyone would be happy, she thought, except poor Eleanor.

She wondered who this Sicilian was that had so stirred the girl. What was he like? He could not be stupid or Eleanor would not have fallen in love with him. Oh, it was all such a muddle.

She looked out of the window again. Her daughter Sylvia was red-faced, shouting something at her brother. Helen shook her head. She wished Sylvia was as nice as Eleanor. She had trouble with Sylvia. Eleanor was everything her mother had never been: warm, unselfish and kind. Sylvia, on the other hand, was a snob. She was selfish and jealous. She was not a very nice person. Helen wondered where she had gone wrong. But there was nothing she could do about it now. Sylvia was what she was. Perhaps if Hugh had lived . . .

Helen's thoughts returned to the dilemma the half-Italian girl found herself in.

'Papa wants me to marry Chris,' she had said when they had finally been able to talk. The girl had been delirious for the first two days. They had gradually nursed her back to health, but she had refused to eat much, and seemed to be sunk in despair. She repeated over and over that she could see no way out.

'Oh, aunt Helen, I adore Chris, you know that. But marry him! He's like my brother. He's the dearest, sweetest person and I'd die for him.'

'Oh, my dear, I'm sure that will never be necessary.' The only criticism Helen had of Eleanor was that she could sometimes be emotionally extravagant.

'But I love Guido! I love him so and Father will never countenance it. Oh, Aunt, I'm so scared and miserable and lonely.'

Helen thought of Hugh. She wished he were here to

help and counsel her. But he was not and she must try to decide what to do. She looked across to where Sylvia and Christopher were standing, croquet mallets in hand. They seemed to have settled their differences and were laughing together.

She glanced at her desk again and laid aside Enrico Domini's letter. She flicked through the invitations awaiting her attention and scrawled a 'yes' or a 'no' where applicable. Lady Roxborough's house party weekend in Devon was not to be missed. Yes. No one went to the Chevalier de Montaigne any more since René had insisted on putting his latest little *in'amorata* at the head of the dinner table dressed in the maid's uniform he liked her to wear. No. Tessa O'Brien Desmond, who gave enchanting masked balls in Cagnes-sur-Mer, wanted to visit in June with her daughter Rosalind. Yes. Archie Florand-Kyte begged to come in June and bring his chum, his bosom pal Freddie Lancing, and could they share a room? He also intended to bring his Siamese and his little peke Tasmin and enclosed a list of special requirements: what the cat liked to eat, and the peke's favourite fare (which was chicken, boiled in *bouillon*, with a little parsley added), and the information that he and Freddie were vegetarians and he hoped she would not forget. No!

She held her pen poised over the next letter, hovering between a "yes" and a 'no". It was from the Duca d'Abrizzio.

> . . . I knew your husband well, we were at Oxford together. I will be in London for the Season and hope to send my son Luciano to visit you. He is, I believe, more or less the same age as your own. I hope you will welcome him at Elm Court. I am sadly out of touch with the socially acceptable young in England and I will not lie to you: I am hoping my son, who in the past made an unfortunate attachment to a young lady in Sicily, will meet under your kind auspices a more suitable set of friends . . .

258

Which meant, she thought, that he was looking for a wife from the aristocracy for his son.

She had been going to refuse d'Abrizzio's request. She had not felt in the mood for visitors who were not old acquaintances. And Sylvia had a bunch of her friends coming down to stay and Helen would have her hands full with that social butterfly crowd.

Then a thought struck her. Visitors might be useful. Particularly the d'Abrizzio boy. He might take Eleanor out of herself. He was Italian, or at least Sicilian. She could insist that Eleanor help her out with him. The girl had a sense of duty. Luciano d'Abrizzio might be just the thing.

She looked out of the window again, then making a quick decision she took up her pen. Yes.

Finally she picked up the handful of letters addressed to Signor Guido Palucci, Via Lombardia, Roma, Italy. She groaned. If in the past she had resented the yoke Enrico Domini had forced upon her, she at least could assure herself that it had its basis in good. The good of Elm Court. She could tell herself that it was merely her pride that was hurt and she hated to be under an obligation to him. But by instructing her to confiscate Eleanor's letters to her lover, he was forcing her into a position of acting dishonourably and that went against her every instinct. Brought up at all costs to tell the truth, this suppression of her cousin's mail revolted her.

She looked sadly at the letters for a long time. Then, unlocking a small drawer of her *escritoire*, she put them carefully inside and relocked it. Then she covered her face with her hands and sat for a long time, alone and silent, listening to the voices of her children in the garden.

Chapter Thirteen

Minouche was crying. Big tears rolled down her cheeks. Far from spoiling her beauty, they made her look prettier than ever before and Mario was totally at her mercy.

'You must be nice to him, *chéri*,' she said, sniffing. 'You must. He is very important. Oh,' she waved her little hand, fluttering it about. 'I know *you* will be, one day. One day soon. You will be more important than anyone in America. But there is time, *mon amour*. Plenty of time. Lucca is old. He will not live forever. While he is alive, I beg you to be careful of him.'

It was what Lucca himself had said and sitting here on the bed, listening to Minouche, Mario conceded the wisdom of the argument. Yet there was a terrible urgency in him, an impatience, that goaded him on almost in spite of himelf.

'Yeah, yeah,' he said, looking at her. 'But that's not what upset you. You don' get excited about things like that. So Lucca gave me a talkin' to. So what? What is it, honey? Tell me. I can't bear to think of you upset.' He kissed her and she clung to him, suddenly fierce.

'Hey, hey, hey,' he said, disentangling himself, 'what's upsetting my girl? Hey? What?'

'Listen, Mario, I have to tell you something. When you're not there they talk, downstairs in the club. They forget I'm there. That I'm your girl.'

'They been rude to you? I'll sort them out . . .'

'No, Mario. It's just that I heard something ... something that frightened me.'

'What, baby?' He looked at her more closely without the eyes of desire and realised that her face was chalk white and her eyes wide with fear. He felt his skin prickle. Minouche was not the nervous type. She was never afraid. It must have been something really serious to upset her like this.

'What is it, baby?' he asked again.

She sat up in the big bed, naked. Usually with Mario, she was gloriously unself-conscious. Now she pulled the sheets up to her chin like a convent schoolgirl. The gesture surprised him so much that he sat back, alert as a cat, watching her.

'Mario, don't get angry, think about what I tell you.' She paused and he waited, tense and expectant. 'I think, *mon chéri*, there is a plot against you. I don't know for certain. It's not exactly clear to me.'

She fixed her large eyes on him. 'Beno was in the club last night. He said, "Mario tries to cross Lucca, he's dead." '

Mario laughed. 'That all? Jeez, we all know that Beno and Zucci say that alla the time. So what's new?'

'Will you listen? It all adds up. Beno says that, then the Ape says, "No. Lucca. *He's* dead. He's an old man, one foot in the grave." Your guy Corino says, "Two feet to look at him." They were shooting their mouths off, you know how they do. Little men talking big.'

He grunted. It never occurred to him that she might include him in that generalization. Then she looked at him again, a frown creasing her forehead.

'Well, then Moses comes in. He's standing listening, you know how he does? Smiling inside, not on his face.' Mario nodded. 'Well, he doesn't see me and he says quietly, "No. It's Mario's who's dead." Everyone looks at him. Surprised. He doesn't talk much, Moses. "How come?" someone says. "He's a dead man," says Moses. "Lucca goin' to blow him

261

away?" the Ape asks, laughing at him, not believing him. Moses shakes his head. "Naw," he says, "Lucca's not that stoopid. Lucca's clever. No. Mario's brother is on his way from the old country to do it for Lucca." '

Mario paled. Minouche leaned forward, peering at him. 'What does it mean, *chéri?* You never talk about your family. Your brother? What does it mean?'

'I dunno. I swear I dunno, sugar.'

'Tell me, Mario, I gotta know what he meant. I can't sleep. You gotta tell me everything.'

He shifted uneasily and she went on, 'Mario, I told you how I killed Aubin. I trusted you with that. My father couldn't be worse than that. Don't you trust me?'

He looked into her worried face and relaxed a little. 'Course I trust ya, baby. Who else could I trust if I couldn't trust you? Well, see, let me tell ya. I left Sicily. I ran away. I caused some trouble. Yeah. OK. But nuthin' to *kill* me for. Shit, I swear it.'

'Tell me, *chéri,*' she urged. 'Tell me everything.'

He thought back, remembering the sunny groves, the lemon and olive trees. It was another world, a world he had put behind him in the city. He thought of his father, of his sisters and brothers. Which brother, for Chrissakes? And kill him? Why? Because of Francesca? He shook his head. Only Maria gave him pause. He did not allow himself to think of his mother.

He told Minouche the whole story. How he had planned it all. Planned to steal the money. His father's money. How he told his family about Francesca and the Duke's son in the woods, watched them leave the house. How he had gone to the d'Abrizzios and informed the Duke of his son's rendezvous.

'Why did you do that?' she asked.

He shrugged. 'Don't remember,' he said. 'Seemed important at the time.'

'Then you went back and stole the money?' Minouche

262

said it matter-of-factly. That was the logical thing to do, and she was totally on his side.

'No,' he said. 'Well, yes. But no. See, that's what I *planned*. And that's what I thought I did. I went back to the farmhouse and I took the pouch the old man kept the gold in. Only it was in the wrong place. I didn' hang about. Got outa there fast.'

It was another world. He tried to recall it. The sun, the countryside, the farmhouse kitchen, the panic. The feeling that someone was watching him.

'Coulda been someone watchin',' he said now. 'Anyhow, in Palermo I found the pouch was empty. Full of stones. No gold, no bank notes. Just pebbles. Jeez, I was furious!' He remembered his rage and frustration. Having to go cap in hand to Sandro Brancusi for help. Travelling like an animal, going hungry often as not. Until he made contact in New York with Luigi Stroza, who sent him right down to Lucca in Chicago. To Lucca and prosperity. Remembering how it had been then, he was suddenly ashamed of his greed. He could lose everything. Go back to that world of poverty he had sworn never to return to. He had hated the desperation he had felt, the hunger gnawing in his belly, the fifteen cent flophouses, sleezy joints off Times Square. He had forgotten how lucky he had been. Forgotten too those first heady days of affluence, and the gratitude he had felt to Lucca for giving him an opportunity.

'So you see, no one has any reason to *kill* me,' he said to Minouche.

'If you had got the money, would they then? Think they should kill you, I mean?' Minouche asked.

He shrugged. 'Yeah, I suppose.' he said. 'I dunno.' He thought of Giuseppe, of his father's probable rage at losing his savings. 'I suppose,' he said again. 'But I didn't.'

'Someone else might have taken the money, *chéri*. Someone who was watching you and guessed your plan.'

'Think so?' He looked perplexed. 'You mean, someone

else took the gold and left the pouch full of stones for me? But who? Who would do that?'

'I dunno, Mario, how would I know? But perhaps someone who was watching took the money and left the pouch for you, and that someone let the family think it was you who stole the money.'

'But why would they think that?'

'Because you were the only one who ran away.' Then she continued, 'I'm just trying to find a reason for your brother to want to kill you.'

'Aw, maybe you imagined the conversation. Maybe . . .'

She shook her head. 'No, *chéri*, I do not think so. Not at all. Why would I imagine someone talking about your brother?' She touched her forehead. 'And if he is coming to kill you, then it is because they think you did it.'

He sat very still, his face drained of colour. 'It is vendetta,' he said.

She knelt up in the bed and put her hands on his shoulders. 'Listen, *chéri*, please. You must find out what happened back in the old country. You must! You gotta protect yourself.'

He did not want to do that. He did not want to think about Sicily if he could possibly avoid it. He had severed all contact with the land of his birth.

He could ask Luigi Stroza. The man might know. Perhaps he and Minouche could work out a letter. He would do that then stop worrying about it.

Besides, he told himself, none of his brothers would actually kill him, even if they thought he had stolen the money. Not for that. He suddenly saw them larking about pushing each other, rough and tumbling it under the pump after work, laughing as they splashed about, shouting to each other. He saw their faces: Guido, Marcello, Paulo. No, they would never try to kill, it was not in their nature. He was the only member of his family capable of killing. He smiled. Then he thought of his father. Giuseppe had probably urged them to vendetta. He grinned. The little man would be beside himself with rage when he found the money gone. Shit! But kill his own son? Never. Mario thought of them again. Paulo who wanted to become a priest? Priests did not kill. Guido? Naw. He was gentle as a lamb, and kind. He loved Mario. Marcello? Never. Marcello was a sweetheart, as Lucca would say. No killer instinct in him.

It was all very confusing and Mario made a snap decision. He would change his attitude to Lucca. Go see him. Tell the old man how grateful he was, tell him about the rumour. Let him know he knew, and lick the old man's ass a little.

Sure, that was what he would do. He looked into Minouche's anxious eyes.

'Sugar, I love you,' he said in a rare burst of tenderness. 'You are somethin' special. Somethin' else.'

She smiled back at him. 'Oh, Mario, I love you too. I love you so much, I'd die if anything happened to you.'

'Hey, hey, what's gonna happen to me? Nuthen, sugar. Listen, I made up my mind. Tomorrow – no, tomorrow's Sunday – Monday, Monday for sure, I'll go see Lucca, 'pologise. Say I'm grateful to the old guy. How's that?'

She threw her arms around him. 'Mario, that would be wonderful! Now don't forget – Monday.'

'Monday, sugar, for sure.'

But by Monday all thoughts of his family, of Lucca and of death threats had evaporated. Mario was far too busy to keep his promise.

Chapter Fourteen

Christopher Wylde stood beside Eleanor. She sat next to the open window, dressed in a satin negligee. Light, gauzy curtains fluttered and the breeze carried the scent of lilac into the room.

'Will you marry me, Eleanor?' he asked, and as she did not answer him he continued, 'I love you terribly, you know that. We would have a jolly time together, you and I.'

His eyes were anxiously pleading, like a little boy's trying to persuade a stern parent to let him stay up late.

'And it would suit everyone, Christopher, isn't that so? Everyone except me.' She turned her face away from him, knowing she was being unfair.

'You know I didn't mean that, Eleanor,' he said. 'It's just that we've always got on well, haven't we? And you've always loved Elm Court.'

She could hear a warbler outside and see the top of the giant copper beech. On the table an arrangement of cultivated bluebells, purple irises and pale mauve stock seduced the eye and ravished her sense of beauty. It was so carelessly exquisite and English. Like the scent of lilac that filled the room.

Her room. For as long as she could remember she had loved this room. Elm Court had meant security to her, a kind of timeless serenity, a tranquil way of life that soothed and calmed her. To live here forever with dear, dear Christopher as the next Lady Wylde was an offer not to be taken lightly. It was very tempting.

She was aware of the fact that Christopher would eventually marry, if not herself, then someone else, and that someone could destroy forever her standing at Elm Court. The next Lady Wylde might not be too friendly towards her husband's ex-girlfriend, might not relish having her spending time there, keeping her room prepared, ready for use.

Eleanor knew her father helped with the finances and upkeep of Elm Court. She did not know to what extent but shrewdly sensed that his support was considerable. The estate was not producing any income. Instead, with constant grooming and tending, it ate up huge sums of money that could have no other source than her father. There would always be a place for her here unless Christopher married an heiress, but Eleanor knew that with her refusal the atmosphere she valued so much would be changed irrevocably. She loved the predictability of life here, the feeling of being at home and at ease, the confidence she had in her aunt's love. She did not want it to change.

If she did not marry Christopher, then that special haven that was exclusively hers would vanish. One way or another it would disappear. Another woman here in their midst would stir everything up and alter it forever. Even a sympathetic wife, a girl who was fond of Eleanor, loved her even, like Francesca Palucci, would change things.

If she accepted Christopher's proposal she could be sure of this refuge forever. Safe and secure. But she was only twenty-one. Her whole life was ahead of her, and out there somewhere was Guido Palucci.

Far from curing her of her passion as her father had hoped, separation had sharpened her desire and longing for her lover. She had had time to think and assess her situation. The memory of her father's brutal high-handedness, her journey by yacht to England, her illegal

267

entry (although she had a perfectly legal passport, she assumed her father thought she might make trouble at passport control) and nightmare journey by fast car to Elm Court, appalled her. She was outraged by the treatment she'd suffered at his hands, and had come, slowly and painfully, to deduce that her father was a ruthless man with power over the Wyldes. She knew he wanted her to marry Christopher. She knew also that she was going to have to just be as ruthless to live her own life and do as she wished which was to marry Guido Palucci. She had finally come to the realization that the sheltered world of Elm Court would be well lost for his sake.

She spent hours thinking about him and writing to him. She was fairly sure her letters were not reaching him, but left that to Aunt Helen's tender conscience. She knew her cousin, whom she called Aunt, well enough to realize that if she was posting the letters Eleanor had given her, she would suffer dreadfully for her own actions.

Eleanor looked at Christopher. He was so sweet and gentle, his head full of poetry and an intense love of nature. His eyes were the kindest she had ever seen and she knew he would always treat her well, as she remembered Uncle Hugh had treated Aunt Helen.

'Dearest Christopher . . .'

'You're going to refuse, I know,' he said fatalistically, looking at her steadily. 'How do I know?' he asked, and sat down beside her. 'How the hell do I know?'

She smiled. 'You know me too well, Christopher. We have always been close. Too close perhaps. I feel about you – love you – like a brother, and I suspect you love me like a sister. You are very dear to me, Chris, but you must realize I'm in love with someone else.'

He looked up, surprised. 'Who?'

'No one you know.'

'There's a problem?'

'My father does not approve, and no one disobeys my

268

father.'

'Why?'

'You always were one to get to the point, eh, Chris? The man I love is a working man. A Sicilian fruit grower.'

'Hell's bells, that's where the money is these days, Eleanor! Don't tell me your father is a snob?'

'Of course he is. And it has nothing to do with money. If Guido were the penniless Count something or other, that would be OK. But the man is not, and I love him. Nevertheless Papa wants me to marry you.'

'Can't say I don't agree with him,' Christopher said ruefully. 'So obviously the thing to do now is get your Sicilian here. Put him among the gents and watch the scales fall from your eyes as he lets himself down.' His eyes twinkled. 'That's what they do in the story books.'

'Christopher, you're outrageous!'

'But I made you laugh, and that's the first time you have done since you came home.'

'I wish I was in love with you,' she said. 'You're so nice and kind and comfortable.'

'How awful,' he said. 'But you know, Eleanor, I'd settle for less.' He caught her eye. 'If you were not in love with someone else. That's why I think it would be a good idea for him – your Sicilian – to come here. No use having you yearning for him all over the place. Situation should be resolved.'

'Papa would never allow it.'

'Your papa need not know.'

'There's something else, Chris. You may not like this.'

'I don't like any of it,' he said, 'but what?'

'I don't think Aunt Helen is sending my letters to Guido in Rome. I think she is keeping them because Father told her to.'

She looked at Christopher. He was staring out of the window. His blond hair fell over his eyes but she could see he was furious.

269

'That is monstrous! Dear God.'

'I knew you wouldn't like it,' she said, crossing her legs and soothing her dressing gown over her knees.

'No, I don't. But I believe you. It's your father's fault, blackmailing her.'

'He's my father, Christopher. And she's your mother. There are faults on both sides. No one is perfect.'

'I suppose you're right.'

'Besides, I can understand them both. Though not my father's violence. It was excessive, drugging me and smuggling me here on a boat.'

Christopher looked up, amazed. 'He did that? Mother never told me.'

'I'm not sure she knew.'

'Good God! I always knew he was a buccaneer but . . .'

She laid a hand on his arm. 'Don't say anything derogatory, Chris, there's a dear.'

He shook his head, looking at her with a perplexed smile on his face. 'Italians!' he said.

'Oh, come on, Chris, the English behave just as badly to each other in cases like this.'

'But not quite so dramatically, so operatically.'

'Well, as I said, I understand them, your mother and my father. Papa came from humble beginnings. He is ambitious for me. He is afraid I'll let him down after the wonderful advantages and education he has given me. What my father is afraid of is ridicule. It is what most self-made men fear. And if I married someone like Guido Palucci, he would be the laughing stock of Rome. Poor man! It is so silly to care, but it's too late to change him. Now if I marry *you*, Christopher, that is a different story. When they call him an upstart and despise him because they are jealous of his wealth, he can say, "My daughter is, or will be, Lady Wylde." '

She looked at him, shaking her soft hair, her eyes troubled.

270

'And Mother?' he asked. 'What excuse have you for her?'

'Elm Court. This place. This lovely, lovely place.' She got up and stared out of the window. The satin clung to her tall slim body. She leaned out, sniffing the breeze. 'We used to argue at school about countries being worth dying for. The English girls were always so patriotic. The Italians, I think, value life more. Life or property, that's what it came down to. And I thought I would run away if there was a war. Run away from violence and bloodshed, destruction and death. No matter what the ideal. Go to some far-off peaceful place. I would not miss England or Italy, never seeing them again. And then I thought of Elm Court, and I was not so sure.'

She looked over her shoulder at him. 'Your mother would consider her life well lost for this place. And that is my father's hold upon her. The struggle is between doing as he dictates or losing Elm Court. It's got nothing to do with me at all. My letters to Guido are incidental.'

'You are very magnanimous.'

'No, I am realistic.'

'Well, I still think my idea is best.'

'Papa would not allow it.'

'He need never know.'

'You think it possible then?' She turned away. Her back was to the light so he could not see her face, but he could sense the hope. She gave it off like incense. He nodded.

'Oh, yes. You have his address?'

'In Rome. Yes.'

'Would he . . .' Christopher paused a second then continued, 'Could he afford to . . .'

'Travel? He never gave me the impression of being short of money.' She smiled. 'Although I'm afraid it is Father who financed him and his sister.' She sighed. 'We never talked about money. But I imagine he could afford to travel, or could find a way.'

Christopher gave a sad laugh. 'You must really be in love.'

She came away from the window and leant over him. 'Oh, I am. I am.'

'Enough to live with him in Sicily?'

'Oh, yes. Anywhere, Sicily, Timbuctoo, anywhere.'

He looked up at her, seeing the passion in her eyes, realizing she meant what she said.

'Then I suggest you write to him, asking him here.' As she began to protest, he said, 'Mother cannot object. She knows nothing about it. We can put him up in the inn in the village if things get sticky. I'll take full responsibility.'

She hugged him, eyes full of gratitude, and he could only wish that her embrace was because she loved him.

'Do think, Eleanor, about what I could offer you. This house. This peaceful life. Don't underestimate it. And I am so fond of you. So very fond.'

She nodded, bent down and kissed him, and he felt her tears on his cheek.

~~~~~~

Guido did not immediately leave for America. Francesca insisted that he first recover completely from the beating he had received. He was still perturbed by Eleanor's disappearance.

'I will find her! I must!' he reiterated as he paced his room instead of lying down. He hit his fist into the palm of his hand. 'I'll find her,' he kept saying. 'I will. I will.'

Francesca heard him. Bringing him something to eat she listened to his footsteps pacing up and down, up and down his room, and the desperation in his voice.

Guido had thought that Eleanor might come to the Via Lombardia. He never stopped hoping. He had put off telling Francesca about Mario being in America. Sick at heart, full of disgust and anger at his brother for what he had done, he nevertheless did not want to execute him.

272

He didn't remember when he first became aware that he did not want to kill Mario. Perhaps love had made him soft. He hated Mario and what he had done, but the realization had grown upon him little by little that killing his brother was not the answer and that he, Guido, was not a killer. Yet he knew too that he had to do it. Gina and Lombardo had sent him to Rome for exactly that purpose. Everyone expected it of him. Gina had written:

Never forget that Mario caused our mother's death as assuredly as he caused Father's, and that it is his fault that our father and mother are not with us today, and that our family is scattered over the earth. Take care of each other. Please give Paulo our love. How is he taking it? We pray for him constantly. I love you and miss you both. Lombardo sends his greetings and asks that you let him know if you need anything. We are making ends meet here. Serena is very disturbed. We are worried about her. She suffers and has black spells when she sits and stares at the wall for days. She misses our mother dreadfully, and cannot accept her death. It was Serena, as you know, who found Mama with her wrists slashed, and I'm sad to say she has never really recovered.

It is a great comedown for us here and we do not know what will happen. The Duke is still away, the land goes untended, the fruit unharvested. It is pitiful to see. Of course there is pilfering, but you know Lombardo. He is far too honourable to stoop to such a mean action. Also he is too angry. You would cry at our humiliation if you were here. However, Cecilia is happy so there is some good. She is to marry Filipo Canona. It is a suitable match and Tomaso is as pleased as we are that our families will be joined. He gives Lombardo work and is glad to have his help.

There was a lot more. Reading, Francesca was assailed by waves of nostalgia and sadness.

They had forgotten Paulo. Forgotten to tell him about

273

Maria's death. So much had happened: Guido's beating, Eleanor's disappearence, their own shock at the news. They wanted to tell him personally, so, once more, made the journey to the monastery.

They took the train down the Appia Antica. They got off and trailed up the steep incline. The Angelus rang as they walked up the dusty hill. Paulo was paler, thinner, more nervous than ever. He stared at Francesca with burning eyes as she broke the news. His face seemed to fall apart. His mouth hung open, his eyes protruded from their sockets, and he fell to the ground in some kind of fit.

Francesca, terribly frightened, pulled the bell. Brother Alonso, the fat little brother they had seen the last time, came in with another priest. Brother Sylvestro was tall and swarthy. He kept tutting, making sympathetic noises in his throat as he tended Paulo who lay on the stone floor, his body jerking, his lips flecked with foam.

'*Jesu Maria*, help him, the poor man.'

The brother put a bar into Paulo's mouth. 'It's to stop him biting his tongue,' he said and smiled reassuringly at them. His eyes were calm and his face kindly. The little brother said, 'He's done this before.' He sounded reproving.

'Ah, now, Brother Alonso, he does not do it deliberately,' the dark Brother Sylvestro said.

'We have been frightened for his sanity,' Brother Alonso continued, unperturbed.

'We had to tell him,' Francesca whispered. 'Our mother died.'

Brother Sylvestro tutted again. 'It's a terrible thing, the loss of a mother,' he said. 'It must have come as a dreadful shock.'

'Nevertheless, he is supposed to have renounced the world,' Brother Alonso sounded waspish, 'and that includes family. His family should now be Christ Our Lord and the Communion of Saints.'

Brother Sylvestro shook his head. He was cradling Paulo in his arms.

'I will give him some laudanum. That will quiet him. Dear Brother Alonso, I only hope Our Dear Lord is more merciful than you, otherwise there is no hope for any of us.' He waited until two lay brothers arrived and lifted Paulo up to carry him away.

'We'll let you have news of your brother, Signore Palucci, Signorina. Please try not to worry about him.'

They had to be content with that. But two days later they got a letter from the Superior of the monastery informing them that Paulo had disappeared and begging them to be in touch if he contacted them, 'for we are naturally anxious about our dear brother who was ill and suffering from a fevered brain and in no condition to go anywhere. We will not rest until we know he is all right. Yours in Christ Our Saviour . . .'

Two days after that Signora Merciano asked them to leave. 'I run a respectable house here and you have been behaving in a most peculiar way,' she said, bursting with righteous indignation. 'Having visitors in your room when you know it is forbidden. Getting beaten up. Thugs coming to my door. Do you think I don't know a thug when I see one? And now staying in all the time. Hiding, more like! From what, I'd like to know? Something fishy. So you have to go. I'll give you till the end of the month, then out.'

The end of the month was a week away. Then Guido got the letter from Eleanor.

~~~~~~

He was ecstatic. Francesca leant over his shoulder as he read the letter.

'Her aunt – well, cousin really – she is sustained, or is it subsidised, by Enrico Domini and did not send the letters Eleanor wrote to me since we have been separated,' he said. 'She's with her mother's family in England, at Elm Court. She wants us to come! Listen, here it is: "Tell Francesca the guest list for next month includes a charming visitor from Sicily, Luciano d'Abrizzio."'

He looked up at his sister. She was so pale he thought she would faint.

'Luciano. Luciano will be there?' she asked weakly.

He nodded. 'So Eleanor says.'

'I don't believe it.' She sat down suddenly, staring at him in shock.

'Well, Francesca, what now?'

'What do you mean, what now? We must go. The two of us. To England. Oh, Guido, I feel so strange, so nervous. Luciano! I've thought of him so often. Suppose he does not love me any more? Suppose he's changed?'

He put his arm around her shoulders. 'Then you'll find out. Don't worry, my dearest, it will be all right.'

She clung to him. She relied on his strength. Looking up at him to say something, she was struck by the remote expression on his face. Guido had come to a decision. He was very clear now what he had to do.

The way it had happened, he thought, was a miracle. He would send Francesca to England. She would take care of Eleanor for him. She would explain that Guido had to complete his mission in America before he could come for Eleanor. He would do what he had to do and no more nerves. He thought of his mother's suicide. He thought of the despair she must have felt and the loneliness. And Paulo, lost and alone, running away from his monastery. Their pain had to be avenged.

Gently, he turned Francesca's face to his. 'You go to England alone. I'll go to America.'

She looked crestfallen. 'Oh, Guido, why? Can't you come to England first? You could spend a little time with us and help me. I need you. I'm not so very brave by myself. Eleanor must be desperate to see you.'

'Don't you realize how much I want to go? How much I want to see her? But if I go to my love, I may never get the strength to leave her and do what has to be done. I have to deal with Mario first. I have to destroy him.' He took her hand. She watched him, listening carefully.

'Francesca, this is something I'll say only to you. Only to you can I admit that I am afraid and sick to my soul about this business.'

'Why, Guido?' she asked, wide-eyed. 'What on earth do you mean?'

'Don't condemn me, Francesca.' She began to reassure him but he continued, 'I don't . . . how can I say it?' He sat down on the bed and put his hands over his face.

She touched his hair, caressing the soft, unfashionably long dark waves. 'You don't want to kill him, is that it, Guido?' she said softly.

He looked up quickly. 'How did you know?'

'Oh, Guido, I always knew,' she said. 'We both hate what Mario has done. We both suffered. Our family has been destroyed. It will never be the same again. Ever. And it's easy to stand and swear revenge. It's easy to *say*, in the heat of righteous rage, that you will kill your brother. It's quite another thing actually to do it.'

'But it has to be done.'

She sighed. 'I suppose so.'

'Everyone expects it. I owe it to the memory of Mother and Father. I owe it to Serena and Marcello and Paulo. I owe it to you, my darling Francesca.'

He put his arms around her waist and laid his head near her heart.

'If it was up to me, I would tell you to forget it. But it is not. There are the others,' she said.

'Yes.'

They were silent a moment.

'You haven't said anything about Paulo,' she whispered.

'I know, Francesca. I've thought and thought about him.

His face has haunted my mind. But no matter how hard I try, I can't come up with a solution.' He paused and rubbed his forehead. 'What can we do?' he asked. 'We can't scour Rome for him. Where could we look? He could be anywhere. He may not even be in Rome.'

'It's true. Oh Lord, Guido, will our troubles never end?'

'I hope so. Sometime in the future it will all be over. But I think that will only happen when Mario is dealt with. I think that will be our catharsis. I pray it will.'

'So you think we should let Paulo go and deal with Mario?'

He nodded. 'Yes. We could spend the rest of our lives looking for Paulo. But he'll know when we deal with Mario. He'll know. I don't know how, but I'm sure of that.'

She looked at him, her lips trembling, 'It seems callous,' she said. 'But I know you are right. Anyhow,' she sighed, 'we have little choice but to leave Rome now.'

'Yes, it is time.'

~~~~~~

Paulo looked about him fearfully. He remembered Fra Anselmo's words, 'Perfect love casteth our fear.'

Fra Anselmo was talking about the love of God. If you truly loved God, trusted him, believed the tenets of the faith, you were not afraid. It was that simple. Neither did you hate. All mankind had the face of God. If you loved God you therefore loved mankind.

Paulo had once loved God like that. But it was gone. The rock that he had held on to all his life had disintegrated. The sure knowledge that had sustained him, that was the very core of his existence, staunch and unshakable, suddenly seemed unreliable.

The Jesuits called it faith. They told him to cherish it, that it was a gift more precious that gold. People who didn't take care of the gift lost it forever, and that was the most terrible thing that could happen. You were in the desert then, lost, thirsty and terribly alone.

It was true, what they had told him. He had lost his faith and was now in a mental and spiritual wilderness. He felt as if he was in an angry sea with nothing to cling to, no raft, no plank, no rock. Tempest-tossed.

He blamed a lot of people for his predicament. He blamed his fellow seminarians for being imperfect, fallible people. They gossiped, they complained, they could be bad-tempered, and he sometimes wondered how they could call themselves Christians, let alone aim to become priests.

Fra Anselmo said that as long as they tried, it was enough, but in Paulo's opinion their attempts were feeble, their ardour half-baked.

He blamed Giuseppe. How dare he commit suicide, when the church expressly forbade it? His father, who had been his model, a truthful, honourable man, a man he could look up to with not a stain on his character, had let him down by committing this terrible act. Giuseppe had been a churchgoer, he could not claim ignorance, Paulo reasoned; he had been at the services and heard the sermons when Fra Bartholomeo spoke of the 'unforgivable sin'. How could he then do such a thing?

He blamed Maria for following her husband's example, but he could not condemn her as much. She was a woman. Signora Palucci would naturally be influenced by her husband. He was the head, the master of the household, his example should be followed, therefore she could not be held fully responsible for her actions.

Nevertheless, she had betrayed everything they had believed in all those years, everything his father had preached. How could his parents, who had said their rosaries nightly, gone to mass and communion on Sunday, lived by the tenets of the Church and brought up their children to do the same, how could they betray them like this, at the first sign of trouble? Their about face had left Paulo doubting, and frightened. It had undermined his

279

security, the very foundation of his life, and left him first bewildered, then resentful, then full of hatred.

He had lost his vocation. Alone in his nightmare, isolated from all he knew and loved, he wandered the streets rootless, homeless, muttering to himself. He slept in doorways. He shared wine and meths cocktails with alcoholics and tramps. He drifted, trying to make sense of life, trying to find a focus, a reason for his existence. He moved in a miasma of unease. He shrugged, he twitched, he shifted within his dirty jacket, he scratched his unshaven face. And in his head the recriminations, accusations and causes of resentment went round and round and round in a whirl.

At last, from the debris cluttering his mind, he plucked out an idea which centred him, gave him a purpose.

He would go and see Enrico Domini. Tomaso Canona had told them to go and see Enrico Domini in Rome. Francesca and Guido had gone to see the man. Perhaps he had an answer. Perhaps he could help.

All Paulo knew was that he had to have a purpose. He had to have an aim. Perhaps Enrico Domini could guide him now. Perhaps.

Chapter Fifteen

New York sweltered in a heatwave. The city simmered under a blanket of suffocating sultriness. The tall buildings trapped the citizens in a torrid, airless cauldron from which there was no escape. Businessmen were doubly stifled in their high collars, their obligatory jackets and trousers covering flesh that ached to be bared.

Luigi Stroza sat behind his desk on the tenth floor of a building near the junction of Madison and Sixty-fifth. He pressed his handkerchief to his neck. A moment later it was wringing wet.

The buzzer startled him

'Yes,' he barked.

'Mr Palucci is here to see you, sir,' his secretary's calm voice informed him.

'Gimme a moment, Pammy.'

He went to the closet off his office where he kept a change of linen. He took off his by now damp shirt and went into the adjoining bathroom where he splashed himself, dabbed himself dry and put on a fresh shirt. He carefully combed his black hair, liberally sprinkled with silver. Pleased with how he looked, he slipped into his striped linen jacket and resumed his place behind his desk. He pressed the buzzer, the signal for Pammy Delacey to send in his visitor.

An urbane and sophisticated man, he viewed violence as the last resort of the stupid. He was a supremely successful financier and life amused him. He liked nothing better than to watch the petty vanities of his friends in the power struggle they all seemed to be engaged in. He was tolerant and charming and completely ruthless.

He wondered what Palucci wanted. It was nearly a year now since they had first became acquainted. Marcello had come into his office, sent by Tomaso Canona for Stroza's protection, and help, and of course eventually to be put to some use in their branch of the Organization. Marcello, he remembered thinking, was a big improvement on his brother Mario whom he had met a short time previously. Both were handsome, but whereas Mario was brash and a little vulgar with his camel coat, his two-tone shoes and greased back hair, Marcello was elegant, well-groomed, and had the refined manners and sculpted good looks of a gentleman. He would look quite at home at a tennis party in the Hamptons or on a yacht on Long Island Sound, whereas his brother belonged firmly in the land of gangsters; the clubs, the fights, the sleaze. Mario also had the thug's lack of vision, a closed mind, the erroneous conviction that violence alone could make him powerful, whereas his brother was intelligent rather than sharp and thought things through before he acted.

Mario had come, cap in hand, green from the boat-trip, penniless and hungry for action, greedy for power, a young man running. Luigi had sent him to Lucca. Let the old war-horse deal with all that raw energy, put it to work where it belonged. Lucca was good with violence, could control the seamier side of life.

Luigi Stroza's environment was finance. He moved in a sophisticated world peopled by financiers, senators and diplomats.

When Marcello Palucci had come to him soon after Mario's departure for Chicago, Luigi had been surprised. The difference between the brothers, he thought to himself, was like Park Avenue and the Bronx. And

282

Marcello had money. Money enough to suggest a hefty investment in a diamond mine in Africa that Luigi Stroza heartily approved of and that made him wonder if the boy knew of his own interests in the African diamond mine, becoming minute by minute more certain that he did. Those light hazel eyes were shrewd and watchful. This boy held his considerable energy in check. It was fully under control and channelled exactly where Marcello Palucci wanted it to go.

They had made money together over the next few months – a considerable fortune. The diamond mine had given them a gigantic initial turnover and they sold before trouble with the miners caused its closure. Then Marcello came up with another investment idea: an oilwell in Nevada. Once more they made a spectacular killing and yet again sold out before the gush became a trickle and the trickle became baked earth. A rubber plantation in the Congo and a coffee plantation just outside Buenos Aires were still yielding a healthy profit and Luigi Stroza congratulated himself on his initial assessment of Marcello Palucci and his association with the Sicilian, which had benefited him enormously and increased his already considerable wealth. He had watched Marcello Palucci with interest as he went from strength to strength, observed him buy the house just off Fifth Avenue and Eighty-fifth Street, right next door to one of the oldest families in New York. Mott Street wasn't good enough for him. Luigi watched him decorate it in exquisite taste, with help of course, watched him become the man of the moment.

The boy was welcome everywhere. Doors were opened for him that should have remained closed. Society welcomed him because of his money, because of his astonishing good looks, and because of his charm, firmly closing their eyes to his doubtful past. The man was ruthless but he hid it behind a buccaneer grin. Women adored him. But Stroza had reservations. He might admire Marcello and take advantage of his business acumen but he was intensely jealous and resented the young man's good looks and charm, the ease with which he achieved his aims. Stroza decided he would encourage Marcello for the moment, reserving the right to swat him like a fly when the time was right. In the cut-throat world they both inhabited it was wise to keep your eyes on the man behind you.

He walked into the room and Luigi leapt to his feet. Marcello came around the desk and shook his hand, smiling broadly.

'Hey, hey, good to see you, Marcello. You look great. Just great.' He indicated the wide leather chair in front of his desk. 'Sit down, relax. It's like a furnace out there.' He glanced out of the window to the narrow canyon of a street below. 'Tell me, to what do I owe the honour?'

Marcello sat down, drew up the legs of his trousers at the knee, and contemplated the toes of his hand-made shoes. He looked cool and self-contained.

For a moment he did not say anything.

'Got another piece of insider information?' Luigi asked, tapping his nose.

Marcello shook his head. 'No, it's not business, Luigi. It's personal.'

Luigi Stroza waited. This was how to get a handle on a man. Let him come to you with his problems, and listen. Don't interrupt.

'See, I heard, contradict me if I'm wrong, but I heard there's a contract out on my brother Mario.'

Luigi feigned surprise. He opened his mouth to speak but Marcello said quickly, 'Cut the crap, Luigi, and don't try to play games with me.'

'Marcello, Marcello, why would I play games?' he asked mildly.

Marcello shook his head. 'OK. If that's the way you want it, Luigi . . .'

Marcello stood up and went and stared out of the plate glass window. It made you feel like God to be up here, so high, looking down on the ants crawling about far below. That was the trouble, Luigi once told Marcello. 'Some of the guys, up in the big offices, they get to think they really are God. They get too big for their boots. They have nowhere to go but down. Don't ever get like that. You'll be dead meat if you do.' Now he watched Marcello intently.

'See Luigi, I heard Salvatore Lucca in Chicago has given his blessing to my brother Mario's execution.'

'Who said so?'

'Never mind who. The source was impeccable. They said Guido was coming from Italy to kill Mario. Said it was vendetta.'

'OK, suppose you're right, Marcello. What's the problem?'

'Guido is comin' to kill the wrong guy.'

Luigi could not see Marcello's face. He was looking out of the window, his back still turned.

'How come?' Luigi asked. 'Story is Mario stole from the family. Caused the death of your father. Something like that.' He spoke softly, fascinated by the conversation, afraid of Marcello suddenly clamming up on him.

'Well, they got the wrong guy, as I said.'

'You mean it wasn't Mario who took the family savings, Marcello?'

Still with his back to Luigi, Marcello nodded.

'Then who was it?'

'That is neither here nor there.' Marcello turned and looked at Luigi. 'What is important is that Guido is stopped.'

Luigi spread his hands. 'How can that be accomplished?' he asked innocently.

'I don't know and I don't care, but you'll have it done, understand?'

The expression in those light eyes frightened Luigi and he was not easily scared.

285

'I'm not too sure I can, Marcello. Have it stopped. No one is in touch with Guido. How can . . .'

'The whole of Chicago is on the lookout for him,' Marcello said tersely. 'You get word.' He banged his fist on Luigi's desk but his voice was a whisper. 'You do it,' he said. He pointed his finger at Luigi and stood silent a moment, looking at him. Then he turned and left the office.

~~~~~~

Marcello walked up Madison, on his way home. He had a luncheon appointment and wanted to change. How the hell Luigi Stroza managed to look so cool with the temperature 90 degrees in the shade he'd never know. Even the cooling system going full blast didn't account for how unruffled the guy looked.

The heat simmered around him, causing his clothes to stick to his body. Shit! Movement was accelerating his pulse-beat, and why the hell was he walking? He had not realized how disturbed he was by the interview with Stroza. He hailed a cab even though he lived only a few blocks away. The taxi smelled of stale cigarette smoke and he wrinkled his nose in distaste and noticed that his hands were shaking. He leaned forward.

'Go round the Park,' he said to the driver who swung the cab left on to Park and drove down Fifth, turning right at the Plaza.

Marcello took off his jacket and dabbed his face with his handkerchief. He had put Sicily very firmly behind him since he arrived in the United States. He had not wanted to dwell on his father's death. He laughed mirthlessly every time he thought how Mario must have felt, bicycling into Palermo and discovering a pouchful of stones.

Mario couldn't come back. Even when he found he had no money, he still had to go on. He had set up such a complicated scenario. He was the one responsible for

286

Francesca's heartbreak and their father's loss of face. Marcello had excused himself over and over again on the grounds that if he had not taken the gold from the pouch, and, like the fairy-tale, replaced it with stones, Mario would have gone off with the money anyway. The result would have been the same. But persuading himself that this theory was *bona fide* was quite another matter. He squirmed under the weight of his own arguments, his mind too clear-sighted not to see the holes in it.

He told himself that he had seen his opportunity and seized it. Which was true. It was his special forte, seizing opportunities. Mario had set it all up. He had seen Mario that night, rutting with Amelia in the doorway like an animal. Marcello had been coming home from a very profitable game of cards in the village but he hung back when he saw the figures of his brother and the servant in the shadows. He waited, saw the light behind the window, saw Mario push Amelia away, saw her go to the grandfather's rocking-chair and sit in it, saw Mario draw back as Giuseppe looked out and laughed, then closed the door of the farmhouse.

Marcello knew what that meant. Papa would count his gold. Ambitious as Marcello was, it had never occurred to him to steal his father's money, but he knew his brother and, as he watched from a distance, he sensed as if he were inside Mario's mind, his discovery of his father's hiding place for the gold and his decision to take it.

Marcello had shivered at the enormity of Mario's greed, at the lengths he was prepared to go to.

He watched his brother closely. He saw him speak to Tomaso Canona and knew what that was all about. Canona had given him, Marcello, the same names, just in case. He was immediately alert when Mario raised the hue and cry over Francesca and waited behind to see what would happen.

They all went to the woods. He could imagine the scene.

He did not need to be there to see Francesca's heartbreak, Giuseppe's shame. Marcello was very sorry for Francesca and his father, but what could he do?

He had known about the love affair. Everyone knew about Francesca and Luciano's assignations except Maria and Giuseppe and the Duke. No one would say anything or condemn them unless they were found out. That was the greatest sin, Marcello knew, being found out, and he realised instantly that Mario would be found out and he would not, for he knew now what he would do.

He had watched Mario ride up the hill to the *palazzo* and come down again, his feet sticking out before him, free-wheeling down the steep incline in the sun, his face a mask of triumph. He guessed what Mario's next act would be.

As fast as he could, Marcello had slipped down to the kitchen door. Waving at Grandfather, he had picked up a fistful of smooth stones. He returned to the kitchen, took out the wrong brick and could not find the pouch. He took out the other one, found and removed the pouch. He took the coins and notes and replaced them with stones and put the pouch back into the wall, but must have put it in the wrong hiding place. Then he went up to his room and waited.

He heard Mario in the kitchen and saw his consternation when he could not find the pouch in the correct niche, then his relief when he located it. Mario left the kitchen and Marcello watched from his bedroom window as his brother pedalled triumphantly away.

Marcello hid the gold and notes in his room in the mattress. It had been easy, so easy. Mario had done all the work for him.

He laughed now to himself as the cab swung along beside Central Park. He had opened the window and the movement of the car stirred the stale skyscraper-trapped air into the semblance of a breeze. He could see the bright

288

dresses of the girls in the park on his right. People seeking the shade of the trees, men in shirt sleeves, tramps and winos, kids playing. Soon the offices would disgorge their thousands of pasty-faced workers and the grass would be littered with the debris of packed lunches, food for the birds and enough rubbish to keep the park attendants busy.

He remembered how the farmhouse had been in turmoil for some time. He had watched events, holding his breath. He had kept strict control over his emotions. His father's suicide had shocked him. He had not envisaged that. Giuseppe's peasant strength, his earthy practicality and ability to adapt, had precluded any such rashness, or so it seemed to Marcello. But it was not his fault, he told himself, it was Mario's. Nevertheless his mother's and his sisters' grief irked him. He could not bear their desolation, and when Paulo left he followed.

'I cannot bear it,' he had said in the letter he had left on his bed, as he followed Mario, Guido, Francesca and Paulo away from Sicily.

But in style. Guido and Francesca had a little money, certainly, but not like him. They would have to be careful, would have to budget. He could travel first-class.

He doubled his money in card winnings during the journey, and made an amazing discovery – when it came to finance, he had the knack. On his arrival in New York he had brought with him the information and the deal that interested Luigi Stroza. He went to see Luigi, but not as a supplicant. He asked him first for news of his brother. He found out that Mario had preceded him and was now in Chicago. Salvatore Lucca had put him in charge of a night-club called the Blue Lady, and his brother, true to form, was throwing his weight about, causing trouble, behaving like a hoodlum. Marcello asked Luigi to be discreet and not broadcast his arrival to Mario. Luigi understood, or thought he did. In the circles Marcello Palucci aimed to penetrate, a brother like Mario was no asset.

Life was sweet. He had everything he wanted. He felt his sins were ones of omission rather than commission.

Why then was his sleep so uneasy? He was sure Mario's was not similarly disturbed. He had to make a conscious effort not to think of the past whereas his brother, he was sure, slept like a baby. Mario probably did not know about his father's suicide. Mario was lucky.

The cab was now passing through a district he was not familiar with. The West Side baffled him.

'Back to East Eighty-fifth and Fifth Avenue,' Mario ordered.

'Sure thing, Mister.'

He could deal with his restless insomniac nature. What he could not deal with was the knowledge that his twin, Guido, was on his way to kill Mario.

Marcello had hoped that the Palucci vendetta would, like many another, become mere histrionics, voices raised in anger, wild threats that were never executed. He had hoped that, given the gentle nature of his brothers and sisters (with the glaring exception of Mario), their aim would in time be blunted; that the literal execution would be indefinitely postponed, become a promise rather than a fact. He felt sure that Mario thought the same.

But that was not what he had heard on the grapevine. And it seemed that the Capos were encouraging it and that alarmed Marcello. Guido, they said, was on his way from Rome, his purpose clear. They said he'd be allowed to shoot the punk and then be left to take the rap.

It would destroy Guido. Marcello thought of his brother, the member of his family he loved the best. Guido had inherited their father's uncompromising honesty and sense of honour, and this would both force him to commit murder in order to uphold the family's honour and to suffer despair and remorse after the deed was done. Guido would not survive the killing of his brother. It was unnecessary for Lucca to lay complicated plans for his capture and conviction. Guido would most probably give himself up.

Marcello was aware of the ripple effect of Mario's action: Giuseppe's suicide, Francesca's heartbreak, Paulo's despair, so abhorrent to the Church. The news of his mother's death had shocked but not surprised Marcello. He had watched her after Giuseppe's death, seen her disintegration. His sister's depression was only another tragic but predictable result of his brother's crime. Up to that point Marcello could do nothing. Or so he told himself. He refused to face the indisputable fact that he could have returned the money and thereby prevented some of the tragedy at least. He preferred to gloss over that fact, telling himself that Mario had set in action a chain of events that had ended in their father's death and that nothing he could have done would have prevented it.

But now he had some power and, he felt, enough was enough. No more havoc should be caused, there should be an end to the mayhem.

They were going through the park again. The grass and the trees calmed the senses and soothed away tension. Soon he would be back surrounded by concrete that reached to the sky.

He wondered if he ought to go to Chicago. If Luigi Stroza did not take the action he had demanded, then he would have to. He would have to stop Guido.

He loved Guido so much. His was the strong arm that had supported Marcello during childhood. His was the listening ear that was always sympathetic. His was the kindness that never teased, was never cruel and never failed to help. Marcello had been loved and guided by Guido all his life and could not see his brother's life spoiled now by this stupid vendetta.

Rounding the exit from Central Park and deftly manoeuvring across and down Eighty-fifth, the taxi eventually pulled to a stop in front of the mansion. Marcello got out

291

and paid the driver.

His heart always lifted when he came home. The quiet dignity of the house elated him. He felt proud to have achieved all this in such a short space of time. He was also seized by sheer delight at the beauty of his home.

The hall was cool. The wide sweep of the staircase sloped gracefully down to the green Carerra marble floor. He took the stairs two at a time. Joshua, his black valet, was taking his shoes down to the servants' quarters to clean them.

'Anything I can do for you?' he asked.

'Yes. Lay me out some fresh clothes. My linen jacket, the cambric shirt. Thank you, Joshua.'

'Will I ask Elizabeth to send you up lunch on a tray, suh?' Elizabeth was Joshua's wife and Marcello's cook.

'No thank you, Joshua, I'm going out.'

He felt a sudden surge of well-being. The comfort of his own home, servants ready to do his bidding, the pleasure of a cold shower and fresh linen, soothed his temper and restored his optimism. It would be all right. He would see it was all right. He would arrange that nothing went wrong. He was rich and powerful. He would organize everything. He forgot Luigi Stroza's strictures against men in his position playing God. In high good humour, Marcello asked Joshua to bring him a whiskey sour and got dressed for his lunch date.

~~~~~~

He was having lunch with Mirella d'Abrizzio. He had been at a party a week ago, bored but doing all the correct things to keep in with the crowd he had chosen to run with, when Mitzi Howard-Colstairs, his hostess, tapped him on the shoulder.

'Here is someone you must meet, Marcello. A young lady from your part of the world. Mirella d'Abrizzio – Marcello Palucci.'

The girl wore a flame-coloured chiffon frock and was stunning in a classical way. He stared at her, openly admiring, thinking that she made all the other girls in the room look cheap. She wore no make-up and her fine skin was golden. The hair framing her face was unfashionably long and wild.

She laughed and her teeth were white against her honey skin. 'Well, well,' she said, 'Marcello Palucci. How nice. It seems we are unable to escape association with your family, no matter how hard poor Papa tries.'

Her face was enigmatic, her tone gently quizzical; he could not tell what exactly she meant by her remark. Whether it was casual, sarcastic, bored or put-upon. He decided not to worry about it or try to interpret it. She had turned to Mitzi, still holding the hand Marcello had proffered in a firm grip. 'He was my neighbour in Sicily,' she said sweetly to Mitzi.

Mitzi Howard-Colstairs's face fell. She had hoped that the Duke's daughter would snub the man she knew to be anything but top-drawer. It would have been a diverting tit-bit to gossip about with her friends over tea the following day. Disappointed, she turned away and left them alone together.

'For a moment I could not place you,' he said. 'We are so very far from home.'

She smiled at him and pushed her heavy hair aside with long fingers. 'Home? Is it still home to you?'

He grinned at her. 'No,' he said, 'I suppose not.'

'You have done well in America,' she said, looking him up and down appraisingly. He blushed. Then, furious at being so gauche asked quickly, 'And you are visiting New York?'

She nodded. 'Yes. Papa is in London. Luciano is in Berkshire in England. And I am here. All staying with different people, and all up to the same thing.'

'And what is that, may I ask?'

She looked at him, a smile lurking at the corners of her mouth. He felt a charge of excitement at the expression in her eyes.

'Take me to lunch next week and I'll tell you,' she said lightly.

They had arranged it. All week, when not thinking about Mario, Marcello was speculating about Mirella d'Abrizzio. The thought of her challenged him. Not just her beauty but her background. He remembered the grand *palazzo* on the hill and marvelled at the change of situation. He felt an upsurge of gratitude to America, to this land of opportunity where any man could meet and talk with any woman. Providing . . . He knew all about the snobbery of money, the aphrodisiac it was, the necessity of it. This was not a land where you could walk barefoot into the drawing-rooms of the mercantile aristocracy and be instantly welcome. This new land had barriers against colour, class and creed. But he had discovered that they could be broken down, whereas in Sicily it would have been impossible. Look at Francesca and Luciano. Here, with money, he had access to the highest if he so chose.

He arrived early. He drank his orange juice, twirled his glass and waited.

The restaurant hummed with muted conversaton, laughter, comings and goings. The atmosphere of New York never ceased to thrill him. One or two people greeted Marcello. He stood up and shook hands and charmed them with his good looks and friendly response. He had the reputation of being bright and tough in business so these men appreciated his deference, genuine or not. He was the man of the moment and they respected his achievements. Marcello loved every minute of it.

The waiter gave him an outsize menu. He knew Mirella had arrived without looking up from it. He felt his pulse quicken and his throat go dry. A little ripple of interest eddied around the room and when he raised his eyes a heartbeat later, there she was, looking incredibly chic in a black Chanel suit and pearls with a diamond spray glittering on her shoulder.

The waiter pulled out her chair for her and she sat, put her clutch bag on the table and commenced to peel off her gloves.

He felt a suffocating excitement at the sight of her and knew that she felt something too. Whether it was as shocking to her as it was to him he did not know. He felt the muscles of his face quiver a little, out of control as he smiled at her.

'Well, well, well,' she said, looking around. 'And I thought you were supposed to be poor!'

He threw back his head and laughed, delighted by her remark. 'I thought you were poor too, but you look like you've come straight from Mam'selle Chanel. The patina of the rich. The gloss. You have it to perfection.'

It was her turn to laugh. 'I am poor. Really quite penniless. You must know, Marcello, that when the rich are poor, they still behave as if they are rich.'

'I think that's immoral.'

She nodded, 'That's the peasant in you.'

'I'd love to know how they do it,' he remarked lightly.

'Well, they run up bills for a start. My father has bills everywhere. All over the world.'

'Do you?' he asked. He wanted to understand and was aware that under her banter there was a grain of truth.

'No, as a matter of fact I don't.' She paused, looking down at her gloves beside the cutlery on the table, smoothing them with one elegant hand. Then she looked up at him, meeting his eyes. 'My mother died, you see. Soon after you left Sicily.'

He lowered his gaze. 'I'm sorry.'

'Don't be. I used to blame Papa for her condition, then I realized she had chosen to be his victim. She *liked* nursing her pain and grievances.' She was staring over his

295

shoulder, a far-away look in her eyes. 'Of course Father was to blame too, but she *enjoyed* suffering.' She looked back at him. 'Anyway she left me – not Papa, not Luciano, but me – a legacy. She said I had more need of it than they. She said women were helpless without money.' She shrugged. 'Anyhow, it was enough to pay some of Papa's more pressing debts and get me groomed and here.'

The waiter was hovering. 'The lobster is excellent today, sir,' he said respectfully. 'Direct from Maine this morning.'

He was Italian, Marcello realized. He was probably an immigrant, proud of his position in this establishment that catered for the rich and famous, looking upon himself as a success. Marcello smiled. There but for the grace of God, he thought. He glanced at Mirella who nodded at him.

'Then we'll have the lobster. Followed by the *carré de'agneau* for me. For you, also?'

Miralla nodded. Then, as the waiter took the menus with a flourish and swept away, she smiled into his eyes.

'How well you order,' she said, and there was irony in her tone. 'One would think you had learned at your father's knee.'

He was uncomfortable for a moment, then realized she was not being malicious.

'French too,' she added.

'We picked up languages easily, my family.'

'Among other things,' she said, and waved to someone in the room then turned back to him.

'I cannot bear it when you do that,' he said, and seeing her surprise added, 'I don't want you to know anyone here except me.'

'You're jealous?' she asked, light as air.

'Yes,' he replied, equally airily.

She covered his hand with hers. 'I didn't mean to offend you just now. I'm agog with admiration,' she said. 'And we cannot boast, my family and I. We are such appalling parasites.'

He did not contradict her and she looked surprised. Instead he said, 'You are very beautiful.' A faint tint of pink coloured her cheeks and she looked at him from under long nut-brown lashes.

'So are you.' He was startled, and more to ease his confusion than really to find out he asked, 'What did you mean the other night when you said . . .?'

'When I said we were all up to the same thing?' She shrugged. 'Why, I meant finding suitable partners.'

She looked at him with a provocative smile on her lips but he did not rise to the bait. He suddenly felt as if he were ploughing through a jungle and at any moment might lose his equilibrium, flounder, and be lost forever. He knew he must keep his head. But she was smiling at him reassuringly.

'Don't worry, Marcello. You are in no danger from me.' She grimaced. 'Papa is looking for a wife for himself and one for Luciano. Whether he will find what he is looking for is open to debate.'

'You realize that I'll tell Francesca . . .' he began, paused and amended himself. 'Let Francesca know where Luciano is.'

'You don't know yet! But it's Berkshire, in England. A house called Elm Court.' She forked some lobster into her mouth and chewed a moment, thinking.

'I don't know if you can understand this but I would be happy for them if they found each other. But, Marcello, Luciano is weak . . .'

'Francesca is strong. Peasant strong. Does it always have to be the man? Couldn't she be strong for both of them?' he asked.

'Of course,' she replied, smiling, 'but Luciano may hurt her. He can be carelessly cruel.' She continued, 'Papa does not object to your family, you know, but he cannot be *seen* to approve. Loss of face, you see. He knows, like I do, that you and people like you are the powerful ones. We are on our way out. A dying breed, clinging together, selling ourselves to maintain a lifestyle that is immoral in this day and age.' She shivered. 'We contribute nothing; our names, our lineage, old piles of stone too large and quite outmoded. Unless we begin to earn our keep . . .'

'Workers of the world unite,' he said, raising his glass with its non-alcoholic contents,

'I'm not a communist, if that's what you mean, Marcello. This lobster is superb. Eat up, do. And forgive me. Sometimes I get embarrassed at my own redundancy.'

'Oh, don't say that. You'll find a way to contribute.'

She shook her head. 'I have no talent. And I cannot see myself as a little stenographer. I was born too early or too late.'

He did not fully understand what she was getting at but he had no intention of letting her know that. So he remained silent and they both gave their attention to their lunch. He wondered if she realized that had their positions been reversed, he would have had no compunction about resorting to any lengths, no matter what, to hold on to that magnificent *palazzo*. He had always coveted it and could understand the Duke's crooked pragmatism. After the lamb they ordered a red fruit compôte which was tart and thick and delicious. Marcello stirred in a dollop of cream but ate absently. He usually enjoyed good cuisine but today was too captivated by Mirella, too intrigued, to give the food his full attention.

'I don't work,' she said, 'neither does Luciano. Neither did Papa or Mother. Or their fathers and mothers. We got others to do it for us. But we did not give them land,' she said softly, 'or payment. They worked it for us for nothing but enough bread to fill their stomachs, and we saw nothing wrong in that. That is what has been happening in our family for five hundred years. It has to change. People will begin to want something back. Remember Garibaldi? Or like your father they'll take advantage of our weakness and buy our land from us. The strength, Marcello, lies with you and not with us any more.'

She was right, he knew. He grinned at her. 'You are talking to a born taker.'

'I know.' She looked at him, unsettling him again with the intensity of her expression. 'I've asked about you,' she said.

'Oh, why?'

'Let's just say . . . let's say I'm interested.' She propped her chin on her hand and looked at him, speaking in their native language.

'Very interested indeed.'

Chapter Sixteen

Francesca arrived at Dover to find Eleanor waiting for her, searching the crowd for the face she wanted to see but Guido was not there. Then, spotting Francesca, she hurried over and embraced her.

'Oh, it's so good to see you!' she cried joyfully, tears in her eyes. 'But where is Guido?' She was looking to right and left over Francesca's shoulder.

'Didn't you get my letter?' Francesca asked, distressed.

Eleanor shook her head. 'I know only what Christopher told me. He said Guido might be going to America, but I was sure he would come here to see me first.' Her heart had plummeted and she felt cold and rejected.

'No. He could not come.' Francesca saw the worried frown on her friend's face and hurried on, 'He *had* to go, you see. He just had to. I'm so sorry, Eleanor.'

She was very disappointed but concealed her sadness under a welcoming smile for fear Francesca might feel as unwanted as she did. And Francesca, aware of this, had to curb her impatience to ask about Luciano. However, Eleanor knew how she must ache for news and said at once, 'Luciano is adorable, Francesca. He's here alone. You will stay with us? Aunt Helen has agreed. She'll be happy to have you at Elm Court, and Christopher, her son, will probably fall in love with you.'

She was holding Francesca's hand in a fierce grip, her voice high and brittle. Once they were in the car, tucked up by Bates, the Wylde's chauffeur, Francesca put her arm around her friend.

'It's all right, Eleanor. I know how you must feel. I went through it myself. Please don't try to be jolly for my sake.'

Eleanor gulped and turned her face to the window.

'It's just that . . . Oh, Francesca, I miss him so desperately! And I'm angry he didn't come with you. I'm furious that he thinks *anything* is more important to him than I am. And . . . I think I'm going to have his baby. Oh, why didn't he come?'

Francesca didn't know what to say. Nothing had prepared her for this news and she simply had no idea how to react.

'Does . . . does anybody know?' she asked timidly.

'Of course not! You're the only one.'

'I wish you'd told us in the letter,' Francesca said. 'I'm sure it would have stopped Guido from going to America and taking risks.' She could have bitten out her tongue.

'I didn't think I was when I wrote the letter. It's only in the last week I've begun to think . . .'

Francesca had sat frozen, hoping Eleanor had missed what she had said, but it suddenly dawned on her friend and she did not finish her sentence. 'What do you mean, taking risks? What risks? What risks do you mean?'

'Oh, forget I said it. I didn't mean it.'

'Oh, God! Guido is in danger. I guessed it. I knew that nothing less than a crisis would have kept him from me.'

'Calm down, Eleanor. There's no real danger that I know of.'

'If it has anything to do with my father, then he is in danger,' Eleanor said with certainty.

She stared out of the car window. The verdant green landscape unfolded as the car moved sedately along country lanes: golden fields of waving corn, lime-coloured meadows, cathedral arches made by the boughs of tall trees closing over their heads. The gentle countryside was

301

cool to the eyes.

Eleanor turned to look closely at her friend. 'I don't think you understand fully what being involved with my father means,' she said. 'I would like you to tell me exactly what you know.'

Francesca sighed. Her mind was full of Luciano, of the apprehension she felt as well as joy at the prospect of seeing him. She knew she should be perturbed about Eleanor but she was too worried about her own situation to work up the proper concern for her friend. She said as much.

'Eleanor, I'm awful, I know, but I'm in such a turmoil about seeing Luciano, I can't think straight. My mind is running around in circles.'

Eleanor turned and gripped her arm. 'I don't care where your mind is! Just get it back here instantly. What we are discussing is a man's life. How can I make you understand that Guido is in mortal danger if he is involved in any way with my father?'

Francesca looked at her, mildly surprised at her vehemence. 'Well, he's not really involved,' she said. She hesitated, then in the face of Eleanor's distress, added, 'It's a family matter that your father said he would help us with. So, you see, Guido is not working *for* him.'

'Francesca, that is how business is done. A favour demands a favour. Oh, never mind.' She took a deep breath. 'Will you tell me all about it? Everything? I love Guido and I'm carrying his child. I told you about Luciano. You owe this to me.' She frowned and muttered under her breath, 'Oh God, I'm exactly the same as my father.'

Francesca looked doubtful and Eleanor pressed on, 'Please. Look, we'll be stopping for lunch at Hye-Over-Hill. Tell me then.'

Francesca nodded. She knew Enrico Domini was a powerful man, but she could not credit that Guido,

302

halfway across the Atlantic, could be in any danger from him now. However, she did owe Eleanor an explanation.

They stopped at the Dirty Duck, an inn which was a little cottage with a tap-room. It was surrounded by hollyhocks and wallflowers, hedges of honeysuckle and cowparsley.

They sat at a wooden table in the garden under an old apple tree. They lunched on homemade pork pie and Stilton in perfect condition, washed down with cider.

The sun sparkled through the shifting branches of the trees, and gnats and horseflies hovered about while butterflies sipped from the lilac and buddleia and bees droned over the wild roses.

Francesca told her story well. She relived the horror of that fateful day. She spoke simply, giving only the known facts; how she had gone to keep her assignation with Luciano in the wood, how she had been so rudely interrupted by her whole family and then the Duke. 'We stood naked before them, Luciano and I, and we were not ashamed,' she said. 'The others said my brother Mario had told them where I was. Told the Duke too. They took me home. My mother put me to bed. She was so gentle. I was dazed and shocked. She stayed with me. Gina said afterwards that Papa was wondering how to save his honour, how he could get us out of the situation. You see, he had killed the servant and needed his savings to pay for a lawyer.'

Francesca told Eleanor about the money, its disappearance coinciding with Mario's, and how the family had put two and two together, realizing that the whole thing had been a diversion created by him so that he could run away with their father's savings while they could not catch him. She told of her father's suicide, the break-up of the family, their mother's death and Guido's undertaking to find Mario and punish him.

'And . . .' She bent her head, unable to finish, unable to say 'and kill him'. It sounded criminal, spoken aloud here under the apple trees with the song of a hundred birds in their ears and the innkeeper's wife, fat and comfortable, hurrying down the crooked pathway, a tray bearing jam roly-poly and custard in her hands. It seemed unreal and lunatic in the peace of this place to say Guido meant to . . .

'Kill him. That's what you are trying to say, isn't it?' Eleanor asked. 'Guido is on his way to America to kill his brother. Oh, my God! My God!' She kept shaking her head from side to side looking at Francesca in horror. 'And you let him go? What kind of a woman are you? You tell me it is nothing, he is not in danger. You little fool! Do you live in a dream? America is not Sicily where everyone understands vendetta. Do you know the penalty if he is caught? The electric chair! The American police are not stupid. Guido is a fool if he thinks he will get away with it. How will he do it? Will he strangle his brother? Poison him? Knife him in the back? Shoot him? Tell me, I'd like to know.'

She was shaking Francesca now. 'Has he thought? Has he worked it out? I doubt it. I doubt it very much. Oh, the fool. I suppose he'll use a gun, eh? Guns are most popular today. Will he shoot him in the street? In his bed? What will the people who hear the shot do? Turn over and go back to sleep? How will he escape? Has he got a get-away plan?'

Francesca was crying, tears running down her face, 'No. I don't know,' she sobbed. 'He didn't tell me.'

'And you didn't ask?'

'No, I didn't. We understand these things in our family. Can't you shut up? Don't you know that I worry too? I'm half-sick with worry. But I have to go on. I have to pretend. Otherwise I'd go mad. And it has to be done. Don't you see that? Can't you see that it has to be done?'

'Why? In God's name why? Hasn't there been enough harm?'

The innkeeper's wife had left the pudding and gone

back into the cottage. She must have heard the noise for they saw her return now.

'You all right?' she called down the path.

'Yes, thank you,' Eleanor shouted, then said softly, 'yes, thank you, we're fine.'

Her voice was so bitter, so sarcastic, that Francesca looked at her in supplication.

'Don't blame us too much, Eleanor. It's our custom.'

Eleanor shot her a withering glance then looked out over the hedgerows to the middle-distance.

'I can tell you one thing,' she said, 'he'll not want to do it. I know Guido Palucci inside out and I know he will not do this. He will try but he will fail. He will not be able to pull the trigger.'

'He said something like that to me before he left.' Francesca dabbed her face with her handkerchief. She looked pleadingly at the tall blonde girl. 'Don't you see that it has to be done? Father and Mother are dead, Marcello and Paulo gone, Serena destroyed – all because of Mario. It is justice. It is expected.'

'Then it is a very bad custom. Do you think that if Guido kills him it will solve anything? When has retribution ever settled anything? Vengeance breeds vengeance. All that will happen is that Guido will end up in prison. Or dead. Or so unhappy and guilty that he is no good to anyone.'

Francesca looked at her with a haggard face. 'What would you have us do?'

'Let him come to me. Marry me. Let me have my baby in peace. Let us live our lives in peace and love.' Eleanor sighed.

'But Mario? He must suffer. He cannot be let off. He has to be punished for what he did.'

'At the cost of my happiness? No. Forget the past. You cannot live there, Francesca. It is a haunted place.'

'*Jesu Maria*, I don't know what to do now. You have frightened me. You have put doubts where there were

305

none before.' Francesca's teeth were chattering. She was pulling the tiny wet handkerchief into shreds.

'I'm glad that you are frightened,' Eleanor said. 'Perhaps now you'll realize how serious this is. You're not children playing at cops and robbers.'

She stared out again over the gentle English country-side. 'I'm frightened too,' she said softly. 'My father hates Guido. If he has told him where Mario is, then it bodes no good for your brother. They'll kill him, or the police will get him.' She looked sharply at Francesca. 'And if he is not caught, if he escapes, how in God's name will he live with himself, with that on his conscience? You know your brother. Think about it.'

They had not touched their pudding. The innkeeper's wife was mortally offended, sniffing loudly as she removed the untouched bowls.

Bates appeared around the corner, his naturally rosy face brick-red. He had enjoyed a couple of pints of home-brew in the tap-room while they lunched.

'What are you going to do, Eleanor?' Francesca asked timidly. She felt out of her depth. Stupid, like a child who has broken a rule she knew nothing of. She had deliberately kept herself from worrying about Guido, not facing the situation in order to protect herself. Eleanor made this seem supremely selfish. Yet she knew in her heart that the other members of her family would understand the need to play such a game. She had not thought of the vendetta from Eleanor's point of view. All her life she had been aware that if your family was insulted, then it meant vendetta. It was the Sicilian way. Eleanor's reaction had shocked her and made her think.

Eleanor stood up suddenly, nearly overturning the bench she sat on.

'What are you going to do?' Francesca repeated.

'I'm going to deliver you to Aunt Helen at Elm Court,' Eleanor said, walking to the car purposefully and getting

306

into it. 'Then I'm going to follow Guido to America. I'm going to try to stop him. I don't care about your precious family's face. I'm going to do my best to stop him. Now get in, Francesca. I'm in a hurry.'

Chapter Seventeen

Minouche buried her head in the pillow. Beside her Mario snored gently, his mouth a little open. It was ten o'clock in the morning and she could not sleep. Bedtime for them was on average three a.m. and they usually rose again at lunchtime. In the morning there was nothing to do in the club while a team of cleaners mopped up the debris of the previous night and set it all to rights for the evening.

Minouche usually slept well. The bed was the most comfortable she had ever known. But recently, since the bad thing had started happening, sleep had proved elusive.

She slid out of bed, her satin nightdress riding up her thighs, and turned, glancing at Mario. Then, as gently as she could, she stood up and shrugged herself into her satin robe and high-heeled mules.

She stood a moment in the centre of the room. The sun would be up by now but the curtains were firmly shut against the daylight. She was dying to open them for the room was full of the musty smell of sleep. Stale air. But if she did she would wake Mario, and he had been edgy lately and she did not want to upset him.

Minouche looked at his head on the pillow. She loved him so much, so very much. She would do anything to keep him. She frowned a little and shivered though the room was hot. She must indeed love him, she thought, otherwise she would not allow that old pig to force her to do those horrible things.

She left the room and went into the bathroom. She opened the little cupboard door beneath the basin where the plumbing was and took out a fifth of bourbon. She took her toothbrush out of its glass and poured the whiskey into it. She drank it quickly, like medicine, then poured water from the tap into the glass and put toothpaste on her brush.

She screwed the cap on the bottle and replaced it in the cupboard, smiling to herself as the fiery liquid hit her stomach and instantly soothed her nerves. She knew it would not last, this numbing sensation, but at least for now it helped.

She began to scrub her teeth. In a moment she would bath and shower. She did both. These days she was constantly bathing. She thought how nice it was that there was so much water in America. In Paris, there had been no water at all in her room. She had had to queue to wash. Here you could have a glass of water whenever you liked, and a bath as often as you wanted.

When she had finished her teeth she looked at her reflection in the glass and thought how ugly she was. She remembered Scarlatti and his taunts. *Mon Dieu*, she thought, I am certainly ugly.

There were circles beneath her large eyes which gave her face a panda look. Her skin was putty white, had lost its sheen, and the light had gone from her eyes,

Suddenly, staring at herself in the glass, she realized there were tears flowing down her cheeks. A sob tore through her, hurting her chest. She stood, holding on to the basin, shuddering and drawing in harsh jagged breaths as if she were drowning. '*Mon Dieu*,' she kept sobbing, '*Mon Dieu*, what will I do? What will I do?'

If only she could tell someone, but there was no one she could trust. Mario would kill if he knew, and if he killed Lucca he would be sent to the electric chair. Or put away.

Pierre too, if he knew, would see red and seek to murder the old man. Then there would be a terrible price to pay.

But she wished him dead, sordid little man, sending for her behind their backs. Lucca would get Pino to bring her to him. She could not believe her ears when, that first time, he had said, 'Down on me, woman. Down.' She saw that his trousers were undone. 'You want to go back to Paris?' he said, leering at her, his eyes terrible in his old wrinkled face. There was a threat in them, and a plea. 'You wanna go back and face a murder rap? You think this is a rough deal? You don't do as I say, you never see Mario again, understand me? You never see Mario again.' He flinched a little from the contempt in her eyes but continued, 'You say anything to anyone about this, you never see Mario again. Unnerstand?'

She had nodded. What else could she do?

'Now down on me, woman.'

His voice was husky with excitement. Her stomach turned in disgust but she had no choice. She knew it was useless to refuse and so she did as he asked, when he asked, and each time it was worse and she was sicker. Now, whenever she thought about it, she had to have a drink. It was the only thing that helped, that numbed the horror.

She had never underestimated Salvatore Lucca. He would ship her back to Paris without hesitation, where she would end up in prison or dead. Worse than that, he would destroy Mario.

Minouche was nobody to him. Unimportant. He would swat her like a fly, and wounded vanity would make him vicious. Those years at the mercy of her father had taught her one thing: not to fight. Do what was asked, get it over with as quickly and quietly as possible.

She was not so much afraid for herself as she was for Mario. He would eliminate Mario and then she would have no reason to live. She knew he was planning to have her man killed but she believed that he would not get rid

310

of him as long as she was servicing him. Without the threat to Mario he had no stick to beat her with. There was no reason for her not to run away. She hoped this would be enough too to force Lucca to intervene between Mario and his brother.

When she was with Lucca she would close her eyes. She would think of her lover. She would pray. She saw nothing incongruous in asking *le bon Dieu* to help her. All her life, stealing, shoplifting, living dangerously, scamming, she had retained a fastidious soul. That pure spirit within her had been despoiled by her father; it was why she had killed him. She had not been intimate with any other man except Mario.

But now this old man was forcing her to do disgusting things. Her soul shrank within her and she felt ill, so she drank to still the pain.

She did what he wanted but her hatred of him grew as her love for Mario increased. She prayed that her lover would never find out.

She could not live without Mario. There was no life for her without him.

She looked at herself in the glass. She loathed herself. She wished she had gone to school, had an education. Then she would have known what to do, how to protect herself. Clever women she saw in the Blue Lady did not allow anyone to treat them like that. Push them around. It was an old nightmare and she had to live through it again.

Yet, she reminded herself, she had Mario. Those toffee-nosed women had rich powerful husbands it was true, but the men were fat and bald.

She sighed. Each day was a bonus, she supposed. She should have been dead a long time ago.

Have a cup of coffee, she told herself. That was the thing. Open the curtains in the kitchen and let the sun shine in. Things would get better. They had to. And some day the old man would die.

Mario woke up when she left the room. He always awakened when Minouche got out of bed and she had been doing a lot of that recently. When she first came to Chicago she had hardly moved from his arms all night and her sleepy tousled awakening was one of his great pleasures.

She'd been a bit odd recently, he thought, a bit edgy. Women! He loved her but he would never let her know how much. Make himself seem weak.

He stretched. Everything in his life was going well, but still he could not shake this uneasy feeling. He didn't know what caused it but it made him irritable and bad-tempered, and was at odds with the charming façade he liked to present to people. It made him unpopular with the customers which was bad for business. The men who frequented the Blue Lady liked to be soothed, made welcome, fussed over, not snapped at. Mario cursed himself for a fool for letting things get to him like this.

What was it that made him look over his shoulder at every unexpected noise? He came to the conclusion that it was what Minouche had said, her warning. She had rattled him with her talk of a brother coming from the old country to kill him. Vendetta? Pah!

It was nonsense. And yet . . .

Minouche had been acting funny too. He could only suppose she was agitated about him because of the rumour, because of what she had heard.

He could hear her in the kitchen, making coffee. He could smell it. It smelled good.

He wouldn't sleep without her, now she was up. He thought he might as well join her, talk a bit. He liked talking to her. Usually she made sense.

He put on his paisley dressing-gown and went into the kitchen. 'Hi, sugar,' he said, kissing her cheek. She smelled of toothpaste, fresh and clean like a little girl. She also smelled of brandy. It must be left over from the previous night, he decided, and looked at her. He could see she had been crying. It did something funny to his stomach. He felt sick at the thought that she might be unhappy, that anyone had been unkind to her. She might leave him. He could not bear it if she did.

'Couldn't you sleep?' she asked.

'I smelled the coffee. You OK?' he asked anxiously.

She nodded, but he knew she wasn't.

'What is it baby? You gotta tell me. I'll find out anyway.'

That was true, she thought. She made a big effort and smiled at him.

'No, Mario. It's nothing. Except, I am worried about you. About your brother, the set-up.'

She could see he was mollified.

'That Moses,' she continued, 'he laughs at you behind your back. He does not like you very much. Be careful of him, *mon amour*, please.'

He folded her in his arms and kissed the top of her head. 'Oh, baby, you gotta stop worrying about me. Here I was thinkin' somethin's upset ya, something's worryin' ya. An' all it is is me! Ya gotta stop it, y'hear?'

She pressed her face against his chest, holding on to him fiercely. 'I will, I promise,' she said, and kissed his bare skin with trembling lips.

~~~~~~

Marcello decided to go to Chicago. Christmas was approaching and nothing had happened.

He had been to see Luigi Stroza again, offering incentives all of which were eagerly accepted. However, there were no guarantees of protection in return, for either Guido or Mario. Only vague promises that Marcello knew were worth nothing. He felt he was wasting his time and his money.

313

Not entirely though. Business was booming and there was Mirella.

Was there ever such a girl? he wondered, exasperated but excited. She was a challenge to him. From the tip of her unvarnished but perfectly manicured finger nails to the toes of her Salvatore Ferragamo shoes she was cool perfection. She had brains as well as beauty, and sometimes he wished profoundly that she had not. He was not at all sure where he stood with her. Sometimes her enigmatic smile irritated and unsettled him. She was provocative and distant all at the same time.

'You could be hitting back at our family through me,' he said ominously to her over dinner one evening. She simply shrugged, not bothering to reply, and went on eating. He could think what he liked, was her attitude, and for him it was an unexpected line for a woman to have. It threw him.

Mirella liked eating. They dined in all New York's most fashionable places, went to the best parties together, were seen at art galleries and charity events; Marcello Palucci could always be relied upon for a large subscription to any of the fashionable charities.

They enjoyed themselves, laughed a lot, shared opinions and ideas. And then he drove her home. He dropped her in front of the Harcourt residence where she was staying and bade her goodnight . . ..and that was all.

She had allowed him to kiss her once. Hardly responding, she then slipped out of his embrace, and touching her fingers to her mouth, threw his kiss back at him, laughing.

'You can't rush me,' she said. 'You're used to eager peasant women, Marcello. Us ladies are more particular. We like to take our time.'

He knew she was teasing but her words angered him.

He was annoyed with her, fed up with her cat-and-mouse game or whatever nonsense she was torturing him with. Did she? Didn't she? Would she? Wouldn't she?

314

He had been spoiled by women all his life. His mother and sisters adored him, pandered to him in every way. At school all the girls got crushes on him, and then later wanted to walk out with him. And, yes, he had to admit Mirella was right; they had been more than eager to lift their skirts, sometimes even when he wasn't. He had never given any of them a moment's consideration.

He lost his virginity to the chemist's wife. A plump, jolly woman, she was highly sexed but frustrated. The apothecary was a dried-up little man at least ten years older than his wife. It had been exciting tumbling in her bed in the afternoon behind drawn drapes, but the thrill soon palled. Marcello had become bored with her constant demands and her rather overwhelming sexual domination of him. He became little more than the instrument of her orgasms. He had to threaten to tell the chemist to get her to desist and leave him alone.

After the chemist's wife he had had a few flings but nothing serious. He had found that he was more interested in the quality than the quantity. He was fastidious. He had never really enjoyed sex for its own sake, feeling that there must be more to it than that.

Since meeting Mirella he was breathlessly waiting to get her into bed but she would not be led there. He was frustrated, slightly irritable for he did not like being thwarted, and was also annoyed with himself for his eagerness. I'm just like a kid, he thought, amazed. He had thought he had complete mastery over his feelings. He did not like being at the mercy of his own emotions. He liked to be in control of what he felt. But this girl, this desirable female, could throw him into confusion simply by raising an eyebrow or licking her lips.

With nothing concrete from Luigi Stroza, and piqued by Mirella d'Abrizzio's elusiveness, he decided to go to Chicago and deal with Mario himself, face to face. He would offer him protection, sort it out with Lucca if that became necessary. At the same time it would give him time to work out what he felt for Mirella, decide on a strategy to adopt with her. It would be easier with a distance between them.

He had an overall plan. He had had it since he left Sicily. This game with Mirella would not interfere with that. In fact, it would add spice. His absence from New York would also, he thought, show what Mirella felt for him. His departure would either upset her or not. It would force her hand, and then perhaps if she would only stop playing games they could get together as more than just good friends. He knew that more than anything he wanted to bed her.

When he arrived home he told Joshua to pack him enough clothes for a few days out of town. Marcello did not tell him where he was going.

'Wha'd I say effen someone ask whe' yo are, suh?' Joshua asked.

'Just tell them 'out of town', Joshua. Say you have no idea. And that will be the truth.'

That night he dreamed of Sicily. He saw the harsh hillsides, burnt-umber under the sun. He felt the dry dusty heat, so different from the humidity of New York. He could see the fruit groves and hear the church bells ring, tolling out their summons. He saw again the Palucci procession on its way to mass: Gina, himself and Guido, Francesca, Paulo, Cecilia and Serena. He stared at Guido, his beloved brother, his twin. And looked again. Mario was not there. There was a shadow where Mario should have been, a silhouette walking beside them. A dark and frightening shade.

Then he realized that he himself was not with the group as he normally was but walking behind them, unable to catch up. He was a child again. His boots were unlaced and his feet hurt and he called, 'Mama! Mama!' But his mother did not look back. She did not turn at his call. He thought

316

his heart would break. He called again. 'Mama! Mama!' But no one heard him.

They had something that he could not get. He did not know what it was, but he knew it was precious and he was excluded, separated from them all. He ran after them, calling to them.

The shadow that walked in Mario's place held out a skeletal hand and beckoned Marcello to join him.

'Come with me. Leave them. Leave them. Come with me.' The phantasm pulled him against his will into the shadows, into the dark, while the rest of the family walked on into the sunlight.

Marcello wakened bathed in sweat. He got up and showered, put on a robe and poured himself a whiskey. Canadian whiskey. The best. Smuggled in for him from Canada. Prohibition would soon be over. He was glad he had had the sense to get his money out of that business and into the more stable areas of oil and real estate.

He thought of his dream, and of his family. 'I took my opportunity,' he said to himself. 'If I hadn't done it, the money would be gone by now anyway. It was Mario not me. It was Mario.'

He sat smoking cigarette after cigarette, sipping his whiskey as he watched the dawn break over Central Park.

Chapter Eighteen

When she and Francesca arrived at Elm Court, Eleanor alarmed everybody by announcing her immediate departure for New York.

'But you cannot do that, Eleanor. What about poor Francesca?' Helen protested.

'Aunt, darling, I must. Francesca will tell you all about it. And she'll be very happy with you. I know you'll take good care of her.'

'But your father . . .'

'Don't talk to me about my father. He doesn't deserve any consideration at all. Now you two really must get to know one other.'

'Well, introduce us then,' Helen said, amused by Eleanor's excitement.

'Oh, heavens, my manners. Aunt Helen, this is Francesca Palucci. She is the dearest person. I leave her in your care. Francesca, this is Aunt Helen.'

And she raced upstairs to pack, shouting for Morton her maid as she went.

Helen was kindness itself to Francesca. She made her welcome, fully aware that the girl must feel bewildered in a foreign place among strangers who spoke another language. She was glad to discover that Francesca's mastery of English was extremely good.

She also tried to dissuade Eleanor from haring off to the States but the girl was adamant. Revitalized, full of energy,

Eleanor was determined to be up and off.

'Can I get a connection at Oxford for Southampton or would it be quicker to go to London?' was all the reply Helen's pleas elicited from the girl. 'I have to catch the next boat to New York, that's all I'm interested in,' she cried, throwing things into a case, while her maid stood beside her trying vainly to fold them. 'Francesca will tell you all about it, won't you dearest? I've told Aunt Helen all about you.'

Francesca nodded and blushed, a little anxious about her friend's departure, and also breathless for her meeting with Luciano. Her whole being felt held in check. Luciano was here. In this building. In this place. He moved here. He breathed the air. She was aquiver with the imminence of the meeting yet glad it was not quite yet. The confrontation was heartbeats away, but not quite yet.

She was afraid. Why? she asked herself, unhappy that it should be so.

She looked up at Helen Wylde. How much did she know? Eleanor said she had told her, but Eleanor herself had not known all the details until a little while ago. The older woman caught Francesca's glance and patted her hand reassuringly.

'We will just have to forgive her, my dear,' she said. 'I can guess what's happened. Your brother, the one she is besotted with, has pitched up in New York.'

'Well then, Aunt, if you've guessed that, what more is there to know? And I cannot think why you are trying to stop me.'

'Your father, my dear . . .'

'He can go to hell,' Eleanor said robustly, and knelt on her case to shut it. 'Is Harland there, Aunt? Tell him to find out about the trains and get me to the station as quickly as possible.'

In her heart of hearts Helen was relieved at the turn of events. Eleanor's action removed her from the sphere of

319

Helen's responsibility. She could not be forced to match-make if Eleanor was in New York and Christopher here. Enrico Domini had not said anything about keeping his daughter prisoner. Helen decided he simply did not have the imagination to envisage her running away from the home she loved. He thought of Berkshire as a region akin to Timbuctoo, and that once there it would be too remote for Eleanor to try to leave. He had the very peculiar idea that England was isolated and access to and from it nearly impossible. The way one thought, Helen mused to herself, of the Outer Hebrides or the Blasket Islands.

Fond though she was of the girl, Helen was relieved that she was going. It gave her a breathing space and she wouldn't have to stop any more of those wretched letters.

They kissed. 'It's all such a rush,' Helen said helplessly as Harland took Eleanor's case downstairs.

'Look after Francesca well,' Eleanor said, hugging her aunt. Then Eleanor kissed Francesca. 'Good luck. I wish I could wait to see how you get on, but you know how I feel. You understand.'

Then she was gone, leaving behind her a curiously uneasy silence.

Francesca and Helen looked at each other. 'Come and see your room,' said Helen, taking the girl's hand in hers. She patted it and returned Francesca's level gaze. Helen liked her eyes. They were chestnut-coloured, their expression trusting and serene. There was something very vulnerable about the Sicilian girl. Helen wondered if Francesca had thought of the possibility of Luciano's rejecting her. Helen had not been very impressed by the young Italian. He struck her as shallow and selfish.

Impulsively, she kissed Francesca's cheek. 'I hope you'll be happy here,' she said, leading her to her room. 'Come down for tea at five. We'll be in the green drawing-room. Any of the staff will show you.' She opened a door off the corridor. 'Here, my dear. If anything is missing, please let me know.' And she left.

Helen had arranged her visitor's room most charmingly and Francesca appreciated the effort that had obviously gone into it. It was very pretty. Bowls of blue iris and fairy's breath and the latest magazines lay on a table draped in blue damask. Pretty lace cushions were scattered about and Helen had left her some books in Italian.

A bath had been run for her. Francesca undressed quickly and lowered herself into the warm scented water. She lay there, trying to relax. She could feel her heart beat, almost see it under the smooth skin. Rushes of excitement vied with acute apprehension as she thought of the meeting before her. She felt the frail vessel of her body could not sustain much more emotion, then chided herself on her lack of faith, trying to calm herself.

What was the matter with her? She *knew* what would happen. She had dreamed of it so many times, visualized every move, every word.

Luciano's face would flood with joy on seeing her, she knew it. He would say: 'Francesca, my beloved' and take her in his arms, holding her as if he would never let her go. Yes, that was how it would be, she told herself.

Feeling much calmer, she carefully dressed, putting on her white lawn and *broderie anglaise*-dress. She knotted the pink silk sash at her waist and looped her hair back with rose satin ribbons.

She decended the stairs slowly. A housemaid showed her the green drawing-room and she entered, alone, and stood at the door, facing all the people gathered there.

~~~~~~

Lady Helen was impressed by Francesca's innate dignity. She needed it to stand there so calmly. She could see the girl's inner tension. It showed in the bright pink patches on her cheeks and neck as she waited in front of them. All

321

conversation had ceased at her entrance and there was silence in the room while the assembled company assessed her. Helen's childrens' friends stared. Like a flock of white gulls they stood about in angular poses, elbows and knees sticking out like storks, dashing and sporty in tennis clothes. They gazed at the newcomer, judging her. Their concentrated scrutiny was both appraising and insolent.

Lucy Braithwaite was the first to speak. Her glance was contemptuous as she took in the details of Francesca's clothes. 'Old fashioned, my dears. Positively *ancien regime*,' she whispered in an audible aside. And, like sheep, the others followed her dismissal of the Sicilian girl. Where Lucy led, the rest of them trotted meekly behind.

Proper little madam, Helen thought. Her mother was ill bred.

She crossed to her visitor, going swiftly to her side and taking her hand. It made no difference, however, the die had been cast. Francesca had received the thumbs down. She had been judged 'not the thing'.

She was aware of it, but only partially. Her eyes were raking the room, searching for the one face she ached to see. 'Come along, my dear,' Helen said, suddenly putting an end to the awkward silence. She could not see Luciano anywhere but he certainly had not come to the aid of the damsel in distress. Helen felt faintly sick. She was aware that she herself had been similarly unkind to others equally unfashionable and vulnerable and now despised herself for it.

She watched the introductions. They had all taken Lucy's cue and greeted the newcomer in that amused and offhand manner that was so crushing. Sylvia hardly acknowledged the girl. She watched Francesca painfully maintain her dignity.

Suddenly she saw the girl's face flood with colour. From the rear of the group the Italian had moved forward to

322

greet her. He had been lurking behind the others, Helen realized. This was the boy Eleanor had said was the lover from Sicily. This was the boy Francesca adored. Helen's heart sank lower as she contemplated the sorry scene.

Helen saw d'Abrizzio bow over Francesca's hand. At least his manners were faultless. But there was something there ... What? Reluctance? Disdain? A withholding certainly. Could it be, she wondered, that he was weak enough not to want to offend the pack? She would despise him if he went along feebly with the group but that was the path he seemed to have chosen.

It was, in any event, a cool greeting, lacking in warmth or emotion or ardour, and Helen saw all the starch go out of the girl. She wilted, drooped, as Luciano moved back to the set, none of whom invited Francesca to join them as they made to go out through the French windows on to the terrace. They talked loudly of another game of tennis before changing for dinner, letting Francesca know by subtly excluding her that she was not welcome.

Francesca watched her lover leave, her face a mask. Only her eyes showed such sick regret and pain that it was impossible for Helen not to feel for her. Francesca sat down, shoulders slumped, and held her hands in her lap, twisting them around each other as if she were washing something.

Then someone detached from the group and went to the rejected girl and took her fevered hands in his own. Christopher had been standing in the window alcove, almost hidden by the green velvet curtains.

'Would you like to see the rose garden?' he asked her. 'Let me show you.'

Helen had never loved her son as much as she did at that moment. Her heart swelled with pride as she watched him take Francesca by the arm and lead her out on to the terrace. 'But won't you want to play tennis with the others?' Francesca asked timidly.

Helen followed them. She stood in the doorway, watching the group, uncertain now, shielding their faces from the fierce light of the dying sun. Her son and Francesca were a little removed from them but still within earshot. When they heard Francesca's question they reached out to Christopher as if to draw him away from her and into their orbit. Sylvia said, 'Come *on*, Christopher. A game of tennis is just what you need.'

He laughed and pulled away. 'Good Lord, no,' he said. 'It would be so boring. Why should I want to play tennis with you lot when I've captured the prettiest girl in Berkshire all for myself? Besides, it's the wrong time of the day for tennis,' he added firmly. 'It's going to be dark soon, you idiots.'

They stared at him, crestfallen and vaguely uncomfortable.

He led Francesca away, out and across the lawn. He kept hold of her hand. Her head was bowed, as if she was staring at the ground beneath her. He bent and whispered something to her. She turned her face to his, the pure outline ivory in the dusk.

Helen shivered. Something was happening and she could not put her finger on it. The group of young people loitered about on the terrace. Sylvia did nothing to help them.

Lucy Braithwaite said, 'Oh, come *on*, you lot. Let's play.'

Someone snorted. 'Don't be daft, Lucy. Christopher was right. You couldn't see anything now. It's too late.'

The group's attention was drawn irresistibly to Christopher and Francesca where they walked by the lake, white-clad, ethereal in the twilight. Christopher picked up a stone and threw it into the water. The noise did not reach them on the terrace, but they could all see the ripples it cast and a thousand fragmented crystals of water shimmering in the sunset.

~~~~~~

That night the band was playing 'Lady Be Good' and the trees were decorated with Chinese lanterns. Elm Court, as always, lent itself beautifully to a party.

Warm yellow light spilled from the house, out over the lawn. The pure silver moonlight touched the lake and set it glittering.

Francesca sat on the grey stone balustrade that separated the terrace from the lawns. She was alone. She stared down to the mirrorlike stretch of water where she and Christopher had walked earlier that evening, and wondered what it would be like to sail across it in a boat. Her chin trembled and every so often she gulped, swallowing the huge lump that seemed to be stuck in her throat. But it would not go away.

It was Luciano, Luciano her love. The fact was, however she looked at it, he had come out badly, a craven weakling.

She knew he still loved her, knew it in her bones. She knew also that he was ashamed of her here, for some reason. Yet Helen and Eleanor were happy with her as she was. She could not work it out. She hated the fact that he had let her down. Her hero had feet of clay. She turned as she heard Christopher behind her.

'And what are you doing, Francesca, out here all alone in the moonlight?'

She blushed and shook her head.

'Nothing.'

'I don't believe you.'

He tilted her chin, scrutinizing her face with its thick arched brows, wide and generous mouth, high cheekbones. It was a sweet face, he thought, and was wondering what colour exactly her eyes were when he saw the tears in them.

'What is it, Francesca? You can tell me.'

'Oh, it's just . . . life can be cruel,' she said faintly.

325

'I know that,' he said, 'but what particular cruelty is making you weep?' He looked out over the lake. 'It's Luciano, isn't it?' he asked. 'Can't you see that he's not worthy of you?'

Her face flushed a brighter red. Her eyes were cinnamon, he decided.

'Don't say anything against him, please.'

He understood. He admired her loyalty even though he felt it misplaced. Yet he was sure of two things: one, that Luciano deserved to be trounced for his cavalier treatment of Francesca, and two, that her sadness was not caused by unrequited emotion but rather regret for the passing of love, sorrow at its loss, and disillusionment that her lover could be so crass.

'He tore it apart like a cobweb in the wind,' she whispered.

'Things change,' he said. She nodded.

'Yes, I know that now. You have to learn things for yourself. People tried to warn me, I would not listen.' She sighed. 'But what is shocking for me, Christoper, is the way my whole life has changed in one day. All that was mine, that made up love and comfort, went . . . poof! I put so much into my feelings for Luciano, you understand?'

'Has it gone or have you just grown up?' he asked. She looked at him, surprised.

'When we are young and innocent,' he continued, 'we see things differently. We fall in love in a selfish way. We are blinded by love, particularly our first experience of it. We see only what we want to see, then we grow up through pain and suffering. Happiness does not help us to grow, you know.

'Then we fall in love in exactly the opposite way. We fall selflessly, thinking more of the other. Our eyes then are opened by love, not closed to our beloved's imperfections. We are aware of the loved one in a new and special way.'

The moonlight dappled her face. Someone called from

326

the house: 'Christopher! Christopher!' but he did not move. He stared at her face, silvered by the moonlight, caught in rapt attention.

'I see,' she said again. 'That's very true. A new idea. Something to think about.'

A gong sounded from the terrace.

'Well, don't think about it now, Francesca. Come, it's dinner time. Walk up with me, please.'

She smiled at him and put her hand in his. 'I would be delighted to.'

~~~~~~

All through dinner Luciano watched her. Francesca wore shell-pink satin. Her shoulders and breasts rose rounded, white and magnificent from a low neckline. The others all had bony necks and shoulders and if Francesca looked dated, Helen thought, she was none the less the most beautiful woman present. Luciano stared at her, not looking into her eyes but seeming to gaze at the cleft between her breasts where an organza rose nestled.

Helen had not known how to work out her placement. To separate Francesca and Luciano after their less than cordial meeting might cause her unhappiness; to put them together might cause embarrassment. So she compromised and placed them opposite each other.

Waves of colour came and went in Francesca's face. She was aware of Luciano's scrutiny, which was at times disconcerting. She felt pinned down, like a butterfly or a moth in a showcase, unable to remove herself from the heat of his stare, unable to protect herself from its almost insolent intensity. She could not fathom its meaning for these were not at all the looks of love she remembered from long ago in the forest.

Christopher, on her right, was attentive and charming and she turned to him more and more, responding to his gentle interest. On her other side a young man, a certain

327

Tommy Ellington-Gore, was asking if she hunted with the Quorn, had dined at Lizzie Corrington's in Eaton Square, had gone to the Duchess of Maltby's bash in Yorkshire, had played tennis at Windsor, or had seen Amanda James jump into the fountain in Trafalgar Square after the Berkley Square Ball? Perhaps she had joined the paper-chase through Harrods? Or had she perhaps wined and dined at the Café Royal? Having to reply to all these questions in the negative was becoming monotonous. 'Missed all the jolly japes then?' he commiserated. 'Dear me. How dreadfully boring.'

She turned to Christopher who had overheard the conversation and whose eyes twinkled in sympathy.

'All that energy wasted,' he said to her, smiling. 'Jumping into Trafalgar Square and paper-chasing through Harrods! Much better employed riding down here. Don't let him rile you or make you feel awkward.'

'Oh, what an old stick-in-the-mud you are, Christopher,' Lucy Braithwaite shrilled from the end of the table where Helen had put her as far away as possible from Francesca. Not one whit deterred, Lucy continued over the others' conversation in her harsh insistent voice, 'This Season has been a great wheeze. But you *chose* not to go. That's different from not being invited.' She shot a malicious glance at Francesca.

The colour stained Francesca's cheeks again and she wished she could disappear. Lucy continued, 'It was the best Season ever, and anyone who was anyone at all was there.'

Christopher laughed derisively. 'That you *know*, Lucy. Anyone who was anyone that you *know* was there. The Duke of Cornwall is in Argentina, Archie Fanthorpe is in Africa, Angeline Beauchamp-March is in Cannes, where it is reported she is having a super time on the Bourbons' yacht. None of them was in London for the Season this year. So, you see, you exaggerate. There's a big world outside ours, Lucy, and I think the best and surest sign of

328

breeding is to be extra polite to visitors. That's what Mama taught me, at any rate.' He laughed lightly. 'Don't you agree, Luciano?'

'What? Oh, yes. Yes, of course.'

There was an awkward pause, then conversation resumed again.

Helen sighed. 'I'm sure some of you young people must find Elm Court dreadfully dull.'

Lucy Braithwaite cried, 'Oh heavens, no. The horses here are the best in the country. Absolutely smashing. The riding here makes a visit more than worthwhile.'

Everyone looked at her. Realization dawned slowly. Horrified, she tried to undo her clumsy mistake but it was too late.

Francesca could feel Luciano resume his scutiny. Those dark eyes, briefly deflected, were now fixed on her again.

After dinner the guests played cards: bezique and piquet. Tommy Ellington-Gore got tight and wandered about with the whiskey decanter under his arm.

Lucy Braithwaite said in an ugly whisper to Francesca, 'If you think I can't see your little game then you're wrong. Coming here all milk and honey and making goo-goo eyes at Chris. Well, your little game won't work, I can promise you that.'

Francesca did not even look at her but went and sat quietly beside Helen, her hands folded in her lap.

Her hostess decided the girl was entrancing. She was beautiful and modest. Lovely qualities, Helen thought. The child did not even pretend to want to be a bright young thing. All Christopher's and Sylvia's friends worked at it so hard, putting such effort into being brittle and bright, shocking and modern, brash and audacious, but to Helen they appeared crass and not a little vulgar. The Palucci girl with her self-effacing ways, her lack of biting repartee and quiet, self-contained beauty, was a refreshing change.

Now and then Christopher came to talk to her, to

reassure her with a smile that lit his kind grey eyes.

They rolled back the carpet, Lucy Braithwaite self-importantly leading them in the new dances, laughing in a high-pitched voice, kicking her legs and flapping her elbows about like windmills. Sylvia was copying her, Helen saw, and wished her daughter had chosen a more attractive friend.

'Do come and join the fun.' Tommy came teetering over and asked Francesca to dance, but she shook her head and explained she did not know how. This left him dumbfounded, and he wandered unsteadily away.

Luciano stood at the empty fireplace and watched her. Stupid, Francesca thought. Stupid to feel so shy before him.

She remembered the clearing in the woods. She could almost smell the leaves and feel the breeze playing on her naked body. She could hear birdsong and the hum from the undergrowth; see the look of love on Luciano's face. Shivering, she looked up and was startled to meet his eyes for the first time that evening. They were full of desire. His look was melting, liquid and soft. She felt suffocated, as if she could not breathe.

Then she looked away, back to the dancers in the hall, back to the butler with his tray of drinks, back to where Tommy sat on the edge of a chair, decanter clutched in his hand, drunken tears flowing down his cheeks, back to Helen's kind face, back to her own hands.

The party broke up soon after that and the guests retired to bed.

Alone in her bedroom Francesca got undressed and into bed and lay motionless, looking at the ceiling.

What did he feel for her, this new Luciano she had met today? For that matter, what did she feel for him? Still something, certainly. She had been aware of his every movement, conscious of and excited by his presence and unwavering interest in her. She was confused by him. The

330

old trust and unselfconscious acceptance of each other had gone. What was this turmoil she felt instead?

He had slighted her at their first meeting, he had hurt her deeply, humiliated her. But at dinner, watching her like that with a passionate gaze . . . what was she to make of it all?

Someone tapped at her door. She assumed it was Helen coming to say goodnight and called out, 'Come in.'

Luciano opened the door and shut it behind him noiselessly. He put his finger to his lips and went over to her and sat on the bed. She opened her mouth to speak but he covered it with his own and she could not make a sound.

The softness of his lips, the fierceness of his arms after such long waiting and thinking and dreaming about him, made her response ardent and passionate. Yet at the same time she wanted to stop him, say, 'Wait! Wait a moment. You are a stranger to me now. You are not the boy I left. Give me time to know you again.' But his scent, his feel, were so familiar her body relaxed involuntarily, trustfully, in his embrace. When she could speak, when he had released her from the heat of his mouth, she murmured the words that summed up how she felt: 'I love you, oh, I love you.'

She felt his hands on her breasts, his soft moan as he kissed her nipples. She closed her eyes. He seemed suddenly so familiar. She gave a gasp of pleasure and slight pain when she felt his hardness in her. Her response was welcoming. She lifted her legs around his body responding to his urgency.

'Now! Now, like that, my pretty. Gently first, then harder. Harder!' he cried.

A cold chill rippled over her body and she put her hands to his chest to push him away. His voice had been impersonal, he could have been talking to anyone. Something in his tone separated her from him. She felt he

331

was not talking to her. She tried to see his face but could not. He was thrusting himself into her now, pulling at her legs, groaning with excitement and pleasure that took no account of how she felt, that mostly excluded her.

'You love me?' she said doubtfully, knowing it was a stupid thing to ask at this time, knowing he did not hear her yet desperate for his answer. She shook his shoulder, certain that he was unaware of her except someone he was using for his pleasure; feeling too that she was being silly and gauche and that Lucy Braithwaite would not behave in such an unsophisticated manner.

'Oh, yes, I love you. Oh, yes. Yes. Now!'

The words reassured and consoled her. She allowed the tide of passion to sweep over her. Feelings she had never imagined possible overwhelmed her. Nerve ends came alive. Her body awakened, responded. She held his hair between her fingers, smelled his scent, felt her body caught up in the rhythm of his.

But suddenly it was over. With a cry he released her and left her quivering and hungry for more. He lay on her for a while, panting. A trickle of sweat slid down his face and she could taste the salt.

'I love you,' she whispered, but there was doubt in her voice. He rose wordlessly, pulled on his pyjamas and went to the door. She could not believe what he was doing. 'Luciano!' she cried but he did not stop. He opened the door and left.

He left her there in bed, her head full of questions, her body aching, curbing a desperate desire to cry.

~~~~~~

'I wanted to see you, Luciano. I asked Lady Wylde if I could talk to you alone.'

They sat in the green drawing-room. A portrait of Hugh Wylde by Sargent stared down at them. The heavy olive velvet curtains were drawn back and it was raining

332

outside. Tiny spattering drops pocked the lake and turned it silver-grey. The trees and grass drank thirstily and became greener as you looked.

Francesca sat in a straight-backed chair. She was wearing a lace blouse and a taupe moirée skirt and jacket. Her fingers played with the frills at her wrists.

Luciano stood in front of the fireplace, a wing of hair falling over his forehead, one arm draped along the marble mantlepiece, his jacket held by the loop over his shoulder, as if he intended to spend only a moment there and was in a hurry to depart. He had not spoken to her since the night a week ago when he had come to her room. It had been a very anxious week, a week of not knowing why he did not communicate with her, why he tried to avoid her, why he was so remote. He had not snubbed her directly but simply slipped out of any room or gathering when he saw her approach.

Frustrated, in an agony of suspense, she had decided on an arranged meeting with Helen's consent. Not that her hostess was aware of what had happened that night a week ago. Francesca was sure that Helen would have been shocked to the core at her guests' wanton behaviour. She herself was appalled by what she had done. In retrospect she could not understand how she could have allowed herself to be so swept off her feet with so little encouragement. She could not rid herself of the idea that it had all been her fault. She wanted to know where she stood. She was determined to find out.

'What do you want?' Luciano asked, his voice neutral.

'I wanted . . .' She hesitated. 'I hope you'd tell me what you . . .' Again she stumbled, the blush mounting in her cheeks. She hated the red stain that suffused her face when she was nervous. It made her feel like a country bumpkin instead of a lady. '. . .what you feel about me now. What you did feel. Whether . . .'

He laughed.

333

'Good God, Francesca, what do you mean, "feel"? What do you expect? What *should* I feel? I like you. I think you are, as the English say, a jolly good sort. So, you ask what I feel? I felt excited by you. I lusted after you, then and now. That's all.'

Tears stung her eyes as she looked up at him. He shrugged looking at her expressionlessly. No amorous glances this morning.

'That was not all. You said you loved me!' she cried.

He slung his jacket over the back of the chair and sat down.

'Oh, for Christ's sake, Francesca, of course I did. What did you expect me to say? That I hated you?' He gave a mischievous grin. 'I'm always in love with a woman when I'm making love to her.'

She could feel physical pain in her breast. She hoped he could not see it, and went on even though she knew she would hurt her even more.

'No, Luciano, you know what I mean. No matter what you say now, I know you loved me then at least.'

He grimaced. 'Yours was a family on my father's estate. Oh, I know your father owned the land, but you were not our sort. We grew up together. You were – are – very pretty.' He paused and looked for a moment like the Luciano she remembered. 'You were my first love. Yes, that's true.' A shade of sadness crossed the selfish mouth; regret at the passing of romance, of hope, of innocence. He shook his head. 'Wet behind the ears,' he said ruefully. 'I was so innocent. What did you expect, Francesca?'

'You keep asking me that, what did I expect, what did I expect?' She was stung into anger. 'I didn't *expect* anything at all. But now I expect you to behave like a gentleman and tell me how you feel about me. Don't play cat and mouse with me, Luciano. I have been through too much to stand that from you. Just tell me the truth. What do you feel now?'

334

'I don't feel anything much,' he said casually, hurting her cruelly. 'I think you are beautiful but I can't forget your background. The peasant Paluccis, always half-way down the hill. The little band of hard-working peasants. So respectable.' He glanced across at her. 'I enjoyed the other night. I had to have you. We're good together. But we're from different worlds. Oh, with you people would never guess. You fit in beautifully here. But in Sicily it would be different. And my children, my heirs, I need to marry a lady for those. In Sicily you'll always be a peasant. Father intends for me to bring a suitable bride back to be next mistress of the *palazzo*.' He broke off and shrugged. 'Oh God, Francesca, you make me sound like a snob, a bastard . . .'

'Well, you are,' she said succinctly, furious with his insensitivity and cruelty. Had she ever really talked to him before? Had young love blinded her to the shallowness of her lover? Helen warned her, but she had mooned about and nearly broken her heart over this selfish, unworthy boy.

'You're not much of a man, are you, Luciano?' she asked him calmly. 'Oh, how could I have loved you so much? How could I have made such a mistake? What a fool I am. And to think I thought that one day we'd be married. That I'd spend the rest of my life with you.'

He looked shocked. 'Good Lord, Francesca, you didn't think I'd ever marry you?' He sounded so incredulous that it was almost comical. 'Can you truthfully see yourself there, mistress of the *palazzo*? A Palucci from the hillside? Good grief, we'd be the laughing stock of Sicily.'

He stood up and retrieved his jacket. 'I love my home, Francesca. I love my position. I'll be a good *padrone*, a good *signeur*. I'll make the land pay. Plots of land will never again slip into greedy Palucci hands. Oh, no. You would be ludicrously out of place there, my dear, so forget your delusions of grandeur and find yourself a more suitable husband.'

He smiled at her, a charming smile belying the warning in his words, and walked out of the room, leaving her alone and very angry.

Chapter Nineteen

Marcello checked into Palmer House Hotel in Chicago. The large lobby was decorated in Art Nouveau style and, sensitive as always to his surroundings, Marcello appreciated the grace of the gently curved staircases and the modern economy of design. Bellboys rushed about. Discreet staff ministered to his every need. Bathed and changed, the grime of the journey washed away, he sat down to work out his next move.

He could not concentrate. Mirella's face imposed itself on his thoughts, blotting out all else and making it impossible to plan.

He picked up the phone, clicked the receiver and asked the exchange to get her number.

'Hello?'

'It's me, Marcello. Mirella, what the hell game are you playing? Whatever it is, it's driving me mad.'

Her laugh was painfully clear. 'Gosh, you sound mad.'

'I am.'

'Then come on over.'

'I'm in Chicago.'

There was a pause. 'Without telling me? Now *I'm* mad.'

'I did it to get away from you. Then I found out I couldn't.'

'Aha!'

'Will you marry me?' It was out before he realized what he was saying. As soon as he'd spoken it he was glad. It was what he wanted. It just had not occurred to him before.

There was silence at the other end of the line. Then, 'Where are you staying?'

'Palmer House.'

'OK.'

'But what about my proposal?'

There was a click as she put down the receiver.

He figured she would need some persuading, but Mirella, he was realistic enough to be aware, was not averse to Cartier jewels and the luxury he could offer her. She was not mercenary but she liked her creature comforts. He would woo her as no woman had ever been wooed before.

Hell, but she could have said something, given him an indication of how the land lay, not just hung up on him like that!

At least phoning her had cleared his mind. He could plan what he was going to do now. He thought he would spend a quiet day, have a light lunch and make a few calls. Then in the evening he would go to the Blue Lady and see Mario. It would be better than going to his home in daylight. Marcello did not know the exact address. He would have to ask, discreetly. Mario might find out and must not be alarmed.

No, best see him in the nightclub which would be packed. Luigi Stroza had said it was very popular. Neither of them would do anything rash with so many people around. Then he could explain about Guido and give his brother enough money to make himself scarce for a while, go to Miami, live it up, have a good time.

He went to the phone, called room service, ordered easy-over eggs, ham, orange juice, hash browns, coffee, cream . . . and a double helping of toast. Then he called an old business buddy and made a date for lunch.

When he had polished off his late breakfast he called another number. The phone was picked up at the third ring, but there was silence at the other end. He said, 'This is

338

Marcello Palucci.'

'Hello, Mr Palucci.'

'Who am I speaking to?'

'What do you want to know?'

'All I want to say is, I've come to see my brother, Mario. I'll take care of him. Is that understood? I am prepared to pay handsomely for the privilege. You take my meaning?'

The voice said, 'Oh, yes. I clearly do. But it may not be possible, Mr Palucci. There is another interested party who is eager to, er, shall we say, take your brother out of circulation.'

'Well, if that happens, you will have blown a fortune. Goodbye.'

'No wait, Mr Palucci . . .'

'Goodbye.'

He replaced the receiver. He found that he was trembling. But there was nothing he could do. It was out of his hands. Either they liked his money more than the nuisance value of Mario or they didn't. He would do his best to take care of things but that, he thought, was all he could do.

~~~~~~

Guido looked out on De La Salle in the mid-afternoon. He stared unseeing at the kids playing around the fire hydrant, the cop talking to the woman carrying a basket of washing, the old man sitting on the porch chewing tobacco.

He was thinking. A deep frown furrowed his brow and his mouth was dry. Earlier in the day he had bought a gun on Clark Street. No one thought it odd when he asked where he could purchase one. Then he bought it, easy. No one questioned him about what he wanted it for.

He felt very uncomfortable with the gun. Very uneasy altogether.

He had not used any of his contacts. He had slipped into

339

the USA via Florida, taken trains up to the Windy City, and felt fairly confident that no one knew he was there. He did not want anyone warning Mario. He did not want anyone to use him as a patsy. He was going to be nobody's fall guy. Part of him said, why keep quiet? Go see the man. Lucca was his name, according to Tomaso Canona. Ask him about Mario. Then he thought, suppose he warns Mario? Suppose he wants to protect him? Suppose . . .? There were too many imponderables. Suppose Mario gets the warning and runs? So then he'd be off the hook. His face lightened. Not to have to tackle his brother. Only deep down he knew he would not be off the hook. He would have to follow Mario.

He'd be committed to following his brother and finding him. He could spend a long time doing that. Better finish it now, come what may. It was decided, it was something he had to do, so he would do it good. Give it his best shot and get out. Back to Eleanor. Try to forget it.

Oh, God. When he thought of her he felt weak as a child. How would she feel about him when she knew he had killed his brother? He punched the wall with his fist until it hurt. Goddamn, how would he feel about himself?

It was too late to think about it now. He picked up the gun, fondling it, trying to get to like it, feel it was his friend. But it was no use. The cold steel was strange and threatening in his hand, would never become part of him as he had seen Giuseppe's rifle become a third arm. This little Smith & Wesson was made for killing, it was not a toy, nor was it an instrument to procure food for the family; its purpose was abhorrent to him, it was a weapon of death.

He lay down on the bed. The room was clean but sparsely furnished. It had a single bed. Curiously like Signora Merciano, Mrs Cutty seemed pathologically determined to keep him alone in it.

'Now don't get me wrong, I ain't no prude, but no one in my house entertains members of the opposite sex. See, there's the question of payment. Ain't fair on me someone gets a free night.'

Guido did not follow her line of reasoning. He was too preoccupied.

He felt very lonely. He longed to hear the sound of his mother tongue. He ached for his own people, their familiarity, their unreserved acceptance of him as one of their own. They knew his reasoning. They knew the validity of his mission. They alone could still his anxiety, stifle his doubts.

He had kept aloof on the ship. He had become more and more isolated, suspicious of everyone, paranoid at the slightest show of friendship. He had spoken to no one and kept himself to himself, difficult in a friendly pioneer nation where everyone greeted each other and easy exchanges with total strangers were the order of the day.

He felt totally alone, and the deeper he penetrated America the worse it got. At last, here in this crummy room on De La Salle, he had reached the depths of isolation and felt lonelier than he had ever believed possible. He was a foreigner here, alien and apart.

He knew he could easily find friendship, or at least comradeship. All he had to do was go into any one of the Italian places he saw, places selling fresh pasta, restaurants advertising dishes from the old country.

But he was not staying and he did not want to advertise his presence in the country. He wanted to get the job done and leave, hurry to Eleanor in England. He dare not allow himself to think what would happen if he were caught.

He watched the light fade with evening, lying on his bed, an arm supporting his head. A neon sign across the street blinked on and off and flooded the room with red, yellow and blue shafts of violent colour.

It was nearly time. He felt sick. He knew that if he thought about what he was going to do, he would not be able to carry on. So he closed his mind, putting all his energy into preparing himself.

He tucked his gun into the top of his trousers and put on his jacket. It was uncomfortable but that could not be helped. He put on the hat he had bought on Clark Street. It shadowed his face, almost concealing it. He looked anonymous, an indistinct, indefinable figure. A shadow.

He looked out of the window, murmuring a half-formulated prayer.

'*Jesu Maria*, help me. Don't let . . .' But he could not go on. There would be no help for him in Heaven. It was time. He turned and left the room and went out into the night.

~~~~~~

'But where is he? Where is he now? You *must* have seen him.'

Luigi Stroza sat back in his deep chair in his New York office and smiled at the beautiful blonde before him. She was a pleasure to contemplate and he feasted his eyes on her long silk-stockinged legs, silken hair so full of light and wide blue eyes.

'I regret to say, I have not.' He spread his hands.

Who would have thought that Enrico Domini could have produced such a dazzling daughter? That squat little man, so ruthless and aggressive, how had he managed to sire such a cool, golden beauty?

She wanted to know about Guido Palucci. These Paluccis, he thought, they're everywhere. They had considerably enlivened New York with their passionate activity. Who was chasing who? Luigi looked with amused eyes at the woman before him. Clad in apple-green and white fox, she looked fresh as a mint julep. Yet the face was a mirror for her thoughts and they were a jumble.

She talked of Guido just as fervently as Marcello Palucci had. Just as wildly she promised him any sum he cared to ask for his protection. Guido, on his way to Chicago to kill his brother, had a lot of people anxious that he did not succeed. What was he like, this brother, twin to the attractive and ruthless Marcello, that others should care so much for his safety and want so badly to protect him?

'He would come to you,' she said.

'Why?' he countered. 'If he had money, why would he need me? Your father has told him Mario's whereabouts. Financed him.'

She made an impatient gesture. 'My father wants to destroy him.'

Luigi Stroza absorbed this piece of information though his bland face gave no sign. So Enrico Domini did not approve of his daughter's liaison with Guido Palucci? Useful information that he was not yet certain how to use . . .

'That is why he told him Mario is in Chicago,' she was saying. 'That is why he financed him. Don't you see? He wants Guido Palucci destroyed.'

'What can I say?' Luigi played for time. He was staring at her legs, so long, so slim, knees dimpled and round.

'I will do what I can,' he said, 'but as I see it there is little anyone can do to stop the wheels that have been set in motion. Guido Palucci will go to Chicago. Find Mario. Kill him.' He sighed and shrugged. 'It is so stupid, Miss Domini. If you ask me, vendetta is outmoded and barbaric. It is evil.' He raised his eyebrows and leaned towards her across his desk. 'Yet if you ask me what I would do if one of my family stole my money like a thief in the night,' he spread his hands again, 'well, I have to admit, barbaric or not, I would probably resort to vendetta myself.'

She looked at him angrily, 'I'm not concerned with the morality or immorality of vendetta. Personally I think it *stupido*. I do not care if Mario Palucci lives or dies. After what he did, he deserves what he gets. But not Guido, Signore Stroza. I want to find Guido so that he does not kill his brother.'

343

'Especially as it is the wrong brother.'

He did not know why he said it. Perhaps to impress her, show her he knew something she did not.

If he had wanted to astound her, he had succeeded. She looked at him, eyes wide, breath held. 'What did you say?'

'I said that Guido Palucci, if he kills Mario for stealing their father's money, kills the wrong brother.'

She kept her eyes fixed on him, an astonished blue stare. 'Mario did not steal it?'

He shook his head. 'I have it on good authority that he did not. Mind you,' he added, 'it was not for want of trying.'

'Then if it was not Mario or Guido, it was . . .?' She left the question hanging on the air.

'Aha!' he said, smiling.

She stood up suddenly. 'Signor Stroza,' she said, 'my father would want you to tell me . . .'

'My dear young lady,' he interrupted her, 'I doubt if your father knows you are here. It is quite unlike him to let you come to New York alone and unprotected, looking for a man hellbent on self-destruction. That does not sound like Enrico Domini at all.'

It was a shot in the dark and he could see at once he had hit the target. She sat down again abruptly, looking crestfallen.

A thought struck him. Enrico Domini, top man in Rome, rich as Croesus, would be grateful to Stroza if he took good care of his daughter.

'Listen, my dear, let us put our heads together and sort out what we can do, eh? Where are you staying?'

'What?' Her thoughts had been far away. 'Oh. At the Algonquin.'

'Suppose I pick you up there in, say, two hours. I'll have finished here by then.'

She was looking at him, faintly surprised.

'We'll have a quiet dinner and talk about getting you to

344

Chicago. Perhaps I can find out what is happening. I think you should have a bodyguard . . .'

She burst out laughing. 'Oh, Mr Stroza, don't be ridiculous. What on earth would I do with a bodyguard?'

He looked at her seriously. 'I don't think you understand the seriousness of your position. Mario Palucci has made enemies. The powers that be are eager to see him wiped out. Guido Palucci will do it for them.'

'And so? Why should *I* need a bodyguard? I have simply come to stop all this nonsense.'

He smiled at her choice of words. 'They will not want you to stop the, er, nonsense.'

'Tough!'

'But, listen, Miss Domini . . .'

She stood up. 'No, you listen. No one will dare harm the daughter of Enrico Domini.'

'They may not know who you are,' he said softly. 'If I were you I would be inclined to take whatever help I could get. You don't know this country. Enrico Domini is not so important here.'

He saw the uncertainty in her eyes and pressed home his advantage.

'You don't know where you are going, where you should look, how to start . . . I do. Do you know where to look for Guido Palucci?'

She looked doubtful. 'I suppose you're right.'

'Of course I am. Now leave it all in my hands. Go back to the hotel. Have a nice bath. I'll pick you up later. We can arrange for you to go tomorrow if need be, fresh as a daisy. Or not. We'll see.'

~~~~~~

Marcello returned to his hotel in Chicago after lunch and a visit to his bank. He had arranged to withdraw a considerable sum of money in cash, and felt conspicuous carrying the attaché case stuffed with bills back to the hotel. He walked

345

up State Street to the Palmer House where he deposited it in the hotel safe. He picked up his key at the desk, took the elevator to the second floor, walked to his room and went in.

She was sitting in the bed, her breasts barely covered by the fine peach lace of her nightdress. Her hair was brushed out. Like burnished copper, it lay on the alabaster white of her shoulders. He gasped and stared at her.

She said a trifle anxiously, 'I came in person to say yes. Did I do the right thing?'

He grinned at her 'Yes,' he said, 'Oh God, yes.'

Relief flooded her face and she opened her arms. 'Then come here, you dope. I'm tired of games.'

~~~~~~

Pino hurried Minouche into the car, for all the world as if she were a piece of shopping, practically slinging her into the back. The sweet sickly smell of the cheap cologne he wore churned her stomach.

'Take her back,' he instructed Moses, and winked at the driver, slamming the door. 'Ol' man'll be peaceful now for a while.'

She could see that Pino dyed his hair and it suddenly struck her that he must be quite old, forty odd, she reckoned. For a moment her eyes met his knife-sharp glance and she shivered. He was his father's son and Mario was mad if he had any illusions about the outcome of any power struggle between them. Pino would win, hands down.

She felt sick and full of hatred for herself, Lucca and his son. A wave of helplessness overcame her. It sapped her courage and left her weak and vulnerable. She ached for someone to champion her. She was often tempted to tell Mario, to lay it on his shoulders and let him deal with it, but she knew the consequences would be fatal. Mario would kill Lucca in a hot-headed fury. Then he would either be caught by the cops or blown away by Pino, probably the latter.

346

She opened her bag and took out the bottle. She gulped down a few deep swallows, screwed on the cap, then replaced it in her bag. She did not notice Moses watching her through the rear-view mirror.

Mario had said to meet him at the Blue Lady. Moses dropped her on Lincoln and she ran up the steps to the front door. She went immediately to the bathroom and, peeling off her clothes, commenced almost to drown herself. Head and all, she immersed herself in water, spluttering and choking as it gushed into her mouth and nose. Then she showered, scrubbing her skin cruelly. She went to the basin and brushed her teeth until the gums bled, then rinsed out her mouth with disinfectant. She went into the living room and over to the bar where she poured herself a large brandy, gulped it down, refilled her glass and took another more civilized sip. She went and lay on the bed naked. Leaving the half-full brandy-glass on the bedside table and putting her thumb in her mouth, she closed her eyes.

She knew she was reaching the end of her tether. The things Lucca was making her do were getting more and more weird. He needed special stimulation at his age, he told her, smiling at her through those lizard eyes. She squeezed back the tears that threatened to flow. One solitary drop ran down her cheek and on to her neck. She was not a prostitute, she told herself, she could not continue like this. She was very near breaking point.

She finished the brandy, got up and went to the clothes closet. She got out the first dress Mario had bought her and put it on. She tried to eliminate the dark circles with make-up and painted her lips bright scarlet to distract attention from her eyes.

Then she went to the club.

A blast of upbeat music, cigarette smoke and noise engulfed Minouche as she entered, giving her an unexpected lift.

347

The place was full and everyone seemed to be having a good time. Jake was tinkling 'Mood Indigo' on the piano and Ella May shifted her weight from one mountainous buttock to the other, inhaled deeply on her cigarette and gave herself another shot of whatever poison was in the bottles labelled '100-year-old Whiskey'. She caught Minouche as she passed.

'How ya doin', hon?'

'Where's Mario, Ella May?'

The black woman shrugged. Her skin was like velvet but she was sweating copiously, the underarms of her dress stained with dark patches. You forgot all that when she sang. Her voice seduced and broke your heart.

'He's over there,' she pointed, 'lookin' fo' you. Oh, honey, you jes wastin' yo' time on that man. Why don' you see the love right under yo' nose.' She pointed to Pierre who stood near the door, ever watchful. Shaking her head she said, 'I'm only tellin' yo', honey, 'cause I'm the same kinda woman myself. Allus pick the wrong dang man.'

But Minouche had seen Mario and was not listening.

He waved her over. Her heart lifted at the sight of him and the concealed impatience in his voice. He had missed her.

'Where ya been, honey? I bin' lookin' all over for ya.'

She smiled at him reassuringly. 'I'm here now, *chérie*. Let's sit down.'

'But where ya bin'?'

'I was resting,' she said.

'I bin' upstairs. You weren't there then.'

She had no energy to think up excuses and the last thing she wanted was to arouse his suspicions, but she was tired to her very bones.

'I was shopping on State Street.'

'You buy that dress? It's sensational, honey. When'd you get home? I was lookin' for you.'

'I got home a little while ago. Moses drove me.'

'Fuckin' Moses! That guy watches me, like you said. You know, you were right about him, sugar. Never takes his eyes off me.'

His attention deflected, thank God, she made one last pitch, not expecting it to succeed but hoping against hope.

'Mario, I'm worried. I heard Moses talking again about your brother coming after you. And Pino. He frightens me. Scares me to death. They mean to get rid of you. Let's go tonight.'

He stared at her as if she was crazy. 'Where?' he asked incredulously.

'Anywhere. California, the Sunshine State. Or Miami.'

He thought of the sun and how he hated it. 'You kiddin'?' he asked. 'Yeah, you're kiddin'.' Then a thought struck him. 'Where'd you see Pino? He never comes here.'

She thought fast. 'He stopped the car on State Street to give Moses a message.'

'An' my brother, that's bullshit. My brother . . .'

His face had changed, total astonishment making his mouth fall open and his eyes bulge.

'Jesus H. Christ. My brother!'

She followed his gaze and knew at once from the family resemblance that this well-dressed man coming down the stairs must be a relative. He was taller than Mario, very different from him in style, but the resemblance was unmistakable.

Mario's hand reached for his gun but the man crossing the room raised his hands, palm upwards, as he walked towards them.

'Watch him, *chérie*, watch him!' Minouche whispered while the tall confident man moved towards their table, hands raised as if for silence or to say 'Stop'.

Mario did not remove his hand from his gun.

'Marcello?' He sounded incredulous. 'I didn't expect you.'

'Yes, Mario, I know,' the tall man said, sitting down.

349

Minouche watched intently as he continued, 'I haven't come to kill you, so relax. I've come to warn you. Where can we talk?'

'Be careful, Mario. Be very careful,' Minouche said.

'It's OK. If Marcello says he hasn't come to kill me, then I believe him.'

'Can we talk?' Marcello asked again.

Mario nodded. He rose and Minouche got up too.

'Alone,' Marcello said.

'Where I go, she goes,' Mario said. Marcello shrugged and followed them out of the club.

The Ape and Pierre were swiftly at their side but Mario said, 'This is my brother. We wanna be alone, OK? Take care o'things for me.'

Pierre looked at Minouche who nodded imperceptibly.

'*Tu es tranquille?*' he asked.

'*Oui, chérie.*'

They went up to the living room of Mario's apartment.

'Fix us a coupla drinks, honey,' he said, not looking at Minouche but keeping his eyes fixed on his brother. 'Mind if I frisk you? As a precaution.' Marcello smiled. 'Sure. Go ahead.'

He was clean. Mario sighed, grinned, and sat down, indicating that Marcello should do likewise.

'See, sugar, I tol' ya. My brothers wouldn't kill me. See, Marcello, she had this cock-eyed idea one of my brothers was comin' to blow me away.' He smiled to himself at the craziness of such an idea and shook his head.

'She's right, Mario,' Marcello said, his voice cold.

'Whaddaya mean?' Mario's head jerked at the softly spoken statement.

'What I said, she's right. Guido is coming to kill you.'

Mario looked at him in disbelief. 'Jeez!' he murmured. 'I don't believe you're tellin' me this.'

'That is why I'm here, Mario. To prevent him. Not that

350

I'd care very much if he did, *capisce*? But Guido is my twin. He's a nice guy, Mario, not like you an' me. He couldn't carry a thing like murder. Too heavy for him. So I've come to stop him.'

Minouche let out her breath. She had been holding it since they entered the apartment. She brought the brothers their drinks then went back to the bar and poured one for herself.

Mario looked at Marcello and laughed. 'Big deal,' he said. 'Think I couldn't take care of myself? Jeez, you wet behind the ears or somethin'? I got goons down there twist your head off soon as look at you.'

'But are you sure they're *your* goons? Not Lucca's? Or Pino's?'

Mario thought of Pierre's barely concealed hatred of him. He thought of the contempt in Moses's eyes, and the fear in the Ape's. He looked at Marcello in surprise.

'How come you know about Lucca and Pino?'

Marcello laughed. 'I know a lot, Mario, and I have a plan. Get you out of it, like a good brother.'

He was being sarcastic. Mario looked at him with dislike. 'Say, just a minute. Why does Guido want to kill me? I ain't don' nuthen to him.'

'He doesn't want to kill you, Mario. That's the point. He *has* to kill you. Vendetta, see?'

'But why?'

'They think you took the money, Mario. See, Papa killed himself, Mama too. Paulo has run away, we don't know where. You ruined Francesca's life in the village. She had to leave. And Serena is sick in her mind. You left quite a legacy behind, Mario.'

He was trying to assimilate what he had heard. 'Oh, my God! Jesus Christ. Papa and Mama dead? Jesus.'

'Yeah. Papa hanged himself. Mama cut her wrists. All down to you, Mario.'

He felt a flood of sorrow rise like a tide within him,

overwhelming him. He was trembling all over. Minouche came to his side and took his arm. He shrugged her away brusquely. He looked around wildly, rubbed his face with his hands, dishevelling the slicked-back hair.

Then he said, 'But I didn' do it! I told you, I didn' steal the money.'

'I know that, Mario. But they don't.'

'He's the one who took it, *chérie*,' Minouche was saying.

Mario didn't look at her.

'*Chérie*, listen, he's the one who took the money. Otherwise how did he know you didn't take it. Think!'

Light dawned on Mario. Minouche was right. If Marcello knew, then he must be the one who had taken it. A murderous rage welled up in him, drowning his sorrow and filling him with a lust for blood.

Before anyone could stop him, he lunged across the room at Marcello, knocking him and the chair he sat in on their backs. Landing on top of his brother, he began to hit his face, pounding him as if to purge himself of the fury within. Marcello could feel the blood pouring from his nose and taste the hot sticky liquid in his mouth. Husbanding his energy he pushed his body forward, knocking Mario off balance. He rolled off and across the floor, hitting his head against the leg of the table and letting out a roar of pain. Minouche was yelling: 'Stop it! Please, stop it.'

Marcello had leapt to his feet and Mario came charging at him like an enraged bull, knocking him over again, pummelling him as he used to do when they were boys. And as they had then, Marcello tried to head him off. Once more he pushed away, got to his feet with far less agility this time, and delivered a stunning left to the jaw under which Mario crumbled. But he still came back like a terrier to hit wildly at his brother. His breath now came in harsh sobs, and Minouche knew that he was, in his own way, suffering from the shock and sorrow of his parents' death as well as the outrage he felt that it was this brother who had, as he saw it, cheated and made a fool of him.

He was hitting out wildly now, sobbing. Marcello held him off effortlessly.

Suddenly all the fight went out of Mario. He put his arms around his brother, weeping on his shoulder. Marcello held him but his face was cold and expressionless.

Then just as suddenly Mario stopped, gulped, pulled himself away and sat down, breathing heavily.

'You bastard,' he said. 'You fuckin' bastard. You set me up for this.'

Marcello had taken a handkerchief from his top pocket. He pressed it to his mouth where Mario had split his lip open. 'You set yourself up,' he said. 'And fighting isn't going to improve things.'

'You took the money, didn't you?' Mario said, not needing a reply.

'Only because you gave me the opportunity,' Marcello said, 'And it's water under the bridge. You did all right without it.'

'But Guido's coming to kill me!'

'Need never happen, Mario. You gotta leave now. Go to Florida or California. My treat.'

'Just what I wanted him to do. Just exactly what I said.' Minouche was eager, relief in her voice. 'Oh, listen to him, Mario. Please listen to him.' She thought of a life without Lucca, a life free of that persecution.

'Go there,' Marcello urged him. 'Lie low for a while. I'll get Guido. Tell him the truth. We'll sort it out between us. Then you can come back here, no problem.'

'I dunno.' Mario sounded doubtful. 'Why can't I explain to Guido I didn' do it? Tell him to lay off me.'

'Because you won't get the chance. I know my brother. Once he's made up his mind to do something, he'll do it good. He'll shoot first. You won't have a chance to explain.'

Mario shook his head. The furniture was all over the

353

place, broken, smashed. Couldn't have been much good in the first place, Marcello thought.

'Please do what he says, Mario, please. He's right. Let's leave here. Go away.' Minouche was repeating over and over, 'Go to California or Florida, like I said.'

'You don't understand. Here I'm somebody. Here I'm a big name. I can't just quit.'

'You'll be a big name OK, front page of the *Chicago Herald Tribune*, shot dead.'

'OK, OK. All right. Maybe you're right. So what do I do?'

Marcello had it all worked out. 'I'll get you the money. I've got it in the safe in the hotel.'

'How much?'

'Enough. More than you would have had if you had got away with Papa's savings.'

'The hell with you,' Mario snarled at him. 'You watch it, or I ain't going no place.'

Marcello shrugged. 'OK by me. It's no skin off my nose. You go, you stay – I don't care. It's not me Guido's aiming to kill. I've warned you.'

He rose to go but Minouche stopped him.

'Please don't go, sir. Please. Mario, don't you *see*? It's the only way. I've told you and told you.'

'Oh, I suppose you're right.' He still sounded reluctant. 'OK, get the money.'

'Money and tickets. Out of town. Tonight. Otherwise the deal's off.'

'OK.'

Marcello looked at Minouche. 'Get him cleaned up. Go back down to the club with him and wait for me. I'll come back in about an hour.'

She nodded.

'Everything must look normal. Otherwise the guys . . .'

'Yeah,' she said, 'I know.'

'I'll be going then. See you later.'

'Fuckin' bastard,' Mario said under his breath as he watched his brother leave.

Chapter Twenty

'What're y' doin', baby?' Mario called from the bathroom.

'I'm packing for you. I've done my own,' she yelled back.

She felt light-hearted, like a feather in the wind. They were leaving Chicago, going away. Mario would get in the big time in Florida or California. He'd forget about Chicago and she would be free of that dirty old man, his power over her broken.

'Well, you can stop.'

She paused, hands suspended in mid-air, clutching the black satin pyjamas he loved so much.

'What did you say?' She could not believe her ears.

'Think I'm gonna leave here? No fuckin' chance.'

She put down the pyjamas slowly. She went into the bathroom, numb with apprehension. She leaned against the door-frame or she would have fallen.

He was putting iodine on a cut above his eye. 'Ouch! Shit. This stuff stings.'

'What are you going to do?'

'Take the money, pretend to fuckin' go. What'd you think?'

'I think you're mad, Mario,' she shouted. 'I think you are an imbecile. A stupid fool.'

He was across the room in one cat-like movement. His hand stung her cheek as he hit her with a violence she was not expecting. He had never hit her before. She stared at him in disbelief, horribly afraid, feeling betrayed.

'Never speak to me like that, y'hear? Never!' he said, and hit her again viciously.

She fell to her knees.

'Now get up. Make yourself look good. You're coming downstairs with me. Pull yourself together.'

She was crying now and couldn't move. Frightened of Marcello, infuriated by the news that his brother had stolen the money, shocked by the family news so bluntly delivered, angry and frustrated at the situation he was in, Mario turned on her snarling, like an animal at bay.

'And don't have any more to drink, y'hear? Think I don't notice? Think I'm some kinda fool? You an' Marcello think I'm stoopid or somethin'?'

Mario was furious. How dare Marcello come here and order him about like a fuckin' bell-hop? Who'd he think he was, dressed Michigan Avenue, like Mario would like to look but never somehow achieved? He could go to hell.

Minouche shook her head, sobbing. Shaken, she was trying to rise but her legs felt like rubber and kept collapsing beneath her.

'No, Mario, you know I don't. Please, please . . .'

'Get up, for Chrissakes. Tidy yourself up. You look like a fuckin' whore. Jeez!'

He glared at her. She looked terrible. He hated women to look anything less than perfect. It made him sick to his stomach to see her now, hair dishevelled, make up all over her face, mascara running.

He went into the bathroom and splashed water on his face. Carefully he combed his hair, slicking it smoothly back into its patent-leather perfection.

He stepped over Minouche where she sat on the floor, trying to pull herself up. He walked across the living-room and went to the bar. He picked up the bottle of Canadian Club whiskey, smashed it against the counter. The liquid spewed out, splashing him, but he did not seem to care. He walked back to her. Holding the bottle-neck and thrusting

357

the jagged edge towards her, he said, 'Don't ever fuckin' tell me what to do again, see? An' if you don't stop swillin' this stuff, you're out. Understand? My meanin' clear?'

She nodded, moaning gently, trying to stop herself, knowing it would irritate him, trying to pull herself up. She knew he didn't mean it, knew he cared about her a lot more than he pretended. Knew that it was his brother he was trying to get at. But she was shaken to the core by the scene, by having her hopes dashed brutally, and by his vicious behaviour. She had seen him being violent before but it had never been directed towards her and she was afraid.

He had gone. Eventually she succeeded in getting to her feet. Her knees felt like jelly and she knew she was going to be sick.

She retched violently until she was quite empty. She pulled off her dress and got into the shower again. Her skin would wrinkle up like Salvatore Lucca's, she thought, if she did not stop all this washing.

She took out another dress, a beaded deep blue number, and put it on.

Her face was a write-off. Circles under her eyes, red nose, and a huge bruise starting on her cheek, she looked like a prize-fighter coming out of the ring after a ten-round bout with Jack Dempsey. She made it up as best she could, painting herself heavily.

She stood a moment in the debris of the living room, went to the door, hesitated, went back to the middle of the room and looked at the bar. She poured a brandy, drank it, shook like a leaf as it coursed through her body and arrived at her empty belly.

She poured another one, tossed it off, then taking a deep breath, she left the apartment.

~~~~~~

As Minouche entered the club, Pierre came up to her.

'What in God's name happened to you?' he asked her in

358

French. His face had gone pale. She could see his knuckles whiten as he clenched his fists. 'My God, Minouche, what has he done to you?'

She looked at him piteously. 'Ah, Pierre, don't ask me. I can't bear it.'

He swallowed his rage. He had never trusted the wop, not for a moment. He looked at that little face he loved so much, the pale skin stained with a purple bruise, and the pools of shadowed misery that were her eyes.

'No,' he said. '*I* can't bear it any more.'

She looked at him anxiously. 'If you love me, don't do anything, Pierre. Please.'

He didn't reply and the slim figure in the beaded dress moved away from him across the room, through the smoke to Mario's table.

He sat there, freshly groomed, flaunting his recent scars. He was telling the table of his run-in, telling them he had won, you should see the other guy! Sitting there, laughing about it.

Pierre watched as he said something to Minouche. He saw her blink rapidly, trying not to cry, and then rub the wrist Mario had grabbed and jerked to make her sit down. Pierre could feel the blood pound in his temples. He fingered the gun in his pocket, hoping he would be given the opportunity to use it.

He saw everything that happened. He had watched and noted since their arrival in Chicago. He had remained on the outside taking it all in. He knew Minouche loved Mario. Knew she was besotted with his superficial good looks and slick appearance. And that was OK. As long as he treated her right, Pierre's love for her was big enough to wish her happiness, even with another man.

He had noticed her drinking long before Mario had. He had then observed her afternoon trips, invariably driven by Moses, to the house in North Southport.

He had been puzzled. He could not conceive that the

359

eighty-year-old man could have carnal designs on Minouche, but the conviction was growing in him that there could be no other reason for the visits and her desire for oblivion afterwards. He knew that was what her drinking was, a desire to escape. Pierre was sure that Mario knew about them. Connived at them maybe. He could not work out any other reason why Minouche would go or why Mario, who was sharp as a tick, would allow her to. His resentment, anger and jealousy grew.

Now the bastard was beating up on her. He clutched his revolver, fingers damp, and looked across the crowded room at his rival. He was showing off, stridently self-important, surrounded by his henchmen, clicking his fingers at the waiter, waving at acquaintances. Minouche was weary and a little drunk. The way her head drooped on her slender neck, how her smile was fixed to her face, set there with no matching joy in her eyes, how that bruise which made him so angry was getting worse by the minute, broke his heart. He wanted to take her in his arms and tell her not to worry, everything would be all right.

When he saw the Ape disappear, he was immediately alert. the Ape was Mario's man far more than any of the others, and he was obviously doing something shifty. It always showed with the Ape. He couldn't disguise it. Now he was slipping out the back way, which meant something was going to happen. Something momentous.

At that moment Pierre saw the man who had been here earlier, the guy who had left with Mario and was obviously his brother, entering the club. He was carrying an attaché case. He walked past Pierre at the entrance and across to the table where Mario sat. Pierre watched, alert.

'You come with the dough?' Mario asked. 'Hey, guys, this is my brother Marcello. Think you know Minouche.'

'We weren't introduced,' Marcello said, politely.

'How do you do, sir?' Minouche said. Her eyes were glazed and she could hardly keep them focused.

360

'Don't call him "sir".' Mario snarled at her. 'He's only my brother, not the fuckin' President.'

'I'm sorry, Mario.'

'Aw, shut up. You got the money?' Mario said to Marcello.

'Sure. And the tickets. I took what came up first. Miami from Union Station.'

'Sounds great. I'll drive down though, I think, Marcello. Prefer the motor car.' He looked at his brother through slitted eyes.

Marcello shook his head. 'Oh, no. I'm gonna put you on the train myself, otherwise no deal.'

Mario shrugged. 'OK, it's all the same to me.'

'Where's your cases?'

'We're not takin' any. Figure we gonna need all new stuff down there, in the heat an' all. Right, baby?'

He looked at Minouche. She saw the disgust in his eyes, contempt for her. It made the ache inside so bad it almost took her breath away. They couldn't stay here, they couldn't! The pain, the horror, would never go away then. The agony would get worse and she would have to drink more and more, and Mario would hate her, look at her always the way he was looking now.

The band was playing 'Deep Purple'. The noise in the room had reached fever-pitch. Sweating waiters were rushing about; the men's faces had turned red and the women's were getting a little slack, a little loose.

~~~~~~

Guido looked down the stairs, trying to see through the smoke and the bustle, to find Mario. They had not been too keen on letting him in. Then he had said his name was Palucci and the guy had looked at him more closely, peering under the Fedora he wore so low over his face.

'Rainin' fuckin' brothers,' the man on the door said, then grinned. 'Gotta believe ya, buster. You're the spit of the other one.'

Guido was not sure what he meant. His resemblance to Mario had never been that pronounced. He stared around the room, searching. He had his fingers on the gun. When he spotted Mario, he would shoot him and run. He bumped into a man on the bottom step of the entrance flight. The man was a giant. He glanced at Guido and said, '*Pardon, Monsieur.*' Then he turned his attention back to the other side of the room. Guido followed his gaze, and saw Mario.

'He's not gonna go,' Minouche said, slowly and distinctly to Marcello. 'He told me. He said he was gonna take the money, pretend to go, and come back here. I'm sorry, *chérie . . .*'

'In that case, goodbye, brother.' Marcello stood up.

'You fuckin' little bitch!' Mario screamed. 'You fuckin' whore.' And hit her across the head, backwards and forwards, screaming at her.

And Guido saw the man beside him raise the gun he held in his hands and pull the trigger, firing once, twice. He held his own gun in his hands but had not had time to raise it. He saw with acute surprise his twin Marcello look back over his shoulder. He was still at the table, turning as Mario fell. Guido was stunned. Everything seemed so slow and distinct. Mario falling. The guy beside him firing the gun. His brother Marcello at the table, looking around.

He heard someone cry, 'My God, he's dead! He's dead! He's been killed.'

He saw the man beside him, the giant, slip away through the crowd of hysterical spectators, into them and away from the entrance, becoming one of them.

Guido turned and ran up the stairs into the arms of the waiting cops. They frisked him and found his gun. Put it in a bag. Handcuffed him. Led him away to jail.

He realized they had been waiting and wondered how they had known they would be needed. He thought they must have been tipped off.

362

The last thing he saw before they drove him away was Marcello standing on the pavement in the shadows, gazing after him.

~~~~~~

Pino said, 'You did us all a favour. Now, scram.' He pushed Pierre out the back way and up the stairs to Mario's place.

They both looked at the debris, the broken furniture and glass everywhere, then Pino gave Pierre a bundle of notes. He stuffed them into his pocket when he couldn't get the Frenchman's hand to close around them.

'The place is crawlin' with cops,' Pino said. 'You gotta split. Walk outa the front door. You'll be OK.'

'I won't go without Minouche,' he said.

'You crazy or somethin'? You gotta few minutes at the most.'

'I won't go without her,' Pierre repeated stubbornly.

'OK, OK. Fuckin' headcase is what you are. Wait here. I'll see what I can do.'

'Won't they suspect you?'

Pino laughed, showing small pointed teeth.

'Jeez, I came with them,' he said. 'The brother's been arrested. Caught red-handed leaving, the gun in his hand.'

'But he didn' do it,' Pierre said.

'Dumb cops don't know that. Yet. They'll let him off when they find out the gun ain't been fired.'

'But he was at the table the whole time,' Pierre said. 'He didn't have a gun.'

'Let the cops sort it out. They don't suspect you, that's what counts. But they might come round to it. So you gotta get out. Lucca says you get treated good. The best, he says.'

He patted Pierre's pocket and gently pushed him to the door. 'You take the money and go. It was comin' to ya. Get outa town. He'll get in touch when it all blows over.'

'But I'm not going without Minouche.'

'So ya keep sayin'. I'll go down now, see if she's there. The

363

cops may have taken her to get a statement.' He caught the wild startled look the Frenchman gave him. 'Hey, hey, don't go gettin' yourself upset. Minouche won't say nuthen. They'll let her go. She's not a suspect. Couldn't be. She was too near when he got it.'

Pierre nodded and sat down to wait. Pino shrugged and left him alone.

They could get no real sense from Minouche. Shocked, drunk, she babbled a lot of stuff about Salvatore Lucca which they did not want to hear. They eventually got her to sign a statement to say that she was beside Mario Palucci when he had been killed, that the shot had come from the entrance but she did not see who fired the gun. She was heartbroken that Mario was dead. He was her lover. Then they let her go.

It took longer to secure Guido's release, even though Pino was prepared to post bail. They held him, convinced he was the culprit. They had been warned that he was on his way to kill Mario in some cockamamie vendetta. They had then been informed that he was on his way to the Blue Lady. They had seen him enter, heard the shots, watched him run back out into the street. Unless someone was trying to pull a fast one, he was their man. Yeah, they were sure of it.

Then Ballistics said his gun hadn't been fired. And not only that – the bullets that had killed Mario were from a different make. Then all the customers there, the staff, waiters, Ella May and Jake, and the people at the table with Mario, said the suspect was sitting right there, at the table, when it happened. Twenty people at least ready to swear to it. And the shot had come from the entrance.

They had to let him go.

Minouche walked about in the rain, holding the thin fur-edged satin coat lightly around her. There was nowhere for her to go. There was no one in the world for her to turn to.

364

The rain stung her cheeks and she thought of how she loved water. She was Pisces, the fish, and fish loved water. She loved the Seine. She showered a lot, she thought, but not because she loved water. No, because she was dirty.

She had killed her father, that man Yves Aubin, because he had defiled her. It was only Mario who had prevented her from killing Lucca. But Mario was dead now. She had cradled him on her lap and her dress was splashed with his blood. They had had to force her arms from around his dead body. She shivered. She would have to go home and change, shower and bathe, but not yet. First she had to kill Lucca. She did not know how she would do it. She did not care. She just knew that she would.

Her legs were soaked, her stockings stuck to her legs, her shoes squelched. Rain ran down the back of her neck from her dripping hair and she remembered another rain-sodden night when she had killed another old man.

She felt in the pocket of her coat and took out a crumpled ten-dollar bill. Mario always insisted she carry a couple, 'Case you get caught short. Little girl money,' he would say. And she would laugh and reply, 'Can't see how I could with you around.' And he would give her that special look, deep and intimate, and she would know that he would make love to her later. She shuddered.

She hailed a cab on De La Salle and told the driver the address.

'Sure, Miss. Bitch of a night, ain't it?'

She didn't reply, sitting on the edge of the seat, dripping all over his cab. So he left her alone.

'You fuckin' bitch,' Mario had said, his last words to her. Her teeth chattered and she thought that he would never have spoken to her like that before Lucca.

She got out when they reached North Southport and she told the driver to wait, she'd only be a moment, she wanted him to take her back to Lincoln Avenue.

Beno answered the bell. She walked straight past him.

He smiled. Pino musta brung her. Ol' man sure was raunchy. Beno hoped he could get it up like that old guy when he was eighty.

Lucca was surprised to see her, then alarmed. Mario must be dead by now. He was about to call in one of the boys when she spoke. Her voice was high and rapid and she moved around the writing-table as she talked. He saw, with relief, that she had no gun.

'Old man, you've had your last fix. You turn my stomach, you know that? You filthy old man. Old body. Nasty breath. Dirty, dirty, dirty! Well, you'll not dirty me again, you filthy old man. Never again.'

He was opening his mouth to cry out when she struck. He realized in a flash she had taken up the paper cutter from the desk and raised it in her two hands. She brought it down in his throat, at the side of his neck, an expert blow.

He had wondered often enough in these later years what death was like and now he knew. It was slipping away, and not wanting to go. More than anything else he wanted to live, but he was on a trip down a long tunnel where it got darker and darker and . . . oh, Christ . . . oh, Hell . . .

Minouche sighed with relief and wiped the knife clean. She walked calmly out of the room, closed the door behind her, smiled at Beno and left. She got into the taxi and asked him to take her back to the apartment, giving him the address.

Pierre was waiting. She collapsed on the sofa. She wanted desperately to sleep but he would not let her.

'Pull yourself together, Minouche. Here have a brandy.'

She shook her head. 'No, I don't want a drink,' she said.

'Minouche, we're going to go home.'

'We can't. We never can,' she said wearily.

'Why not?' he asked, aching for her to say yes, to give them permission. Paris. Beloved Paris.

'I'm wanted there for murder. And now I'm wanted here for murder. I've had it, Pierre.'

'They'll have forgotten by now. *Gendarmes*'re not going to go on looking for the killer of an old soak like Aubin.'

'Scarlatti won't have forgotten.'

'He could help us.'

'Not now I've killed Lucca. Everywhere I go, they'll be looking.'

'You killed him, huh?'

'Yes, I did. And I'm not sorry. Only I don't know what to do now.'

'We'll think of something. We'll take it a step at a time. Now we gotta get outa here. Go someplace else. Disguise ourselves.'

She laughed mirthlessly. 'You? Me? The giant and the midget? How can we disguise ourselves?'

'We gotta try, Minouche. We gotta. Help me, please.'

He was shaking her and she said, calmly enough, 'OK, Pierre, we'll try. I don't think we have a hope in hell, but we'll try.'

She gave him a faint smile, 'You really care for me, don't you?'

He nodded, unable to speak.

'How awful I am, taking you for granted.' Then she said, 'Where'll we go?'

'I thought Paris.' She shook her head and he said, 'Then Florida. I thought we'd try anyway.'

'OK, I suppose it's the only thing to do.' She touched his hand gently. 'After all, it's what I wanted to do all along.'

Chapter Twenty-One

Francesca's slow awakening to Christopher's kindness was watched, sometimes with apprehension and sometimes with nostalgia, by Helen. Her son was so very like his father and she remembered when she fell in love with Hugh as if it were yesterday. Remembered the feelings: the awkwardness, then the tremulous awakening. She had held Hugh's hand as Christopher held Francesca's. She had walked with him, looked up at him from under the brim of her hat, as Francesca now looked at Christopher. Luciano, Helen could see, was quite put-out at the romance blossoming under his nose. He did not want her, Helen mused, but he did not want anyone else to have her either.

In the meantime she watched and wondered if the two main protagonists were aware of what was happening to them. She thought, too, how wonderful it was to fall in love; how she wished she could put the clock back and go through it all over again.

Helen was still bitter that she had lost her husband in the war that was to make the world safe for democracy. She reflected, sadly and somewhat shamefacedly, that she really would prefer to live under the most terrible regime than live in freedom without her darling. She would sell her soul to have him at her side again, but sadly that was impossible.

Over the weeks Christopher and Francesca had become

inseparable. He took her riding, she was his tennis and dance partner; at first tentatively, then with growing confidence. They sat under the lilac tree together and drank lemonade. He punted her across the lake and played the latest records to her on the phonograph. Most important of all, in Helen's view, they laughed together. Christopher had taken Francesca gently by the hand and led her effortlessly into his world, and she was blossoming under his tender care.

She was a girl made unhappy by conflict. She could not bear cruelty. She needed looking after. She was not, in spite of her past, used to the harsh aspects of life.

She had told Helen all about herself. The hillside in Sicily became real to the older woman; the crime committed by the brother Mario revolted her. But the appalling consequences of that crime – the break-up of the Palucci family and the terrible vendetta – shocked her. She felt as strongly as Christopher the need to protect Francesca, somehow to make up to her for all the pain she had suffered and guard her from future trauma.

Aware of the hurt inflicted by Luciano d'Abrizzio, Helen had tried to winkle him out of the house party and unload him on one of her friends. As quite a number of them were desperate mamas with unmarried daughters, this proved easier than she had imagined. When he left she was glad to be rid of him and Francesca hardly noticed his going, so preoccupied was she with Christopher.

Helen had already said goodbye to Lucy Braithwaite, Tommy Effington-Gore and the rest of that set. Sylvia was furious and decided to go to Maude Oglyve's with them, so Helen was left alone with Francesca and Christopher in the peace and beauty of Elm Court.

Autumn was coming. The red leaves of the maple Uncle George had imported from Canada on Hugh's birth mingled with the bronze of the copper beech and the yellow sycamores. Then, as the weeks went by, they all

369

began to shed their leaves and Christopher and Francesca wore scarves and woollen gloves when they went walking in the woods.

Helen felt at peace, reprieved. With Eleanor in New York or Chicago, haring off after Francesca's brother, who by all accounts was hell-bent on killing his brother, Helen could evade responsibility for her young cousin. She hoped she would not be blamed for Eleanor's headlong flight to the USA but decided that by the time Enrico Domini found out, the girl herself could deal with her father. But for the moment life was peaceful and Francesca excellent company.

The young people revelled in their privacy. Francesca got letters from Gina telling her all the news. They had heard that the Duke had sold off a great deal of land to outsiders:

> We don't know who he has sold it to and we are very alarmed about it. A stranger coming here, so close to us. And what will he do with the acres he has bought? Will he continue to cultivate the orchards, the vineyards, or will he cut down all the trees and build houses? Oh, you don't know how anxious we are.

Gina was expecting her first baby, she said. The *palazzo* had fallen into ruin. During the summer the land had become parched and over-run with weeds. Lombardo was in good health and he and Filipo Canona worked all the hours God gave to keep body and soul together. They had scrimped enough to buy some land adjacent to the Canona property.

> Which is lucky. It gives Lombardo and Filipo work and a purpose. And Cecilia blooms. She is so much nicer now, loving Filipo suits her. Poor Serena causes us much anxiety. Her mind wanders. She falls into dark depressions and we cannot seem to shift her out of them. Paulo is still missing. No one knows where he is. The good brothers have stopped

370

writing. However, the nice thing is that Marcello has written. Can you believe? He is in New York and apparently doing very well.

No news about Guido's mission. I often think we were wrong to send him. Was it a wicked thing to do, Francesca? Yet what else could we have done? I question myself often. We had to avenge Papa and Mama, didn't we? Lombardo says it's woman's fancy, that Guido will be all right, but I'm not sure. Lombardo says the honour of our family is at stake, but I don't know any more. What is honour? Did the Duke behave honourably when he cheated Papa? And why is there a different rule for him? How will Guido, our gentle Guido, feel with that deed on his conscience? I wonder and pray. Oh, Francesca, I pray.

Tell me if you get any news. Tell me too what is happening to you. You don't say much about how you feel. I don't understand how Luciano could treat you like that. It shows how selfish and irresponsible the d'Abrizzios are. Are you terribly unhappy? You don't sound it and I hope you are not, dearest sister.

Oh, I'm not unhappy at all, Francesca thought, hugging herself. She could not have believed she could recover so quickly and find herself supremely content in so short a space of time. She was ashamed of herself and felt she should at least have a broken heart.

She had not known what it was like to be truly loved, for herself, for her faults as well as her virtues. Christopher knew her, really understood her, and loved her all the same. Not in spite of, but because of, he said. He was interested in what she thought about things, really listened, paid attention to what she said. It was like heady wine to her. No one had ever really listened to her before. Perhaps Guido, but no one else. Christopher drew her out and sometimes she surprised herself with ideas and feelings she had not known she possessed.

She felt freer than air and filled with a peace, profound

and trusting. She had heard Fra. Bartholomeo say that 'perfect love casteth out fear' and knew now what he had meant. She laid her love at Christopher's feet in the sure knowledge that he would treat it with respect and would not let her down. There was no danger in this love. He gathered it up tenderly and carefully and gravely gave her his. Their happiness was mutual, depending upon each other's well-being. Francesca did not worry that she might not be worthy of him. Unlike Luciano he gave her confidence, gave her permission to be herself, and loved her exactly as she was.

Helen welcomed her, and that, Francesca realized, was the biggest hurdle taken successfully. Only Sylvia was peeved when she returned from the Ogylves to find her brother engaged to the stranger from Sicily.

Aware that the girl was jealous, Francesca set about reassuring her, and far from separating the family tried to show Sylvia that she would do her best to keep them all close together. But the girl was not so easily won over.

'I expect Eleanor will never forgive you now,' she remarked after lunch one afternoon as they lingered over coffee. Francesca looked surprised. Eleanor had not told her about Enrico Domini's hopes that she should marry her cousin.

'Why shouldn't she?'

Helen said, 'Sylvia, please,' and Christopher covered Francesca's hand with his.

'Let me tell you about it, Francesca,' he said, but his mother interrupted,

'No, dear boy, let me. It's more my muddle than anyone's.' She looked at her daughter. 'I'm disgusted with you, Sylvia.'

'Please don't be cross with her, Lady Wylde. She didn't mean it.'

'Oh, but I did,' Sylvia said spitefully. 'My brother, no matter what he may say now, was wild about Eleanor. But

372

she refused him and now he gets you on the rebound.'

'I'm not at all worried about Christopher's past, Sylvia,' Francesca said quietly, 'and I am very confident of his love for me now. Eleanor is terribly in love with my brother. I've seen them together and there is no doubting their love for each other. What hurts me is that you hate me enough to try to upset me so. That you dislike me so much that you would try to destroy our love.'

'Christopher and Eleanor grew up together, Francesca, rather as you and Luciano, and in a similar fashion they came to understand that they were not really suited to each other. They loved each other like brother and sister,' Helen finished lamely. Sylvia was mortified at the position she found herself in. Cornered, in a foul mood, jealous of Francesca, she turned on her now, reserving her unkindest thrust 'til last.

'There was nothing brotherly and sisterly about what she and Luciano were doing in her bedroom here one night!'

The colour left Francesca's face. It surprised her that she did not blush nowadays. At Sylvia's words she could feel all life draining out of her and fear gripped her.

Everyone looked at her.

'It's true, Sylvia, Luciano was in my bedroom. He . . .' she stammered, when Christopher leapt to his feet.

'And I have often been in Eleanor's. Francesca, you don't have to explain to me. I don't expect you'll quiz me on everything I did before we got engaged, and I'll not bother you. Your past life is over.'

He smiled at her and took her hand in his firm clasp.

'Yes, but . . .' Sylvia began.

'That is quite enough from you, my girl,' Helen said severely, 'I'm disgusted with you. I don't want to look at you just now. Go to your room.'

Sylvia's face crumpled as she realized the enormity of what she had done.

'I'm sorry, Mother. I only wanted Christopher to know

373

the kind of girl he's marrying . . .'

'He knows very well the kind of girl he is marrying and can manage beautifully without your help, thank you, Sylvia. You have been unduly influenced by that dreadfully common Lucy Braithwaite and I am thoroughly ashamed of you.'

'If that kind of malicious gossip is encouraged by your friends, Sylvia,' Christopher said, 'then I'm afraid they are not the right sort. Just rather sad, sick, jealous people.'

Helen agreed. 'Exactly. Christopher is quite right. I don't know what the world is coming to when young people imagine they can be cruel and unkind. It's sheer bad manners.'

Sylvia went to the door then turned, delivering her parting shot.

'You'll lose our home, Mummy, if you let it happen. Enrico Domini will take it away from us, you know he will.' And she went out, slamming the door behind her.

Understanding had dawned in Helen's eyes.

'That is why she was so beastly to you, my dear,' she said to Francesca. Then, 'Look at her, Christopher. She's as white as a sheet. Get her a drop of brandy. There, there, my dear, you mustn't let Sylvia upset you. She's really a nice girl but she's obviously sadly scared. She's afraid we'll lose Elm Court and she loves it here so. Not always for the right reasons, I'm afraid. Sylvia is a snob. But she's behaving badly because of that, not because of you.' She took the brandy from Christopher. 'Now drink this, there's a good girl, and you'll feel better.' Helen reflected a moment. 'Poor Sylvia,' she said, 'I never really looked at it from her point of view. She'll lose her horses and that's what she lives for.'

'Why should she lose her horses?' Francesca asked. 'Why should you lose Elm Court? What has it to do with Enrico Domini?'

'Ah, my dear, it's a long tale, but I'll tell you all about it, then you and Christoper and I will put our heads together and pool ideas to find out what's to be done.'

'Couldn't we ask Sylvia to help us? It would help maybe to . . .' Francesca said shyly.

'What a splendid idea,' Helen interrupted, and added, 'you really are amazingly tolerant. A peacemaker.'

'We were a big family. You have to mend quarrels all the time or nothing would ever be done.'

'Why don't you go to her, Francesca, and ask her yourself?'

Christoper pressed her hand and she went up and fetched her future sister-in-law. The girl was sitting in her room crying. She turned away when she saw Francesca enter.

'Sylvia, I'm not your enemy,' Francesca said. 'Please will you come down and join us? We are going to hold a family conference to decide what best to do. Won't you help us?'

Sylvia sniffed and nodded. 'OK,' she said. 'But if you think you can win me over like that, you're wrong.'

Sylvia gave her assistance reluctantly but by the end of the discussion, during the course of which they had been unable to think of anything they could do to escape from their predicament, she had forgotten herself enough to ask Francesca to play a game of croquet with her the following day.

'Weather permitting. Hope it doesn't rain,' she said, then hesitated. 'I'm sorry, Francesca, if I was gruesome today after lunch. It's just that, as you know now, we're all very worried about what to do. Don't you see? It would have been perfect if Christopher had married Eleanor. All our troubles would have been over.'

'It would not have been perfect for Christoper or indeed Eleanor,' Helen said tartly.

'I love Elm Court and my horses. It might all have to go. Just to make Christopher happy.'

She stared at Francesca, willing her to understand.

'I know. But we'll find a way out.'

'As long as you stay away from that dreadful Lucy Braithwaite,' Helen muttered.

'Let's leave it now, Mother,' Christopher said firmly.

Which was what he also said to Francesca in front of the fire the next morning when she felt impelled to explain about her liaison with Luciano.

'Let it alone,' he said. 'I have no desire to be a Father Confessor or grovel about in the rubbish of the past. So let's leave it, darling, eh?'

She nodded, glad enough to do as he asked.

The sun was pale, misted over with wispy veils of cloud. It had rained during the night and the croquet lawn was soggy. Sylvia, Christopher and Francesca had gone for a gallop instead of playing a game and when they had returned the horses to the stable for a rub-down, Francesca and Christopher went into the library for elevenses.

It was Francesca's favourite time, the unfamiliar custom delighting her. Whatever they had done in the morning, to meet in that mellow room, have a quiet chat or simply read the latest magazine or newspaper, gave her the deepest pleasure.

In the last week the fire had been lit in the mornings and welcoming flames leapt in the wide grate, filling the room with the scent of pine.

'Darling,' Francesca said, wrinkling her brow, 'I've been thinking.'

'Umm.' Christopher did not look up from *Country Life*.

'Well, there's nothing to stop you from making this place a paying proposition. Then you could do without Signor Domini.'

'How do you mean?' he asked, still reading.

'Well, if Papa could do it, so could you.'

Christopher put down the magazine. 'Do what, darling?'

'Make Elm Court pay. Make it self-supporting.'

'Like having the public in, you mean?' he sounded disgusted.

'No, no. Like Papa.'

'But how? This isn't Sicily.' He glanced ruefully out of the window at the rain which had just started, a thin grey drizzle. 'The sun does not shine here all the time, ripening olives and figs and grapes.'

'Well, what does grow? Apples?'

Christopher laughed. 'Apples? Darling, if we covered the whole estate in apple trees we wouldn't make enough money to pay for food for the table, never mind all the rest.'

'Then what? Think! There must be something you've got that others want, need, would be willing to pay for.'

'Well, I can't think what it could be. Now I've got to leave you. What will you do until lunch?'

'Helen has promised to give me an advanced English lesson.'

'Your English is perfect. Don't let her spoil your delightful accent. Promise?'

'Oh, I won't. But I want to understand perfectly what you are all saying. Things I don't understand, like "silly mid-on".' He laughed. 'I want you to be proud of me.'

She smiled up at him and he bent and kissed her. Her lips were soft as rosepetals beneath his and he held her fiercely for a moment.

'What will you do?' she asked.

'Check that Dunhanny and Liberty are all right. Lady Roxborough wants to send over her mare to Dunhanny . . .' He paused in mid-sentence and Francesca, who had followed his line of thought, got to her feet. A brilliant smile illuminated her face.

'Darling,' he cried, 'a stud farm!'

'That's it,' she said in delight. 'Oh, Christopher, that's it.'

'You're right. Elm Court has been used as a stud farm, but without fees, for a long time.'

'Well, it's time you changed all that. You've got to make a living.'

'There's no one around here who will object to that. And, Francesca, we'll stock up on horses. Breed. Let Sylvia run a riding school. We could do that as long as we're cautious. There's money to be made.'

'Yes, and plenty of room to expand into out at the back, without spoiling the view or anything.'

He lifted her up, swung her around. 'You're a marvel, darling. It would never have dawned on me, without your help, to make money that way. And Sylvia will be so pleased. Oh, let's tell Mother and Sis right now.'

He turned an excited face to her. 'Sylvia will be ecstatic. Horses are her thing. She loves them. If it were possible, I think she'd marry her horse. Oh, you are a clever little thing, and I love you.'

And so saying, he kissed her again.

Chapter Twenty-Two

As soons as the cops let him go, Guido had slipped
through the wet streets to his lodging house, making sure
he was not being followed. He wanted nothing more than
to leave now. Mario was dead. It was over. And he had not
fired the shot. He wondered who the huge man who had
stood near him at the entrance to the Blue Lady was, and
why he had killed Mario. He had pumped two bullets into
Mario before Guido could even get his gun out.

Mario was dead and he hadn't had to do anything. He
had been cleared. The police didn't like letting him go but
they had no evidence. They said his gun had not been
fired. But that was not enough. He could have used the
other gun, the one he had seen in the big man's hands, the
one the giant had dropped when he ran away. But all
those people said he was sitting at the table with Mario
when the shots were fired. They had mistaken him for
Marcello.

Guido had not seen who else was at the table. All he had
seen was Mario. All he had looked for was Mario. It was
over so rapidly.

Guido had felt tired, walking home to his room on La
Salle. Tired and relieved. Mario was dead, there was
nothing more to be done. *Finito*. He would go back to his
room, rest a little maybe, then get out.

He was not followed. The police were obviously not
suspicious of him. He got to his room, opened the door,

and outlined in the hall light behind him, in the blue and red of the neon across the street, flashing on and off, he saw a shadow. The dark mass of someone sitting, back to the window, the head outlined with alternate halos of navy and scarlet.

He froze. His hand went for his gun, then stopped as he realized he was a standing target. 'Don't shoot me, Guido. It's Marcello.'

Relief flooded him, emotion overwhelmed him and all tension evaporated at the sound of the dear familiar voice. Joyfully he stumbled into the room, arms open, and folded his twin in a bearhug.

'Oh, it's good to see you, Marcello. So good.'

They slapped each other's backs, kissed cheeks, patted faces, and gently punched each other on the chest.

'Oh, so good. So good,' Guido said, hugging Marcello again. Then he asked, 'How come you're here? We worried about you, didn't know where you were. It's good . . .' He stopped and laughed.

'I heard you were looking for Mario,' Marcello said. 'I came to stop you. I'm sorry I was too late.'

Guido looked surprised. 'What d'you mean? I didn't shoot Mario.'

'I saw you, Guido. I came to stop you.'

'Why?' he asked. 'But I told you, I didn't shoot him.'

'It was me those people saw in the Blue Lady tonight, me they swore was you. We're so alike, eh, Guido?'

He turned on the light. A naked bulb swung on its cord, to and fro. He looked at his brother – elegantly dressed, well-groomed, fingernails manicured.

'You did well,' he said, smiling fondly at him, admiring him. 'I always said you'd succeed. Gee, it's good to see you.'

'Don't be too sure of that, Guido.'

Guido looked surprised. 'Why? Don't you know I love you, you fool? Don't you know I'm always glad to see you? And now, when I'm lonely for the family, lonely for Sicily, you appear. Don't you realize the joy I feel?'

He paused. Something was wrong. Marcello's face was closed, his eyes shuttered.

'What did you mean when you said you came to stop me shooting Mario?' Guido asked. 'Why did you do that? You knew it was vendetta.'

'Because you would have killed the wrong brother. I'm bad, Guido, but not that bad.'

'I don't understand,' he said, puzzled.

'It's very simple, Guido. I took Father's money, not Mario.'

He watched understanding dawn on his brother's face. 'Oh, Mario planned to,' Marcello said, explaining, 'I realized it. Then I filled father's money pouch with pebbles, and I took the savings. It was that simple.'

Guido buried his face in his hands.

'Ah, God, no,' he said. He took deep breaths of air, gulping it down as if he were choking. 'Ah, Jesus, no.'

'I'm afraid I did, Guido. The question is, what are you going to do now?'

But Guido was incapable of talking. 'Shut up,' he moaned and got up off the bed to begin pacing up and down in the small room. Marcello had to pull in his feet to let him pass. 'I came to help you escape. The police will find the gun eventually,' he persisted.

'I told you, I did not shoot him,' Guido said impatiently. 'The man beside me did. Big guy. French.'

'Pierre,' Marcello said. 'Well, well, well.'

'Why was Mario hit?' Guido stopped his pacing and turned to look at his brother.

Marcello shrugged. 'Mario didn't change. He was playing a little power game with his boss, hand in the till, something like that. Guy you said shot him is in love with Minouche, Mario's dame.'

'Oh.' Guido went to the window and stared out. The rain had turned the pavements black, the sky was slate

381

grey. The neon sign was suddenly switched off. Guido laid his forehead on the cold glass.

'Jeez,' he said. 'Why did you do it, Marcello?' Marcello flicked a speck of dust from the knife-crease in his trouser leg.

'I was always ambitious, Guido, you knew that.' He glanced sideways at his brother. 'I'm not apologising for what I did.'

'It killed Mother and Father. It destroyed Serena and Paulo. I saw Paulo, you didn't. Oh, don't apologise, Marcello, we don't want your apology. It won't bring Mother and Father back. It won't mend Serena and Paulo.'

There were tears on his cheeks as he spoke and he could feel a hard lump in his chest. Marcello carefully avoided meeting his eyes.

'I couldn't know that would happen.'

'Oh, don't give me that,' Guido snapped.

'Question is,' Marcello asked, 'are you going to shoot me?'

Guido sighed and turned around. He looked sadly at his brother.

'I pity you, Marcello. Look at you. Ambitious? Yeah, sure. You've got everything except peace of mind. Am I going to shoot you? That's what you want to know? Well, the plain truth is, I don't know. You'll have to wait and see. Every time you go in or come out of your house, you'll wonder am I in the shadows, waiting. I just don't know, Marcello. I'll have to make up my mind. And if I do decide to do it, you're the last person I'll tell.'

Marcello shrugged. 'OK,' he said, 'I'll just have to live with it.'

'Like the way you live with the fact you were responsible for our parents' death.'

Marcello winced. 'Not really,' he said.

'Get out. Just get out of here. Now.'

Guido knew if his brother stayed a moment longer he'd hit him.

Marcello rose. 'Goodbye then, Guido.'

He went to put his hand on his twin's shoulder but Guido jerked away.

'Don't you touch me.'

'I'm sorry. I wanted to help you. Can't I help you to get away from here?'

'No, I don't need help. Even if I did, I wouldn't take yours. Get out now. Just get out.'

Marcello looked at Guido. He felt wave after wave of loss sweep over him. He felt empty. Scenes flashed before his eyes. Guido's firm hand pulling him from the river. Guido taking him out in the boat to catch fish. Guido's friendship and comradeship. Guido whom he loved, and who up to this evening had loved him. It was gone now. There was silence and hatred between them. Coldness and strangeness. A vast gulf. He put out his hand but his brother did not touch it. Guido laid his forehead against the window pane and Marcello turned and left.

~~~~~~

When Marcello returned to Palmer House it was late but the hotel was jumping. There was a dance in progress. Couples were laughing, running hand in hand from ballroom to lobby and back. There were shrieks of excitement, an orchestra playing; the place was alive with activity.

Marcello had his collar turned up against the cold wind from the lake and the driving rain. As he entered the lobby he shook himself like a dog.

He found Mirella sitting in the lounge sipping tea. Her long legs were crossed, her thick hair fell in a cascade over a blonde chinchilla coat that was loosely draped around her shoulders. She wore a light wool Mainbocher dress, and was smoking. She was causing some havoc in the foyer, Marcello noted with amusement. All the men, coming and going, from the oldest down to the youngest, registered

383

her presence in the lounge, registered it with approval. Women plucked sleeves, rebuking spouses or escorts, urging their attention away from Mirella. An elegant guy ogling her walked into a pillar and said, 'I do beg your pardon' to the marble column before he realized what he was doing. This made a little runt of a bell-hop almost kill himself, snorting into his sleeve. A waiter clicked his tongue against his side teeth as if he were urging a horse forward every time he passed her.

'Well, you're causing quite a stir,' Marcello said, sitting down beside her, becoming the envy of all the men in the lounge.

She shrugged and the coat fell off her shoulders, dropping on to the floor. She paid no attention to it, her large golden eyes searching his face.

'Any luck?' she asked.

'Mario's dead,' he said simply.

He had told her all about it last night in bed, the whole story. Her pale amber skin glowing in the lamplight, their bodies entwined, hot from passion, she said, 'I want to know all about you. Keep nothing back. Nothing. I am your woman, now and forever. Yours.'

She had taken him in her hands, had aroused and released him in ways he had not known possible.

'I am yours, any way you want me. Anything you dream or imagine, I'll do for you, my love,' she had said, kissing him, and he could taste his own body on hers.

He had learned the scents and secrets of her body. He had seen her heavy-eyed with the intense gathering of her nerve-ends before she came, eyes open wide, crying with ecstasy. He had felt himself grow, become engorged, until he could hold the pulsating excitement no longer and flooded her deeply with his love.

'I know your body,' she said, 'I want to know your soul.'

Sheets tangled, bed-clothes on the floor, they lay exhausted at last. She lit a cigarette and watched him as he lay with closed eyes.

'I don't talk much about myself,' he said.

'I know,' she said, 'I know instinctively all sorts of things about you, as if I've known you in another life.' Then she asked, 'Tell me why you're here?' She murmured it against his cheek. She licked his mouth, her tongue soft as silk, then held his bottom lip lightly between her teeth.

He opened one eye. Her face swam close. He could see the pores of her skin beaded with sweat.

'It's a long story.'

'I'm not going any place,' she said, smiling.

He told her the whole story, leaving nothing out. She listened, giving him her full attention, not interrupting or asking questions until he had finished. She shook her head then.

'It's terrible,' she said.

'It's been my fault, so much of it. There, that's the first time I've admitted it. I caused . . .'

She put her hand over his mouth. She would be fiercely partisan. 'You did what you had to do. Call it what you will, it had to be. We are all to blame anyhow. My father. Luciano. Mario. Who knows what your father would have done if Mario had not told mine. Your father killed himself because he lost face in front of my father and the village. Not because Mario robbed him, or because you robbed him. It was an accumulation of things and we all contributed. I'm not minimizing your part in it, beautiful man, nor my father's. I'm just telling you not to be so hard on yourself. It's over now.'

He shook his head. 'No,' he said softly, 'it's not over. Would to God it were.'

'What do you mean?' She was alarmed by his tone.

'Guido is coming to kill Mario and I have got to stop him. This cannot go any further.'

Whatever he had decided was all right with her.

'You do what you have to. I'll be here for you, waiting. I

love you, y'know?' She looked at him intently. 'Really love.' And she had wrapped herself around him. By now he was open to her, he responded as if to a switch. Their bodies merged, blended like butter, soft, melting, growing and pulsating, their climax long and complete.

That had been earlier. Now she was watching him anxiously.

'What happened?' Her voice was sharp with concern.

'Some stranger shot him,' he said, 'it was extraordinary. Guido was there, I saw him. He saw me. So strange. In that room, the three of us, so near, so far apart.'

His eyes had a far-away look. He was remembering things from the past, precious recollections, things shared with his twin, private things. She waited, watching him, not interrupting his memories. At last he roused himself and glanced at her. 'The police arrested him. Let him go. Thought he was me. Didn't realize there were two of us. At least I did that much good.'

She looked at him, her eyes asking the question.

'I was sitting beside Mario. The shot came from the entrance across the room. I was too near to have done it. I thought it was Guido but it was a Frenchman called Pierre. Guido and I are almost identical. We both wore raincoats.' He shrugged. 'All hell broke loose. Guido was standing at the entrance in shadow. When the police arrested him, people thought it was me. I left, then I called the police. Guido is free.'

She did not relax. 'There's more,' she stated.

He sighed. 'Yes.'

'Well?' She leaned across the table, covering his hand with hers. 'Always remember, I'm your woman, darling, flesh of your flesh, bone of your bone.'

He could feel the tension inside him melting. He looked into her amber eyes.

'I went to see Guido,' he said. 'I waited. Followed him.'

'And?'

'Told him the truth. That Mario was the wrong guy.'

'And?'

'I think he's going to try to kill me.'

~~~~~~

All Guido wanted was to leave Chicago. He suspected the police might decide to question him again when they found whoever had fired the bullet that killed Mario Palucci and where it had come from. If they could do that, he did not know. But he thought they would probably want to know whether he had seen the man beside him in the Blue Lady and if he could identify him or not. He did not want to hang around and become involved. He wanted out.

He wanted Eleanor. Suddenly with all his strength he wanted Eleanor. He wanted to get away from concrete, away from the smoke of exhaust pipes, away from the noise of horns hooting and sirens tearing at the silence of the night.

He felt cut off in America, the great Atlantic Ocean separating him from everyone and everything he knew and loved. He wanted to get away from the country that held Marcello and the corpse of his brother Mario. He wanted to leave. Run away. He wanted to get to Eleanor.

He missed her. He had put her out of his thoughts on his journey to the States, and during the time he had spent in Chicago he had put her firmly into another compartment of his mind and closed the door. Now he told himself he could think of her again. The barrier he had erected fell and thoughts of love preoccupied him. They took his mind off his twin.

He could not bear to think about Marcello; he wanted only to get to Eleanor and sanity. Afraid he might bump into his brother at the station, he waited until the following morning, then packed his case, put on his raincoat, paid the greasy little desk-clerk and went to Union Station. He took the first train to New York.

387

What impelled him he did not know. Why New York? He told himself that he could reach England faster from there but in his heart he knew that this was not the reason.

On the train he fought the memory of the scene last night. He tried to suppress the recollection of it, but in vain. Marcello's face intruded between him and the countryside flashing past. Like a reflection of himself. The twin image, the split brothers, closer than others could conceive. And struggling to the forefront of his mind was the realization written across his vision of his twin – or was it of himself? – 'You must die.'

He would have to kill Marcello. He owed it to his father and mother, he owed it to Paulo and Serena, and in a strange way he owed it to Mario. Bad as his brother had been he had not committed the crime that he had been condemned for and that had led to his family's downfall.

Guido sighed. He felt the burden of responsibility weigh heavy upon him again. Good God, would it never end?

He did not want to do this terrible thing, yet however hard he tried he could see no other way. He wished with all his heart that Marcello had not confessed to him, but there was no going back now. What was done was done. Slowly and painfully the resolve had been forging itself in his mind. Reluctantly, he acknowledged that the execution was inevitable.

Marcello had to die. Nothing else made sense.

He squeezed his eyes shut and took a deep breath. The man beside him, an agitated little salesman by the looks of him, edged away from Guido nervously. He smiled at the man to reassure him, but far from being reassured as he had hoped, the man took out a spotted handkerchief and mopped his brow. He was staring at Guido's hands and, glancing down at them, Guido saw they were bleeding. He had dug his nails into his palms so hard that there were crimson half-moons of blood like a stigmata on them. He quickly folded them but the little salesman got off the train at the next station and Guido guessed that far from reaching his destination he had simply changed compartments.

It would be difficult, his task. Marcello would know what his twin had decided to do and would take every precaution. He would enjoy the contest. There had always been a fierce streak in Marcello that had missed his twin. He knew how Marcello would behave and knew he would do the same if their situations were reversed.

He knew too that it would be dangerous. He had been questioned by the police about one murder. It would be too much of a coincidence if his name surfaced in connection with another. He would have to be careful. He did not know whether the police in Chicago would be in touch with the New York cops. He wondered if they exchanged information.

He was worried about the FBI. He knew there was a big crackdown operation mounted against the Mob, and as Mario was indubitably connected with Lucca he was not sure how wide the net was and how much information gathered about anyone connected with him would be passed on, documented by J. Edgar Hoover's lily-white boys.

He decided he would use an assumed name, Palucci was becoming uncomfortably well known in America. He would be as anonymous as he could, drawing no attention to himself, as near as he could looking like the millions of average men in New York City. It should not be too difficult, he told himself, and shivered again. He wished he was travelling in another direction. He wished he was home in Sicily. He wished he was with Eleanor. He wished most of all that what he knew he had to do was avoidable.

And he knew it was not.

~~~~~~

Marcello and Mirella went to Los Angeles and got married.

They hired a plane out of Chicago and flew to Santa Monica, stopping once to refuel.

It was a rushed and perfunctory ceremony but they planned to marry again, in church, in Sicily.

Los Angeles was unreal, Mirella said, and she loved it. But she had to admit she would have been happy anywhere with Marcello.

After the ceremony in downtown LA they got the Super Chief to New York. They had a de luxe sleeper, and for five days travelled in bliss.

'You can have the grandest wedding when we go home,' he told her, kissing the fronds of amber-coloured hair on her brow.

'Father will disown me,' she giggled at him.

'Yes. I think he will,' Marcello laughed.

'Don't,' she said.

'I'm laughing at something else,' he said. 'I love you.'

'I'm carrying your child,' she told him, and he laughed again although there was a lump in his throat.

'You can't know that yet,' he said. 'We've been together only a short time.'

'I knew at the moment you came. I knew when you shot into me. I knew then. I said, "That is the boy Marcello wants." ' He held her a moment, oh, so tenderly, in his arms.

'Where will we go in Sicily, Marcello?' she asked. 'Where will we live?'

'I have something to tell you, my darling,' he said, his eyes twinkling. 'It's what I was laughing about before. I don't know whether you'll like it or not.'

She kissed him. 'All yours, remember,' she said huskily. 'I'm your woman now. Whatever you do is right.'

The train was rocking them with its rhythmic movement.

'Well, here goes.' He looked at her. 'When I first came to New York I started to buy up the land. The *palazzo's* land.'

'Our home?' she asked. 'Our land?' She pushed him back.
He nodded.

'The d'Abrizzio *palazzo*?' she cried, eyes wide.
He nodded.

'How?' She searched his face.

'I knew your father needed money,' he explained. There was silence in the compartment except for the rumble of the wheels on the tracks. Outside they could hear the hooting of the train in the night. They were insulated from the world, cocooned in darkness.

'I knew it would not be long before he began selling the land he took back from my father,' Marcello raised himself on his elbow and ran his forefinger down her cheek.

'You know he cheated Papa? My father trusted him. He paid him good money for that land, earned by the sweat of his brow.' Marcello's voice was even, casual almost. 'The Duke had no right to take it back when Papa died. It was a con.'

For a moment their glances challenged each other, then she shrugged.

'You would have done this no matter how I felt. Am I right?'

He frowned. 'Yes.' She nodded, satisfied. 'Go on,' she said.

'Well, I know how your father behaves. His pattern is predictable. He runs out of money – he sells some land. Right?'

'Right,' she said, folding her hands behind her head. 'And I know that my father is a cheat, and a gambler.'

'Well,' he continued, 'I decided I would be there. Waiting. I set up a connection to let me know if any of the d'Abrizzio land came on the market. It did. Sooner than I expected. Couldn't wait, your father, no patience.'

She shook her head. 'No money.'

'Well, anyway, he took it back from us and right away put it out for tender.'

'He needed the money to finance Luciano and me, and his own gambling in London, Monte Carlo and Cannes.'

'Well, there were not too many people interested. Vineyards, olive and lemon groves an hour outside Palermo, in the hills, away from everything.' He shrugged. 'Who needs it? No big demand. So the land was not snapped up and I bought it quite reasonably, for a fair price, even though it was morally if not legally mine already. Or my family's.'

She seemed fascinated by what he said. 'Go on,' she demanded.

'Well, then I let it be known I was interested in taking out a mortgage on any large residential property with land in the vicinity. Using the name of another company, of course.' He grinned. 'I did not expect any interest. I did not think that even your father would go so far. After all, the *palazzo* has been in your family for generations.'

She closed her eyes. 'Don't tell me,' she said. 'He leapt at it.'

'Yes.'

'I know my father, Marcello. He's a spendthrift. It's a disease. He would have sold Luciano and me if he had been offered a high enough price. He took your bait, hook, line and sinker, I suppose?'

'Yes. I am now the owner of the d'Abrizzio *palazzo* and surrounding land, but your father does not know yet. He has no idea who the buyer is. And, my darling, it is yours. I'll take you there as my bride.'

She looked at him seriously, her eyes dark. 'Poor Papa,' she said. 'Poor, poor old man. How sad it is.'

'But you can have your father to live there, if you wish,' he said. 'And Luciano. Just as long as they remember who is the owner now.'

'Oh, you are the most gorgeous man,' she said. 'You're so satisfactory. So absolutely grown-up. Oh, darling, all the men I've known are boys compared to you.'

392

Mirella looked at him closely. She clasped her hands in his, their fingers laced.

'But you must be careful, *mi amore*. If Guido plans to kill you . . .'

'I know my brother, darling. If he comes for me, I'll know. We can read each other's minds. Besides, Guido is no killer. He will not pull the trigger when it comes to the crunch. He could not kill anyone.'

'Let me go and see him. If I explain what you have done . . .'

'No, my darling. This is a family matter,' he said gravely, pushing her arms back, fingers still clasped, until he rolled over on top of her.

'If anything should happen to me . . .'

She cried out, unlaced their fingers and put her hand across his mouth.

'No. Don't say that.'

'I have to, dearest. If anything does, I have made a will. I've left it all to Guido. You have to understand.' He looked at her, his eyes pleading for her to understand. 'Not to you. Do you see? It has to be in Palucci hands or there's no sense to any of it. He will look after you, Guido will. I left all the instructions. OK?'

She nodded wordlessly, then he suddenly grinned at her and slapped her rump.

'Now come here, wench. Your husband wants you.'

She turned him over, pushing him sideways, until she was half across him, legs apart, mouth on his, whispering; things that made him hard as iron, things that made him forget his family and the vendetta, things that made him forget everything except her, the deepness of her, the welcoming endless pleasure she gave him.

Later, watching her cross the little compartment, he said, 'You realize it is almost Christmas? I'm giving a party on Saturday. It's been planned for a long time. I phoned Joshua from Santa Monica and told him it would be a welcome-home party for Mrs Palucci. What do you think of that?'

The smile she gave him was radiant.

Chapter Twenty-Three

Paulo had become an island. He had cut himself off from all normal associations. He moved about remote and unconnected. But these days he did not drink with winos. He shaved and his clothes were clean if shabby. He had a mission.

He had an aim now. He was obsessed. In the same way as he had been fanatical in his passionate affiliation to his Church, his God, he was now dedicated to the execution of his brother. The execution of Marcello.

The monks had understood nothing, nothing at all. His Lord had deserted him. His mother and father had gone to hell and his sister was driven mad. The monks kept telling him to forgive. Talking nonsense. How could he be expected to do that? Forgive the destruction of his family, the pain they had endured? How? And now Guido had killed the wrong brother. Marcello was guilty of the crime and he was getting off scot-free. Mario was dead and everyone thought that justice had been done.

He had read it in the papers. Banner headlines.

GANGLAND SHOOTING IN NIGHTCLUB.
Mario Palucci, gangster and gunman, friend of Salvatore Lucca, was shot last night in his nightclub, the Blue Lady, by person or persons unknown. Police questioned the deceased's brother, Guido Palucci, but found no evidence against him . . .

Such injustice could not be allowed to triumph. The turmoil bubbled and surged inside him like an erupting volcano. He had to hold on very fiercely to the deep roots of himself or he might boil over.

He had to be careful. The emotional hiatus engendered by Enrico Domini's amazing news that Marcello was the thief, was eventually channelled, then honed into a single purpose. He prayed that, in his aimless wanderings, cast out and abandoned, he would find a mission. Now his prayers had been answered. 'Mario Palucci is dead,' Domini said. 'Shot by your brother, Guido.' He showed Paulo the headlines in the papers and waited for Paulo's reaction.

Enrico Domini was lashing out around him like a wild and wounded animal. He wanted to hurt and didn't care which one of the Palucci brothers he damaged. They cared so much about each other that to hurt one was to hurt all. Stroza, always stirring things up, always careful to allow no man pass him by, and jealous of Marcello, had lost no time telling him of Eleanor's visit. It had enraged Domini and when this Palucci brother came to see him he was just about ready to create havoc. 'Guido fucked my daughter Eleanor. I'll never forgive him.' Domini said. Paulo looked at the silver-framed photograph on Domini's desk. It must be the daughter Eleanor. She was tall, a blonde woman with long legs and shining hair. There was a portrait of her on the wall. She was beautiful, Paulo thought, with an unforgettable face. 'My friend Stroza tells me that it was Marcello who stole your father's money. Not Mario.'

The pugnacious face pushed itself across the desk, nearer to Paulo, the thick tanned neck bulging, colour staining his mottled cheeks. 'But it was the wrong brother.' Enrico stabbed the desk with his finger. 'The wrong brother. Did you know? It was Marcello who stole the money. I give you that information for what it's worth.'

Enrico Domini swivelled his chair around and looked

out of his window where the cold statues were forever frozen in flight. 'Where is Marcello?' Paulo asked. Domini shrugged, 'He is alive and well, as far as I know. He is giving a party in a week or two, according to Stroza.' He swivelled his chair around, facing the Palucci brother again. He looked into his feverish eyes and decided this one was mad. 'I want his address.'

Domini stared at the ex-monk speculatively. It could be interesting. He scribbled on a piece of paper then slid it across the desk to Paulo. 'Go see Stroza,' he said, 'You'll find him here. He'll help you.' Paulo had found a mission. He was not concerned any more with the problems of daily life. He did not feel hunger or thirst. He did not feel heat or cold. The sun had no jurisdiction over him, nor the rain.

Enrico had given him money to pay for his journey. He travelled silently, a man who moved in shadows. He burned with resentment. It eroded his logic, the facts changed imperceptibly. The story shifted in his tortured mind and assumed another shape. Giuseppe was killed by Marcello. Maria was killed by Marcello. Marcello had sent Serena mad. Marcello had debauched their sister Francesca. He saw Marcello, taller than in life, more powerful, a gigantic figure of evil, dark as a spectre, laughing as he pushed his father's body to and fro as it hung there, suspended from the rope that strangled him. He saw the gigantic image of Marcello bending over Maria's bleeding wrists. He thought how Marcello must be laughing at them all, thinking that the family was easy to deceive. Well, he, Paulo, would put a stop to that. Single-handedly he would fight the evil.

He had debated with himself whether Enrico Domini had told him the truth. He had decided that the man could have no reason to lie to him. Why should he invent something like that? Tomaso Canona had said to trust him, so he must be trustworthy.

He went to Luigi Stroza in New York. The man seemed nervous of him, looked at him suspiciously.

'Palucci,' he said and sighed.

'I want my brother Marcello,' Paulo had told the great man in his great office. 'I want Marcello Palucci.'

The man shrugged. 'I am not sure where he is.'

'Enrico Domini said you would tell me.' Paulo was insistent.

Luigi Stroza was very uncomfortable. Pammy, his secretary, had told him through the intercom that a Signore Palucci wanted to see him, sent by Enrico Domini. He was fed up with Paluccis but did not wish to offend Enrico Domini. He wished they would all go away and stop bothering him. Even Marcello who was usually good news was fucking things up in Chicago. Had to go down and stick his nose in when the other two brothers would have knocked each other off, no problem, and saved everyone a lot of trouble.

He would see Marcello on Saturday. At his party. He would tell him to calm his family down. He would explain about Eleanor.

Luigi shuddered when he remembered last week, the girl, the dinner. The pass. She had seemed sophisticated enough, seemed to know her way around. Tall, golden and cool. He had been wrong. He had totally misread the situation and that was unlike him. And he had thought he had done his best for her.

He had tried to find out for her where Guido was in Chicago, but it was an impossible task. No one had heard of him, least of all Salvatore Lucca who had been waiting impatiently for his arrival in the Windy City.

'Mario, yes,' he had said to Luigi on the phone. 'Guido, no. Not yet.'

Stroza had taken Eleanor to Ciro's. She was wearing a slipper-satin sheath that did not leave much to the imagination. Her body moved in it freely. It clung only to her

398

breasts and hips.

They had dined well. Eleanor enjoyed her food. She laughed at his jokes, his weary descriptions of the New York social climbers who would kill to enter the right doors, commit suicide if they were not invited. She told him about society in Rome; the battle-axe Roman matrons who were just as ruthless about such matters in the Eternal City. They were relaxed together, exchanging views, finding that they agreed.

He had got the call then, returned to the table and told her: 'Mario Palucci has been iced.'

Her face went white and she twirled the wineglass around and around between her fingers.

'Oh, Jesus,' she whispered. 'Oh, Jesus.'

'It's OK,' he reassured her. 'They took Guido to the police station, the cops, but they let him go. I don't understand it. Word was out to make him the fall guy but he walked.'

Relief flooded her face. Then she asked, 'How shall I find him?'

He shrugged, 'Dunno. Lucca was taken out tonight too. Salvatore Lucca gone. Jesu Maria, what a day! To think I'd live to see this. It will be interesting to see what develops. How long Pino will last. A cold man Pino. Lethal.'

But she was not interested. Those people were simply names to her.

'Can't they tell you where Guido is?'

'No one knows,' he replied. 'No one at all. Though he will have left town. So, I think . . . well . . .'

He looked uncomfortable and signalled a waiter. 'Let's get outa here.'

'There's something else?' she said.

'Yeah. Remember I told you that Mario was not the right brother? Well, now they think Guido Palucci will be coming here to New York, to kill Marcello.'

Luigi looked at her, then away. 'That's what they think,' he finished feebly.

'Give me Marcello's address,' she demanded. She pestered him until he did, and when the bill was settled they rose to leave straight away.

'Marcello Palucci is giving a party on Saturday,' he told her. 'Everyone is invited. He hasn't cancelled, so he must intend to be there.'

He offered her a lift. In the car he had asked her back to his apartment for a night-cap. She agreed! What the hell was he supposed to think? How was he to know she wanted to talk about Guido Palucci? He did not know Guido Palucci. He did not *want* to know Guido Palucci. If he never heard the Palucci name again it wouldn't bother him one bit.

Inflamed by the nearness of her, by her iridescent beauty, by her perfume and the scent of her hair when she got into the car beside him, he had grabbed her.

He cursed himself for a fool. He should have used more *finesse*, waited perhaps until they were looking at the Manhattan skyline from his living room. However, he had been in too much of a hurry and now he cursed himself.

She had shrieked loudly and slapped his face. Abel, his chauffeur, had glanced in the mirror, surprised. Luigi had apologised. Said he had made a mistake. But Eleanor insisted on Abel's drawing over to the curb and stopping. She got out of the car, shouting about telling her father, Enrico Domini, and her fiancé, Guido Palucci. Either way he could be dead.

Now, a week later he stared at the latest Palucci brother to pitch up. He surveyed Paulo with distaste and also, he had to admit, with fear.

This one was mad. This one burned with hatred. This one was dangerous in a way the others were not. This one would not be selective.

Luigi did not want to have any truck with Paulo Palucci. Apart from anything else, he did not want him cluttering up the office, looking only one step away from the gutter.

This one was a looser from way back, Luigi decided, and probably very bad news to have around.

He had not heard much of what Paulo said. His accent was heavy and he was not very articulate. He was not at all like Marcello. He was driven by some inner fire and sometimes stammered, unable to get his words out. His dark eyes burned in his ravaged face.

'I've told you, I don't know where your brother is at the moment,' said Stroza.

'But you must! Enrico says you know. You to tell me, Mister, or I'll break your arms.'

'Hey, hey, hey! Don't be so eager. Keep calm. No need for that.'

'I'll leave you like pulp if you don't tell me,' Paulo threatened and Luigi believed him.

The hell with it! He was fed up with the Palucci family. Let them fight it out between themselves. And their women. He didn't owe Marcello a thing. And this guy was a head case.

'Here. Here's the address of your brother Marcello. Now are you satisfied? It's the only one I got for a Palucci. And rumour has it that Guido is on his way there.'

'Now go,' he said as civilly as he could, but noticed that his hand was shaking. 'Good day.'

He watched with relief as the gaunt figure slid out of his office, leaving behind the musty smell of fear.

~~~~~~

Eleanor did not know what to do, how to handle it. She had to find Guido, stop him doing anything more. She could not go to Luigi Stroza after his disgusting behaviour in the car. Putting his hand up her skirt – ugh! He made her want to vomit. Who'd he think he was, anyway? And what kind of girl did he imagine her to be that, talking to him about her lover, she would allow him to crawl all over her like that? She shook her head in disbelief each time she thought of it.

401

How to find Guido? How to stop this senseless vendetta and wrap herself in the warmth of his embrace forever? How? She had knocked on Marcello's door a couple of times but the black servant there had told her he was away. She saw that there were preparations underway for a party in the house. Obviously the guilty brother was doing all right.

She was going crazy in her hotel room. She would scream if she had to remain inactive much longer.

Kicking off her shoes she rang the exchange, asked for Marcello's number, got it, asked to be put through to the Park number. A male voice that she recognized as the servant's answered.

'This the Palucci rez-i-denz. Yas'm?'

'I want to speak to Signore Marcello Palucci.'

'Sorry'm. He not here. But he's due back for the party Saturday.'

Well, at least that was a certainty. He would be back on Saturday.

'Yes, well, I'm one of the guests. What time should I be there?'

' 'son your invitation, 'm.'

'Well, I seem to have mislaid it. You know how it is.'

'Yes'm. Well now, guests arrivin' bout eight o'clock. Mister Marcello, he 'spected at nine sharp. He say so.'

'Thank you. Thank you very much.'

'Pleasure.'

At least knowing Marcello would not be there until nine on Saturday night meant that nothing would happen until then.

Eleanor would have to wait. Be patient. She would be there at nine o'clock. Guido would be there too, she thought. He had to be.

~~~~~~

Guido sat in the dark interior of a cab. The last act was about to be played. He would go to the party. No one would refuse him entrance. He was his brother's double.

He felt quite comfortable in his hired evening clothes. The collar was a little tight but the jacket fell easily over his gun, concealing the weapon.

He was tense as a violin string as the cab drove through the traffic to his brother's house.

Afterwards, he thought, he would hurry to Eleanor in England. He would marry her as soon as possible. He was glad she was out of all this.

He looked out of the cab window. Snow spattered against the glass, melting as it fell. It was a cold night. He thought about Giuseppe and Maria. The good old days, days of sun and sweat, toil and labour and good will. Days when food tasted flavoursome, and laughter and music were part of the fabric of life. After tonight, by the crime he intended to commit, he would bar himself from such warm innocent feelings forever. Was that fair to Eleanor? But it was too late to think about it now. Much too late.

He felt as if he had been primed to act in a certain way, that he had no control, no real choice, that it was all arranged beforehand and he was only obeying orders.

He peered out of the cab window, noting the grandeur of the houses in his brother's neighbourhood. His ill-gotten gains had been put to good use.

Eight for nine o'clock the servant had said over the telephone. It was snowing out there, but it was lighter now.

The cabby said, 'Fifth and eighty-fifth, sir.'

'I'll get off here. Walk the rest.'

'Not a good night for it, Mister.'

The cabby drew up and Guido paid him. He envied him. The man was chewing gum. He smelled of garlic and peppermint. He was probably going home to a cosy apartment with wife and family, and Guido wished more than anything else that he was going home too. To Eleanor.

He walked down the narrow street, his collar up against

the softly falling snow, then turned into the street where Marcello lived.

He could see a procession of cars lining the street and looked across just in time to see Marcello getting out of a limousine and going up the steps to his house. He looked debonair and handsome. A shaft of pain shot through Guido's heart. Why did he have to do this terrible thing? Yet another part of him knew he had no option. His senses were hyper-aware. He could feel the sting of the snow on his cheek, hear the carol singers down the road.

Next, to his surprise, he saw Mirella d'Abrizzio stepping out of the limousine, looking breathtakingly lovely. She was running up the steps to join Marcello.

The next moment he thought he must be asleep, having a nightmare. His stomach seemed to heave up and down as if he were on a carousel. He could see Eleanor standing there in the street, a square of lace covering her shining hair. Eleanor in New York? He was dreaming for sure.

Her face was a mask of anguish. Why? What was the matter? He tried to grasp what was happening.

His own distraction drowned the sound of the shots. He did not hear them. He watched appalled as Marcello slowly crumpled on to the steps. There was blood on his stiff white shirt. He saw Eleanor reaching his twin at the moment he dropped and then she too fell. He felt his face, stiff and dry, mouth open in a scream. A silent scream. Mirella stood over the now still bodies on the steps, her mouth, too, open in a scream. Then he saw Paulo in a tattered raincoat, pause, throw away the gun and slink away. Was it really him, with mad unfocused eyes turning away and sliding into the dark places of the night?

Guido felt the sobs well up in his chest. His mouth was dry as a bone, his brain numb.

She was gone, he knew it. He felt her absence. It was no use going to her on the steps. Only her shell lay in the snow beside his dead brother.

He had not fired the shot. Again he had been prevented. By fate? Divine Providence? Who knew? But he was guilty all the same, just as guilty as Paulo. He had had the intention. He had been going to do it in cold blood. Only a quirk of Fortune had prevented him.

He moved back. Sirens were screaming, automobiles clogging the roads. He heard the sound of someone crying in the cold street, a wild lament. Then he realized it was himself.

~~~~~~

Paulo took a cab to the Hudson Bridge and paid off the driver. The wind whistled a low moaning whine. His hand shook as he counted out change. The cabby looked at him suspiciously.

'You OK?'

'Sure.'

'Cold here, pal. Wouldn't hang about if I was you.'

But his customer was not listening. He had turned his back and was walking slowly away. The cabby shrugged. It was nothing to do with him. Last time he had interfered he had very nearly ended up behind bars. He revved the motor and drove away.

Paulo shivered. He did not seem able to stop shaking. His teeth chattered like castanets and the muscles in his neck jumped.

He walked to the middle of the bridge. There was no one about. The night was a dark cloak. The lights of the city sparkled, gaudy man-made stars, lacking the subtlety of the heavenly kind.

Paulo did not see the stars. He did not really see the city lights. He was looking at the water. It lay below him, turgid, dirty and velvet-black. It seemed calm, a flowing, welcoming dark blanket, a depthless tomb into which he could sink.

He had done what he had to do. It was over and there

was nothing left. God had deserted him. Heaven had closed its doors on him and his family. There was no tomorrow. No love left. No hate to sustain him.

He stopped shaking. There were tears on his cheeks but he felt quite peaceful.

He dropped like a stone into the darkness and was swallowed up forever.

Chapter Twenty-Four

Christopher and Francesca became officially engaged at Christmas. There was a huge tree in the hall at Elm Court, lit by a hundred candles. Under it, amidst the multi-coloured packages that were the family's gifts to one another, lay a tiny box from Christopher to Francesca. It held an emerald circled in diamonds and it fitted perfectly.

Helen was in an exultant mood. Her family had helped and supported her in the enterprise that they had all set their minds and talents to. Not least Sylvia, who had thrown off all her unfriendliness and sourness and suddenly become the prime mover in making a success of the stud farm.

It was not very long before Helen felt confident enough to write to Enrico Domini in Rome:

> I find I can now support Elm Court and have no more need of your financial help which you may stop on receipt of this letter. I would like to express my gratitude for your past assistance . . .

'Mother, we just *have* to manage without him.' Sylvia had said to her, 'Even if we sell off the fields at Haydock-cum-Hoe, does it really matter? All the signs are good and Francesca is a marvellous organizer. We'll make it, never fear.'

'Yes, Mother, Syl is right. We can do it. Francesca has a wonderful instinct about it all,' Christopher said, smiling.

Helen had watched Francesca and what she saw there reassured her. There was nothing airy-fairy about Francesca. She came from the land and understood it. She would wrest everything available from it. And she would put back what she had taken. Helen sighed, profoundly happy, and sent up her usual message to Hugh.

'It's going to work, my love, I really believe it's going to work. All these years without you I've been so afraid. Terrified. It took a young stranger, a farm girl from Sicily, to show me that the land will never let you down. There is always something to be had from it, and I need never be frightened in that way again. Your son and his wife-to-be are taking over and they will succeed. I can sit back and relax until it is time for me to join you.

She looked up from her desk and glanced out of the window. Christopher and Francesca were walking up to the house. They had such an air of belonging together. The girl jumped up to catch a branch of a tree they passed under, laughing at something Christopher said. She snapped off a twig and threw it for Mosquito, the Yorkshire terrier pup, who ran frisking in delight after it. Christopher bent and kissed her on the lips. Francesca touched his cheek tenderly, then ran ahead of him up to the house. Helen smiled and put the letter in its envelope.

A moment later the young couple burst into the room. Francesca came and stood on one side of her chair, Christopher the other. They each kissed a cheek.

'I've written the letter, children,' she said. They did not need to ask which one.

'I'm glad, Mother,' Christopher said quietly. Mosquito came whirling into the room and Francesca scooped her up, kissing the frisky little ball of fluff.

'It was really all due to you, Francesca,' Helen said, smiling fondly at the girl.

'Oh, no. You would have thought of it for yourselves, I'm sure,' Francesca replied. 'Besides, it was Christopher really.'

'No,' Helen said decisively, 'we needed new blood. We might have thought of it, though you must give me leave to doubt that, but we would never have *done* anything about it. You motivated us.'

'You've both made me so very happy.' Francesca looked into their kind faces and gave a little squeal. 'I'm so happy,' she said, and laughed, and they all joined in, even Mosquito pirouetting about in excited glee.

'There is a lot of hard work in store for us,' Helen said.

'But that only makes it better, not worse. Makes it more satisfying,' Francesca said.

'I'll post this tomorrow,' Helen said eventually, 'It should reach Rome within a week. I wonder how Signor Domini will take the news. Ah, well, it doesn't really matter much, does it?'

~~~~~~

Enrico Domini read the letter in disbelief, realizing that his ties with Elm Court were now irrevocably cut. It was all over. Alice had died for him again, and all the pain had returned.

He had truly loved her. Loved her but never won her. As long as he supported Elm Court he was in some way still connected with his dead wife. Now that tie was severed. He hit his fist on the desk. Alice. Tall golden Alice. To this day he could not think about her without pain. Alice, so blonde that the hair on her body shone platinum in the light, like silk.

Alice would vanish forever with Elm Court gone from his life. Alice would die.

Death had been on his mind lately. Death and

destruction. Goddamn the Paluccis! He cursed the day he had first heard of the tribe of destroyers.

He had heard that Guido Palucci was the new *padrone*, the new *Signeur* of the d'Abrizzio *palazzo* and estate. He was going to return in triumph, to Sicily, to the *palazzo* on the hill, rich from his brother's will. It was totally unbelievable. Incredible. Enrico Domini squirmed in his chair. Jesu Maria, what was the world coming to?

Guido Palucci was too powerful now to risk crossing. Story was that he killed his two brothers to get the money and the estate. Mowed them down in cold blood. Well, Enrico could see how a man could kill for that inheritance. But his own family?

Why should he feel so angry about it? Enrico wondered. He was blindingly furious. He had never really spent any time at Elm Court, never even visited Sicily, and he had no desire to do either, yet the news put him into a towering rage.

His judgement had been completely wrong. That was what he could not understand. Everyone said Enrico Domini was a great judge of character yet he had made so many mistakes about the Palucci family.

Guido Palucci had struck him as gentle and honourable, a man who would not be ruthless enough for the cut and thrust of big business, certainly lacking the killer instinct. Now look at him. Sitting on a million in a *palazzo* on a hill. At least he would be soon, they said. For now he was still in New York.

Enrico stood up. He would have to get out. He decided to visit his mistress Olympe. Only she could soothe away his tension. Only she could restore his sadly diminished confidence. Only she could persuade him that he had not lost his youth, his reason, and was in fact surrounded by incompetents and fools. It was someone else's fault that Guido Palucci and Lady Helen Wylde had proved not to be dupes. At least, Enrico thought, there was one good

410

thing about all this – Eleanor was not involved. She had not been mentioned in all the gossip. She must have recovered from her infatuation with Guido Palucci. For that one thing he was grateful.

The phone rang. He picked it up and listened. Sat down again abruptly at his desk. His face turned putty-coloured and he took out his handkerchief and mopped his brow.

What was the man trying to tell him? His daughter dead? Eleanor, dead? Shot with Marcello Palucci outside a mansion in New York.

Eleanor was dead. His golden girl, the light of his life, was now lifeless.

His hand closed around the telephone and with a great cry of anguish he wrenched the instrument out of its moorings, pulled it away from the wall and slung it violently to the floor. Then, burying his head in his hands, he prayed for the first time in over forty years.

When he stood up, he had the bearing and haggard face of an old man.

Chapter Twenty-Five

'I'm going to have a baby, Pierre.'

'I'm pleased, Minouche. Very pleased.'

'Are you? I thought you might mind.'

He shook his head. 'All I ever wanted was your happiness, Minouche. You know that. Mario, if he made you happy, could have you. When he stopped, he could not. Do you forgive me now?'

'You had to do it, Pierre. We all have to do these things.'

They sat on the balcony of their little wooden shack on Castle Beach, California.

Minouche had arrived there and thought herself in heaven. 'I've died and gone to Paradise,' she kept saying. She fell in love with the ocean, the beach, the flowers. She had never seen so many flowers in her life. And the water! She was Pisces and here was the whole Pacific Ocean. She stood with her feet in the breakers until Pierre pulled her away.

She loved it more each day. She had never been able to visualize such a life. She could not credit that there was such peace, such beauty, such fulfilment. She had become as brown as a native, spending all her days barefoot on the beach. ' "Beach bum" they call you here,' Pierre said.

They saw no one and were happy. At first Minouche was frightened. She missed Mario. She was scared that the Mob would find her and exact vengeance for Lucca's death. They would be acting within their code if they did.

She and Pierre went to extreme lengths to avoid drawing attention to themselves.

Then one day, after strolling on the beach, they had returned to find two men waiting for them. They wore white suits, black shirts and Panama hats. They were smiling.

Minouche, in torn shorts, shoeless, brown from the sun, her hair bleached white as cotton, caught Pierre's arm and reckoned that their last hour had come. She sent up a silent prayer of thanks that she had had a taste of this Paradise before she died. She would have run if Pierre had not caught her around the waist and held her firmly. He knew that on that golden spread of sand they could be picked off like black crows in a cornfield and there was no escape for them. Better stand still and try to talk their way out. He cursed that he wore only swimming trunks and was totally unarmed.

The duo looked at them for a moment in silence. 'We bin' told to tell ya, you did good,' one of them said eventually. He had a toothpick stuck between his front teeth. He took it out to speak to them, then put it back. The other one had a shy smile and ice-water eyes.

'Pino senta message. Said it was time his ol' man met his maker. Pino said there's a time for everythin'. Pino is boss now. Doin' great. Said to pass on the message.'

Minouche and Pierre stared at the duo transfixed, hardly able to believe their ears.

'No need for you to worry. Relax.' The shy one smiled, freezing eyes staring, trying to project warmth, failing.

They turned to go. The one with the toothpick said over his shoulder to Minouche, 'Wanna job in the movies?'

She shook her head. '*Non*. No. Thank you, no.'

He looked at Pierre, 'You?'

'Well, I gotta do something soon,' Pierre said. 'Pay the bills.'

'OK. You're on.'

413

They left.

Pierre got a job as a stunt man and stand-in and was occasionally asked to appear as an extra.

Minouche was for the first time in her life totally relaxed. She felt secure on her little slice of beach. She had everything she wanted and was blissfully happy.

No one bothered her. They were too afraid of Pierre. She spent her days swimming, lying in the sun on the sand. When Pierre was home they went fishing. He had bought a little boat and they spent hours pottering about, content as cats.

Occasionally Minouche would be haunted by memories of the past. Her face quivered, pain and disgust chasing each other. Pierre was instantly at her side, cradling her in his big arms.

'Don't, honey. Don't upset yourself. Listen, will ya? You forget Lucca, OK? You put that animal out of your mind. You just forget all about the past. Forget it, see? Every time it comes up, you think of something else. It's all over and done. You're safe with me, honey. You forget all that shit. Just be here, with me.'

He would press her forehead with his thumbs, then draw them to her temples, pressing again. It was something he had learned from an Indian stage-hand in the 'Vie en Rose' years ago. This old guy could get rid of any pain just by pressing. Pierre would firmly massage the back of Minouche's neck. He would see her limbs, tanned from the sun, slacken and grow limp, her body relaxing under his hands.

'No one ever loved me like you do,' she said one day as he lifted her up in his arms, and kicking open the swing door carried her into the bedroom and laid her gently on the bed.

She looked at him intently, her dark eyes trying to convey everything he meant to her.

'You know, Pierre, all the others took. Any man I've

414

ever known, took. Took my soul, my centre. You give. Oh, *chérie*, you give me so much, so much. You just don't want anything back, do you? You ask nothing of me?'

He shook his head and she tenderly caressed his hair, pushing it back from his forehead.

'Oh, but I do, honey. I want your love. You have made me so happy. But I want your love.' His mouth was over hers, kissing her softly.

'I like the way you make love to me. I like the way you consider me. The way you think about what pleases me.'

'Mmm. Well, it's no use. Today I want you to please me.'

She laughed, finding this exciting. She began to caress him, listening to him as he murmured to her. She thought of Mario's quick grunting climaxes. She smiled and Pierre kissed her.

'I'll be a good father to this kid,' he said. 'I'm making good money now. We'll give this baby a great life. Here, on the beach.'

She grunted contentedly in his ear and sighed softly under his caresses, cuddling up to him, rubbing her cheek against his arm.

He said, 'I can't wait any longer,' and moved to her soft centre. She was moist, ready for him, and gave a little chuckle. He leaned up over her, his back arched.

'You laughing?'

'I was thinking,' she said, 'I'm happy. Who would ever have thought it could be? Minouche Aubin with Pierre inside her. Living on a beach. Beside the sea. In the sun. Who would ever have thought I could be so happy? Oh, yes, Pierre, yes. Now.'

Chapter Twenty-Six

Guido had travelled down a long tunnel of despair.

Marcello was dead. Mario was dead. Eleanor was dead. Giuseppe and Maria were dead. Paulo was probably dead. A long list since this terrible thing had started.

He had relentlessly persued his brothers, ready to kill, determined on vendetta, but he had killed no one. Yet he was guilty. He knew that although he had not pulled the trigger, he was guilty. There was no escaping it. He was as culpable as Mario or Marcello. His was the sin of intention. Only lack of opportunity had prevented him from pulling the trigger.

And so he was consigned to Hell. He had lost that carefree innocence that a clear conscience carries with it, the capacity for happiness.

Stark terror held him like a vice. Sleep was impossible, delirium constant. Days and nights passed interchangeably, unnoticed. Nightmare visions haunted him, denying him any respite.

Giuseppe swinging from the beam in the barn, an ugly, pop-eyed gargoyle. His beloved father reduced to that. Francesca's pain and Paulo's insanity, for he was sure now that it was his younger brother who had killed Marcello and Eleanor.

Eleanor, his silky, golden girl. The marvel of his life, so fine, so lovely. Gone. Blown away forever.

He remembered little of that night in the street, just a few disjointed images, glimpses of a scene so tragic and terrible that he could not bring himself to remember it in its entirety.

Pandemonium had broken out yet he had stood still, unable to move, watching Paulo's shadow disappear. Ambulances screamed. The cops were all over everyone. The guests were crowding the corpses, eager to be horrified.

Mirella had plucked him out of it all. Guido jumped when her hand grabbed his coat. He looked down into her tragic face, her eyes dark pools of despair yet still with a glint of compassion for him. Why? What had he ever done for Mirella d'Abrizzio that she should come to his rescue?

For it would not have taken the police long to take him into custody. Guido, carrying a gun, could not have talked himself out of that one.

During the long weeks that he lay between madness and sanity, hell and reality, Mirella was there. She was with him every moment, beside him in his delirium, suffering with him. When he cried out Eleanor's name in agony, she echoed, 'Marcello'.

When he could hear her, she said, 'They're out there somewhere – Eleanor and Marcello. They're trying to help us to heal.'

It was Mirella who talked to the cops. She was gracious and calm. She told them that she knew nothing. No, her husband had no enemies that she knew of. They had just been married in Santa Monica. They had been on honeymoon in the Super Chief for the past week. The police could check. No, Marcello had not met with anyone on the train.

She was visited occasionally by the New York Police for a few days and all the time Guido was in the house, laying low. She cared for him, sharing his grief.

They had seen each other defenceless, with all barriers down. They clung together, healing each other, finding solace in each other.

'You'll need me,' she said.

'I know.'

'You can't do without me.'

'I know. And you can't do without me.'

He could open his heart to her about Eleanor. She never tried to be evasive, never shirked the emotional upheaval these confidences engendered.

He let her talk about Marcello, his twin. They talked and talked until there was no more to say.

After Marcello's funeral, she went to Luigi Stroza. 'I want a passport with an exit visa,' she told him. 'For . . .'

'I don't wanna know,' he said, holding up his hands.

'OK, but I want the papers soon.'

Guido could not stay forever in the house, hiding. He wanted more than anything to get back to Sicily.

'It'll cost,' Luigi said.

She shrugged. 'That's not important. Money!' She looked at him curiously.

'How did Marcello make his?' she asked casually.

'Don't ask,' he said. 'Don't even think. It's nothing to do with you,' he added, shrugging, 'I'll get the papers.'

Guido and Mirella ate by candlelight in the basement, Joshua serving. In case someone called, Mirella said. The servant's ebony face was impassive, as if what they were doing was the most natural thing in the world, as if everybody ate in the cellar rather than the beautifully appointed dining room upstairs. He accepted it all, doing his work efficiently, without query. He often wept when he was serving, and they pretended they did not see, but sometimes Mirella wordlessly squeezed the old black hand with affection. Joshua missed Marcello very badly. Guido had said to her, 'I have to go home.' She knew his hunger, his great need for his native land. She shared it. 'I know,' she soothed him, 'I've got your papers. We can leave when you want. When you are ready.'

They sat in the basement surrounded by a bizarre

collection of antiques, stored here by her husband. He had understood instinctively their beauty and value. His brother did not. Guido was ignorant of the treasures that lay around them. Mirella smiled ruefully as she recognized a pair of Ming vases, the exquisitely shaped leg of a Chippendale chair, and peeping from under a dustsheet the corner of a Braque. Guido did not glance twice at them, but she could teach him, he would learn.

I want him, she thought. He is so like Marcello, physically so very alike. And I can come to love him. I will learn to understand him. He needs me. He needs my strength now to survive. If he is left alone he will become crazed and unstable like his brother Paulo. And I need him for the way he looks, the way it squeezes my heart and makes my knees weak. I need him for the baby, Marcello's child's future. And I need him for the *palazzo*. For me. I want him for me.

He could be persuaded, she knew. He was lost and lonely and in need. His family had been destroyed and he was left with a terrible emptiness only she could fill.

As if he read her mind he said, 'Marcello wanted us to marry.' Marcello had left clear instructions. It was his wish, 'if agreeable to both parties' that they should marry. 'He felt he would die,' Mirella had said to Guido, 'It was almost as if he had been aware of an icy hand on his shoulder.'

She looked at Guido now, her eyes clear as pools.

'He did not know about you and Eleanor,' she said, 'but it is a good idea. Listen, Guido, we must be practical. It might be a very good thing for us, marriage. We share so much. I loved Marcello.' She smiled. 'You're not him but you're near enough. I'll never be Eleanor for you, but I'll be the next best thing. And you must remember, I am a d'Abrizzio. I know about the running of the estate. I'm the only one who does. You'll need me and I want to live there again. At home. I love it, you see, Guido. I've resented my father's cavalier treatment of our beautiful heritage all my life.'

She thought of her dream which nearly came true, of

living there with Marcello. That dream was now blasted forever. But she had this alternative. His twin brother Guido now owned the d'Abrizzio *palazzo*. Marcello had willed it so. He knew she would grieve and without him might die. He wanted her to survive, to continue not just because he loved her but because of the baby. His baby. The son she had told him she carried long before she could verify its conception.

He knew too that she would want Guido; his 'other half' as Marcello called him. He knew she would settle for second best when there was a brother so physically similar that she would have no trouble getting to like, then love, the gentle Guido. She already did. It was impossible not to.

It would be good for Marcello's son to have a father. And she could go home to Sicily, to the *palazzo* with more money in her pocket than she knew what to do with.

They would take over the estate, the olive groves, the vineyards, the sweet lemon trees, the warm and beautiful land. The red earth was calling her. With her knowledge of the estate and Guido's love of the land, they would survive and prosper.

Epilogue

It was spring. In the *palazzo* high in the hills outside Palermo, Guido sat on the throne. The golden eagle behind him stared endlessly out through the French windows into the distance. The eagle looked above the wisp of smoke rising from the chimney of the Palucci farmhouse. It stared fixedly over the vineyards and olive groves, above the village church, above the groups of pink-roofed houses where the people lived and laughed and loved. Its blind gaze was forever fixed on the empty sky.

Guido Palucci had his head turned in the same direction. His eyes held the same expression as the birds': intense yet curiously vacant. His gaze was towards the exact same spot the eagle seemed fixed upon: the tip of the mountain. The boundary of his property. He stared at the rosy tip until his eyes watered. But his eyes were blind. Like the eagle he saw nothing.

Below the dais where he sat, the others waited. Mirella, proud and pregnant, sitting nearby, a thick streak of white winging her bronze hair on either side. She sat on a high-backed chair parallel to the throne. Widowed in one week, remarried before the month had passed, no one could read the expression on her beautiful, remote face. But it was her presence that kept this meeting formal and restrained.

Gina and Lombardo sat uneasily on a sofa in front of the

throne. Gina held an infant in her arms. She cooed to it every now and then, apprehensive lest it should cry, defiant in the face of the Duke's contemptuous snorts. They could see how happy she was. Nothing could detract from her glowing love for Lombardo. Their unity was visible to all present. The bonds that linked them were firm and would hold, growing stronger over the years.

Cecilia and Filipo Canona stood, ill-at-ease, near the window. They held hands, fingers interlaced, nervous in this grand place.

Luciano stood near the throne. He looked remote and distant, as if he would rather have been anywhere else. There was a white line of tension around his mouth and his nostrils quivered. It was the only sign of his inner turmoil. He stood behind a high-backed chair that matched the one Mirella sat on. The old Duke reclined upon it, struggling to preserve the last shreds of his dignity and pride.

The Duke was not so very old, Guido thought in surprise. He was a few years Giuseppe's senior. Yet he looked a hundred. His hands shook. He leaned heavily on his silver-headed stick. The fierce old eyes peered at Guido every few moments, shooting fire, hatred, and outrage. He's trying to frighten me, Guido thought, and remembered the last time he had stood in this room, nervously awaiting the judgement of the great man. Now the tables were turned. He was lord and master here. But Guido remembered too that this was not a time for vengeance. There had been too much of that already. The old man had suffered enough. His humiliation was complete.

The Duke hated to be kept waiting so Guido decided to begin.

He drew himself up, marshalling his innate dignity and strength, the proud peasant blood of the Paluccis, to aid him in this interview.

'Sit on the throne,' Marcello's will had commanded. 'Sit on the throne with all the others, family and d'Abrizzios, before you and let them know what I have decided.'

Serena was not there. They had left her with Amelia. She liked Amelia and sometimes thought the maid was Maria. Francesca was now happily married in England. She had written to say she would not be there. She belonged with strangers now. Paulo was lost. Guido felt, deep within him, that his brother was dead too.

The Duke could wait no longer. He leant forward and banged his stick on the marble floor.

'Well, don't keep us waiting all day. What have you got to say?'

'You all know the terms of my brother's will,' Guido said. 'It was one document you could not manipulate.' He glanced down at the old man. 'You know he wished you all to attend this meeting.

'My brother acquired this *palazzo* and all its lands. He has left it to me with certain provisions. One is that his widow, now my wife, Mirella, is given a joint but not controlling interest in this place, and is treated as its mistress.'

'Well done, Mirella,' the old Duke sneered. 'Feathered your nest at the expense of your family, eh? You're no better than these upstarts.' He glared around at Gina, causing her to blush, at Lombardo, and at Cecilia, and Filipo who shrank back into the shadows. Mirella did not answer him.

Guido rapped, 'Remember your position here, sir.' He paused a moment then continued. 'This meeting is not of my choosing. It's a condition of my brother's will. Please remember that.'

He was not enjoying himself. He thought how Marcello would have loved every minute of it. With his theatrical sense he would have told them their fate with relish, let them see who was boss, overlord, master; he would have played the part to the hilt. Well, Guido thought, it is not my idea of satisfaction, but what has to be done, has to be done.

'Sir,' he said to the Duke, 'you know you have a home here as long as you wish, but you'll have to earn your keep. My brother expressly stated that you should not be asked to do anything that would be too taxing, too demanding, or that might damage your health. But you will have to contribute to the life of the place.'

The Duke said nothing. His shoulders drooped and his head sank lower on his chest. He was trembling. There was no way out for him.

'It is outrageous. Outrageous!' he whispered.

'You brought it all on yourself, Father,' Mirella said crisply. 'You cannot go around selling things and still expect to own them.'

'The same conditions apply to Luciano,' Guido said, his mouth tightening. He had been so close to Francesca's suffering brought about by this handsome boy with the petulant face. 'If you stay here, you work. Hard. To make this pile of ancient stones and neglected land prosper and flourish. For I promise you all, it will.'

Luciano looked at him through half-closed eyes. He appeared to be about to say something. Guido could see that mentally he was not with them any more, though he still stood there in his immaculate whites, his long fingers on his father's shoulders.

They would not stay, Guido thought. They were incapable of bending their stiff necks, of accepting humiliation as the Paluccis had had to do over the years. They would travel, exiles doomed forever to roam the earth, dependent on others, guests in strange homes where their hosts craved the reflected glory of housing a title. It would be sadder and more humiliating than staying here and fighting for survival on the land they came from, but they did not have the humility required. Eventually they did not have the courage.

'Gina and Lombardo are bequeathed in perpetuity the old Palucci farmhouse below. It will be known as the Lombardo Demarro farm from now on. Marcello wanted your forgiveness, and that your well-being should be ensured. He wanted to thank you for keeping the family together for otherwise we would have been scattered over the earth. He said that Lombardo, if he wished, could become overseer and manager of the d'Abrizzio estate, which would from now on be known as the *Palazzo Palucci*.

'Amelia can stay on at the farm, and Lombardo and Gina are required to provide for her well-being until such time as she marries, when she will receive a substantial dowry. Serena too is to be cared for. Cecilia and Filipo will build themselves a home, and have a share in the profits of the Demarro farm and vineyards, the lemon groves and the olives.' Guido raised his head and looked at them closely. 'And it is my brother Marcello's wish that the Palucci vendetta dies in this room, at this time. Dies and is buried forever.'

There was silence. A bluebottle droned, banging itself against a window, fruitlessly trying to escape. Sunlight slanted through the window, the beams full of dancing motes.

At last the Duke rose, tapped his stick on the marble floor and looked up at Guido.

'And you will be the *Signeur*? You will be the *Padrone*? You?' His voice dripped contempt. 'A Palucci from the valley?' He shook his head.

'He will make a better one than you ever did,' Mirella said calmly.

The Duke blew out his cheeks, speechless with rage. Then he turned and walked slowly and majestically down the long room to the door. Luciano followed him.

'Don't let them make you lose heart, Guido,' Mirella said, standing up. 'They were doing the only thing they are good at – looking down their noses. You have guts and a love of the land they never had. Don't confuse it with love of the *palazzo*, love of position, love of power. You have a love of the very earth, of the trees and plants, of all that grows and is produced from the land and is so necessary.'

She looked very beautiful, he thought, pregnant and glowing. She was a strong woman. His spirits lightened. With her at his side, he could conquer this place.

Gina stood, sighing. 'We must go home, Lombardo.'

She was so like Maria that Guido's chest tightened and he swallowed hard. He wished he could go with her, go back and find Maria waiting to scold him, Giuseppe in the fields calling to him or Marcello. And Marcello looking towards him, white teeth flashing, a twinkle in his eyes. Paulo and Serena, Gina and Lombardo, Cecilia, and Grandfather in his rocking chair under the eucalyptus tree. Even Mario who had started it all, having a grumble about the dullness of life here. Perhaps he could have said something to make him see that you have to pay for what you take. But it was too late now. Too late to think of it. Too late to go back. Would home, he wondered, always be the farmhouse half-way down the hill or could this stifling, echoing palace ever take its place? Well, he thought, the first thing he would do would be to plant eucalyptus trees all around the *palazzo*, bring some much needed shade. Then he would install fans in all the rooms. Cool the air.

Gina said, 'We are very happy, Guido. Marcello has our forgiveness. It is all over now.'

She mounted the few steps that led up to the great carved chair where her brother sat, and kissed him. Then she went over to where Mirella stood. She touched her cheek to her sister-in-law's.

'Welcome,' she said. 'Welcome, Mirella.'

Lombardo had followed her. He shook Guido's hand.

'Thank you,' he said simply. Guido nodded. Their

attitude to him had changed subtly. The old camaraderie had gone and in its place was respect and an acknowledgement of his new status.

'Come, Lombardo,' Gina said. They too left, followed by Cecilia and Filipo who shyly nodded to Guido and Mirella before they went. They were left alone. Mirella went and sat on the step at Guido's feet. She laid her head on his knees.

'It's about time we had a wedding party,' he said. 'Give the village a celebration. Help them to grow accustomed to my living here again. Let them know I am still one of them.'

She kissed his hand. 'Very wise,' she said.

'Do you think often of Marcello?' he asked, stroking her hair.

'I will learn to love you, Guido, as much if not more as I loved him,' she said. 'It will not be difficult for me. You are so very alike. But you have more depth than your brother. You are more serious. Perhaps I need that now.'

She looked at him through slanting golden eyes. 'But for you, it will be difficult. I am not Eleanor. I am not in the least like her. You will have to meet me half-way, Guido. You will have to help me.'

'No, you are not like Eleanor. I don't think she would have fitted in here. We would have had a different life if she had lived.'

He thought of the social creature Eleanor had been. The glamour of her. The style. 'Of course I'll help you,' he added. 'We'll help each other.' He paused then said, 'We'll have the wedding here, the religious ceremony here in the *palazzo*. We'll invite everyone. And Fra Bartholomeo will perform the ceremony. Would you like that?'

'Yes,' she replied, 'I would.'

He slid to the floor beside her and put his hand on her belly.

'I feel it's mine,' he said.

'It is, in a way.' She kissed him. 'And you'll have your own after Marcello is born.'

427

He looked at her, surprised. 'Marcello?'

'Yes,' she said, pressing his hand to her body, 'I will call this boy Marcello. Then you will have yours. I want a lot of children. I want this old place to ring with the sound of children, running about, quarrelling, laughing.' She glanced up. 'How about you?'

'Oh, yes,' he said. 'Yes.'

'Do you think a vendetta is ever really over?' she asked quietly.

'No,' he said regretfully. 'It goes on once it's started, that's the tragedy. Hatred is hard to kill. It has an existence of its own, like a cancer. Mean men, frustrated men, thrive on it. It feeds their ego. Or sometimes their despair. No, I don't think a vendetta ever ends.' He frowned. 'But this one, maybe.'

He smiled at her, and in imitation of a courtier placed one hand behind his back and raised her up with the other.

'Will you have tea on the terrace, Signora?'

She moved gracefully to the bell-pull. 'Yes,' she said. 'I think that would be a lovely idea.'

'Before we go out,' she held him back a moment, 'do you think you will ever love me, Guido? Apart from needing me, liking me?'

'I would not be a man if I did not.'

Together they went out on to the terrace that overlooked the whole valley. They sat beneath the shade of a canvas umbrella that flapped in the wind.

'Your domain, Guido,' she said, smiling at him.

'Let's hope we can bring peace and prosperity here,' he said. 'There have been enough deaths.'

He remembered how he and Francesca had stood here before the Duke on another sunny day when the tragedy was new and unresolved. He could never have forseen its ending like this. He was no longer that gauche country lad. How had he changed, he wondered, and had sorrow made him wise?

He looked at the woman beside him. She would not be hard to love and she would guide him through the pitfalls that lay ahead. She would be strong and loyal and true. They were held together by so much.

'Amen to that,' she said, smiling into his eyes. 'Dear Guido, Amen to that.' And felt the child, Marcello's son, move within her.